ALLIANCE

THE BELLATOR CHRONICLES: BOOK FOUR

CLARE LITTLEMORE

BRIT ALERT!

If you are reading this book and not from the UK, a brief warning that I am a British author and use British spellings throughout. In Bellator, the pavements have 'kerbs' rather than 'curbs', the students of the Danforth Academy may be disciplined for their bad behaviour (not behavior) and one or two of the characters might, on occasion, have to apologise (rather than apologize).

Happy reading!

Contents

Chapter One: Faith

T he library was eerily silent.

Moments ago, there had been action and activity. Now, shock hung thick in the air, choking the room's inhabitants. As nausea threatened to overwhelm her, Faith glanced at her companions.

Blake was frozen, her eyes fixed on the darkened screen. Beside her, Madeleine's eyes were like saucers. The warmth of the room was stifling.

"What–" Faith wiped the sweat from her forehead with her sleeve, attempting to make sense of things. "What *happened*?"

There was no immediate reply. The only sound was Blake unplugging and reconnecting wires, repeatedly swiping a finger across her datadev.

"I'm not sure." Madeleine shook her head. "A bomb of some kind."

They had heard the explosion before their screens went blank. More powerfully, the ground beneath them had shaken, a booming sound echoing out across the city. Whatever it was had happened close by.

Blake gestured at the still-blank screen. "Whole system's down."

Her words jolted Madeleine into action. "Check the power supply. We have to get it up and running again."

Moving to the door, the leader hauled it open. She gestured through it as Blake stared at her, breathing hard.

"*Now*!"

Cowed for once, Blake got up and hurried off down the hallway in the direction of the fuse box. The fresh air from the hallway wafted in, a welcome reprieve from the stuffiness. Faith took a deep breath, trying to steady herself.

"Faith?" Madeleine's voice was sharp. "With me."

She disappeared into the hallway without waiting for a reply. Dazed, Faith stood up and followed her. Madeleine headed for the stairway which led to the public area of the library. One of Faith's favourite places, right now the books would not offer their usual comfort.

The first-floor windows would certainly provide answers. But Faith wasn't sure they were answers she was ready for.

She struggled to keep pace with the Resistance leader. Madeleine was surprisingly fit for someone who spent most of her days buried in an office.

As she passed the door to the dorms, she remembered Sophia. Her best friend, newly rescued from Danforth's clutches, was on the other side of it. Faith was desperate to see her. But she had to find out more about the explosion. So many lives hung in the balance.

Promising herself that she would visit Sophia the minute things were calmer, she followed Madeleine up the stairs.

This wasn't the first attack the city had suffered. A couple of months earlier, a bomb had gone off at the Bellator Hospital in the middle of the night, completely destroying the fertility stores. On that occasion, there had been no casualties.

This time, in a city packed with people attending the Liberation Day celebrations, it wasn't a case of *if* there were casualties, but how many.

At the top of the stairs, she caught hold of the door Madeleine had abandoned just before it collided with her shoulder. The Resistance leader strode across the room, pausing briefly to glance out the first window on her right as she passed.

"Business district looks untouched." She hurried on.

Faith followed her example, trying to focus on key locations as she moved to the opposite side of the space. Reaching the window, her eyes searched for the place she had at one time called home.

It was serene as always. She closed her eyes briefly.

"Academy's okay."

"No damage to the square either." Madeleine sounded breathless. "Looks a bit chaotic, but the buildings are still standing."

Faith ran through the mission plan in her head. Diane's team was safe from the explosion, as well as Flynn and Helen. She heaved a sigh of relief.

But Madeleine had stopped abruptly at the next window.

Faith abandoned her position. *The hospital!* She stumbled to Madeleine's side. For a moment, she couldn't see the building where Noah was stationed. She felt a trickle of sweat make its way down her spine as her eyes searched the horizon. Finally, they settled on the shining glass frontage. It was untouched.

He was safe.

But the sky to the north was ominously dark. Pushing Faith out of the way, Madeleine moved into the Records Room. The window there offered a view from the end of the building rather than the side.

Faith followed close on her heels. As she reached the window, she echoed Madeleine's horrified gasp. Dark clouds of smoke billowed into the sky in the distance. This was a far more powerful explosion than the one which had enveloped the fertility stores.

Her eyes searched the horizon, trying to make sense of the skyline. Where was the smoke coming from?

And then, it hit her. She was facing a building she had looked out at only a few days ago. A building of great importance to Danforth and the city as a whole. Matriarch House.

The perfect place to hit the chancellor where it hurt.

For a second, relief flooded over her. And then her thoughts flew to the only Resistance operative working within the government building.

Ella.

Only a few hours ago, Ella had sneaked into the control room to help Blake bypass a firewall which was preventing her from broadcasting Faith's speech.

Had she been caught in the explosion? Was she, even now, lying in the rubble of the devastated building?

Faith squinted at the smoke. From this distance, it was impossible to assess the severity of the blast. But as she trailed back downstairs, Faith's nausea returned full-force.

Chapter Two: Noah

A siren split the air, wailing through the hospital wards and hallways.

"Emergency Protocol!" a disembodied voice barked. "All staff, adopt emergency protocol immediately."

Noah hurried back down the hallway on autopilot, wheeling the cleaning trolley in front of him.

He hadn't been able to stop shaking since Flynn had appeared on the stage. His father was here, in Bellator, in broad daylight. He'd been standing right next to the city's chancellor.

But he'd hardly had a chance to process the fact before a shockwave had reverberated through the building. Noah had spun to face the window as the deafening noise rolled across the city. In the distance, he had seen a column of smoke rising into the air. But the hospital was right in the centre of the city, surrounded by towering skyscrapers making it difficult to see which area the explosion had affected.

When he'd looked back at the screen, the feed had been cut. Instead of a view of the stage, he'd been faced with a message scrolling across the empty space: transmission loading... transmission loading...

But it never did.

As he made his way back towards the hospital's main thoroughfare, Noah searched his mind for possible targets.

The square? Liberation Day was an important event. Anyone wanting to have a big impact on the city would know it was a prime day to attack. But the security around the stage had been tight when Flynn and Helen had made their way to the stage. *Surely*, that would make it an impossible target.

He ran through other possibilities. The academy? One of the medcentres? The library?

If Danforth had discovered the Resistance's hiding place, she would waste no time destroying it. With Faith inside.

His heart pounding, Noah dodged a tech striding in the opposite direction. As she passed him, she barked orders into her wristclip.

"Call in all off-duty staff." Her voice faded as she retreated down the hall. "Expecting multiple casualties. Matriarch House employs hundreds of people and..."

Relief flooded over Noah. The bomb's target was not the library or the Liberation Day Ceremony, but Danforth's central operations building. Filled with Danforth's employees, but no-one that he–

He forced himself to keep walking. Ella had been working undercover in Matriarch House.

How badly had the bomb damaged the building? Was his friend, even now, trapped under the rubble? His promise to Ruth came back to him. She'd asked Noah to keep an eye on Ella, to be there for her as she transitioned into the alien world of Bellator.

He curled his fingers into his palm. He had let Ruth down. If Ella was dead, she would never forgive him. But how could he have kept his promise, in a city where men were powerless? Worse still, he couldn't attempt to rescue his friend, or even discover what had happened to her. He was trapped.

He paused at a set of doors to allow a group of medics through.

"...at least forty" "still getting people out" "almost completely collapsed" "rear of the building"

Breathing through his nose, Noah left the group behind. With no real idea where he was going, he ploughed ahead. If he kept moving, surely people would assume he had a specific purpose.

A new question nagged at him as he plunged forward. *Who was responsible?*

His prime suspect, had it been the library gone up in flames, was unlikely. Danforth was hardly going to destroy her central government building. It wasn't the Resistance, unless Madeleine had an undercover team that she hadn't revealed to the rest of them. And destroying Matriarch House would hardly further the Resistance's cause. In the old days his prime suspect would have been Eremus, but that was in the days when...

And then he knew. Jacob. The ex-Eremus leader hated Danforth with a passion. Destroying the chancellor's central operations base would have a major impact on her. And Noah had never managed to get to the bottom of Sarah's appearance the previous day. What if she'd been in Liberty Park to scope out a location? A bomb had certainly been Jacob's weapon of choice in the past. And the park was only a five-minute walk from Matriarch House.

Noah's thoughts returned to Ella. If this was Jacob's doing, he had potentially killed one of his *own* citizens in his efforts to get revenge. Not that he would care.

As Noah passed through a door, he glanced around.

His heart almost stopped. Without realising, he had wandered into the main reception area, an extremely busy part of the hospital. And not one that drudges frequented without a specific purpose.

He had ended up here once before. Almost given himself away. Cursing his stupidity, he considered potential escape strategies.

The reception was chaos. Medics and techs hurried in and out, calling out requests to one another. A line of hospital out-patients stood around the desk, clamouring for attention. Numerous pieces of equipment were being brought through the space on their way to the Emergency Department: trolleys, wheelchairs, an item Noah recognised from his ma's medical books as a blood pressure monitor, and several machines he could not even begin to identify.

The ever-present siren meant everyone had to shout to be heard.

"Sending home non-urgent cases." "Multiple casualties expected." "Have to get them out of here."

Noah took a deep breath. None of his training had prepared him for this. He found himself wishing he was with Liam, the drudge who had helped him with his quest to free Sophia. *He* would know what to do.

But Liam would be with the other drudges, presumably already engaged in whatever drudges were supposed to do in an emergency.

Steeling himself, he pushed Ella from his mind. He couldn't afford to let his guard down now, no matter who might have been hurt. He'd be useless to his friends if he was caught. He shrank down even lower than usual, hoping that the patients and staff had better things to think about than an errant drudge. He had to get somewhere quieter, somewhere he could use his comms device to contact the Resistance and ask what he should do next.

He continued through the reception area, his eyes searching the ground for other drudge feet. There were none. Numerous shoes hurried past, but none of them wore the plain grey shoes of the drudge.

At least the alarm was still blaring. He stood a chance of passing through unnoticed when everything was so hectic.

He had almost reached the door which led to the wards when the siren stopped. Noah froze. The sudden silence shocked everyone for a second. And then a tech to Noah's left took charge.

"As you've no doubt heard, we have a major emergency on our hands. Any outpatient and non-urgent appointments will need to be rearranged for a later date." He could feel the woman gesturing towards the main exit, her hands drawing a broad semi-circle in the air. "Please accept our apologies. The hospital will be in touch as soon as we've dealt with the current situation."

Grumbling and muttering, the patients began shuffling towards the main doors. Some seemed fearful of leaving, but the tech was determined, herding the citizens outside with ruthless efficiency. Within seconds, she had cleared the lobby, and Noah no longer had the luxury of hiding in plain sight. Sensing the lost advantage, he began moving towards his intended exit again.

He had barely taken three steps when one of the technicians blocked his way.

"What are you doing?" Her tone was accusatory. "Shouldn't you be in the Emergency Resource Centre right now?"

Noah froze. This was what he'd been most afraid of. In Eremus, when he was in a sticky situation, he'd have attempted to talk his way out of it. But a drudge speaking was tantamount to a crime. Bowing his head low, he hoped the gesture conveyed some sense of apology.

But the tech tapped her foot. "There shouldn't be any drudges *here* right now. You should be stocking up the operating rooms. Or waiting with trolleys for the incoming patients."

Noah said nothing. He was trying to decide whether to step around the woman and move away like he knew where he was going, or stay and receive a sanction, when she sighed.

"Are you...? Let's see." She studied the datadev she held. There was a pause as she tapped the screen several times. Eventually, she took a step back. "Come with me."

His legs like jelly beneath him, Noah shadowed the tech out of the lobby and into one of the quieter hallways. They hadn't gone far when she stopped. Noah braced himself for more harsh words or a physical punishment. Remembering Liam's swollen eye, he braced himself.

But the woman seemed to simply want rid of him.

"You!" Her voice rang out down the empty corridor.

Noah knew from the sharpness of her tone that she was speaking to another drudge. It was only a matter of seconds before a pair of shoes identical to his own approached.

"This one must be new." The woman was dismissive. "Show him what he's *supposed* to be doing."

The woman spun on her heel and was gone. The drudge who stood to his left moved off in the opposite direction, his silent footfalls contrasting sharply with the tapping of the technician's shoes on the polished floor.

Noah followed the drudge across the hospital, where he led Noah to a familiar thoroughfare which housed the main equipment and storage rooms. Once there, the drudge headed for the largest of the supply rooms, which was housed in a separate building. Though he didn't dare glance at the sky, Noah could smell the smoke in the air. In the distance, numerous sirens were wailing. As they passed through the doorway into the space beyond, he prayed that Ella had not been inside the building when the bomb had gone off.

"This becomes the Emergency Resource Centre during times of crisis." The drudge's voice was low. Noah had to strain to hear him. "That's where we get our assigned jobs. Different than the usual ones."

The drudge led Noah to a small door at the back of the room which he hadn't noticed on any of his previous visits. It was standing open, revealing a small anteroom.

The drudge led him inside. "Wait here."

Curious, Noah obeyed. All around him, the bustling sounds of the drudges paired with their frantic footsteps as they hurried in and out of the room. Their urgent movements contrasted with their usual calm invisibility. Apparently, some of the drudge rules were relaxed during emergencies.

Noah sighed. The Resistance had not been in touch since Robyn had left with Sophia. But the explosion had happened not long after the team had left him. Clearly those left in the library would be busy dealing with the fallout. They would check in with him eventually, but he wouldn't be a priority.

Not like Ella.

He considered contacting headquarters himself. He'd done it before. But he didn't want to take their attention away from Resistance members who might be in immediate danger. And he was in the middle of a busy drudge thoroughfare. He could hardly whip out his hidden comms device without attracting attention. He had no idea which of the drudges he could trust.

No. He'd wait until later, when he could snatch a moment alone.

But what would they want him to do? His mission was complete. But would the Resistance prefer to keep someone on the inside at the hospital as the emergency progressed? Or should he use the chaos in the city as a cover to sneak back to the library?

A pair of drudge shoes with a familiar teardrop-shaped stain on them appeared by his side.

"I've had all the drudges on the lookout for you." Noah's heart leapt at the sound of Liam's voice. "Knew you'd show up in the end. You can raise your head." The man nudged his shoulder. "It's permitted in here. Has to be, so we can access the Jobs' Board."

Noah looked up. The most commanding feature of the room they stood in was a large screen fixed to the wall. Instead of broadcasting the news, it displayed a list of tasks.

"I hear you almost got yourself into trouble back there. Let me show you what to do." Liam led Noah closer to the board on the wall. "Protocol for an emergency takes precedence over your usual role. Jobs are displayed here." The drudge pointed to a column on the left of the screen. "With a location here." His finger moved to a second column. "And an individual code at the end. Makes sure everything gets done in order of priority. Today, it will mostly be about making sure the medics don't run out of emergency supplies. Oh, and ferrying the new patients about."

He gestured to a number of datadevs fixed to the wall beneath the screen. They were all currently occupied by other drudges, so they waited until one came free. Stepping forward, Liam glanced up at the board.

"Enter the next code on the board." He demonstrated. "Take note of what the job is and where you need to be. Then key in your ID number."

He modelled what to do, typing in his ID, then gestured at the board again. The job had disappeared.

"Got it?"

Noah nodded, then, remembering that he could probably speak here, said, "Yes."

The drudge pointed at the datadev. "Show me."

Figuring he needed to keep up the pretence until he'd managed to contact the Resistance, Noah took a note of the next job on the board: a delivery of bandages to the Emergency Department. Appreciating that Liam had stayed to make sure he knew what he was doing, he hurried to type in the code.

Liam leaned closer. "You got that girl out? The keycard... it worked?"

Noah considered the question. Had Robyn's team managed to get her back to the library through all the chaos? The idea of the mission failing in its final stages was devastating.

Realising Liam was still waiting for an answer, Noah nodded. "It did. The Resistance came and collected her. Thank you for your help getting the keycard." He paused, aware of the other drudges waiting behind them. "With everything that's happened since they left though, I'm not sure that..."

"You did your part." Liam nudged his shoulder. "Stay strong. Trust that the others will do theirs."

He gestured for them to move away from the datadev. "Heads down again now. Follow me." Liam led Noah back into the main supply room. "Today... that girls' speech... the disruption in the square..." He kept his voice low. "Was that also...?"

"The Resistance?" Noah followed his lead, speaking at whisper-level. "Yeah."

The drudge gave a low whistle. "Impressive. And that man from Eremus. I heard him speak. Brave move."

Pride surged through Noah. From the moment Flynn had laid down his weapon and ascended the steps to the stage, Noah had been terrified for him. But he'd had to admire his father's courage.

Flynn had been unprotected. Surrounded by heavily-armed guards. Yet when he had opened his mouth to speak, both his voice and his facial expression had been calm. Noah knew the image he would want to project was one of peace. To convince the women standing in front of him that he wasn't the type of male they'd been brought up to fear.

The women's expressions had ignited a small flame of hope in Noah. Whilst many were still hostile, as Flynn continued to speak their expressions softened, became curious, began to trust what he was saying.

Following Faith's speech, Flynn had been totally believable. What he'd said tied in with and supported what had come before, and with Helen's help, it would have gone a long way towards showing the Bellator citizens that he meant what he said. But Helen had never gotten the chance to speak.

"Did the Resistance honestly blow up Matriarch House?" Liam's incredulous voice brought Noah back to the moment.

"Well, no." Noah hesitated. That, he was pretty certain, hadn't been the work of the Resistance. "I don't know who that was."

"Forces outside the city then? Are they…?" Liam hesitated. "Are they on our side?"

Noah shrugged. "I'm not sure. I'm sorry."

"No matter. Anything that brings Danforth down is good by me." The drudge gestured to a shelf of boxes. "The bandages are at the top."

Noah fetched the ladder from where it rested further along the shelving. Placing it in position, he climbed the rungs until he could reach the relevant shelf. Aware that Liam was waiting for him, he tried to hurry. The box was a large one, and it was difficult to balance and still keep hold of the ladder rungs with his free hand.

On the way back down, his foot slipped. Fighting to stay upright, he tumbled down the last few rungs and landed awkwardly on his left arm at the bottom.

"Are you alright?" Liam took a step closer. "Your arm… is it?"

Noah scrambled to his feet, aware of the spectacle he had caused. "I'm fine."

He rubbed his arm. It would no doubt be bruised, but there seemed to be no permanent damage.

"Alright then." Liam gestured to the box Noah had abandoned. "Take the bandages to the Emergency Room, then hurry back. Repeat the process with another task from the list." He stepped away. "Try not to kill yourself next time."

Before Noah could work out if he was joking or not, Liam turned and hurried away.

Noah made his way to the Emergency Room, rolling his sore shoulder. He'd been careless. More than once, now. He had to focus on keeping up the drudge act, at least until he was back at the library and out of harm's way.

He was in a safer place than many of the people he cared about. His thoughts spun from one person to another: Sophia, on her way to the library; Ella, potentially trapped in a burning building; Helen, perhaps even now on her way back to the academy.

And, finally, Flynn.

Had his father managed to escape during the chaos following the explosion? Or had Danforth's guards captured him? He'd been so daring, so selfless, coming to Bellator to speak to the women. Noah closed his eyes.

Was Flynn going to pay the ultimate price for his bravery?

CHAPTER THREE: FAITH

"**G**o help Blake."

Madeleine's tone did not invite discussion, but as Faith passed the door to the dorms, she hesitated.

"Could I just look in on Sophia? I'd like to–"

"No." Madeleine turned to glare at her. "You saw the damage up there. Matriarch House is in ruins. And whilst the damage doesn't seem to extend beyond the government building, it's *imperative* that we discover what's going on out there."

"But I–"

"What if there's a second explosion?" Madeleine snapped. "What happened to Flynn and Helen in the wake of the bomb?" She strode off down the hallway, clearly expecting Faith to follow. "Our operatives have been instructed to check in with us as soon as possible in the event of an emergency, whether in person or via walkie-talkie from one of our safehouses." She held a hand up as Faith attempted to speak. "First, we have to know if we lost anyone."

"Ella." Faith's throat constricted. "She was at..."

"Yes." Madeleine's expression softened slightly. "She was closest to the explosion. Most likely to–" Abruptly, she turned and started walking again. "We have to hope she got out.

And..." her voice hardened, "the only way to find out is for you to start contacting the safe houses. "

Faith had to admit that the leader was right. The only way they were going to find out if Ella was alive or not was to start asking questions. Sophia was safe right now, Ella was not. With a final glance at the door to the dorms, she retraced her steps to Blake's office.

When she arrived, the tech genius was fuming. Her efforts to get the systems up and running had so far come to nothing, and she was pacing the tiny room like a caged animal.

"Madeleine sent me to help you." Faith hovered in the doorway. "Says we need to check in with people."

Scowling, Blake flung herself into her usual chair. "We're going to have to do it the old-fashioned way."

She gestured to the walkie-talkie in her hand. Usually, they were used for contacting Eremus. But until the communication systems were working again, they would be the only method of contacting the safehouses. It struck Faith as ironic that the people of Bellator were forced to revert to Eremus-style technology when their own high-tech equipment failed them.

"You coming in?" Blake yanked open a drawer in the desk. She pulled out a second walkie-talkie and thrust it in Faith's direction. "You're supposed to be helping me, yeah?"

Faith crept inside. Accepting the device, she took a seat beside Blake and awaited further instructions. For several moments, Blake rifled through another drawer. Eventually she drew out a folder stuffed with papers. Slamming it down on the desk, she began sorting through it.

"This should have all the information we need." She stopped at a page towards the back. "A list of today's mission objectives, for example." She sniffed. "Madeleine makes me do a hard copy as a back-up. We've never needed it before."

"I'll bet you're glad she had you do it, this time."

Blake grunted in response, continuing to pull papers from the folder.

"Shall we get started then?" Faith inched forward, her concern for Ella outweighing her fear of the techie's death stare. "I'm worried about–"

"Ella." Blake cut her off. "I get it."

She pulled another couple of sheets out of the folder. Smoothing them out on the table, the techie jabbed a finger at the top one.

"This is a list of call signs. One for each safehouse." She pointed at a second sheet. "This has specific times and places linked to the mission. Which operatives were stationed where. Unfortunately, we're going to be limited to contacting the safehouses. We have to hope that our people have been able to make it to one of them without getting caught. It makes sense to assume that people will have headed for the safehouse closest to their position during the mission."

"What about existing operatives?" Faith's thoughts went to Ella, and then Noah. "People not directly involved in the mission?"

"We'll just have to hope they're safe, and that their cover is still in place." Blake met Faith's gaze for the first time since she'd opened the door. "Contact them in due course when things calm down."

Blake's hands strayed to the keyboard. She began to type, then glanced up at the still-blank screen. Her face fell. "Dammit!" She slammed a hand on the desk. "I can't believe we trusted them."

Faith frowned. "Who?"

"Eremus."

Faith placed the walkie-talkie on the desk. "What do you mean?"

"The bomb!" Blake's tone was incredulous. "Seems like this is their handiwork."

A bolt of anger shot through Faith. "Really?"

"Yes, *really*." Blake's eyes were filled with fury. "Flynn's little *peace* stunt was clearly a decoy. Make everyone look the other way, while they target another key building in the city."

"That's not... They wouldn't..." Faith struggled to find words. "Flynn's not like that!" She recoiled at Blake's pitying glance. "He's *not*!" She stood her ground. "You don't know him."

Halting abruptly, Blake spun to face her. "Maybe not. But as I recall, this kind of stunt is *typical* of Eremus. Have you forgotten they blew up the fertility stores a few weeks ago?"

"Yes, but that was–" Faith stopped, horrified. "That was Jacob."

Blake's eyes widened. "You mean–"

Nodding, Faith picked up the walkie-talkie again. "This is just like the man I met in Eremus. But... he's not *with* them anymore. He went rogue, remember?" She fiddled with the volume on the device in her hand. "I told you. This isn't Flynn. Jacob's out there, somewhere. With minimal support, but a good number of weapons and explosives. We know Noah spotted Sarah in the city only days ago. Maybe she was planting explosives."

Calmer now, Blake sagged back in her chair. "Jacob would do anything to get at Danforth, right?"

"From what I've learned about him, yeah, anything."

"I guess that makes more sense." Blake tapped a finger against the list of call signs thoughtfully. "It's just a shame that the Bellator citizens won't distinguish between the actions of a rogue male and the community as a whole."

Faith's heart sank. "So–"

"Obviously, Danforth will take charge of the narrative. Blame *the rogue men of Eremus* for the explosion. She'll have the citizens believing her version of events within the hour." Blake scowled. "And anything positive that Flynn said will be forgotten."

"But–"

Blake waved a hand, as though the mission's failure was too painful to consider any longer. "Listen, I need to try and get the systems back up." She thrust the call sign list at Faith. "Think you can work your way through this list while I focus on that?"

Faith took the paper. "So I just..."

"Contact each safehouse. Or respond if they call in. Check who's there." Blake thrust a pen and notepad at Faith before turning back to her keyboard. "Mark people as safe once you've spoken to them. Ask whether they know the where-abouts of anyone who might be missing. Or any information about the explosion."

Faith was glad to have something to occupy her. Shifting a few papers aside to make some room, she found a map of Matriarch House. Blake had asked her to note camera locations on it the previous day, when they'd been instructing Ella to disconnect a firewall in the government building. Now it lay in ruins, the map was useless.

"The explosion must have destroyed the servers at Matriarch House." Noticing the discarded sheet, Blake had come to the same conclusion. "I'm guessing that's what's causing the issue." She swiped a finger back and forth across her blank screen. "But the chancellor needs them up and running as much as we do."

"She can't broadcast her version of events without them, right?"

"Right." Blake chewed her lip. "They have a back-up server we can connect to though, once it's up and running. Danforth's tech team *must* be trying to activate it. If they're still alive, that is."

"They're still alive." Noting Blake's confusion, Faith pressed on. "Remember when we spoke to Ella earlier? She said the tech team was leaving as she got to the Control Room."

Understanding dawned on Blake's face. "Oh *yeah*. They'd been called to the square, right?"

Faith nodded. "Lucky for them, I guess."

"*Very* lucky." Blake went back to her datadev. She held her finger down on the power button. "I'll do another hard refresh, see if it makes a difference. They *have* to get things back online again soon."

Faith turned her attention to the walkie-talkie. Turning it on, she consulted the list, running her eyes down it until she found her friend's name.

"There's no way for me to check on Ella, is there?" She glanced at Blake. "I mean... she's the most likely to be..."

For a moment, the techie didn't respond. When she finally looked up, her eyes were surprisingly sympathetic. "I know you're worried about her. But until Ella makes her way to a safehouse... or shows up here, there's no way we can know what's happened to her." Blake glanced at her datadev longingly. "At least, not until the communications systems are back up and we can use the wristclips. Sorry."

"I should..." Faith swallowed hard, "keep busy, right?"

"Exactly." Blake patted Faith's shoulder awkwardly. "I find it's better to distract myself when I'm worried." She pointed at the papers. "Check off as many people as you can." She gestured to a couple of names halfway down the list. Both had thick pencil lines scored through them. "Call came in from the Red Six safehouse just before you showed up. I've already checked off the operatives who made it there safely. Let's hope everyone else calls in just as quickly."

As Blake went back to her screen, Faith ran a finger down the list. The first safehouse was located in the middle of the city and was the one closest to the square. Her hands shaking, she raised the walkie-talkie to her lips.

"Come in Red Three. This is Red One. Are you receiving me?" She released the button and waited. There was no response.

Beside her, Blake tensed. "Try again."

Faith pressed the button again. "Red Three, come in. Can you hear me? Is everything alright over there?"

Blake leaned across, consulting the list. "I'd expect there to be at least a *couple* of people at the Red Three location. The team from the square should have relocated there as soon as the trouble started. Unless something–"

Not finishing her sentence, she gestured to the walkie-talkie again. Faith gritted her teeth. Blake wasn't making the calls herself, yet she didn't seem able to keep her focus on her own task while there were Resistance members at risk.

Faith was just about to press the button again when the device crackled to life in her hand. She was so startled that she almost dropped it.

"Red Three receiving you loud and clear. We are alright. I repeat. All operatives in Red Three are fine."

"It's Olivia." Blake waved an impatient hand. "How many others? Ask for names."

"Good news, Red Three." Faith tried to keep her voice from shaking. "How many of you are there?"

"Three." There was a slight pause before the woman continued. "Olivia, Grace, and Evelyn." There was a crackling sound, as though something was happening in the background. "Make that four. Diane just arrived."

Faith's heart leapt at the news. At least one of her close friends was okay. Diane had been with the team in the square, right in the centre of the Liberation Day celebrations. And right under Danforth's nose.

"Glad you're all okay." Faith scanned the list of names. "What about Flynn and Helen?"

"Negative." Faith recognised Evelyn's voice. "They were on the stage when the bomb went off. I couldn't get near them."

"Did you see where they ended up?"

"No. But they were pretty close to Danforth, so..." There was a pause. "I'm thinking she's got them."

Faith sagged against her chair. Knowing the failure to protect her assigned subjects would weigh heavy on Evelyn, she moved on.

"Any sign of Ella?"

"No." Evelyn's tone was brisk, but she knew why Faith was asking. "Sorry."

"Alright. Thanks for the information. Madeleine's instructions are to stay put and keep this frequency clear until we're able to contact all the safehouses. We'll be in touch when we know the full extent of the situation."

"Roger that. We'll be waiting." Evelyn signed out.

Faith was about to move to the next name on the list when Blake stiffened beside her. "Yesss!"

"What–" Faith began, but closed her mouth, understanding.

The screen in front of Blake was no longer blank. Muttering to herself, Blake tapped furiously at the keys, more alive than she had been for the past hour now that her precious technology was showing signs of revival.

"If I can just establish a connection…" her eyes roamed over the screen as various commands appeared and disappeared in the code. "Almost there… just need to…" she frowned, "that's it… aaaand…" she pumped a fist in the air, "*that's* what I'm talking about!"

Her celebration was cut short, however, when the Bellator news site loaded. Already, they were reporting on the explosion at Matriarch House. The image on the screen showed what was left of the main entrance, its façade in ruins as plumes of smoke curled out into the street.

Guards and firefighters swarmed around the entrance with purpose, setting up barriers and attempting to usher a few curious bystanders away. So far, there was no sign of anyone being brought out of the building.

"Could people survive that?" Faith braced herself for Blake's response. "Looks bad."

"It was definitely a sizeable explosion." Blake sighed. "That building houses at least a hundred workers on a daily basis. Some of them might have been in the square watching the speech, but..." she shrugged. "...there'll be a fair number of body bags."

Faith shuddered. "Could you..." she gestured to Blake's wristclip, "is it possible to..."

"Contact Ella?" Blake was already raising the clip to her lips. "You have her details?"

Faith pushed the paper towards her, pointing to Ella's number. Far faster than Faith at using the equipment, Blake dialed it in seconds.

She held her breath as they waited for the call to connect.

Chapter Four: Noah

Noah's head was spinning. He'd spent the past hour ferrying resources from the Emergency Resource Centre to various locations around the hospital. He'd lost count of how many jobs he'd taken from the screen, but he was glad to have been kept busy. It gave him less time to worry.

Frustratingly, the comms device the Resistance had given him wasn't working. He had attempted to use it several times throughout the morning, to no avail. The soreness of his aching arm was compounded by his growing certainty that he had damaged the tiny device in the fall.

He still wasn't certain whether remaining in the hospital was his best course of action. In all the chaos, it would have been easy for him to slip away. But he suspected the explosion had Danforth's guards on high alert. Being out on the streets of the city right now would be suicide. Better wait until things calmed down. Or at least until darkness fell.

The screens around the hospital had remained dark, so there was no additional news of the explosion. The only new information came from the gossip that had begun to circulate in the hospital hallways, and he had no idea which of the rumours were true.

One medic whispered that the explosion had destroyed the entirety of Matriarch House. Another claimed many of the buildings around it also lay in ruins. There were numerous other bombs planted in key locations around the city just waiting to be detonated, if you believed what the various techs in the Emergency Department were saying. And Danforth was either injured, dead, or in hiding.

The rumour mill was in full flow; the citizens of Bellator were fascinated and terrified in equal measure. There was one thing the women all agreed upon though: Eremus was responsible. It made Noah sick. After a while, he'd taken to reciting all the prime numbers in his head to tune the babble of voices out.

Eventually, the ambulances began arriving from the bomb site. Instead of filling supplies, drudges were now directed to transport patients from the emergency room to the various wards in the hospital, or, more tragically, the morgue. In the space of an hour, Noah had taken five trolleys to the depressingly large room located on the far side of the hospital.

The number of casualties was shocking. Many of the women being brought in were severely injured. Some had lost their fight on the way from the bombsite to the hospital. Others had been treated once they arrived, but had quickly succumbed to their injuries.

When he arrived back at the Emergency Department, he was dismayed to see the familiar black tag on the rail at the base of the trolley he was assigned.

"Another one who didn't make it." The tech's tone was emotionless, and Noah couldn't look up to see if her facial expression differed. "Take her down and get back here quickly. There are more on the way."

He nodded his understanding, not judging her. One way to cope with the death which stalked the hospital was to mentally distance yourself. Many of the medics had struggled with this, their voices cracking as they dispatched bodies to the morgue. More than one had broken down in tears, but it didn't help those who were still alive. The women who needed saving required a clear head and a steady hand.

Noah respected those who could stay focused. They reminded him of his ma, who always seemed to keep a cool head in a crisis. Over the years he had witnessed her treating many sick and injured Eremus citizens, always fighting to save lives with the limited resources she had available.

The only time he'd ever seen her crack had been when Dawn, Ella's ma, had been shot. Even then, Anna hadn't let her terror stop her. Where many would have frozen, she had somehow managed to push through, drawing on some inner strength as she attempted to stop her friend losing blood and barked commands to those around her.

Only when Dawn had succumbed to her injuries, had she allowed herself to break down.

A wave of loneliness washed over him as he began to push the trolley along the now-recognisable route. As he had with every victim, he glanced at the woman, wanting to pay his respects. And also, though he wouldn't admit it, to check that the body on the trolley wasn't familiar.

This woman lay on her back, her head facing away from him. Her features were hidden by her hair. Her *long, blonde* hair, which was stained red.

His heart stopped. Ella had long blonde hair.

His eyes roamed over her, desperately searching for other clues. She was young, he could tell by the skin on her hands. But the fingers were curled inwards, so he couldn't see whether they were roughened by work, the way all the Eremus citizens' hands were. He tried to work out her height, but it was difficult to estimate when she was lying down.

He didn't dare move her hair away from her face in such a public place.

As he approached the lifts, he prayed that there wouldn't be anyone else waiting. Finding the area deserted, he pressed the call button and waited, willing it to arrive quickly. It seemed to take an age, but finally the doors swished open. Waiting for a couple of medics to exit, he wheeled the trolley in as fast as he dared, angling it so the woman's head was underneath the camera.

He pushed the button for the basement. Clutching the rail which ran around the trolley, he waited until the doors had swished closed. He didn't want to check, but if he didn't do it now, he might not get another chance. Inching forward, he slid around the side of the trolley so he was out of the camera's view.

As he got closer to the woman's head, he could feel a line of sweat trickling down his back.

Let it be someone else. Please. Let it be anyone but her.

His fingers were trembling as he reached forward to brush the woman's hair out of her face. The skin was cold to the touch, the hair brittle. A devastating wound ran along the woman's forehead and snaked down her left cheek.

But it wasn't Ella.

His entire body sagged with relief. Even with the injury, he could tell. The face was too angular, the cheeks far wider than those of his petite friend. He closed his eyes.

The woman in front of him was dead. She had died violently, painfully. She wasn't his friend. But she'd been *someone's* friend.

For a moment, he thought he was going to throw up. Sucking in a deep breath, he replaced the woman's hair as gently as he could and backed away.

I'm sorry. He opened his eyes. He made himself look at her. *I'm so sorry.*

The ping of the lift jolted him back to reality. He managed the rest of the journey on autopilot, then escaped the grimness of the morgue as fast as he could. On the return journey, he ducked into the rudimentary drudge bathroom for a brief moment of respite.

As he stood in front of the sink, he inhaled deeply. The woman had not been Ella, but she had been similar to his friend. Young, innocent, full of life. She hadn't deserved her fate.

And Ella might still be brought to the hospital in the same state.

Noah clutched the rim of the sink, dread and fury coursing through him in equal measure. The earlier nausea returned, making his head spin.

He'd faced illness and injury before, in Eremus, but never on such a scale. Back home, his ma would have allowed him to assist with treating the patients, as he had with Dawn. Be active, play his part.

He rolled his shoulders up and back. His right arm had already felt tender after his fall, but now his entire body was stiff with tension. He was nothing but a lackey here: fetching and carrying items for the people who were trying to save lives, desperate for news of his friend.

He closed his eyes as a darkness descended over him. Letting go of the sink with one hand, he flexed his fingers. Curled them into a fist. Raising his hand, he rested it against his forehead. Willed himself to breathe. He moved the fist away, then brought it back into contact with his skin. Repeating the movement, he increased the pressure each time, until he was pounding his fist against his skull over and over.

When he stopped, his head hurt. But the nausea had abated. He could breathe more easily. He was able to move again.

Leaning down, he splashed his face with cold water, willing himself to retain control. If this was Jacob's doing, it was something he could never forgive. The death of so many innocent Bellator citizens was inexcusable. And all the while, the women of the city blamed Eremus, cursing the *vicious brutes from the forest*. Destroying the fragile trust the Resistance and Eremus had attempted to build through Faith and Flynn's words.

He hadn't allowed himself to think too hard about his father yet. Flynn had been on stage right beside Danforth when the bomb had exploded. Unarmed. There was no way the chancellor would let him walk out of the city unscathed. Not if she blamed him for this, which she no doubt did.

Quashing the frightening thought, Noah dried his face. Exiting the bathroom and heading back to the Emergency Department, he steeled himself to resume transferring bodies to the morgue. But when he got there, the next patient he was assigned was still alive.

And very familiar. Lying on the trolley, her eyes closed, was Helen. Praying she wouldn't open them and let a flash of recognition give them away, Noah glanced at the note on the board. Ward A9.

As he transported her through the hospital, he wondered why she had been brought in. She hadn't been anywhere near the bomb, and at a glance, appeared to have no injuries. But the fact that she was being taken to a ward implied she required treatment.

So far, she hadn't moved. *Was she unconscious?* He couldn't touch her to check. Hoping it was a pretense to avoid awkward questions, he waited until he was in the only place it was safe to converse.

Entering the lift, he pushed the button to go up to the wards. This time, he made sure he stood directly under the camera in the corner. As they began whirring upwards, he took a breath.

"Helen? It's Noah." Her eyes flew open. "Stay still. Don't react."

She closed her eyes again.

"I'm here working undercover. Are you okay?" She moved her head slightly. A nod. "That's good."

She rolled her head away from him. "Danforth wanted the medics to check me over."

She was turning away to hide her mouth from the camera. Encouraged by her astuteness, he asked the question he dreaded the answer to.

"What happened to Flynn?"

"Arrested." Her voice was muffled, as though she was moving her lips as little as possible. "We were separated as soon as they brought us off the stage." She shuddered. "The guards who hauled him away were pretty rough."

"So Danforth blames him?"

Helen inclined her head again.

Noah's heart sank. "Do you know where he's been taken?"

This time, Helen shook her head. There was a silence, as Noah considered Flynn's plight. There was no way Danforth would let him get away with this. But what could be done to save him?

The lift's whirring sound increased. They were approaching the ward floor. On the trolley, Helen shifted her body slightly.

"What about Sophia?"

"Resistance took her from the hospital earlier today." He wished he could be certain that the rescue had been a success. "She was on her way to Resistance headquarters when the bomb went off. I just hope they made it."

"And Ella?" Helen's voice was filled with trepidation. "Flynn said she was working undercover. Is she–?"

The question hung between them. Noah hesitated, not wanting Helen to have to shoulder the burden of dread alongside him. Admitting where Ella had been working would have Helen jumping to the same conclusion he had. But he didn't want to lie.

"Don't shield me." Helen's tone contained an undertone of steel. Gone was the frightened rabbit he'd first met in the tunnels of Eremus. "I need to know."

"I don't know where she is," he admitted.

As Helen fought to keep the emotion from showing on her face, Noah steeled himself to admit the truth.

"She'd... she'd been working at Matriarch House."

Helen's eyes were open, her stare filled with alarm. "And that's where–"

"Yes." He searched for words which might offer comfort. "I'm sorry. I've no idea if she was there today. She might not have been working, or she may have been in an area of the building which wasn't affected."

"But she might have been right at the centre of it all."

Noah's mind travelled over the battered and broken bodies he'd witnessed entering the hospital over the last few hours. The blonde woman's face appeared in his head, morphing into Ella's. Shaking his head, he tried to stay positive.

"To my knowledge, she hasn't been brought in." He fought to keep his voice steady. "I'll keep my eyes open for her. I promise."

As the lift pinged open, Helen closed her eyes again. This time, to mask the pain. He manoeuvred the trolley out of the lift and wheeled it to the ward doors. Pressing the buzzer to indicate their arrival, he waited until one of the medics inside opened the door.

Nodding briskly, she gestured for him to follow her. He pushed the trolley along the ward, wanting desperately to offer Helen comfort, but knowing that he couldn't risk speaking. It was torture. When he helped to transfer her into the bed, he squeezed her hand tightly, hoping it conveyed his support.

As he exited the ward, a weight lifted from his shoulders.

He couldn't assist with saving the women who had been caught in the explosion. He couldn't help rescue Ella or save Flynn from Danforth's punishment. But he had helped get Sophia out.

And now he could be here for Helen. For the first time since the explosion, he was certain he should stay.

Promising himself he would find some way to get back to check on her later, he took a deep breath and headed back to the Emergency Department.

Chapter Five: Faith

"**C**ome in!"

Nerves fluttered in Faith's stomach as she pushed open the dorm door.

After three hours contacting the various safehouses, she and Blake had confirmed that all the Resistance operatives were safe. Apart from Ella. Numerous attempts to contact the young Eremus woman had gone unanswered. And while Blake had given many plausible reasons as to *why* Ella might not be responding to their calls, it was difficult not to think the worst.

As news filtered in about the explosion, a picture was forming. The only building affected by the explosion was Matriarch House. Set amongst fairly extensive grounds, the government headquarters was a fair distance from other locations, so the damage was limited to Danforth's command centre. But it was extensive.

The front of the property had been decimated, rubble scattered across the lawn and amongst the trees which fringed the grounds. Parts of the rear were still standing, but fires were raging among the debris, making it difficult for emergency services to rescue people. The thought that Ella might be lying among the debris haunted Faith.

When Blake suggested she take a break, she suspected it was only to get rid of her. But Faith had been desperate to see her friend ever since Sophia had arrived at the library, so eventually she took the techie up on her offer.

Now that she was at the door to Sophia's room though, she was nervous. After years of spending a large part of every day together, it had been weeks since they had last seen each other. So much had happened to them both in that time.

Faith had no idea what to expect.

Taking a tentative step inside, she scanned the room. All the beds were empty except the one at the far end under the window.

Robyn and Lily stood at the foot of it, conversing in whispers. A figure bent over the bed, ministering in some way to the patient. It took Faith a moment to recognise Rowan, the drudge who Noah had replaced at the hospital. She supposed it made sense that he was being put to use in this way. He was comfortable in a medical environment.

As the door closed behind her with a click, Robyn and Lily looked her way.

"Any news on Ella?" Robyn looked hopeful.

Faith shook her head. For a moment, their expressions were sombre, then Lily stepped forward with a smile.

"She'll turn up soon. Guess you've been permitted to see the patient, at last." She beckoned to Faith. "Don't be shy."

"If you're all set, I'd better get going." Robyn turned back to Lily as Faith headed towards them. "I'm sure Madeleine has things for me to do." She glanced down at the bed, her eyes darkening. "Keep me posted, please Lil? I don't want to let the situation get away from us."

"Of course."

Faith turned to the senior Resistance operative. "What situation?"

"Nothing for you to worry about." Robyn passed Faith on her way to the door, but refused to meet her gaze. "Good job on the speech, by the way. I heard it went well."

"Thanks." Faith tried to smile. "Pity its effect was ruined by the bomb."

It was true. As Faith had been speaking with the operatives in the safehouses, Blake had been gathering information on the events which had gone on in the city. The media was already up and running, and the news was bleak as far as the Resistance was concerned.

True to form, Danforth had been quick to blame the explosion on Eremus, making it seem like Flynn's appearance had been nothing but an elaborate diversion. It wasn't true, but so far, it looked like most of the Bellator citizens were swallowing the story. Jacob's little stunt had blown apart their efforts to change the minds of the city's women as surely as it had destroyed a large part of Matriarch House.

Danforth had appeared on the news already, repeatedly reassuring her citizens she was doing everything she could to keep them safe. Word on the street was that most of the women were *grateful* for her intervention. Evelyn had returned to headquarters via a circuitous route, listening to conversations on the way. Her report suggested that the incident had made the women more afraid of the Eremus men than ever.

Worst of all, both Flynn and Helen had been captured by Danforth. The chancellor had Flynn in custody. His badly bruised face had been flashed up all over the news, along with reassurances that he wouldn't be allowed to get away with what he and his people had done. Faith hoped that Noah hadn't seen the footage. She knew what it would do to him, witnessing the only father he'd ever known at the mercy of the devil herself.

As for Helen, they were all concerned about Danforth's plans for her. Faith thought she might become a replacement for Sophia. Once Danforth discovered her prize guinea pig's absence, she would need a substitute. Madeleine assumed she would be shipped back to the academy. Her reappearance in the city had been so public, Danforth wouldn't dare treat her as casually as she had Sophia. But sinister things were happening at the school, so there were no guarantees she would be safe in either location.

"We'll have none of that." Robyn stopped as she reached the door. She turned to face Faith, this time looking her dead in the eye. "Your words may have been overshadowed. They won't be forgotten, though. We can't expect to change people's minds overnight. It may take years. But every single person we cause to question Danforth's rule is a step in the right direction. Don't you forget that."

"But I–"

"No buts. People were listening. Perhaps the next time they walk past the academy, they'll think twice about what's going on behind those gates. And maybe," Robyn added, "the next time they have dealings with a drudge, they'll be kinder."

With a kindly smile, Robyn left the room. Faith stared after her. Was she right? Or was she simply trying to make Faith feel better?

"Come closer." Lily's voice broke through her thoughts. "She's been asking for you."

At Lily's comment, Rowan backed away from the bed. It was an instinctive move for a drudge, to subjugate themselves when women were present.

"Thank you, Rowan." Lily smiled widely. Faith was glad that the Resistance women did not treat Bellator's serving class the way the rest of the population did. "You can try again in a little while."

As the drudge turned away, Faith caught a glimpse of the bowl in his hand. It looked like it was filled with soup. Had he been trying to *feed* Sophia?

As Rowan left the room, Lily grasped Faith's arm, ushering her closer to the bed.

"Look who's here!" she trilled. "Seeing your best friend will be just the medicine you need. I know you're..."

But Faith's eyes had found Sophia's. For a moment, they were back in their dorm, at the academy, about to go down for breakfast or out for a walk in the grounds together.

"Hey, Soph." Faith lowered herself onto the bed, careful not to jostle her friend. "How's it going?"

Sophia's eyes brightened at Faith's voice. "I *knew* you wouldn't abandon me."

Sitting bolt upright, she flung herself forward. As Sophia's arms tightened around Faith, she realised for the first time how skinny her friend was. And, as she pulled her closer, she felt the gentle swelling of Sophia's stomach.

Guilt crept over her. Sophia had been in Danforth's clutches for too long. Yes, they had got her back, but at what cost? She had been subjected to numerous experimental treatments. Spent hours alone hooked up to machines which monitored her every move.

And she was pregnant.

Feeling Sophia wince, Faith relinquished her hold. "What is it?"

"It's nothing." Sophia proffered her arms. There were numerous sores on the white skin on both. "I'm just a little sore, that's all."

"What on—?"

"They're from the tubes that were attached to me in the hospital." Sophia pressed a finger to one of them. "Noah had to take them out."

"Noah did this?" Faith tried to keep the horror from her voice.

"He did." Sophia beamed. "I almost fell out of bed when he walked into my room at the hospital. *Noah*, in *Bellator*?"

"It was a good job he was there." Lily stepped forward, pressing a bandage to the wound. She turned to Faith. "You know we were majorly delayed in getting to the hospital. If Sophia hadn't been ready to go when we arrived, we may not have gotten her out at all."

"So Noah was..."

"Quick-thinking, resourceful, heroic?" Sophia raised an eyebrow. "Most definitely."

"She's right. We'd have been lost without him." Lily bent closer, examining the broken skin. "I know we've already cleaned these up, but I might just go grab some more sanitiser and give them one more dousing. Just to be certain." Moving away, she headed for the door. "It's great to see you with a little more energy than you had earlier. I told you seeing Faith would do you good. Won't be long."

Left alone, Faith turned back to Sophia. "I'm so glad Noah was there for you." She took hold of Sophia's hand. "I'm just sorry that *I* couldn't be."

"Don't be silly." Sophia dismissed her apology. "I knew you'd be playing your part in the rescue mission." She leaned closer. "I hear it was a pretty big part, actually."

"Not really."

"Lily was telling me all about your speech. How powerful it was." Sophia insisted. "That's so much more than rescuing a single person."

"I'm not sure it did us much good, though."

"You don't know that yet." Sophia squeezed Faith's hand. "Hey, I heard you and Diane staged a breakout from Eremus to come and get me." Faith smiled at her change of subject. Sophia had always been intuitive. "You'll have to tell me about it."

"I will... sometime." Faith managed to smile. "But, for now, I'm more interested in what's been happening to you."

She sat back, allowing her gaze to roam over her friend properly. Sophia was pale, her skin almost translucent in the light from the overhead bulb. The pregnancy had rendered her stick-thin, aside from the belly which protruded more than Faith had expected for someone who could only be a few weeks pregnant. Her eyes were hollow, enveloped by haunting dark circles which contradicted Sophia's cheerful words.

Faith choked back tears. "How does it feel?" Her eyes lingered on Sophia's stomach. "I mean... did you know that you were...?"

"Pregnant?" Sophia dropped her gaze. "Not at first. I overheard a couple of conversations. They were whispering about cycles and fertility. I kind of got an inkling of what they wanted. But one day they came in all excited. And when they took me for the scan, I knew what they were looking for. When my stomach started to..." she gestured to her belly, "it just confirmed what I'd suspected."

"How is it?" Faith shifted a little closer. "Do you feel different?"

"It's draining." Sophia sagged back against the pillows. "I'm very tired all the time. And I'm..." she faltered for a moment, "I guess I'm a little nervous. This pregnancy isn't an ordinary one. The drugs they were giving me... I don't know what effect they've had." A tear rolled down her cheek. "Faith, I thought I was never getting out of there."

"You're here now, though." Faith reached for her hand. "We'll look after you."

"I know." Sophia brightened. "Robyn said they've assigned Lily and Rowan to me permanently, until I get better. I feel *very* special."

It was true. Lily had limited knowledge and experience, but was the closest the Resistance had to a medic. And with no other Resistance operatives in the building to help Lily, Rowan was an obvious choice to assist her.

"You are very special." Leaning forward, Faith enveloped her friend in another hug. "I'm so pleased I have you back. I just hope…" she pulled away, "I hope that you–"

"I'll be fine." Sophia was smiling, and looked more like her old self. "With a couple of weeks' rest, I'll be grand. Now that I'm off the drugs, how could I fail to get better?"

Faith didn't want to mention the baby. No one knew how Sophia's pregnancy would progress when it was the first of its kind. But her friend looked so much more positive now; Faith didn't want to ruin her mood.

A knock made them both turn.

"Up for another visitor?" Diane popped her head around the door.

Faith leapt to her feet. "When did you get back?"

"Just now." Her friend hovered in the doorway, grinning. "Bit of a delay on my way back. Streets are pretty busy, what with the clear up from the explosion and all."

"What's so amusing?" Faith frowned. "It's not like the mission went exactly to plan, is it?"

"Well, no." Diane sobered. "But let's just say I'm grateful for small mercies."

"*Small–?*" Faith shook her head. "Would you come inside? *Why* are you hovering in the doorway like that?"

"Because…" Diane glanced at Sophia. "I wanted to check if the patient could cope with multiple visitors."

Sophia and Faith exchanged glances.

"I can manage two people." Sophia rolled her eyes. "It's hardly a crowd."

"Well, actually, it would be three." Diane shrugged. "But I figure the third visitor's someone you'd be happy to see."

Diane stepped aside. In the gloom from the hallway, Faith couldn't make out the figure behind her. But when she stepped into view, Faith's heart soared.

"Ella!"

"Hey." The young woman's clothes were filthy, her face stained with sweat and dirt, but she looked unhurt. Her face reflected an exhaustion beyond measure, but she managed a small smile. "I hear you've been looking for me."

Chapter Six: Noah

Pushing an empty trolley in front of him, Noah exited the lift for what seemed like the hundredth time that day. It was early evening, and the flow of victims from the bombsite seemed to have subsided. Thankful that there were no more bodies to move to the morgue, Noah had been happy to keep busy with the multitude of other tasks that had arisen since the explosion.

The operating rooms had been in constant use all day, as the doctors worked on patients who had been brought in with various wounds. Though at the beginning of the day Noah had never been inside the operating suites before, they were fast becoming familiar.

On his eighth visit, he hurried in with a pile of fresh scrubs for the medics.

"Wait there," one of the techs barked at him. "Op's almost over. You can clear the area before the next patient comes in."

Noah didn't ask questions. Placing the scrubs on the half-empty shelf, he backed away and stood as unobtrusively as possible in the corner. He had never been asked to clean out an operating room before, and found himself thankful it was one of the tasks Rowan had run through in their brief training session.

First: collect the detritus left over from the previous operation. Bag it up to be taken to the incinerator. Next, fetch the sanitising machine (kept in the blue storage unit at the side of the room). Connect it to the power supply and place it centrally in the space. Ensure the room is empty before pressing the remote detonator. Put signage on the door to indicate the ten-minute re-entry period. Leave area, taking any rubbish away with you.

His palms were sweating. He didn't enjoy spending long periods of time around medical personnel. And the outer room of the operating suite was small. There were two techs present. He counted the legs, hoping the operation would finish soon so he could get the job done and leave.

At least the techs weren't paying him any attention. It meant he had fooled them. Drudges were infamously invisible. As the conversation between the techs continued, Noah knew he was playing his role well.

"Thank goodness Sanders managed to patch this one up," one tech exclaimed. "Not sure I could have taken another one down to the morgue."

"It's too much," the other replied. "Those bastards have got a lot to answer for."

Noah tensed, trying to tune out the conversation. It wasn't hard to work out who the *bastards* were. Obviously, the blame was already being placed at the Eremus door. He shouldn't have been surprised.

"Which ward is this one bound for?"

There was a pause as a set of fingernails clicked on the keyboard of a datadev. "C7. Needs to be watched carefully for signs of infection. And not–"

The woman broke off as the door from the outer hallway burst open. Noah worked hard not to flinch at the sudden entrance, knowing it would attract unwanted attention. But he needn't have worried. The techs' attention was firmly focused on the newcomer.

"Susie?" Shock pervaded the tech's voice. "What is it?"

"Need to see Sanders. *Now*."

Noah recognised the shoes at the same time as the voice. This was the medic who'd been assigned to look after Sophia. And Noah was willing to bet he knew exactly what shocking news she had to tell the doctor.

"She's in the middle of an operation! Can't it wait?"

"How much longer will she be?" Susie was panting. "It's pretty urgent."

The tech tapped at her keyboard again. "She's just closed the patient up. Won't be long now. Want to leave her a message?"

"I need to tell her in person."

The tech sighed loudly. "She should be done any minute now."

Susie tutted, but fell silent. Noah heard her shoes padding across the room. He suspected she was heading for the viewing window which would allow her to see what was happening inside the operating theatre. Holding his breath, he waited, hoping he'd at least get to witness Sanders' reaction.

"Look at that..." One of the techs had turned back to the datadev. "*Another* press conference."

The other crossed the room to peer at the screen. "What do you think Danforth's got to say this time?"

"Not sure." The tech tapped at the screen of the datadev. "Let's hope the news is more positive."

As the volume increased, Noah could hear a reporter's voice. *Chancellor Danforth herself will be here in just a few moments. We're all eager to hear what she has to say about...*"

The reporter was drowned out as the inner door banged open and a medic rolled a trolley into the space. The two techs jerked away from the datadev, hurrying to deal with the new arrival.

In the doorway of the operating room, another set of feet appeared.

"Know where this one's going?"

"Yes, Doctor Sanders."

"I've removed all the metal, flushed out the wound and sewn her up, but I want half-hourly checks on her vitals. No point in me saving her life for her to die of sepsis. Tell the lead medic to–" She broke off. "Susie? What are you–?"

"Need to speak to you. Now."

Sanders seemed flustered for a moment. "Half-hourly checks, okay?" She dismissed the techs. Crossing the room, she began washing her hands. When the door had swung shut, she turned to Susie. "This had better be important. I don't have long."

"It's important." Susie took a step forward. "She's gone."

"Who's gone?" Turning off the water, Sanders began to dry her hands.

"Sophia." Susie's voice trembled. "I think she's been tak–"

"Stop." Sanders cut Susie off. Moving across the room, she stopped a foot away from Noah. "I assume you're here to sanitise the operating room. Get on with it!"

Noah obeyed. Sanders waited until he was on the other side of the sound-proof glass before she spoke again. But as Noah donned a pair of gloves and moved around the room, collecting the abandoned swabs and bandages, he chanced a glance through the glass panel.

Sanders and Susie were paying him no attention. Instead, they were locked in an intense discussion, their faces horrified and their gestures wild. Lowering his head again, Noah hid a grin. Without Sophia, Danforth's experiment would fail. It had to.

No matter how badly the rest of the mission had gone, they'd succeeded in removing the chancellor's only successful subject.

He continued with the task, bagging up the rubbish and placing it at the door. Wincing at the twinge in his left arm as he picked up the heavy sanitising machine, he set it down at one side of the operating table and turned it on. Retreating to the door, he flipped over the *Keep Clear for Ten Minutes* sign. Then he pulled it open and stepped through, closing it before pressing the remote detonator.

A quick scan of the ground showed Noah that the outer room was empty. The techs had yet to return, and Sanders and Susie were gone, no doubt to report Sophia's disappearance.

The datadev lay on the counter, still open on the news channel. Noah chanced a couple of steps towards it, raising his gaze just high enough to view the screen. His eyes caught on a bright red tickertape running along the base: *Chancellor Danforth speaks out.*

Noah placed the bag on the counter, fiddling with the neck of it, so it looked like he was completing a legitimate task. As Danforth appeared on the screen, he tensed. Seated behind an official-looking desk, she was dressed smartly, her face its usual mask of calm.

"Citizens of Bellator," she began, "I know the past two days have been stressful for us all."

Noah peered at the screen. Danforth's comfortable surroundings could not be located in Matriarch House, if the reports on the extent of the bomb's damage were to be believed. *Where was she?* Her ability to rebound and relocate was impressive.

"This press conference aims to allay your fears and reassure you that this kind of attack will not be tolerated by your government." She paused for a second, letting her words sink in. "As you know, the leader of the band of rebels which threatens our town is already in custody. And whilst the number of males in the forests surrounding Bellator appears to be larger than we perhaps suspected, I have guard teams combing the area right now to find and bring in any other stragglers."

Noah's heart sank. Additional guards in the woods would put Eremus under a great deal of strain. He said a prayer that his ma and Paulo were managing to keep everyone at home safe.

On the screen, Danforth was listing the additional security measures she had put in place to protect them all. "...bringing in a city-wide curfew, for your own protection of course; additional guard presence on the streets, day and night; the latest bomb-detection technology in *all* our public buildings." She stared directly into the camera. "I will personally make sure that Bellator remains a safe place for us to live."

Of course, she would spin the tragedy into something which made her look good. Noah clenched the rubbish bag too tightly, cursing Jacob's actions. How much damage had he wreaked with his ill-thought-out scheme?

The threat of rogue males in the woods had always made the Bellator citizens nervous. Today's explosion had terrified them. And Danforth, as always, would use their fear to control them. She would claim that everything she did to counteract the threat was for their own protection.

And they would believe it.

He cast his mind back to Faith's speech. To her magical words, which he knew some of the audience had listened to. Believed. How powerful was Danforth, that she could destroy that fragile seed of truth with a few well-chosen words? Noah hated her.

At the sound of footsteps in the hall, Noah lowered his head. He picked up the rubbish bag, ready to leave if necessary. But the footsteps passed by, ignoring the room altogether.

Relieved, Noah allowed his eyes to wander back to the screen. Danforth had moved away from the desk and was walking across the room. The camera followed her. On the far side, a chair came into view. She circled it as the camera zoomed in. There was a figure sitting in it. Noah's heart started thundering as he recognised his father.

Flynn's face was bruised and bloodied, his arms bound behind his back in what must have been tight bonds, given the tension in his body. The expression on his face was one of anguish, but realising he was on display, he raised his eyes to the level of the camera.

"...no doubt you recognise this face." Danforth stopped directly behind him. "This is the man who tried to weasel his way back in with the Bellator women yesterday. And while his words *sounded* kind and reasonable, let's not forget that his associates were working away in the background, planting and detonating a lethal bomb in what they *knew* was a vital city establishment."

Despite his injuries, Flynn was somehow managing to retain an expression of calm. It was his way of trying to convince the Bellator public that Danforth was wrong, Noah knew. But would any of the viewers look beyond his masculine appearance and his bloody face? He doubted it.

"Remember," Danforth continued, "the male of the species is built for violence and cruelty. No matter what pleasant façade they hide behind, they are rotten to the core, and will turn on the female without warning if they are permitted even a modicum of power."

She walked around the front of the chair and took Flynn's chin in her hand. Forcing his gaze up to meet hers, she scowled and turned back to the camera.

"As you can see, this man has already been physically punished for his crimes. But the attempt to dupe us into submission while he murdered so many of our citizens is..." she paused, enjoying Flynn's discomfort, "unforgiveable."

"To that end," she released her hold on Flynn, permitting him to drop his gaze, "and because I am aware how many of you lost people in yesterday's attack, I am planning a public memorial ceremony this coming Thursday. It will be a time when we can come together as women to mourn our losses. As part of the healing process, to show you that justice has been done for all those women who died, this male will be present."

With a growing sense of dread, Noah stared at the screen. Thursday was less than a week away.

"He will be present," Danforth crowed, "so he can see the depth of our sorrow for the women he murdered. So he can witness the extent of our hatred of his gender, our determination to never again let men rule over us. And present, so we can all bear witness to what happens to men who seek to undermine and destroy us."

She was building to a grand finale. Returning to her position behind Flynn, Danforth took hold of his face, placing her hands on either side of his cheeks. She pulled his head up sharply. Noah winced at the pained expression which crossed his face at the movement. Making sure that he faced the camera, Danforth paused, her face a twisted mask of vengeance.

"The memorial will leave any other rebels with no doubt as to how we deal with threats and traitors to our city." She gave a definite nod before delivering the final blow. "It will show the people who is in control, who will come out on top. *Every. Single. Time.*"

She paused once again, her eyes zeroing in on the viewer.

"Because it will end..." she let the sentence hang in the air for a moment, "...with a public execution."

CHAPTER SEVEN: FAITH

The following morning, Faith woke with a start, a sheen of sweat covering her entire body.

Leaving Sophia to rest the previous night, she and Diane had holed up in the hub with Ella. Arming themselves with steaming cups of coffee, they had listened with growing horror to her story.

By complete chance, Ella had been outside the building when the explosion had gone off. Many of the canteen staff spent their breaks in the canteen itself, grabbing some food and chatting. Usually, Ella joined them. Part of her mission was to infiltrate the normal Bellator citizens, and break-time chatter was a perfect way to do this.

But yesterday, Ella had been anxious about the mission. She had chosen to go for a walk during her break, rather than join her colleagues, fearing they might sense her nerves and ask awkward questions. Leaving the admittedly-pretty grounds of the government headquarters, she had opted instead to pace the streets nearby, wanting to avoid contact with any of Danforth's staff and let off some steam away from prying eyes.

She had been on her way back when Matriarch House had exploded. Though the surrounding streets had been mostly free of flying debris, the force with which the ground had shaken told her how powerful the blast had been. Horrified, she had raced towards the building. When she'd arrived, she discovered that half of it was gone.

"It took me a while to get my bearings." Tears streamed down her cheeks. "There was so much damage. I couldn't even work out where the front entrance had been."

A circuit of the building had told her that the canteen lay in ruins. In deciding to take her break away from the building, she had escaped death. The main reception area had been decimated, as well as numerous offices and meeting rooms. The rear of the building was still standing, the Control Room included, but she suspected there would be a lot of smoke and water damage to the equipment.

In the short time that she'd been in the job, Ella had made numerous friends. When the emergency services arrived, she had volunteered her support, hoping she could help them. Though she hadn't been permitted close to the building after that, she had been able to assist with comforting the survivors who had been brought out, administering some basic first aid, and communicating with the medics in the ambulances when they arrived.

"I made a list of survivors, and attempted to catalogue their injuries. Tried to triage them, until a medic turned up to take over." She had sniffed loudly. "Later, I tried to help identify the deceased. With some of them..." her voice dropped to a whisper, "it wasn't even possible."

Though it had crossed her mind early on that she should check in with headquarters, Ella's wristclip had been out of action. Later, she had been too busy to check if it was working again.

"In all the time I was there, they only brought two of the canteen staff out alive." Ella had choked up. "It could so easily have been me. I... I stayed as long as they would let me. In the end, one of the medics told me to go home and get some rest." She had blinked several times. "At that point, all I could do was put one foot in front of the other until I got here."

She had swayed in her seat, her eyes fluttering closed. Between them, she and Diane had escorted Ella to one of the dorms. Before she succumbed to sleep, Ella had grasped Faith's hand.

"It was terrible." Her eyes were haunted. "All those innocent women..."

Remembering her words, Faith gritted her teeth. Yes, Ella was safe. But so many others were not.

In an attempt to work out the true damage inflicted by the bomb, Resistance operatives had been asked to check out various key locations all over the city on their way back to headquarters.

Olivia had been assigned to check out the situation at the hospital, but hadn't been able to get past the main lobby, let alone make contact with Noah. Slipping around the side of the building, she had witnessed the arrival of numerous emergency vehicles, filled with dead or severely injured citizens. Danforth's claims on the news channels had not been exaggerated. It made Faith even more concerned for Noah's safety.

How was he doing? After Olivia's failure to get inside, they had repeatedly tried his comms device, but it wasn't working. Had he even gotten any rest last night, with all the casualties from the bombing? And had he found out about Flynn's arrest yet?

He had to know, she reasoned. There were too many television screens around the hospital's public areas for him to be oblivious. She hoped he wouldn't plan anything rash.

Flynn's arrest, in addition to the deaths of so many Bellator citizens, had been devastating for the Resistance. Danforth's damning words had put the nail in his coffin, destroying any hope that the women of Bellator might believe Faith's claims about the Eremus people.

The other person no one had managed to track down yet was Helen. Despite several Resistance operatives poking around in likely places, nothing had been seen of the academy student. No one was certain what had happened to her after Flynn's arrest. The one thing in her favour was that she had appeared in Bellator very publicly. It meant, unlike Sophia, that the Bellator citizens knew of her existence. Hopefully, it would offer her some level of protection from suffering the same treatment as Sophia. But that was cold comfort to Ella, who had already lost so much.

After a quick shower, Faith made her way to Madeleine's office. Today, Professor Kemp was visiting the Resistance for the first time since her return to the city. She'd insisted that she wanted to see Faith and Diane during her visit. The curfew which Danforth had implemented was making movement around the city far more of a challenge, since the streets were supposed to be empty at night. As a result, the professor was having to visit them during the day, which had an additional element of risk to the journey.

When Faith entered the office, Kemp was already there.

"...forced to take an extremely circuitous route to reach the library," she was saying to Robyn as Faith entered. Turning towards the door, she beamed. "Good to see you, Faith. Great job on your speech." Her eyes flicked back to Robyn before Faith could respond, taking up seamlessly where she had left off. "I was certain that at least one Bellator guard was following me." She sighed heavily. "Now, I'll have to return before dark to ensure I don't get caught out by the curfew."

It was odd to see the professor seated here in the office. Her expression was calm, even after her difficult journey. She appeared unflappable under the most stressful of circumstances, which, Faith presumed, was what made her so good undercover. She could see why the Resistance had wanted her back.

A noise behind Faith made her turn.

"Ah, you're already here." Madeleine swept past Faith with Diane in tow. "Come in, come in. Let's get started."

Faith and Diane closed the door behind them and took the last available seats as Madeleine sat down in her usual chair and turned to Professor Kemp. "*Tell* me you have something positive for us."

Kemp frowned. "I'm afraid not."

The mood in the room took another nosedive. Madeleine let out a hiss of annoyance and Robyn leaned forward, her face tense.

"The second she realised Sophia was missing from the hospital, Danforth got in touch with Anderson. I'm afraid things at the academy are about to get even worse."

For several hours after the explosion, there had been no word on Danforth's reaction to her most promising subject's disappearance. But Robyn had listened to a conversation in Anderson's office late the previous night which had left no doubt as to the level of the chancellor's panic over the loss. Danforth had been furious, speaking several times of *dramatic measures* now being necessary.

She hadn't been specific about the measures, but, clearly, they were being implemented fast. Tighter security at the hospital was only the first step. Now, it seemed, the academy would also be affected.

"As you know, Anderson already has every single senior girl on femgazipane." Kemp's tone was even as she delivered the facts, but there was a stiffness in her shoulders which conveyed her concern. "But none of them have been delivering results like Sophia's. As you know, despite the lack of success with the femgazipane, Danforth attempted to trial some of the girls on metraxilone, with catastrophic results."

Faith shuddered as she remembered the two girls who had died. Across from her, Madeleine shifted in her seat and Robyn stiffened. The guilt they felt at failing to make the drug switch earlier weighed heavy on them.

"The placebos you provided have prevented any similar occurrences," Kemp rubbed a hand across her chin, "but we have no idea how much longer we'll get away with using them."

"No one's questioned why they're not working yet?" Robyn cocked her head to the side, concern etched on her face.

Kemp shook her head. "Not so far. But they'll work it out soon, when nothing happens to the girls who are being given it. And now Danforth's lost her prime subject, she's getting desperate. I'm afraid we'll have more deaths on our hands, unless something is done."

Beside Faith, Diane went rigid, no doubt thinking of her friend Serene, who had also died as a result of the chancellor's experiment. Faith fought the urge to take her hand, knowing the tough older girl would not appreciate the gesture.

"What's Danforth's latest plan, then?" Madeleine asked.

"She's had Anderson raise the quantity of femgazipane being given to all senior students," Kemp continued, "and reduced the number of days in between doses."

"Damn her!" Madeleine slammed a hand on the desk, making them all jump.

Unfazed, Kemp continued. "She's also instructed that *all* the seniors be given metraxilone. Anderson has just put in an order for another five boxes of the stuff. We were running out of placebos with the limited number of students on the metraxilone. With all the seniors taking it, we'll run out in a matter of days. Which means..."

"Unless we get a new delivery of placebos to the school pretty damn quickly," Robyn was almost whispering, "we'll be looking at a lot more fatalities."

The reaction in the room was palpable. Momentarily, Kemp glanced down at her hands, folded in her lap. Her fingers were almost white. Robyn buried her face in her hands.

"Anderson *told* you this?" Madeleine narrowed her eyes. "I thought you'd said they were being careful what they said in front of you."

"They are. But I overheard a conversation between two of the other professors. And I've managed to sneak a look at a couple of the documents lying around the academy." Kemp shrugged. "It hasn't been too difficult to piece it all together."

"But *why?*" Robyn was pacing the room now. "When she knows that the metraxilone doesn't work until the femgazipane levels are right, why put the girls at additional risk?"

"Is she really *that* desperate to solve the fertility issue?" Diane spoke for the first time.

"Frankly, yes," Madeleine snapped. "She's hung all her hopes on managing to successfully reproduce without male seed. "And I think she's frightened by the Resistance's recent success. She's convinced the experiment will cement her power for good if it produces results. Sounds like she's willing to sacrifice anything to achieve that goal."

"You're right. Now that Sophia's gone, she doesn't have a choice but to keep trying with the other students." Kemp hesitated. "Sophia was Danforth's *only* success. There have been no other pregnancies. Many of the older girls' bodies are showing permanent signs of damage from the prolonged exposure to femgazipane. Add the metraxilone into the mix and... who knows how it will impact those girls."

"The femgazipane's killing them. Right?" Diane clenched her jaw. "Just more slowly than it did Serene."

"It looks that way." Kemp nodded. "I heard Anderson describe the seniors who've been badly affected as *useless*."

"So they're infertile." Robyn had stopped pacing. Her face was a mask of horror. "That's–"

"You mean... they can't ever–?" Faith butted in.

"Reproduce? Unlikely." Madeleine was clenching and unclenching her fists. "Which would be bad enough. But if what you're saying is correct," she turned to Kemp, "many more of the girls will end up dead, if she carries on this way."

Kemp's expression was bleak.

"We can't let her get away with this!" Diane burst out. "We have to find evidence. *Show* people. If the citizens knew, they'd never forgive her."

"You're wrong." Kemp's tone was harsh and Diane flinched. "If she manages to get this to work, people will forgive the methods she had to use."

"*Methods?*" Faith couldn't stop herself. "You mean sacrificing the lives of young girls?"

Robyn nodded. "With the right end result, she'll just spin it. Make herself the saviour. If Bellator can breed without the need for male input, the women of the city will support her."

"They'll *thank* her," Madeleine added. "For saving them all from the wicked, wicked men."

Faith shuddered. The lengths to which Danforth was willing to go to ensure the fertility experiment worked were terrifying. But the idea of the citizens condoning it was even more disturbing.

But Kemp wasn't finished. "Sadly, that's not all." She hung her head. "Danforth wants to start testing the juniors."

"What?" Robyn sprung to her feet. "But they're–"

"Young?" Kemp smoothed a hand over her hair. It was a habit of hers, Faith knew. A subconsciously anxious gesture. "I know. I was as horrified as you are. But it's happening. This morning, Anderson asked the professors to start selecting a number of younger students who might take the place of the seniors in the testing programme."

"Sounds like she's *expecting* fatalities," Diane said bitterly. "She wants to have replacements all lined up, so it doesn't slow her progress."

Madeleine shook her head. "The effect those drugs might have on the body of a pre-teen."

"How can we leave them in that situation, suffering like that?" Faith asked. "I mean... can't we get them out?"

Madeleine's face remained emotionless. "If we move them, where would we put them? Safely? Danforth would be sure to know we were behind it."

"So?" Faith had burst out. "Isn't that what the Resistance is *for*? To protect people? Isn't there *somewhere* we could take them?"

"Moving that many girls?" Madeleine had raised her eyebrows. "Without detection?"

"Could you at least think about it?" Kemp's tone was softer. "I mean, Arden and I will do what we can to protect them from the inside. But it won't be enough. And when they realise that the metraxilone pills are placebos... which they will, in the end... they won't hesitate to replace them with the real thing."

"Those girls are in terrible danger," Robyn's face was serious, "As are you, professor, when Anderson starts asking questions about where the placebos came from."

"Alright." Madeleine gave a tight nod. "I suppose the safehouses might be an option. I'll see what I can do."

"Thank you." Kemp stood up. "Security's getting tight at the school. This might be the last time I can get out for a while. Could I see Sophia briefly before I leave?"

"Of course. Faith can take you to her." Madeleine also got to her feet, mirroring the professor. "Don't stay too long, though. Better you get out of here long before the curfew starts."

The Resistance leader walked around the table, surprising Faith by enveloping Kemp in a tight embrace.

"Take care of yourself." Madeleine pulled back, meeting the professor's gaze. "Keep a close eye on the girls, but don't endanger yourself unnecessarily. We'll work out a solution as soon as we possibly can."

Chapter Eight: Noah

For a moment when he woke up, Noah was still lost in his dream. He'd been walking though the woods close to Eremus, hand in hand with Faith. The sun had filtered down through the leaves, casting a warm light across her face. She'd turned to him and smiled, and all was right with the world. And when she leaned in to kiss him, he felt the trees around them whispering their approval.

He kept his eyes closed, trying to hold on to the emotion. It faded all too quickly though, and was quickly replaced by a gnawing ache.

The narrow bunk he slept on was uncomfortable and cramped, but no worse than he was used to back home. The drudges' food was basic, but he was never hungry, as he had been in Eremus. His body had even grown more used to the uncomfortable posture he had to adopt throughout his waking hours. But the pain he felt wasn't due to his drudge position.

It was rooted in the fact that Flynn was going to die.

Since the announcement about Thursday's memorial service for the fallen Bellator females, the staff and patients of the hospital seemed to have nothing but admiration for the chancellor. Noah had been forced to bite his tongue while the women heaped praise on Danforth for taking such decisive action, for her devotion to protecting them, for the multiple measures she was putting in place to ensure this *heinous crime* would not be repeated.

He'd lost count of the number of times he'd had to force himself to walk past people spewing hatred about Flynn and his followers. Curl his hands into fists to stop himself from lashing out at the women who cursed the males of Eremus for something Noah was certain they were innocent of.

Damn Jacob's insistence upon violence. He'd ruined everything for them.

After a quick wash in the tiny bathroom, Noah headed out. His shift would be long and tiring. The panic of the initial emergency was over, but the patients injured in the explosion would no doubt require frequent attention, which meant additional food deliveries, more sheets and towels, and extra meds. Noah didn't mind the work. The busy day would keep his mind off Flynn's situation.

Leaving the dorm, he lowered his head as he crossed the alley which ran between the drudge quarters and the hospital. He'd only made it halfway across when a strange hissing sound made him stare into the shadows on his left, where a row of waste bins was ranged along the wall. As if the drudges didn't already know their lack of worth, the positioning of their lodgings served as a daily reminder that they were trash.

He walked a few more steps before the hissing sound came again. On instinct, he moved closer to the first bin. Stooping to pick up a stray paper which had fallen out of the bin, he glanced at the space between the bins. Sure enough, there was someone standing there.

He raised the lid of the bin to cover his actions. "Who's there?"

The reply was instant. "Diane. There's a camera on the wall to your left. But it rotates. Wait until I say, then get in here while it's facing the other way."

Noah took his time dropping the paper into the bin. As he lowered the lid, she spoke again.

"Now!"

Without hesitation, he squeezed into the narrow space. Once there, he looked up.

Diane didn't waste any time with pleasantries. "How long before you're missed?"

"Not long. Five minutes. Ten, at most. We're still really busy with the fallout from the explosion, so there's a lot of–"

"Fine." She cut him off, her eyes urgent. "Let's get this done. I'm here to check in with you. Make sure you're alright. Swap relevant intel." She tapped her wristclip. "I'm going to record our conversation so I can report it back accurately."

"Okay."

"We expected you to check in with us. Use the comms device we provided." She tutted. "Not for us to have to lie in wait to speak to you."

"I tried, but it's not functioning." Noah fingered the tiny device concealed in the sleeve of his drudge tunic. "Not sure if it's damaged."

"Could be something to do with the extra security measures around the hospital, I suppose." She peered closely at him. "You look tired."

"I'm exhausted." He shrugged. "The emergency has taken a toll on all of us. But I'm coping. Once I–"

"Are you in danger?" she continued. "Sick? Injured?"

"I'm okay." Noah flexed his arm. It still ached, but the pain was easing now. "Just tired, as I said."

"I assume your cover's still intact?"

"As far as I know. I did have one sticky moment, but–"

"Do you need us to extract you?" Her eyes flicked to the alley beyond and back to him. "We'd rather not, but if you feel your position is a dangerous one, we can–"

"It's fine." He shook his head. "I know the ropes now, and I have a drudge on my side. He'll help me out where he can."

"That's good." She nodded. "So you're safe, for now."

As he nodded, it struck Noah how well Diane had adapted to the Resistance life. For Madeleine to send her on a mission without a partner so soon was impressive. But things were difficult, right now. Perhaps desperate times had called for desperate measures.

"Thought you'd want to know that Sophia's safely back at HQ." Diane waved away his response. "No time to celebrate. But Madeleine conveys her thanks for your part in the mission."

Noah felt a small surge of triumph. One thing had gone right with the mission, then. "Is Faith—"

"She's fine. Happy to have Sophia back, obviously." Diane pressed on with total focus, seemingly unaware of Noah's emotions. "You know about Flynn?"

"Yes." The gnawing ache returned. "What are you—"

"We're working on a solution." Her voice contained an urgent quality. "You are, under no circumstances, to attempt any kind of rescue. Leave it to us."

Suddenly, Noah understood the main purpose of Diane's visit. Not to check on his status. Or to share intel. But to make sure he wasn't planning any rash moves to save his father that might mess things up for the Resistance.

"I won't." He sighed. "It's not like a single unarmed male would stand a chance of getting into a maximum-security government facility. I'm assuming Danforth has him locked up somewhere?"

Diane dropped her gaze. "We think so."

"You *think* so?" Noah lowered his voice as the door to the drudge quarters banged open. "You mean the Resistance doesn't know where he is?"

"We haven't been able to locate him yet." Diane paused, allowing the drudge to pass by before continuing. "Things have been crazy at headquarters. Trying to check in with all our operatives, working out who was behind the bombing, looking after Sophia, figuring out what we're going to do about the academy situation."

Noah frowned. "What academy situation?"

Diane's face darkened. "Kemp paid us a visit. Seems since Danforth discovered Sophia missing, she's decided to intensify the testing regime. Give *all* the seniors metraxilone." She held a hand up, anticipating his question. "We're working on sending a new batch of placebos, but we're not sure when we can get them in."

"That's–"

"Shocking, right? Danforth's even suggested they start testing the junior students! We're looking at ways to get the girls out as soon as possible. But we also have people looking for Flynn. We're confident we'll find him soon. And we're looking at ways to retrieve him when we do."

It was cold comfort. But the Resistance was Flynn's best hope right now. All Noah could do was trust that they would find him before the memorial service. Aware of the time ticking away, he moved on to another matter which had been plaguing him.

"Is Ella..." he couldn't finish the sentence, "I mean, has she..."

Diane's face softened slightly. "She turned up late yesterday."

"And she–"

"She's completely fine. Physically, at least." Her eyes clouded over. "She's a little traumatised, but she'll recover, in time."

"She witnessed the bombing then?" Noah remembered the violence and chaos of the Fertility Unit explosion. That time, there had been virtually no casualties. "Must've been horrendous."

"She stayed to assist with the clean-up too." Diane's tone was admiring. "Many of the victims were people she knew, so..."

It was just like Ella to stick around and offer support in an emergency. Noah could imagine the horror of finding people she had been working with only hours before dead. He shuddered, remembering the blonde woman he had taken to the morgue. Fearing the worst, not knowing whether the people you loved were alive or dead, was horrible.

He changed the subject. "Helen's here. In the hospital."

"She is?" Diane's eyes pierced his. "I'll let headquarters know."

"Tell Ella too. She must be out of her mind with worry."

"You've seen her, then?" Diane's eyes flashed with concern. "Is she injured? Sick?"

He shook his head. "Think they just want to keep her for observation, for now. As for what Danforth intends to do with her next…"

"I know." Diane held his gaze. "It's one of the things we're concerned about. Madeleine wanted you to stay in position and await further instructions anyway. But I'm pretty certain when she finds out Helen's here she'll definitely want you to stay. It's been very difficult to get people inside the hospital, what with all the extra security.

"How will I get a message to you?" Noah frowned. "If I need to?"

Diane shrugged. "Sounds like our only option is to send someone here in person again. Contact might be a little sporadic for the time being. But we'll do our best to get someone to you when we can."

"Alright." But Diane's words had not been comforting. Noah glanced at the alley behind him. "I'd better go."

Diane nodded, but as he backed away, she grabbed his arm. "Be careful in there." It was the most emotional the young woman had been since they'd started talking. "Keep a close eye on Helen. I'll let Faith know you're okay."

She released him, craning her neck until she could see the security camera. For a moment, she stared at it in silence.

Noah held his breath, readying himself to leave. When she finally waved a hand, he slipped across the alleyway and into the building as fast as he could.

Once inside, he got to work immediately, attacking tasks from the jobs' board like a man possessed. When he finally stopped to catch his breath, two hours had passed.

He was desperate to let Helen know that Ella was safe. But he had to have a good reason to visit her ward. Another hour passed without a suitable opportunity, but eventually Noah spotted a job on the board which would take him to A9. A patient needed to be taken for a scan. Hoping he'd be able to pass by Helen's bed and check on her at least, he snagged the task.

When he reached the ward though, the patient being taken to the scanner was Helen herself. Unable to believe his luck, he focused on keeping his head low and his movements smooth until he had her trolley in the lift. Echoing his actions of the previous day, he stood out of sight beneath the camera.

"I was hoping it might be you." Helen angled her head away from him again, disguising their conversation. "Any news?"

"Ella's okay." Noah felt a surge of warmth at delivering the good news. "She wasn't in Matriarch House when the bomb went off."

"Thank goodness." Helen exhaled audibly. "How did you–?"

"Diane showed up this morning." He glanced at the numbered lights indicating the different floors as the lift ascended. "Apparently Ella stuck around though helping with the aftermath of the explosion. She didn't get back to the library until quite late last night."

"Typical Ella, putting others before herself." Helen tensed. "It must have been awful for her."

"Yeah. I found it hard enough seeing all the dead bodies brought in here yesterday." Noah grimaced. "But they were strangers. To deal with the bodies of people she'd been working with... that she knew..."

He stopped talking as Helen brushed away a tear.

Gathering herself, she continued. "Any other news?"

"Apparently, they're working on a plan to help Flynn. And the girls at the academy." He sped up, knowing once they reached their destination, he would be silenced. "Kemp says they're making changes to the experiments *again*. They're upping the dosages for some of the seniors, even considering giving the drugs to the junior girls."

"The *juniors*? But they're–" Helen visibly paled. "Has Danforth gone mad?"

"Sounds like it. Sophia's disappearance must have sent her over the edge."

There was a brief silence. On the trolley, Helen shifted on to her side so she was facing completely away from him. Noah stayed quiet. Perhaps she needed time to digest what he had said. But as the lift began to slow, she spoke again.

"I'm frightened, Noah." Her voice was thin, shaky. "I heard the medics talking this morning. They're pretty satisfied that there's nothing physically wrong with me. This scan is just to double check there are no hidden issues. They're also waiting for some blood samples they sent up to the lab, but if they're clear..."

She broke off. The lift was coming to a halt now. Noah prayed she would finish what she had to say fast.

"If they're clear..." she was visibly trembling, "they're going to send me back to the academy."

Before he could respond, the lift doors sprang open. Noah wheeled Helen the rest of the way to the scanning department in silence. As he handed her over to the tech, he felt an overwhelming sense of guilt. Diane had asked him to look out for her. Already, he was failing.

He headed back to the supply building with a heavy heart. When he arrived, Liam was waiting in line to pick up a new job of his own.

For a moment they stood in silence. But as the line shuffled forward, Liam dropped back slightly so he stood almost next to Noah. Glancing around, he made sure that there was no one behind them.

Then he leaned a little closer. "Grab a task in the laundry room."

The man's voice was muffled behind the mask, but Noah understood. Giving a very slight nod, he did as the drudge instructed.

Ten minutes later he entered the laundry. Located at the rear of the hospital, it was staffed almost entirely by drudges. When Noah had first arrived, he'd dreaded coming down here. In Eremus they washed everything they owned by hand, and he'd had no prior experience with the large machines which did the job for the Bellator citizens. He'd had to closely observe the other drudges to discover the process.

Now, however, the room was one of his favourite places. The noise and steam which filled the room made it the perfect place to talk without being caught.

Liam was waiting for him just inside the entrance. "Look busy."

Pulling open a bag of dirty sheets emblazoned with the green star emblem of the hospital, he pushed it towards Noah, then moved to open the next one himself. Noah loaded the bag into the machine, filling the drawer with soap as he waited for the drudge to speak.

"You need to be careful." Liam emptied the second bag of laundry into the machine next to Noah's. "Sanders is on the warpath."

"I know." Noah folded the laundry bag and placed it on the shelf above the washing machine. "I was there when she found out yesterday. She didn't look happy."

"She's trying to work out who's responsible."

Noah felt a finger of panic curl inside him. "Do they know how Sophia got out?"

"Not exactly." He turned to face Noah. "Apparently there was an issue with a camera that went blind for a few minutes. I'm pretty sure you had something to do with that."

Dread settled over Noah as he considered Liam's words. "Do they know a drudge was involved?"

"Rumour has it they do. As for which one..." Behind the mask, he grimaced. "We're all the same to them." He shrugged. "But I think you need to be prepared for them to start questioning us all. Looking at which one of us might have been in the hallway when that camera went out."

Fighting a rising sense of panic, Noah collected another bag of laundry and began loading the next machine. "You think I should run? *Before* they start asking?"

"Maybe not." Liam snapped the drawer of the washing machine shut and turned it on. "They haven't started questioning us yet because there are so many patients at the moment. They're busy, so they need the drudges more than ever." He shrugged. "You probably have a couple more days before they start to investigate properly. But I heard that Danforth already has people checking the other camera feeds."

"Do you think there are drudges who know it was me?" Noah wiped his sweaty palms on his uniform. "Other drudges, I mean – who might give me away?"

The other man stared back at him, his gaze piercing above the mask. "I've spread the word that you're to be left alone. That you're on our side. Drudges are a pretty loyal sort. I think the others will know it was you, but they're unlikely to give you away." He inhaled a slow breath. "The administration isn't stupid though. They'll work out who it was in the end."

"Then I–" Noah found he couldn't look away. "I should run. But–"

"But what?"

"I received instructions this morning to stay. For now, at least. There's a patient in the hospital... the Resistance thinks I can help her." He shrugged. "I don't want to let them down."

"Fair enough." The drudge took the laundry bag from Noah's hand and folded it, adding it to the pile of empty bags on the shelf. "But don't risk staying here too long. And as I said, if you need me to cover for you in some way..." he shrugged, "let me know. I'll do my best."

"Thanks." Noah leaned closer, touched by the man's support.

"No problem."

"Don't take this the wrong way," Noah waited until another drudge passed by behind them, "but why would you risk your life to help me?"

Liam turned to face Noah. "You... the Resistance... you're trying to change things. Do something positive. That girl who spoke at the ceremony the other day?" Noah nodded. "She spoke for us. For *drudges*." He held Noah's gaze steadily. "No one else ever has."

Before Noah could reply, the drudge had begun to walk away.

"Wait here a couple of minutes before you leave. Probably best if we're not seen together."

Noah emptied a couple of machines which had finished their cycle and folded the sheets neatly, giving Liam time to get away before he headed for the exit himself.

As he headed back along the hallway in silence, he considered the effect of Faith's speech on the drudges. Aimed at convincing the *women* of Bellator that Danforth was bad, it had inadvertently had an impact on the servant class. Who, just maybe, were willing to join in the fight to remove Danforth from power.

It was encouraging news, and he found himself wishing he could share it with Faith. A pang of sadness hit him. He had no idea how long it would be before he could speak to her again. He was willing to bet she didn't believe her words had had any impact, after the explosion had overshadowed them.

As he headed out of the laundry room, he felt a strange mixture of fear and elation. They were making a difference, no matter how small. But he was in more danger here than the Resistance realised. How much would he have to risk before they permitted him to leave?

And how long would it be before the Resistance located Flynn? Attempted a rescue?

Thursday was five short days away. In a city with so many people, could Madeleine's team find him before then? Noah had no answers.

With a shiver, he put his head down and headed back to the storage room. Stay busy, he repeated to himself. Perhaps it would keep him sane.

CHAPTER NINE: FAITH

"**Y**ou're certain he wasn't in danger?"

"For the last time, he said he was fine!"

"And you told him Madeleine has plans to rescue Flynn?"

"I did." Diane took a swig of coffee. "Though I'm not sure what they are."

The hub was quiet. It was two days since the failed mission ended with the devastating explosion. Although the majority of the Resistance operatives had returned to the library, the whole place was shrouded in an air of misery. So many dead Bellator citizens. The potential for so many more, with the situation at the academy. And the impact of Faith's and Flynn's speeches totally destroyed by Danforth's recent declaration.

It was no wonder everyone was depressed.

On the opposite side of the table, Ella flung a piece of toast down on her plate. "Has Madeleine even managed to locate him yet?"

Diane shook her head. "No sign of him. Danforth's not prepared to lose her scapegoat. She's put him somewhere very secure."

"Could the situation get any worse?" Faith sighed. "A few days ago, it felt like things were looking up. But now, what with Flynn and Helen getting caught, and the situation with the academy students…"

"And what are we doing about it? Diane spat out. "Nothing!"

"Has anyone even told Eremus what happened to Flynn?" Ella asked. "I mean… they deserve to know."

Not for the first time, Faith thought of Anna. Did she already know what had happened to her partner?

A noise at the far end of the hub made them turn. As though their complaints had summoned her, Madeleine emerged from her office and made her way towards them. She looked tired, her face was pale, but there was a determination in her eyes which hadn't been there the previous day.

"Ladies." She didn't waste time on pleasantries. "We must continue with our work. Robyn, Blake, and I have been attempting to put a plan together." She turned to Diane first. "I need you to go on a scouting mission today. Various locations."

"I'm looking for Flynn, right?"

"You are. Blake has drawn up a map of likely locations. You can collect your specific assignment from her as soon as you've finished breakfast. There are a few of you, searching different parts of the city. Evelyn and Olivia are trying to source more placebo pills for the academy as a matter of urgency, though how we'll get them inside, I'm not sure yet." Sighing, the leader turned to Ella. "We'd like you to return to Matriarch House."

Ella's eyes widened. "But–"

Madeleine waved away her protest. "Danforth appears to have her people salvaging what they can from the sections of the building which are still intact. They're moving to a new location. Since you're one of the few surviving staff members, I'm sure they'll be happy to have you back. You may even find yourself assigned a more central role, which could be very helpful."

Faith could see Ella struggling with the idea. Her experiences in the aftermath of the bombing had been horrific, and she obviously had no desire to return to a place which held such terrible memories. But it didn't look like she had much of a choice.

"Would I..." Ella sat up a little straighter. "If I set off early, might I be able to go via the hospital? I was wondering if there was some way I could... get inside... check on Helen, see if she's–"

"Absolutely not." Madeleine cut her off. "We have enough to do at the moment. Diane returned from the hospital only yesterday. There's no need for anyone to go there today or tomorrow. It would put you in an unnecessary amount of danger for no practical reason."

"But I'd really like to make sure that–"

"I said *no*." Madeleine's eyes were steel. "You're to go to Matriarch House, as instructed. I'll expect a full report from you this evening when you're back. Okay?"

Ella's eyes darkened, but she nodded.

Satisfied, Madeleine snapped her focus to Faith. "As you know, there is little you can do outside of this building. But you shouldn't sit idle. Lily tells us Sophia seems a little stronger today. I'd like you to interview her about her time at the hospital. See if you can get more details about the people involved in her care, the drug dosages she was on, any other aspects of her treatment we may not know about. No detail is too small. It could prove vital when we attempt to extract the girls from the academy."

"No problem." For once, Faith's assignment was a pleasing one. "I'll head to the dorms right away."

"Good. We all clear, then?" Madeleine's eyes rotated between them. When none of them argued, she gave a sharp nod. "I'll catch up with you later."

Without further fuss, she moved across to another group of Resistance who were sitting on the opposite side of the hub to repeat the process.

Ella leaned towards Faith. "Wish we could switch assignments. I'm not sure how I'll..." she bowed her head. "It's just..."

"We get it." Faith grasped her hand. "You don't want to go back there."

"But we need you to." Diane's expression was resolute. "If we're going to continue to work against Danforth, we have to keep trying."

"I know you're right." Ella straightened up. "I just wish I felt reassured about Helen. If I knew she was okay, I'd feel a lot better about everything."

"I'm sure Madeleine will send someone over there in a couple of days." Faith attempted to comfort her friend. "For now, I suppose we'd better do as we're told."

The three of them stood up and collected their dishes. After washing them and putting them away, they all headed for the door of the hub. Before they got there, it opened.

Lily stood on the other side. Taking a step into the room, she waited for the person standing behind her to catch up.

"You're out of bed!" Ella was the first to rush forward as Sophia took a tentative step forward.

"Woah there." Lily shot out a hand to stop her. "She's still pretty weak. Don't overwhelm her."

A smattering of applause rolled around the room as Sophia made her way to one of the tables. Her face flamed with embarrassment as Lily helped her onto the bench.

"Got to go." Diane was smiling as she headed for the exit. "Great to see you up and about though."

Ella retraced her steps until she was standing behind Sophia. Bending down, she squeezed the younger girl's shoulders gently. "Seeing you out here has made my day. How are you feeling?"

As the pair continued to chat, Lily approached Faith. "I'm going to get her some porridge. Would you sit with her while I make it? Keep her company?"

"Of course." Faith was beaming. "Madeleine wants me to talk to her anyway."

Lily leaned closer. "She's still not A1. I didn't want her up out of bed, but she insisted."

Faith glanced over at her friend, who was saying goodbye to Ella. "She looks okay."

"She's barely eaten anything in the two days she's been here." Lily frowned. "And she keeps throwing up."

Faith eyed Lily. "Isn't that normal with pregnancy?"

"It is, but..." Lily shrugged. "There's just something I can't put my finger on."

"Fair enough." Faith accepted the other woman's concern. The unofficial medic was not usually overdramatic. "I'll keep an eye on her."

"Thanks." Lily moved off towards the kitchen. "Back in a minute, Soph."

Faith took a seat opposite her friend. Searching her face, she noted how pale Sophia looked. Perhaps Lily was right to be worried.

"You okay?"

Sophia nodded. "Sick of staring at the walls. I want to be helpful."

"There's no need. You should rest, take your time to get better. You've–"

"Been through so much?" Sophia's usually gentle features creased with annoyance. "If I hear one more person tell me that..."

"I'm sorry. It's just..." Faith searched for the right words. "We've waited so long to get you here, we want to make sure you're fully recovered before–"

"I get it." Sophia sighed. "It's just... I keep hearing about how hard the Resistance has been working to fight Danforth. You, Noah, Diane, Ella, even Flynn! I want to be part of that." She sagged a little as she finished speaking. "Instead of feeling like a burden."

"You're not a burden." Faith insisted. "I have the perfect way for you to be helpful. Madeleine wants to know all about your experience in the hospital. She thinks it will help us with the other girls who are still stuck at the academy in similar circumstances. Think you're up to a few questions?"

"Of course!" Sophia brightened slightly. "If you think it will help. And... I have a few questions for you too."

"Okay." Faith settled back in her seat. "What did you want to know?"

"Firstly, where are we?" Sophia gestured to the room around her. "I barely remember being brought here. We're underneath the library, right? But how big is this place?"

"I'll give you a tour later, when you're feeling up to it," Faith said. "But for now, you're in the hub. This is where the Resistance folks eat. And socialise, obviously."

Sophia stared around, more comfortable now that the other women in the room had gone back to their own conversations. "So, how long have you been here?"

"Um, less than an hour." Faith was puzzled. "We just ate breakfast."

"Not today." Sophia gave a gentle laugh. "In *total*."

"Oh. You mean when did we get here in the first place?" Faith remembered how little Sophia knew. She considered. "I guess... almost a month ago."

"And you left Eremus...?"

"As soon as we could after we knew Danforth's guards had you."

Sophia closed her eyes briefly. "Figured you'd do something crazy."

"Crazy?" Faith faked offence. "I'll have you know we thought our plans through very carefully." She winked. "You should be proud."

Sophia smiled. "I am proud. Can't believe you got all the way here without getting caught."

"Oh ye of little faith." She smirked to herself at the pun. "Seriously, though, it was pretty scary. I've never been so relieved as when we got here." Noticing Sophia's worried expression, Faith reached over and squeezed her hand. Shaking off her concern at how cold and clammy it felt, she continued. "It worked out in the end. Are you up to telling me more about what happened to *you*, now? I mean after you were taken from the forest?"

Pulling her hand out of Faith's, Sophia sank back against the bench. "Not much to tell... not really. Hammond's guards carried me through the woods to a waiting Jeep. They put me in it... drove me to the hospital."

"You weren't taken anywhere else first?" Sophia shook her head. "What happened when you got there?"

"They s-stripped me. Even took my academy pendant." Sophia's voice turned bitter. "Then they examined me. *So* humiliating."

"I'm sorry." Faith leaned forward. "You don't have to talk about this if you don't want—"

"You said it would be helpful. So I'll tell you. As much as I... I can remember, anyway." Sophia's voice was a whisper. "When the medics knew that I wasn't sick... or injured, they dressed me in a gown and stuck me in a bed. I was... was the only patient in the ward." She sucked in a breath, as though the memory caused her pain. "That was the..." she paused, breathing deeply through her nose, "the first thing which made me suspicious."

She broke off as Lily approached, a steaming bowl of porridge in hand. "Here you go." She placed it in front of Sophia. "I put lots of honey in it, build up your energy. Eat as much as you can manage, okay?"

"I'll try."

"I'll be sitting right over here when you want to go back to your room." Lily gestured to a table on the other side of the room. "Just holler when you're ready."

Sophia waited until Lily had moved off before picking up her story. "I tried to find out why I was... why they had me in the ward, alone..." She broke off, staring at the bowl in front of her. "But they wouldn't... no one would tell me anything."

Faith peered closely at her usually-lucid, intelligent friend. *Did she seem confused?* As Sophia continued, she leaned closer, her concern growing.

"Only medic who spoke to me said I was there for... for *assessment.*" Sophia rested her chin in her hand, as though her head felt heavy. "Whatever th... that meant."

Faith's heart went out to her friend. Having suffered similar treatment when she had been imprisoned in the academy, she understood Sophia's fear.

"First, they put one tube in. Here." She gestured to a small scar on the back of her hand. "Said they were giving me fluids... rehydrating me, that it would make me feel b-better. *Told* them I didn't feel ill, but..." Tears shone in Sophia's eyes. "Thought if I didn't struggle, they'd treat me better." She closed her eyes. "Sh-should've tried to fight them off."

"How could you have?" Faith was shaking. "You were totally alone. Terrified."

Sophia's eyes focused suddenly, zeroing in on Faith. "*You* would have fought."

"Maybe." Faith shrugged. "But it wouldn't have done me any good."

"After that, it's pretty hazy." Sophia bit her lip. "Don't know how long I was there. There's a huge section of time where it's all... blank."

"They lied to you. That first line they put in wasn't fluids. It was a sedative," Faith explained, through gritted teeth. "Once you were unconscious, they could do what they wanted to you, without fear of you putting up any kind of fight."

"As if I'd've f-fought them off," Sophia choked out. "I was too scared. When I woke up, I was...I was..."

"You were out cold. For days." *How much should she tell her friend?* "No wonder your concept of time got muddled. Once they'd put multiple lines into your body, there really wasn't any chance for you to escape." She eyed her friend. "I can't believe Danforth made you *pregnant.*"

"Me neither." Sophia moved a shaky hand to her stomach. "Something's not right, though. I can feel it."

"It does seem odd that you're showing so early." Faith agreed. "You can only be a few weeks gone, right?" She steeled herself. Her friend would want the truth. "Which means the pregnancy isn't... *normal.*"

She fell silent, not wanting to voice her fear. No one knew what would happen to Sophia as the pregnancy progressed. But Sophia wasn't stupid. She had to be thinking along the same lines.

Sophia was quiet for a moment, and Faith let the conversation lapse. There was a lot for her friend to process, and platitudes were not going to bring her any comfort. Eventually, Sophia sat forward, placing her elbows on the edge of the table. The movement seemed to take a lot of effort.

Glancing down at the porridge, she picked up her spoon. "How many of the academy girls are pregnant?"

Faith took a deep breath. "None of them."

"You mean..." Sophia paused, a spoonful of porridge halfway to her lips. "I'm Danforth's only *success?*"

"Yes. That's why it was so important that we got you out." Faith leaned forward. "You won't believe what's been happening at the academy. They have *every* senior on femgazipane now. But they haven't had any other success. They've even started to give metraxilone... that's the second drug, the one which caused your pregnancy... to some of the girls when they weren't ready for it. Despite the fact that..." she steeled herself to tell Sophia the truth, "two of them died recently."

"No!" Sophia gasped. She dropped her spoon back into the bowl, untouched. "That's... how could she—?"

Faith gave a heavy shrug. "She's desperate to make a success of the procedure. Madeleine's working on a way to rescue the girls, before the situation gets any worse. That's why she wanted me to talk to you." She paused, noting the still-full bowl of porridge in front of Sophia. "Are you going to eat that?"

Sophia sighed. "I'm never hungry."

Picking up the spoon again, she shovelled some into her mouth. She chewed it for several minutes, as though she had to psyche herself up to swallow. When she did, it was with a grimace.

She turned back to Faith. "What we need to... we need to..." she hauled in a breath, "we have to work out what makes you and I... different."

"What do you mean?"

Sophia took another hesitant mouthful. "Why did the femgazipane work...on us..." she chewed resolutely, "and not on anyone else?"

Faith shrugged. "I've no idea."

"There must be a reason." The quest for information seemed to give Sophia renewed energy. "Let's go over it again." Glancing down at the bowl, she pulled a face, but took another spoonful. "I was taken to the hospital..."

She closed her eyes, a sheen of sweat glazing her forehead.

"You said they stripped you and gave you a sedative, right?" Faith prompted her friend, desperate to distract her from the discomfort the food seemed to cause "Presumably, that's when they started you on the femgazipane?" Sophia nodded weakly. "That's different than my experience. I wasn't sedated." Faith shuddered, remembering the tiny room Anderson had kept her in. "And I was only given a single dose."

"But they... they saw promising results," Sophia replaced her spoon in the bowl. "We m-must..." She lowered her head to the table, resting it on her arms. "Must have..."

"Do you want to go back to bed?"

"No." Sophia waved Faith's concern away weakly. "Just a little... dizzy, that's all." She gritted her teeth. "We must have... have something else in common."

A thought struck Faith. "You said they took your pendant when they stripped you, right?"

"That's right." Sophia's hand drifted to her bare neck.

"And you were never given the pendant back."

"No." There was a flicker of determination in Sophia's eyes. "And you... you–"

"I *lost* my pendant. At the hospital. So when they gave me the drug, I wasn't wearing it. And neither were you." Her eyes locked on Sophia's. "But that's stupid, right? I mean, how could a *necklace*–"

"S'definitely an anomaly." Sophia muttered. Her head was still pillowed on her arms, but she forced herself to continue. "*Must* be significant."

"Yeah. I think it's worth checking out." Faith glanced at Madeleine's office door. "Alright. I'll mention it, see what they think." Faith turned to Sophia. "See? You're proving useful already." She stopped. "Are you okay, Soph?"

"I'm just so tired. And I feel a little... queasy." With a Herculean effort, Sophia raised her head. "Think maybe I should..."

"Let's get you back to bed." Faith placed a hand on her friend's back. It, too, was clammy. She tried to smile, not wanting to frighten her friend. "You've done enough for to-day."

Faith gestured to Lily, who hurried over, her eyes clouded with concern. Her eyes went to the half-full bowl. "Porridge not going down very well?"

Sophia didn't reply. Bending down, Lily slid an arm around her. "Help me get her back to her room?" Lily gestured to Faith. "I'm afraid it's becoming a familiar cycle. She'll probably throw up, then need to sleep off the effects." The medic's eyes were clouded with worry. "I was hoping we wouldn't need to put her on IV fluids, but I think now's the time to take that step."

Faith took her position next to her friend. As they helped her back along the hallway, she noted how much support Sophia needed. She could barely support her own body.

Lily was right. Sophia was not well. And if she couldn't eat, how would she ever build up the strength to recover?

CHAPTER TEN: NOAH

Noah's heart pounded as he approached the doors to Helen's ward. He hadn't seen her since she'd been brought to the hospital. Too long, when he'd decided his role was to watch over her. After waiting almost two days for a chore that would take him in her specific direction, he'd finally taken matters into his own hands. Grabbing a fresh bale of sheets, he'd headed off, praying no one would question his behaviour.

When he reached his destination, a technician was on the way out. Timing it just right, Noah held back to let the woman pass, then slipped through the doors just before they swung shut. Inside, as he slowed his breathing, he noted the lack of noise. It should have been a comfort that so few people were about in the evenings. But as he ventured further in, he was trembling.

Most of the patients were sleeping. After checking the ward was empty, Noah headed towards the private room at the far end, where Liam had told him Helen was. He passed the technician's office, where there was a low hum of chatter. Rounds were completed by this time of day, and staff were usually taking a well-deserved break. It was the reason Noah felt able to risk a slight detour from his usual duties.

As he approached Helen's door, voices floated from within. He froze. Leaning closer, he caught a snatch of the conversation. First, Helen's voice, her tone far more positive than it had been the previous day. And then, another female voice, one which was even more familiar.

At first, he couldn't place it. And then, it hit him. Inching closer, he peered inside. Sure enough, seated on the edge of Helen's bed was *Ella*.

Checking the ward was still empty of people, Noah ducked inside. Both girls spun to face him. He kept his head low, but imagined their faces were emblazoned with panic.

"It's Noah." Thinking quickly, he pushed the door closed with his hip, then placed the bale of sheets on the dresser. "Aren't there cameras in here?"

Ella recovered first. "I've taken care of it."

Noah's head jerked up and their eyes met. Hers were gleaming.

"But how—?"

She reached into her pocket and pulled out a small device which looked a little like a pen. "One of Blake's creations. It scrambles the signal within a five-metre radius." Grinning broadly, she put it away. "No one can see into this room via the camera right now."

Noah didn't add that a real-life technician or medic could come in at any moment.

He jerked his mask down. "When did—"

"She just got here." Helen didn't seem to be able to take her eyes off Ella. "Seems like she's becoming quite the undercover expert."

Ella chuckled. "Not sure about that."

"*I* am." Helen's eyes were bright. "You're fitting into Resistance life really well."

"What are you *doing* here?" Noah stared at his fellow Eremus citizen. "I mean, it's good to see you, but..." He moved a little closer to the bed, keeping his voice low. "Did Madeleine send you? Are you here on a rescue mission?"

"Not exactly." A flush crept up Ella's cheeks. "I asked Madeleine if I could try to get inside the hospital today… see Helen." She gritted her teeth. "She said no."

Noah could well imagine the Resistance leader refusing such a request, which was purely personal and served no practical purpose. But he kept quiet.

"But she did send me on a mission. Which I completed." Ella looked up, meeting his eyes. "Figured it would be acceptable to make a stop on the way back."

Helen's eyes were saucers. "She doesn't know you're here?"

"I needed to see you." Ella tilted her chin upwards. "She refused to let me come. So I made my own arrangements."

Noah finally took in Ella's hospital gown. "Are you a *patient*?"

"For now." The older girl pulled the neck of the gown to reveal a circular pad stuck to her chest. A wire trailed from it.

"What's that?"

"It's called an *electrode*, apparently." Ella shrugged. "It's a sensor, attached to a little monitor which is measuring my heartrate. It's strapped to me. Here." She pointed at a slight bulge at her waist. Catching Noah's look of concern, she smiled. "Don't worry. There's nothing wrong with me. I had to give them something real when I came to the Emergency Department."

For a moment, Noah couldn't form words. When he did, they burst from him more loudly than he'd intended. "What did you—?"

"Shh!" For the first time, Ella shot a nervous look at the door. "Are we likely to get a technician visiting at some point?"

Helen shook her head. "Not unless we attract their attention. In my experience, unless there's an emergency, the technicians on duty drink coffee, watch TV, and do as little work as possible." She glanced at Noah. "Keep your voice down and we should be fine."

Noah breathed in deeply, steadying himself. "How did you make them believe you had a heart issue?"

Ella scuffed a foot along the floor. "Took some of Blake's pills on the way here. She takes them to keep her awake. They're mostly caffeine, but I took more than I should have." She shot out a hand at his horrified expression. "It was a means to an end."

"A dangerous means to an end," Helen muttered.

Ella squeezed Helen's hand, then turned back to Noah. "When I arrived here, I told them I had severe chest pains." She shrugged. "The caffeine pills I'd taken made me pretty convincing. They put this thing on my chest... stuck me in a bed overnight for observation. Once they stopped watching me, I swiped one of the technician's schedules. I figured out where they were keeping Helen and," she swept a hand across the room, "here I am."

"So you're here *all night*?" Noah looked between them. "You don't think the Resistance will worry when you don't report in?"

"I'm sure they will." Ella dropped her gaze to her wrist. "I've turned my clip off for now. Didn't want any of the techs to get curious if it keeps buzzing away." She sighed. "I didn't intend to be here overnight, but it seemed to be the only way..." Her tone was defensive. "Look, it was important to me to see that Helen was okay." She relinquished her hold on Helen's hand. "And now I have. When my heart rate is normal in the morning, they'll let me out. I'll be back at the library before anyone gets too concerned."

"You'd better apologise when you get back," Helen said. "I get why you're here, but causing them all even more worry when they've only just got you back after the bombing..."

Ella nudged Helen's shoulder. "Madeleine should've *let* me come and see you. If she didn't want me taking matters into my own hands." She broke off, concern settling on her features. "It's a good job I did. If they're talking about sending you back to the academy soon, we have to do something about it."

Noah glanced at Helen. "Any news on that?"

She shrugged. "My initial scan was clear, but they're still waiting on some blood results. Apparently, the lab is backed up. All the extra patients from the bombing."

"So you're okay until…"

She nodded. "Until the results come back. But I'm not sure when that will be."

Noah turned back to Ella. "Any news on Flynn?"

"None." Her face fell. "Madeleine has people out scouring the city for him, but they've had no luck so far. Danforth's put him somewhere very secure."

"So Madeleine doesn't know where he is?"

Ella shrugged. "Not so far."

"And is there a plan to try and rescue him?" Noah fought for breath.

"How can there be, if they don't know where he is?" Helen's eyes were wide.

"They're going to keep looking." Ella admitted begrudgingly. "I know Madeleine has a lot on her plate, but she did sound like she'd do everything she could to get him back."

"I really hope that's true." Noah glanced back at the pile of sheets he'd left on the dresser. "I'd better go soon. Don't want to get caught up here." He turned back to Ella. "You said you were on a mission. What did Madeleine have you doing?"

"She sent me back to Matriarch House." Ella's face darkened. "Not that I particularly wanted to go, but…"

Noah understood. Back in Eremus, he still struggled with passing through the section of tunnel where they had attacked the Bellator guards. "Did you discover anything useful?"

"Not really." Ella shook her head. "The canteen was completely destroyed, but some of the offices survived. One of Danforth's senior advisors assigned a group of employees to help with the clean-up, before we move to our new place-ments. I managed to wrangle myself a spot. We were asked to retrieve any resources which had survived the blast. I was there for hours today, but I didn't find anything implicating the chancellor." She turned to Helen. "I did come across a stack of old papers about the academy though, in one of the waste bins outside."

"Really?" Helen sat forward. "What were they?"

"Not sure." Ella shrugged. "I haven't had a chance to look at them yet. They're a little smoke-damaged."

"They'll be throwing them away because they have digital copies now," Helen mused.

"They could be useful to the Resistance, though." Noah glanced at the door. How much longer could he stay?

"That's what I thought when I stashed them in my bag. I'll pass them to Madeleine tomorrow." She turned back to Noah. "And I'll go back, keep working on the clean-up, accept a job wherever they move us to. There *has* to be hard evidence somewhere of what Danforth is doing to the girls at the acad-emy. If I'm working inside the new government building, I'll be best placed to find it."

A shadow crossed Helen's face. "You think you could find something before they send me back to the academy?"

"I'll do my best."

Leaning forward, Ella put her arms around Helen. Noah glanced away as they held each other.

Eventually, Ella pulled away. "I won't let them send you back. I'll break you out of here myself, if I have to."

Helen smiled, but the expression didn't quite reach her eyes. Her future was still uncertain, and she knew it. Ella's declarations were useless without the Resistance to back her up.

"I'll do my best to watch out for you," Noah picked up the bale of sheets. "Come up here as often as I can. For now, I'd better go though." He looked at Ella as he moved towards the door. "Wait a while before you go back to your own ward, okay? Give me a chance to get clear."

Ella nodded. "Will do."

He hesitated. "Don't fall asleep in here, will you?" He turned to Helen, who was blushing. " I'll try and check on you again tomorrow."

"Thanks."

He turned to Ella. "Safe journey back to the library. Tell them I'll keep an eye on Helen." He nodded at Ella. "Keep looking for damning evidence against Danforth. I'll keep my ear to the ground here for the same reason."

As he retraced his steps through the ward, he felt a renewed determination. There had to be something they could use to take the chancellor down. They just had to find it. And soon.

Chapter Eleven: Faith

Faith's eyes fluttered open. For a moment, she wasn't sure where she was. Her back was stiff, and her head rested forward on something soft. It was still dark, but she didn't remember going to bed. Sitting up, she massaged her aching neck.

Then it hit her. She was in Sophia's room.

She sat up and checked the time on her wristclip. It was almost midnight. Beside her, Sophia was sleeping, her breathing so light that Faith couldn't hear it until she leaned close. When Faith took hold of her hand, it was no warmer than it had been in the hub at breakfast.

They had managed to get Sophia back to the dorm and into bed. But Lily's prediction had been accurate: within ten minutes, she had thrown up the porridge. Rowan had cleaned her up and settled her back in bed, while Lily fetched a cannula and section of tubing, which she had managed to insert into Sophia's arm.

"We have to rehydrate her," she had muttered to no one in particular.

Lily had been slightly happier once the fluids were flowing into Sophia's system, but her expression was still bleak. She was out of her depth, and she knew it.

The effort of walking to the hub and back, plus the vomiting episode, had taken its toll on Sophia. Since their return to the room, she had laid on the bed, her body limp and listless. Faith had stayed with her, hoping that a combination of rest and fluids would help her to heal, but neither seemed to have made much difference. Sophia was just as sick as she had been the previous day.

Tears pricked at Faith's eyes. All she had wanted for weeks was to have her friend back. Out of Danforth's clutches, away from the drugs, safe in the haven of the library. She'd pictured their happy reunion so many times. But she'd never pictured this.

Part of Faith was glad to be there to support her friend in her time of need. It was what you did for the people you loved. But another part of her hated every moment that she sat there, staring at her friend's wasted body. The coward in her just wanted to run away. If she wasn't in this room, she could pretend Sophia was going to get better.

But she had to face this. Be honest about what was happening to her friend. Looking at her right now, it was difficult to believe she would ever recover.

She had refused offers from both Lily and Rowan to watch over Sophia through the night. Either of them would have taken over, she knew. But she hadn't wanted to leave Sophia with people who were virtual strangers. Not when she was so sick.

Desperately thirsty, Faith reached for the glass of water which rested on the nightstand. She slurped at it greedily before setting it down. When she turned back to the bed she was shocked to see that Sophia's eyes had flickered open.

"Hey!" Faith fought to keep her voice upbeat. "Welcome back to the land of the living."

"Time is it?" Sophia whispered.

"It's late." Faith smoothed down the covers. "How are you feeling?"

Sophia grimaced as she shifted her body slightly. Trying to hide her concern, Faith leaned forward, adjusting the pillows until Sophia looked more comfortable.

"Feel up to trying a little food?" Faith gestured to a bowl on the nightstand. "I have a bowl of yoghurt and berries here, or I can go and make you toast if you'd like?"

Sophia leaned forward, glancing at the contents of the bowl. She blanched, bringing a hand to her mouth.

"Maybe later." The nausea had clearly returned. "When I'm less... when my stomach is..."

"You have to *eat*, Soph." Faith put the bowl back. "You have to build your strength."

"I know... I just... I can't." Sophia sank back on the pillows. "You saw what happened today. I keep t-trying, but nothing stays down."

"Okay." Faith tried to soothe her. "We can try again tomorrow, when you're more rested."

"Maybe." A lone tear trickled from Sophia's eye. "Thought I was improving."

"I'm sure you are." Faith insisted, not believing it. "It'll just take a little time, that's all."

Sophia sniffed loudly. "D-don't lie to me."

Faith grasped hold of Sophia's hand. "I'm not lying!"

Pulling her hand away, Sophia struggled to sit up. "Could you..." she gestured to the bed next to hers, "...another pillow, please?"

Glad of the excuse to diffuse the tension, Faith moved away. By the time she brought the pillow back, Sophia seemed calmer. Placing an arm around her, Faith assisted her into an upright position.

When she was settled, Sophia took a deep breath. "Thanks. And I'm sorry. It's just... difficult to stay p-positive...." She sighed. "Tell me about your speech."

For a moment Faith hesitated. But she could see her friend was trying to change the subject, think about something more positive.

"Um. It felt good, I guess." Faith felt herself blushing. "Like... like I was actually having an impact."

"You *were*." Sophia's eyes glowed. "Diane said... she said the women were really l-listening."

"Maybe." Faith shrugged. "But the bomb ruined all that."

"Not necess-essarily." Sophia paused, closing her eyes briefly. Faith leaned forward, concerned, but Sophia recovered and waved her away. "You made them... made them doubt. It's a good start."

"I suppose." Faith inhaled deeply. "What we need now is some solid proof of what I told them. Something that will convince them once and for all. But how do we get it?" She tried to keep the despair out of her voice. "Security at the hospital is crazy now. Matriarch House is in ruins. The curfew makes it more difficult to move around the city at night, and—"

"There has to be a way," Sophia whispered.

Faith chewed on her lip. "Persuading them that the Eremus people aren't their enemy will be too hard. The hatred of men is too ingrained. And with the explosion causing all these deaths..." Faith shook her head. "Can you imagine the Bellator women *ever* accepting them?"

"What if we could get someone... someone inside the academy..." Sophia drifted for a moment. She blinked slowly, coming back to the conversation. "I m-mean to take f-footage of the experiments..."

"Possibly." Faith was doubtful, but didn't want to discourage her friend. It was the most enthusiastic Sophia had been so far. "I guess Kemp might be able to do something, though she said at her last visit she didn't know when she'd get away again. They're still watching her pretty closely."

"What about me?"

Faith frowned. "You?"

"I'm a prime example of Danforth's ex... per... experiment." She gestured to her body. "Just s-show the citizens the state I'm in!"

"You're not well enough." Faith's heart lurched. "We just got you *out* of danger. You go public, you'll be putting yourself in a huge amount of danger."

"It's worth... worth considering." Sophia's eyes fixed on Faith's. "Isn't it?"

"I suppose you're the only one who reacted the way Danforth wanted to the femgazipane," Faith conceded. "But we'd need to be very careful how we did it."

"Keep meaning to ask what Madeleine..." Sophia took a steadying breath. "What did she say about the n-necklaces?"

Faith's hand flew to her mouth. "I didn't... You were sick, and it went out of my head."

"Tell her today." Sophia's gaze drifted to the darkened window. "S-soon... soon as she gets up."

A noise at the door made them both turn. Rowan poked his head inside.

"Want me to take over?" He glanced at Faith. "You've been up most of the night."

"No, I'm fine, I–"

"No, you're n-not." Sophia's expression was fierce. She stared at Rowan. "Yes please. Faith needs to rest." She glared at Faith, challenging her to argue.

"Alright." Faith pushed her chair away from the bed. "If you're sure you'll–"

"I'll be fine." Sophia reached for Faith's hand, squeezing it tightly. "Rowan will take care of me."

Reluctantly accepting Rowan's offer, Faith walked to the door. When she got there, she turned to look back at her friend. Sophia had already sunk back on the pillows and closed her eyes. The animation she'd had a moment ago was gone.

Pushing through her exhaustion, Faith headed for Madeleine's office. It bothered her that she had forgotten to pass on the theory about the pendants and she wanted to see if the Resistance leader was awake, as she so often was at night. The hub was quiet, given the early hour, but raised voices from inside the office disrupted the peace.

One of the voices stopped her in her tracks.

"What are you *doing* about it?"

Unable to stop herself, Faith burst in. Anna stood opposite the Resistance leader, her fists clenched in fury. She spun to face the door at the interruption, her face moving from anger, to shock, to relief.

"Faith!" She stood up and moved forward, enveloping Faith in her arms. The embrace was warm and genuine. When Anna let go, Faith missed the contact.

"You're here because of Flynn, right?"

Anna nodded, the brief glimmer of happiness disappearing from her eyes. "When he didn't come back, I got worried." She turned back to Madeleine. "And we've had no contact from your operatives since the day he headed into the city."

"The curfew has made things very difficult for us," Madeleine said stiffly.

Anna glared. "You left me no option but to come here myself. And now I discover from some poster on the streets that Danforth has sentenced him to death!"

"As I said, we're *not* taking this lightly." Madeleine waved an impatient hand at Faith. "Did you want something?"

It didn't seem like the right time to interrupt, but Faith steeled herself. She couldn't put off telling Madeleine a second time.

Taking a step into the room, she plunged ahead. "Sophia and I were just talking, and–"

"Sophia's here?" Anna's face brightened. "The rescue went as planned, then?"

"It did." Faith's mind returned to her friend's condition. "But–"

"Is she any better?" Madeleine's tone was hopeful.

"Better?" Anna's gaze flicked between them. "What's wrong?"

"She's pregnant. But she's also sick." Faith blinked rapidly, fighting to remain calm. "We've no idea what's–"

"What symptoms does she have?"

"She's constantly nauseous and very weak." Faith fingered a thread on the sleeve of her sweatshirt. "She's so tired she can barely hold her head up. And she can't eat."

Anna tapped a finger against her lip. "Are the rest of the girls at the academy similar?"

Madeleine shook her head. "None of them are even close to being pregnant, according to Kemp. It's so strange. They're–"

"Sophia and I have a theory about that." Faith seized the opportunity. "We think it may have something to do with the academy pendants, that they–"

Madeleine turned to her, frowning. "Pendants?"

"Neither of us were wearing them when we were given the femgazipane. The girls at the academy will all–"

"I hardly think the *jewellery* worn by the academy girls is relevant right now." Madeleine gave a dismissive wave of her hand.

"But I–"

"I'll get Blake to look into it later." Madeleine's glare cut right through Faith. "I think, at the moment, we have more *pressing* matters to deal with."

Faith felt her face flushing. Obviously, Sophia's health was the most important thing right now. She opened her mouth to apologise, but Madeleine had turned back to Anna.

"Do you think you could take a look at Sophia? We're extremely concerned about her."

"Of course." But Anna's face hardened. "Can you spare a few minutes to answer my questions first? It won't take long."

"Sure." Madeleine nodded, reluctantly. "What is it you want to know?"

"My son." Anna took a breath. "Is he–?"

Faith watched the Resistance leader's face closely.

"He's fine, as far as we're aware. Still at the hospital. Diane checked in with him just yesterday." Madeleine smiled. "It seems he's done an excellent job of blending in so far."

"He played a *vital* part in rescuing Sophia," Faith added.

Anna barely blinked. "Where's Danforth keeping Flynn?"

Noah's ma wasn't usually so demanding. But Faith could imagine how her frustration had grown as she'd hurried through the darkened city. Of course she was insisting on getting to the truth before she helped them.

Faith vowed to keep quiet. The faster Anna was satisfied, the faster she would go to Sophia.

"We don't know." Madeleine held up a hand at Anna's protest. "*Yet.* Rest assured, we have operatives out looking."

"And you're certain he's not already dead?" Anna demanded.

"As you saw on the poster, Danforth has announced a public execution. Faith's speech – the one Flynn was planning to arrive during – it went well." As Madeleine ploughed on, Faith felt herself blushing under Anna's grateful gaze. "The women were starting to believe what she said. Danforth's worried she's losing them. Trying to further demonise the Eremus men to bring the Bellator citizens back onside." Madeleine shook her head. "There's no way she would kill him in secrecy. She wants an audience."

"And the execution is scheduled to take place this Thursday?"

"Yes. At the memorial."

"Memorial?"

"For the women lost in the bombing." Madeleine's face changed. "I guess you don't know about that."

Anna regarded Madeleine with a raised eyebrow. "You forget all our news comes from you."

Madeleine sighed. "The day Flynn brought Helen into the city, a bomb went off at Matriarch House. Right in the middle of the Liberation Day Celebrations. Killed more than forty Bellator citizens."

"That many?" Anna turned to Faith for confirmation.

Faith nodded. "It was awful."

"Jacob's work, of course." Madeleine continued. "But Danforth wasn't slow to take advantage of the situation for her own ends." The leader shook her head. "Damn that man. Things would look very different right now, if it wasn't for him."

"Wait." Anna's brow furrowed. "You think the bomb was *Jacob's* work?"

"Who else?" Madeleine raised her eyebrows. "He's gone rogue. There's been no news of him for days. Given his past behaviour, we assumed–"

But Anna was on her feet, pacing the room. "This was the night Flynn came to the city, you say?"

Madeleine tutted. "Yes. Why?"

"Then it couldn't have been Jacob." Anna turned to face them both, her eyes wide. "Because he was in the forest that night."

"What?" Faith sat forward. "He came back to Eremus?"

"They broke in and stole some more supplies." Anna's tone was bitter. "Waited til people were gathered in the canteen for dinner. Snuck in through the sky cave. Ruth was on duty at the entrance. They knocked her out before she could radio for help."

Faith's hand flew to her mouth at the mention of Noah's best friend. "Is she okay?"

Anna nodded. "She had a major headache, but no lasting damage. She's furious, though. Jacob's group was in and out within half an hour. Took some batteries. Food. A little extra ammunition."

"And they were *all* there?" Madeleine's tone was urgent. "They couldn't have left someone behind in the city to detonate the bomb?"

Anna shook her head. "Ruth accounted for them all. Jacob, Sarah, Carl, Harden, Denton, Sil."

Faith stared at Anna, her mind spinning. "If they were in the forest, then who–"

I know exactly who." Madeleine's face was dark. "Someone who has benefitted from the horror that's swept the city since the death of so many of its citizens. Someone who has capitalised on the women's fear ever since the explosion."

"You mean–?"

"Someone," Madeleine shook her head, "who will stop at nothing to keep the women of this city in the dark."

Anna's gaze levelled at Madeleine, understanding. "Danforth."

Chapter Twelve: Noah

He was exhausted. The evening shift was always a killer, and this one had been more eventful than most. Ever since he'd left Ella and Helen, he'd been racking his brain for how he might get into the Fertility Wards again. Finding proof of Danforth's experiments was another way he could make himself useful to the Resistance. But the drudges on duty had been kept busy all night, and he had yet to come up with a viable plan.

It had been difficult enough to steal Susie's keycard the first time. Now Sanders was on the warpath, and there was no doubt that additional security measures had been put in place. If the authorities were actively looking for a drudge who had assisted with Sophia's rescue, Noah needed to stay under the radar more than ever. But it was agony to be so close to the place where the evidence was most likely to be and not try to access it.

Thankful that he had finally finished work, Noah headed along the rear hallway in the direction of the drudge quarters. The hospital was usually deserted this late at night, so he was surprised to hear someone walking along the hallway behind him. Whoever it was kept an uneven pace, hurrying one moment and slowing the next, as if they weren't certain of their destination.

The medics always walked rapidly, with a certainty that demonstrated their expert knowledge of the hospital layout. Drudges moved more slowly, but had a quiet, regular footfall. This woman followed neither pattern. But it was unlikely that a *patient* would be out of bed so late.

Curious, Noah slowed his pace. When the woman was almost upon him, he moved aside, bending to tie his shoelace as she passed. Moving off again, he judged the distance between the cameras carefully. Timing it just right, he angled his head a fraction higher so he could study the woman more closely.

She looked familiar, but he couldn't work out where he knew her from. She wore a dark coat, not a gown, so she definitely wasn't a patient. Her pace was even more erratic now, as though she were nervous to have someone so close behind her. She hurried along, glancing up at the signage on the doors as though she were lost.

Noah picked up the pace as much as he dared, hoping another glimpse might help him to place her. As he gained on her, something about her posture brought back a memory. An Eremus citizen in the clearing, glancing nervously into the forest right before the bombs had gone off.

Fury surged within him. It was Harden's friend Sil. A member of the group that had run away with Jacob. Who had detonated the bomb which had landed Flynn in Danforth's clutches.

He sucked in a deep breath, steadying himself. When he'd followed Sarah, he'd almost gotten caught. There was the same danger here. As a drudge, he shouldn't approach a woman. In the hospital, he was even more trapped than he had been on the streets, where there had been numerous alleyways he could slip into.

There were other dangers too. He knew Jacob had plenty of guns and ammunition. Sil was no doubt armed. If he accosted her, at best he would blow his cover. At worst, he'd end up dead. But no matter how precarious his position, he knew he couldn't let Sil leave without confronting her.

The question was, how could he speak to her without attracting attention?

In the end, Sil solved the problem for him. Stopping abruptly, she turned to face him. "Excuse me. C-can you help me?"

His heart pounding, Noah moved a step closer. For her own sake, it was a good job there were no other Bellator citizens within earshot. The way Sil had spoken to him, a drudge, was far too uncertain and polite to be convincing.

Ignoring her error, he inclined his head to indicate he was at her service. Any cameras which recorded their conversation would look like a Bellator citizen giving commands to a drudge. An everyday occurrence which wouldn't attract much attention, as long as Noah was cautious and kept his temper in check.

There was a short pause. Had Sil recognised him? When she continued speaking, he knew she hadn't.

"I'm looking for..." she fished in her pocket and consulted a piece of paper which might have been a map. The lack of wristclip gave her away. "The pharmacy?"

It was a strange request. The pharmacy was closed at night to anyone except the medics, but Noah ignored the fact. Inclining his head again, he moved off down the hallway, knowing she would follow. His mind was racing. Was she after drugs? Why? But he couldn't ask her.

Confident that Sil knew little about the hospital layout, Noah led her to a small walk-in storage room on the far side of the hospital. When they reached it, he pushed open the door. Sensing her hesitation, he hurried her inside, grabbing hold of a sheet from one of the shelves before closing the door behind them.

"This isn't–" she began, as the room went dark. "Where are we?"

Keeping his head low, Noah moved to the corner where he knew there was a camera. Using the shelving as a ladder, he looped the bedsheet over the lens before jumping down. Returning to the door, he snapped on the light and pulled down his mask.

"Noah!" Her face flooded with recognition. "What are you–?"

"Be quiet. We haven't time for this." He stepped closer. "What are *you* doing here?"

She bristled at his question. "Why should I tell you?"

"Because I want to know what Jacob's up to. After recent events, I think we've a right to–"

"What Jacob does is no concern of yours anymore." She tossed her head. "Eremus rejected him. He owes them nothing."

Noah felt his hackles rise. "I'm sure that's how he sees it. Is that why he blew up Matriarch House? That was a *real* double-whammy! Piss off Danforth *and* increase the hatred of the Eremus people?"

Sil narrowed her eyes. "Blew up...? Wait. You mean that big government building that was destroyed? I saw the ruins earlier today." She tilted her head to one side. "You think Jacob was responsible?"

"Well, wasn't he?" Noah hated her denial. "It's just the kind of thing Jacob loves to do."

"Not that I'd confide in you under normal circumstances," Sil snapped, "but that had nothing to do with us. I can assure you we were nowhere near that government building the other night."

"I don't believe you."

"Believe what you like." She scowled. "I'm telling you we weren't there."

"Well, what exactly are you doing here then?" Noah spat out. "Why wander the hospital in the dead of night?"

"None of your business." She moved towards the door.

"I wouldn't do that if I were you."

Sil stopped, her hand on the handle. "Why not?"

"Because," Noah stepped towards her, "you're doing a lousy job of pretending to be a Bellator citizen. And if you're caught..."

She turned to face him. Her face was still defiant, but he could tell he'd rattled her. "Lousy... how?"

He almost laughed. "The fact that you're wandering the hospital in the middle of the night with no good reason is enough. The only people up and about in the hallways at night are people who work here. How did you even get in?"

She shrugged. "It took me a while. I watched the Emergency entrance all day today. Eventually, two ambulances came in at the same time. I sneaked past while the staff were distracted with the new arrivals." She chewed on her lip. "I figured I could move around at night without being seen though."

Noah pointed at the sheet hanging from the ceiling. "There are cameras everywhere."

She shuddered. "Really?"

"Yeah. *Really*. We're watched all the time." Noah shook his head. "Putting that aside, the biggest issue you've got is the way you spoke to me out there. A total giveaway that you don't belong here. Any Bellator citizen would know you were an outsider."

She blanched. "But why?"

"I'm a *drudge*. The Bellator women give us orders. They don't speak to us with respect."

"I see." Sil shifted from one foot to the other. "I didn't realise. I guess there's a lot I don't know about the way things work in the city."

Noah snorted. "There certainly is. Now, will you tell me what you're doing here?"

"I will not." Sil folded her arms across her chest. "It's none of your–"

"Fine." Noah pushed past her, heading for the door. "I'll leave you to get out of here on your own then."

Sil grasped his arm. "Don't go."

He stopped. She looked like an animal in a trap. For a moment, he felt sorry for her. And then he remembered the bomb.

"Did you hear what happened to Flynn?" He took a step towards her. She flinched, but didn't reply. "He was *blamed* for the explosion. Danforth's planning his execution as we speak. All because of Jacob's little stunt."

"I keep telling you." Sil shook her head in disbelief. "It wasn't us."

"You expect me to believe that?" Noah scoffed.

"Yeah. I do." Sil's entire body sagged back against the shelving. "Since we came to the city, things have been pretty difficult. We have few resources, the men in our group can hardly move around the city without being spotted, and Avery's a royal pain."

Noah remembered the arrogant senior girl who had been kidnapped by Jacob after his recent split from the Eremus community. As a prisoner in the caves, she had been demanding and unpleasant to his own community and most of her fellow students, but even she didn't deserve to be Jacob's hostage.

"...we've had to scavenge for food or steal it, and to cap it all–"

She broke off abruptly.

"Go on?" Noah prompted. "Don't leave it there."

She sighed. "I'm telling you, with everything we have going on, we wouldn't have had the opportunity to blow up such an important landmark. And, as I keep saying, we were elsewhere the night the bomb went off."

Noah stared at her. *Was she telling the truth?*

"Where were you, then? If you weren't here."

Her face closed off. "I won't say."

Noah tried a different tack. "What do you want with the pharmacy? Was that just a ruse, or did you really want to get some drugs?" He took a step closer. "One of you get injured in the bombing? Got a nasty wound you don't want to get infected?"

"We had nothing to do with that." Sil sighed. "We do need drugs though. Avery's sick. A cough which refuses to go away. The little princess isn't used to roughing it, I guess."

Noah was glad that the group appeared at least to want to keep Avery in good health.

"What does Jacob intend to do with Avery?"

"I don't know. Use her to get to Danforth, somehow? Avery is one of her *precious* academy students, as she keeps reminding us." Sil shook her head. "I'm not even sure Jacob knows himself. But her being ill is just another of our many issues." She glanced around the store room. "I'm guessing this isn't where they store the drugs?"

"Definitely not." Noah gestured at the shelving. "This cupboard stores various supplies used by the drudges. Cleaning fluids, mops and buckets, cloths, bleach, spare uniforms–"

Sil picked up a mask from the shelf Noah had indicated. "You wear one of these things all the time?"

"Every minute we're in public."

"And the uniform?"

Noah nodded.

"What are *you* doing here?" Sil began to walk along the shelving, running her hand across the contents of the shelves. "Why are you pretending to be a drudge?"

"I'm working for the Resistance now." Noah deliberately kept it vague. "I'm undercover here. It's a useful place to be."

Sil accepted his response without question. "Can you get me some drugs?"

He laughed. "No chance."

Her face fell. "Jacob will kill me if I come back empty-handed. He's pretty desperate."

"Sorry. They don't let the drudges near the important stuff."

He found himself feeling sorry for her. Jacob could be cruel, especially when backed into a corner. Sil's fear that he would take out his frustration on her, or Avery, was not unrealistic.

"The only way you'll get drugs is by stealing them from the delivery van." He sighed. *Was he doing the right thing?* "It's dark blue. Drops off deliveries at the rear entrance of the hospital every other day. If you can somehow be there when the drugs are being brought inside, or if you got in a comcar and followed the van when it left, you might work out where the warehouses are that store the drugs. Maybe you could break into them more easily."

Sil's eyes were wide. "Why would you help me?"

Noah shrugged. "Because I don't want Jacob to punish you. Or Avery."

"Thank you."

"Don't thank me." Noah closed his eyes. It was the right thing to do. Faith wouldn't want Avery to suffer, even if she disliked the young woman. "Just promise me you'll try and keep an eye on Avery. Look after her."

"I will."

"Alright. Now if I were you," he leaned close, "I'd make my way out of here the same way you came in. Quickly. Before someone catches you and identifies you as an Eremus citizen."

Sil gave a weak smile and gestured to the door. "Could you...? I mean, will you check that...?"

Sighing, Noah edged past her and eased the door open. The hallway outside was empty.

He turned back to Sil. Her breathing was rapid and her arms were wrapped tightly around her chest.

"All clear. For now. But hurry."

As Sil disappeared into the darkness, he wondered if she was telling the truth. Because if it hadn't been Jacob, he had no idea who was responsible for the bombing.

Chapter Thirteen: Faith

"I still can't believe it." Robyn's face was bleak. "That Danforth would murder so many of her citizens just to—"

"Believe it." Madeleine cut her off. "She's capable of anything. All the more reason for us to get those girls out of the academy as soon as possible."

It was 8 a.m. and Madeleine had called the Resistance members together in the hub. After a disturbed night, Faith had reluctantly dragged herself away from dozing at Sophia's side to attend. Despite Anna devoting most of the night to examining her friend, they were no nearer to finding a reason for Sophia's sickness. Which meant they were no nearer to treating her.

In fact, she seemed sicker than ever.

As a sleepy-looking Olivia entered the room, Madeleine stood up.

"About time." She gestured to Olivia to sit down before turning to the others. "I know we're busy, but a lot of things have happened since the explosion. I want an update on all ongoing missions, so we can figure out our next steps." She turned back to Olivia. "Firstly, any sign of Flynn yesterday?"

The petite Resistance operative shook her head. "None at all." She glanced around at the others who had been assigned the task of searching for the Eremus leader. "We've combed the city... all the government buildings we're aware of. Any locations that Danforth is associated with. There's no evidence that he's in any of them."

Faith felt Diane stiffen beside her. She had been out for multiple hours the previous day with the search team, but they'd found nothing. It rankled that they had failed.

"She has to be keeping him somewhere off-grid." Madeleine sighed. "At the moment, it's looking more and more like the first time we'll actually be able to get to Flynn is at the memorial service itself." She held up a hand at the gasps which followed her words. "I know, it's not ideal. But as the service creeps closer it's what we're facing. We can't let Danforth murder him in cold blood without attempting a rescue."

Faith raised her hand. "Sophia had an idea."

After Madeleine's abrupt dismissal of the pendant idea, Faith was reluctant to make any bold new proposals, especially those which put her friend at risk, but Sophia had been insistent. Since it was the only idea her friend had shown any enthusiasm for since her near-collapse, Faith felt bound to offer her suggestion. She braced herself for further rejection as she opened her mouth.

But Madeleine raised an eyebrow. "Oh, yes?"

"We need hard evidence of something criminal that Danforth's done, right?" Faith glanced at the crowd around her. "And we're not having much luck finding any so far. Sophia suggested *she* could be the evidence. We record her – do an interview of sorts – and then–"

"Broadcast it during the memorial service!" Robyn's face lit up. "Like we did with your speech."

"That's right."

Robyn turned to Blake. "We could hack into Danforth's feed again, right?"

"I'm not sure whether..." Blake pulled a face. "It might be difficult to..." At the hopeful looks on the others' faces, she squared her shoulders. "Of course, I can try."

"Let's look into it, at least." Madeleine turned back to Faith. "Is Sophia feeling better, then?"

Faith's stomach lurched. After her initial examination of the patient, Anna had instructed Lily to increase the amount of fluids Sophia was being given. It had made little difference so far. Sophia still wasn't able to tolerate food without throwing up, and she'd developed even more disturbing symptoms overnight. Hot sweats, shivering, intense muscle pain. She'd also been having disturbing visions which made her cry out in terror.

"No." Faith choked out. "If anything, she's worse."

Faith had been horrified at her friend's deterioration, but the anguish on her friend's face during the hallucinations had cut her to the bone.

Madeleine glanced at Lily for confirmation. The unofficial-medic was nursing a cup of coffee, her face as pale as Sophia's. She was exhausted.

"'Fraid so." The young woman's usually bright features were drawn. "We're doing everything we can for her, but..."

"Shouldn't we be calling her a doctor?" Olivia asked. "I know taking her to the hospital is too risky, but don't we know anyone who could come here?"

Madeleine shook her head. "I'm sorry. There's no one that we'd trust. No good risking everything to rescue her just to have her fall straight back into Danforth's hands. Anna's our best bet, for the moment at least."

"Who's with her now?" Robyn's gaze glanced over Lily and Faith. "She's not alone, is she?"

"Of *course* not." Lily stiffened. "Anna's with her. Like Madeleine said, she knows a lot more about medicine than

I do. And Rowan's in and out all the time." She gestured at her coffee cup. "I'll go back and check on her when we're done here."

Robyn's face softened. "Leave her with Anna for a while. Go get some rest yourself. You look shattered."

Nodding gratefully, Lily hunched over her coffee again.

"Moving on." Madeleine turned to Evelyn. "We've heard nothing from the academy, but if things are as bad as Kemp said, we have to be ready to act soon. How are the plans coming along?"

"Alright, I suppose." Evelyn sat forward. "We have a fresh batch of placebos to replace the first ones, but even if we can get them inside with the increased security, I'm concerned someone will figure out they're fakes. As for the long-term effects of femgazipane, or the fact that Anderson has been instructed to give it to the juniors now..." She shrugged. "Basically, Robyn's been looking into getting the girls out as fast as possible."

"We're concerned the girls won't be able to walk far in their current condition." Robyn took over from Evelyn seamlessly. "I've arranged a number of comcars which we can use without much warning."

"The biggest issue," Evelyn interrupted, "is where we hide them once we get them out."

Robyn sighed. "We don't have a suitable solution to that yet. We considered the safehouses, but even if we use them all, there isn't enough space to house that many people."

"Not to mention," Evelyn warned, "the disaster that would occur if any of them were spotted within city limits by Danforth's guards."

"It would be so much better if we could keep them together." Robyn added. "Somewhere on the outskirts of the city, where there's less chance of them being seen."

"Keep looking." Madeleine frowned. "I'm sure we can come up with something." She peered at the other faces around the room. "Where's Ella? I wanted feedback on what's going on at Matriarch House."

Diane and Faith exchanged glances. "Did you–?" "I didn't–"

In all the worry about Sophia, Faith had forgotten about the young Eremus woman.

Madeleine's face paled. "Are you telling me she didn't make it back last night? Did no one notice?"

"I guess..." Faith searched for the right words, terror over her friend's second disappearance freezing her brain. "Maybe she... She must've–"

A noise at the tunnel exit made them all jump. They froze as the door began to open. When Ella emerged, Faith sagged back in her seat.

"Where have you been?" Madeleine's tone was accusing. "You should've been back hours ago."

Ella shrugged. "I had to make a detour on my way home."

Robyn raised an eyebrow. "Did you go via *Eremus*?"

The Resistance operative was smiling, but Madeleine looked anything but amused. Rummaging in her bag, Ella took a step towards her.

"They're relocating the staff from Matriarch House over the next couple of days. I managed to get a role in the offices this time. Might help me get closer to Danforth. I also spent a lot of time helping with the clean-up operation. There's a lot of damage." Pulling some papers from her bag, she held them out with a flourish. "No hard evidence against the chancellor yet, but I did find these."

Madeleine eyed the papers suspiciously. "What are they?"

"Records. Something to do with the establishment of the academy." Ella flipped through them. "They were being thrown out, but I rescued them when no one was looking. Figured they might be revealing."

Madeleine's expression had softened, no doubt because of the potentially damning information Ella proffered. Faith had a sneaky feeling that the presentation of the documents was a deliberate move to distract the Resistance leader from her questions. *Where had Ella been all night?*

"Can you make it a priority to look over them today?" Madeleine's eyes were bright. Ella's ruse had worked. "Take Diane and Faith up to the library. Go through them with a fine toothcomb." She glanced at Faith. "Maybe there'll be something in there about the pendants you mentioned?"

"Um... maybe." Faith blinked.

Madeleine had paid attention to her suggestion after all. But going through the documents would take her away from Sophia.

"Faith?" Madeleine's tone was sharp.

"Yes. Of course we'll look the documents over." Faith glanced at her friends. "Right?"

"Sure thing." Ella and Diane exchanged glances. "We'll get started right away."

With Sophia so sick, Faith was reluctant to join them, but she didn't dare argue, especially when it appeared that Madeleine was actually considering her idea from the previous day.

"Does anyone else have relevant information to contribute?" Madeleine ran her eyes around the room. When no one spoke, she waved a hand. "Alright, meeting dismissed. You know your assigned tasks. Get on with them and report back anything of relevance immediately." She gestured to Robyn and Blake. "We will be in the office if anyone needs us. We have other matters to discuss."

As Madeleine swept out of the hub with her two lieutenants behind her, the hub emptied quickly. Faith trailed along the hallway behind Ella and Diane. At the door to Sophia's room, she stopped.

"I might just..." she gestured.

"Sure." Ella nodded her understanding. "Give her our best, will you? But come up soon. I've lots to fill you in on."

"Will do."

As Diane and Ella disappeared up the library steps, Faith said a silent prayer that her friend would be sitting up in bed eating a bowl of stew. The moment she stepped inside the room, her hopes were dashed.

Sophia lay in bed. Her eyes were closed and her face waxy and pale. At least she was no longer in the throes of some horrific hallucination.

Rowan was nowhere to be seen. But sitting by Sophia's side, her hands resting gently over Sophia's, was Anna. She smiled as she spotted Faith and beckoned her closer.

"How is she?" Faith glanced at the bowl of cold soup which sat on the nightstand. "No better, I suppose?"

"I'm sorry." Anna shook her head. "I would have expected the fluids to have picked her up a little by now, but she doesn't seem to be improving. She's in quite a lot of pain too."

"Pain?"

Anna nodded. "Cramps in her stomach. Possibly linked to the vomiting, but they seem to be worsening."

Faith stared down at her friend. "Has she been awake?"

"Not much." Anna picked up a bottle of pills from the nightstand. "I've had to give her a couple of these over the last few hours. They're pretty strong."

"Are they painkillers?"

"Yes, but not standard-strength ones. These are powerful. Strictly speaking, I can only give her one or two per day, and I have to space them out carefully. Any more could kill her. But nothing else will touch the pain."

"*That's* how bad it is?" Faith recoiled. "What's *wrong* with her, Anna?"

Noah's mother shook her head. "I've never seen anything like this."

Refusing to let Anna's assessment get to her, Faith gestured at the bedside. "Want me to take over? Lily went to get some sleep, but I can sit with her, if you–"

"It's fine. I'm happy to watch over her." Anna came around the bed and took her hand. "I *promise* I'll come get you if she wakes. Lily tells me you've barely left this room over the past few days. Give yourself a break."

"Alright. I'll be in the library. Ella came back from Matriarch House with some documents. Madeleine wants us to look them over."

"Sounds like it might take your mind off things here." Anna grasped Faith's hand. "Just for a little while. It doesn't mean you don't care."

"If you say so."

"How was the meeting?"

Faith shrugged. "It was fine. There's a lot going on, but... honestly? It feels pretty hopeless right now." She dropped her gaze. "They didn't find Flynn yet."

A dark shadow crossed Anna's face. "What else was discussed?"

"The memorial service. I told them about Sophia's idea." Faith glanced at her sleeping friend. "If we record her looking like this the Bellator women will have no choice but to believe us." She bit back a sob and forced her gaze back to Anna. "We talked about the girls at the academy. There are plans to get them out as soon as Kemp makes contact, but they're struggling to find somewhere for the girls to go."

"I suppose they can't bring them all here." Anna's eyes lit with a spark of interest. "I wonder... How many of them are there likely to be?"

"I'm not sure, but we definitely wouldn't have the facilities to host them all here. And we want to keep them together, if possible." Faith shrugged. "I'm sure they'll think of something."

"I'm sure they will. Maybe we could look at taking them to the caves."

"Really? You think..." Faith chewed her lip. "I mean... would the Eremus people be okay with it?"

"They might. I mean... it's worth a try." Anna gestured to the door. "Anyway, you go. Give yourself a break. I'll take good care of her."

Faith turned to leave, but turned back and flung her arms around Anna. For a moment, the older woman didn't respond, but then her arms tightened around Faith, pulling her close. When they let go, Anna's eyes were also filled with tears.

"What was that for?"

"A thank you. For knowing what I need." Faith cast an arm around the room. "For being prepared to sit here with her when it's all I can do to..."

"I know. This is your hell." The older woman shrugged. "But sitting with Sophia makes me feel useful. It gives me something to do. To keep my mind–"

She broke off, but Faith knew what she meant. The two people she was closest to in the world were in danger. And she couldn't help them. That was *her* hell. Anna needed distracting too.

Nodding her understanding, Faith turned to go. The light in the hallway was brighter than inside the sick room, where the curtains were permanently drawn to keep Sophia comfortable. Faith paused for a moment, allowing her eyes time to adjust. When she could see again, she set off in the direction of the library.

She found Diane and Ella seated at one of the desks in the Records Room. Their heads were bent close together; the folder of papers was lying ignored on the table. Clearly, whatever Ella had to say was more interesting than their contents.

At the sound of Faith's footsteps, Diane turned. "Ella's so-called detour took her to the *hospital.*"

Faith hurried to join the pair. "*What?*"

"You know what it's like to be separated from someone you love, right? You understand?" Ella raised an eyebrow and Faith felt herself blushing. "I knew I wouldn't be able to rest until I saw Helen was alright for myself, so..."

"You *saw* her?" Faith pulled out a chair on the opposite side of the desk. "How did you–?"

"Faked an issue with my heart. Got myself admitted overnight." Ella frowned. "Madeleine won't be happy when she finds out, but I figured it was worth it."

"How were things at the hospital?" Faith sat down. "Did you–"

Ella anticipated Faith's question. "I saw Noah. He's okay. Keeping an eye on Helen, as best he can. Apparently, there are some suspicions about drudge involvement in Sophia's rescue, but no one has pointed the finger at him yet."

Faith felt a surge of relief. "What about Helen?"

"She's okay. No injuries, and she's not sick." Ella's face darkened. "In fact, they're considering sending her back to the academy."

"Really?"

Ella nodded. "I figured I'd have to try and persuade Madeleine to sign off on a rescue, but now that we're planning to bring the girls out of the academy, I guess I can wait til then."

"I'm guessing you'd like to be part of the group on the rescue mission?" Diane leaned back in her chair. "Be Helen's hero?"

Now it was Ella's turn to blush. "I'm not sure she'll let me after the stunt I just pulled."

"How about you try to get back into her good graces?" Faith elbowed Ella. "Let's get looking over this stuff you found, like she asked us to." Leaning forward, she grasped the folder of papers. "Where did you say you found it?"

"It was in a waste bin at the back of Matriarch House. They were dumping stuff that had been damaged in the explosion, but a lot of the papers looked perfectly readable."

"There'll be digital versions of all this stuff now..." Diane picked up the pile and began sifting through it. "Looks a little smoke-damaged, but it's definitely legible." Dividing it into three equal piles, she passed one to Faith and one to Ella. "Let's get started."

Two hours later, they were still reading. The documents were mostly reports: applications to the government gaining permission for the academy's set up, mission statements, endless pages of information about the academy's purpose and lists of the regulations Danforth planned to follow as it developed. Faith had scanned page after page of text, many of which were composed in extremely complex legal terminology. Her eyes hurt. She was considering suggesting that they take a break when Diane stiffened beside her.

"Wait... No!"

Startled from her reverie, Faith bolted upright. "What?"

"Look." Diane jabbed a finger at the page in front of her. "This is a catalogue of specific requirements of the girls chosen for the academy. We're not specially selected because of our intellect or promise. It's purely down to genetic make-up. They pick us because we're more likely to produce strong babies." She grunted with disgust. "And *this* describes the ways the academy ensures that every girl stays in tiptop condition. To maximise the chance of pregnancy."

"So it's been about the fertility experiments from the very start." Faith felt sick.

"There's something else." Diane squinted at the page. "Weren't you and Sophia wondering about the pendants?" Faith nodded, and Diane moved the page closer. "Resources the academy will provide every student upon entrance to the school." She jabbed her finger at the list. "Academic equipment, numerous items of uniform, full sports kit for a range of different activities and..." she pointed to an item at the bottom of the list, "the Danforth Academy Pendant."

Faith leaned closer, reading aloud. "Pendant will be given to all students on entry at the age of ten. Made from a special porous alloy, the pendant contains a slow-release pellet of hormones intended to enhance the girls' fertility." She turned back to Diane. "*What?*"

Diane's face was dark. "The pendants aren't about school pride. They tell us they're to unite us as one proud body of Danforth Academy students." Diane hadn't worn her pendant since the moment she'd become part of the Resistance, but her hand went to her throat all the same. "It's bullshit! They were a way of getting drugs into our systems without us even knowing."

"So... the hormones in these necklaces..." Ella was frowning as she spoke, "they do something to your body... something which makes it easier for you to get pregnant?"

Diane sighed. "That's the idea."

"But..." Faith burst out, "it doesn't *work*! The only two people the femgazipane has *ever* worked on are me and Sophia."

"And *neither* of you were wearing the pendants when you were given it." Diane's eyes glittered with fury. "They got it wrong."

"So you're saying," Ella's tone was incredulous, "that the pendants are preventing the femgazipane from working. That, unless they remove the pendants, the other drugs will *never* work."

Faith shook her head. "That's exactly what we're saying."

"We have to tell Madeleine. Now." Diane pushed her chair back from the desk. "And we'd better hope the medics at the school don't make the same connection before we can get the girls out."

Chapter Fourteen: Noah

He woke the next morning in a cold sweat. After the encounter with Sil the previous night, he had not slept well. Had she been lying to him? He didn't think so. But if Jacob wasn't responsible for the bombing, who was? He'd found it impossible to stop his mind from racing through the possibilities. A rebel group from outside the city? Madeleine, without the rest of the Resistance's knowledge? Danforth herself, even?

When he'd finally drifted off to sleep, it had already been getting light outside.

His head was pounding when he woke, and he had a horrible sense that something was wrong. After a quick shower and hurried breakfast, he entered the hospital half an hour early for his shift. Despite throwing himself into the work, taking as many of the physically demanding tasks as he could, he still couldn't shake the unsettled feeling.

It was eleven a.m. before there was a task on the board which took him to Helen's ward. Cutting in front of another drudge to snag the job, he gave the man an apologetic look and hurried away. A patient needed transporting to the scanning department. He found himself hoping it might be Helen once again.

Grabbing a wheelchair from the lower floor, he fought the urge to fidget as he waited for the lift to arrive. Once inside, he tried to stay calm while various medics and technicians got in. The lift seemed to stop on every floor as it ascended. Finally, it came to rest with the familiar bump on the correct floor.

When he arrived at Ward A9, the doors were closed, and the technicians on duty took their time responding to the buzzer. When the door finally swung open, Noah stepped inside and waited for instructions.

"Patient's in the private room at the end." The technician jerked her head. "Needs a scan."

Noah's heart soared at his wonderful luck. Checking on Helen today would be easy.

Beside him, the technician was tapping a foot. "Don't dawdle!"

Bowing his head in apology, Noah followed the technician along the ward. *Why did Helen need another scan when they'd suggested her last one had been clear?* When they reached Helen's door, it was standing open. Lining the wheelchair up outside, Noah waited for further instructions.

"Transport's here." The technician's voice was cheery. "Ready for your scan?"

There was a rustling of covers and the sound of feet landing on the floor. The usual fumbling, as a pair of shoes and a robe were pulled on. Noah waited patiently, his eyes cast down, until the figure clambered into the wheelchair.

A hunched-over figure, with greying hair and wrinkled hands.

A figure that was definitely not Helen.

Panic seized him. As he moved on autopilot through the ward, Noah's mind was racing. At the door, he paused, waiting for the technician to release the door lock. Once the doors began to swing open, the technician turned to go back to the office. Noah glanced around. The ground in the immediate vicinity was clear of feet, and whilst there were murmured conversations going on in the main ward, there was nothing to suggest that anyone other than himself and the patient were close by.

Praying he wouldn't be caught, Noah glanced up at the patient progress board. There was one on the wall at the entrance to every single ward in the hospital. Scanning it as fast as he could, he found Helen's name at the very bottom.

Next to it, in large capital letters, was a note:

TRANSFERRED TO DANFORTH ACADEMY.

Chapter Fifteen: Faith

"My name is Sophia. I am a student of the Danforth Academy. A few weeks ago, I was taken from the city by some of the citizens of the Eremus community... and..."

Faith bit her lip. Her friend was finding it difficult to even sit up now, but she was determined to get through the speech.

It was Tuesday. With no knowledge of Flynn's whereabouts, and Thursday's memorial service creeping ever-closer, the Resistance was running out of options. They had reluctantly accepted that Flynn's rescue would have to take place during the ceremony itself. And Madeleine felt that Sophia's declaration was their best chance to create a distraction. While Faith agreed that Sophia could provide damning evidence of Danforth's guilt, she wished the recording did not have to take place while her friend was so sick. But without a distraction, their chances of getting Flynn out were extremely limited.

The previous day had been devoted to preparing for the missions to come. The Resistance were stretched thin, between the issues at the academy and the upcoming memorial service. After discovering that Faith's claim about the pendants was correct, Madeleine had moved up the deadline for the academy rescue. She had also assigned more people to the mission, hoping that more hard evidence of Danforth's experiments might be found inside the academy.

Anyone not assigned to the academy assignment was busy preparing for the memorial day rescue. Robyn had been drawing up plans for the operative who would be in the square itself, assigning people to various positions close to the stage. Blake had shut herself away for the entirety of the previous day, attempting to work out how she might hack into Danforth's feed again, now that security had been increased. Even Sophia had managed to compose a speech, enlisting Diane to type it up on a datadev borrowed from Madeleine's office.

And now, they were filming her attempt to deliver it.

"...but the abuse and mistreatment I have suffered since... since m-my return to Bellator," Sophia was struggling, "since my so-called rescuers brought me back here, has been so much worse."

Sophia paused, struggling to catch her breath. Anna had dialled back the amount of painkillers she was on so that she was coherent for the speech. But the reduction came at a price: the pain was returning, full-force. A vivid orange pill lay on the nightstand ready for Sophia the moment she had finished delivering her message.

"Take your time," Blake's voice came from behind the camera. "I can edit this out."

The techie was being far more understanding than usual. But one glance at Sophia was all it took to see why. Her skin was almost see-through and had a permanent sheen of sweat. Her hands shook constantly and she couldn't stay warm. Despite numerous attempts to tempt her to eat, she seemed incapable of keeping any meaningful sustenance in her system.

Anna had devoted herself to caring for Sophia. Between Lily, Rowan, and Noah's ma, Sophia now had round-the-clock care, yet she still wasn't improving. Faith had offered to record the speech in Sophia's place, but she'd had to admit that it wouldn't have the same impact.

"Please." She had clasped Sophia's clammy hand to her chest. "I don't think you're strong enough to do this. Not yet."

Sophia had closed her eyes. Her response, when it came, had been no more than a whisper. "What if I never am?"

"Don't talk–" Faith had swallowed hard. "Don't talk like that. We have one more day before the memorial service. Tomorrow, you'll be–"

"Tomorrow might be too late." Sophia's eyes flew open. "I *have* to do something, while I still can."

There had been no changing her mind. And now, Faith stood by helplessly, while Sophia gave the performance of her life.

Drawing in a deep breath which seemed to exhaust her, Sophia pushed on. "For the past few weeks, under Chancellor Danforth's orders, I have been kept isolated in an experimental fertility ward at the Bellator Hospital. Only a select few people know about these experiments, which aim to investigate new methods of reproduction. An *honourable* goal, if we are to believe our chancellor." Sophia stared right into the camera. "But a goal which I believe she has taken to extremes."

She broke off, clutching a hand over her mouth. Hurrying forward, Faith held out a bucket, stroking her friend's back as she retched over and over. Vomiting had become an almost hourly occurrence. Even though there was barely anything in her stomach, the nausea had a powerful hold on her.

When Sophia was finished, Rowan hurried forward to wipe her face with a warm cloth. As he resettled her on the pillows and backed away, Faith turned back to her friend.

"You sure you want to–?"

Sophia nodded firmly. "I do."

"Ready when you are," Blake called out. "Promise I'll edit out the puke section."

Faith shot the techie a dark look, but when Sophia managed a weak smile, she was grateful for Blake's attempt at humour. It felt like her friend hadn't smiled for days.

Was Blake serious? She couldn't decide. The broadcast, Faith admitted, would be far more powerful if it showed Sophia's true state.

Eventually, Sophia began to speak again, her gaze cast downwards.

"Whilst a *prisoner* on this ward, under sedation and against my will, I was injected with numerous experimental drugs. The result?" She paused, looking directly into the camera. "A pregnancy."

Placing a hand on her stomach, she sighed. As they had rehearsed, Blake zoomed the camera out so she was showing the whole bed rather than just Sophia's face. Waiting just the right amount of time for the shocking revelation to sink in, Sophia continued.

"Yes, Danforth achieved her goal. But at what cost?" With effort, she pulled the blanket away to expose her body. Beside her, Blake swept the camera along Sophia's emaciated body, zooming in on the swollen stomach which sharply contrasted the rest of her. "This pregnancy is not a normal one. I'm told the foetus is growing too fast. I shouldn't be this big at such an early stage."

Sophia broke off, sighing deeply. Faith and Rowan exchanged worried glances as Sophia forced herself to continue.

"I'm a *s-shadow* of the girl I used to- used to b-be." Sophia's voice broke. "I can't eat, so... I'm wasting away, and—"

Her heart aching, Faith took a step towards her, but Sophia waved her away. With great effort, she continued.

"I have..." she sucked in a deep breath, "...c-constant stomach pains. I throw up almost hourly." Blake panned back to her face as the tears started to fall. "I am carrying a foetus, y-yes." Sophia was whispering now, and Faith had to strain closer to catch her words. "But I fear it's not a normal one. And if... for whatever reason... I don't carry it to term, what's the point?"

Horrified, Faith turned away, her eyes filling with tears. She had promised she would keep it together, but hearing her friend deliver the speech, her tone raw and the words brutal, was too much. Clenching her hands into fists, she dug her nails into her palms so hard she was sure she'd drawn blood.

The *one thing* she'd promised to do for her friend: bear witness. Be strong.

And she was losing it.

Suddenly, there were arms around her. Faith turned, burying her face in Anna's shoulder.

Noah's ma had told them she would keep checking on them, *in case she was needed*. And Faith needed her now. Anna didn't speak, but enveloped Faith in her arms. The contact was comforting, sending waves of silent strength coursing through her body. This, Faith thought, was what it was like to have a proper mother.

Somehow, she found the strength to turn and face Sophia as she continued.

"Citizens of Bellator, *please* listen to my story. Believe... *believe* me when I tell you that your chancellor *does not* have your b-best interests at heart. She lies to you. She makes decisions based on her own twisted ambitions, and only... only reveals what *she* w-wants you to know." Drawing on some desperate strength, Sophia pulled herself forward, lifting her body from the pillows as she delivered her message. "For my sake, *question* what you're told. *Insist* on the truth. If we don't *do* something, and s-s-soon, I won't be the only one forced to suffer like this. Your chancellor has ma-many more subjects like... like me... waiting in the wings at the Danforth Academy. They don't d-deserve this any more than I do." Her voice was impassioned, rising in volume. "Rise up and support the Resistance. There *is* a better way."

Spent, Sophia collapsed on the pillows. A heavy silence filled the room. No one wanted to break the powerful spell Sophia's words had cast. Eventually, Blake turned off the camera and moved towards the bed.

In an uncharacteristic show of kindness, she reached out and she took Sophia's hand. "You did it. Leave the rest to me. I'll easily have this edited together by tomorrow. You can relax now."

As Blake exited, she shot Faith a concerned glance. The sympathy was so out of character, it felt as shocking as someone else yelling at her would have done. It was a testament to the severity of the situation.

Faith couldn't move. Beside her, Anna came to life, saving the day again. Crossing the room, she removed some of Sophia's pillows, allowing her to rest more comfortably.

"That was *so* powerful." Anna reached for the tiny orange pill and glass of water. "But you've done enough now." Reaching an arm around Sophia, she supported her into a sitting position. "Take this."

She pressed the pill between Sophia's lips and helped her to sip the water. When she had swallowed, Anna lay her back down on the pillows. Tucking the blankets around Sophia, she somehow managed to smile.

"You'll start to feel better in a minute. The pill will help you sleep."

Sophia was struggling to keep her eyes open. "Is Faith still here?"

"I'm here." Jolted into action at the sound of her name, Faith crossed the room. Anna faded into the background so Faith could take her place by her friend's side. "That was... *incredible.*"

Sophia managed a weak smile. "At least... I know I did something..." She trailed off. "Not much, but something."

Faith took in Sophia's pale skin, her laboured breathing, her tiny form. The speech had taken everything out of her. She opened her mouth to speak and found that she couldn't.

"It was enough." From the other side of the bed, Anna spoke for her. "You did enough."

Sighing softly, Sophia let her eyes close. Within seconds, her breathing deepened and she was asleep.

Anna glanced at Lily. "You up for taking the next shift? I need to speak to Madeleine."

"Sure." Lily drew the curtains again. "I'll make a note of the time, so we know when she can have the next dose."

"Shouldn't the pain be getting better?" Faith asked, her voice dull.

Lily and Anna exchanged glances.

"It should, yes." Anna put her arm around Faith. "Those painkillers aren't the everyday type. They're very powerful." Her face darkened. "Let's hope she doesn't need another dose too soon."

She guided Faith out of the sickroom and down the hallway. When they reached the hub, Madeleine was standing drinking a coffee with Olivia.

"Is it done?" she called across. "The video, I mean. Did she manage?"

"She did." Anna drew Faith with her across the room. "We have a lot of very powerful footage. Blake has gone to edit it." She gestured towards Madeleine's office. "Okay if we speak to you for a few minutes? I have a proposition for you."

Madeleine nodded and they followed her into the private space. Once inside, the Resistance leader gestured at the chairs as she took her own seat.

"Still no message from Kemp," she muttered. "No idea what's going on at the academy. I only hope her cover hasn't been blown." She took a sip of her steaming coffee. "But Kemp is good. No news is probably good news. As in, she's not been in contact as she's working to stay under the radar and doesn't want to risk a message."

She gave a sharp nod, as though she were trying to convince herself.

"What's this about a proposition?" She eyed Anna. "I don't have a lot of time, so spit it out."

Anna sat forward in her chair. "I heard you were struggling to find a place to keep the academy girls together when you get them out? I may have a solution."

"I'm listening."

"What about if we took them to Eremus?" Anna waited while the suggestion sank in. "Not forever, of course. But temporarily, if they were given shelter in the cave system, they would be safe. Danforth is unlikely to consider it as a place of safety for the girls. She still doesn't know our location, and as long as we could get them out of the city at night, without being seen, we'd stand a good chance of keeping their location a secret."

"And you'd be prepared to do that? Eremus would be happy to house a large number of young Bellator women?"

"I've spoken to Paulo and a couple of the other council members and I think we can make it work. With proper planning and preparation." Anna paused. "You'd need to supply us with the resources to support them, of course."

Madeleine was silent for a moment. "Do you think the academy girls will feel safe there?"

"After what they've been through, I should think anyone who shows them kindness and doesn't pump them full of damaging drugs will be a hero." Anna shrugged. "When the truth comes out, Eremus gets to play the hero who sheltered these vulnerable young women. It could rewrite history in terms of the way that Eremus... that *men* are perceived to treat women."

"What would you ask in return?"

"*I* think the rebranding of Eremus will be reward enough. Flynn and I have always wanted the Bellator citizens to change their minds about us." She hesitated. "But the others might require more convincing. How about you make sure you're ... generous with the supplies you send for the girls? If there are plenty of leftovers to share among the community, that would go a long way to silencing any protests."

"Done." Madeleine didn't hesitate. "Anything else?"

"On a personal level, I'd ask you to do your best to save Flynn's life."

"You have my word." Madeleine gave a solemn nod. "Are we agreed, then? Can we assume that–"

A sound at the door made them turn.

"Sorry to interrupt, but I thought you'd want to know." Robyn paused to catch her breath. "Been listening in to the conversations in Anderson's office. I've just heard Anderson and Danforth talking. They mentioned Helen."

Madeleine stiffened at the sound of the young student's name. "Go on."

"Seems like they're planning something." Robyn gestured to the headphones strung around her neck. "She wasn't specific, but Anderson mentioned something about a publicity stunt."

"At the hospital?"

"She didn't say." Robyn grimaced. "All I know is, we don't have much time to find out more."

"Why not?"

"Because," Robyn rubbed her forehead exhaustedly, "whatever they're plotting, she obviously wants it to happen *before* Thursday's memorial ceremony. It's happening tomorrow."

Chapter Sixteen: Noah

H e was crouching behind the reception desk in the main lobby when the news report caught his attention. The hospital was quiet, and the technicians on duty had stepped away for a minute so he could clean up and restock the cupboards at the rear of the station. The television in the waiting area was always on, but one of the technicians had turned up the volume while they waited for him to finish.

"...our special report on Helen Matthews," the reporter was saying, "who recently returned to Bellator after a terrifying ordeal at the hands of rogue males in the forest surrounding the city. Despite the long-awaited memorial service happening tomorrow, Chancellor Danforth *herself* took time out of her busy schedule to welcome the young woman back to the academy."

Noah had been racked with guilt since Helen's disappearance, though he wasn't sure how he could have prevented her transfer. His only hope now was that Helen could avoid the testing programme. If Danforth was using her publicly to rebuild trust in the academy and its aims, surely she wouldn't be subjected to the experimental drugs?

After pondering who the perpetrator of the bombing could be for most of the previous day, he had come to the only logical conclusion: Danforth herself.

She was the only one who benefitted from the explosion. Her campaign to keep the Bellator citizens in the dark *depended* on them continuing to hate and fear the men from the forest. Staging a devastating incident which could be blamed on Eremus was a surefire way to make sure the city's women continued to believe her. To trust her.

Even if it meant sacrificing a few of their lives.

Noah shifted his position, craning his neck so he could see a portion of the screen without attracting the attention of the technicians. Onscreen, the reporter stood in front of the school, her face serious.

"It's certainly nice to report something positive for a change, especially with all the distressing news the city has had to bear recently." She paused before continuing, bowing her head in respect for the fallen Bellator citizens.

When she spoke again, her tone was far more positive. "The chancellor is eager to dispel recent rumours about the school's true purpose. Citizens claiming they belong to a rebel Resistance group cast doubt on its methodology and have tried to bring the academy's name into disrepute. But today," the reporter gestured to the gates behind her, "our chancellor invites you inside the gates of this prestigious institution to see what really goes on."

On the other side of the desk, one of the technicians cleared her throat. "Think she's for real?"

"I guess we'll see."

A faint creak suggested the pair were settling into chairs. Noah turned his attention back to the desk, refilling the box of patient ID bracelets in the drawer and wiping down the surfaces with a cloth spritzed with disinfectant.

In the background, a new voice boomed from the screen.

"Welcome to Danforth Academy. I'm the principal, Joanna Anderson." He imagined her beaming at the camera. "Today is a very special day."

Classical music played faintly in the background, and when Noah sneaked another glance at the screen, a tall, dark-haired woman was walking into the academy's main reception. When she was standing in the centre, surrounded by shining marble pillars and expensive-looking paintings, she turned to face the camera.

"A few weeks ago," her voice had taken a sombre tone, "several of our students were taken from us. Kidnapped by men from outside the city limits. This incident was horrific, and..."

"Building's beautiful, isn't it?"

The technician's voice jolted Noah from his reverie. Startled, he refocused his attention, pushing a broom across the floor behind the desk. If one of the women decided to check on him, he had to make sure he was doing the job he was here to do. But as the technicians' conversation continued, he relaxed. Clearly, the news report was far more interesting than he was.

"I'd have given anything to be selected for the academy." The woman's tone was wistful.

"You really think it's as good as it seems?" The other technician was less convinced. "Even after the rumours?"

"I don't know. I mean, it *looks* good. They get to live in a gorgeous building, their education is second-to-none, they're guaranteed a great job when they graduate." The woman hesitated. "But I guess, I mean if the rumours are *true*..."

On the screen, Anderson was still speaking, her voice sugary-sweet. It set Noah's teeth on edge. "Today however, we get to bring one of those students back. And who better to welcome her than our namesake, Chancellor Danforth!"

One of the technicians snorted a laugh. "It's like a game show."

"Shh!" She yelped as the other technician elbowed her. "I want to hear it. They've *never* allowed cameras inside before."

Noah moved around the desk, using the task of emptying the bin into a large disposal bag on his cleaning trolley as an excuse. A sideways glance at the technicians told him they both had their backs to him. Otherwise, the waiting room was empty and the desk blocked him from the view of the camera on the wall. Pushing his luck, Noah glanced up at the screen again.

He was just in time to catch sight of Danforth, gracefully ushering a shaky-looking Helen into the reception. The chancellor had hold of her hand and appeared to be pulling her forward, closer to the camera.

"She doesn't look like she wants to be there," the more sceptical technician commented.

Noah had to agree. But Danforth more than made up for Helen's hesitance, the wide smile on her face giving her the impression of an alligator waiting to attack.

"Good morning, Chancellor!" Anderson trilled. Noah tried hard not to react to the falseness of her tone. "And *Helen*," she swept the girl into an awkward embrace, "welcome home. I'm sure you're eager to be back in the fold once again after your distressing experience with the beasts who took you from us."

"What do you think they *did* to her?" One of the technicians asked, her voice hushed.

"I dread to think what she's been through." The other one shuddered. "Those *men*... who knows *what* they're capable of."

"No wonder she looks so distressed."

Noah had to bite his lip. The reason for Helen's reluctance was nothing to do with the men from Eremus, and *everything* to do with the place she was being forced to return to. And the women who were forcing her to return.

On the screen, Danforth faced the camera, a satisfied smile on her face. "Eremus has proved to us, over and over, how vicious they are. With the kidnapping, and with the recent bombing of our beloved city." She paused, shaking her head slowly. "But I assure you, bringing Helen home is the first victory of many for Bellator. We fully intend to make sure that these brutes are punished for their actions, and that you, my citizens, can feel safe again in your homes."

Noah inhaled sharply. The chancellor had always been capable of justifying the method, no matter how brutal, as long as it helped to achieve her goal. But the fact that she had engineered this... *publicity stunt*... was pretending to care about a single female citizen mere *days* after her actions had murdered more than forty of them... it beggared belief.

The woman was despicable. As Danforth finished her speech, Noah fought to control his feelings. *Never* had he hated her more.

As the trio walked out of the reception area, the camera zoomed out. It followed them into a large, circular vestibule, out of which led a wide staircase. The grandeur of the space elicited a gasp of wonder from the technicians. The two women sat up, straining closer to the screen.

Aside from Danforth, Anderson, and Helen, the area was completely empty, despite it being nine a.m., a busy time of day for any academic establishment. Obviously, it had been kept clear on purpose. *But where were they hiding the other girls?*

"As Helen rejoins the school community," the news reporter had taken over the narrative again, "we've been offered the chance to take a tour of some of the school's grounds. This is an unprecedented opportunity, and one we're sure you'll find fascinating."

Classical music swelled as the reporter finished speaking. Shaking his head, Noah moved behind the desk again. He was willing to bet that they would only show the public certain areas of the academy. Those which would give the Bellator citizens the impression that the building provided well for its students, and the staff there had the girls' best interests at heart.

He moved to the side of the desk, refilling a bottle of sanitiser which was fixed to the wall for universal use. On screen, the camera was panning up the staircase. As Anderson led her guests to the floor above, the image faded, replaced by a montage of shots from around the school: the enormous sports' fields and running track; the state-of-the-art gym; the art and graphic design studio, filled with the latest technology; the canteen, also curiously empty.

As the montage ended, the music decreased in volume and the camera returned to Helen and the two older women. Now they were sitting in a bedroom, a pleasant, airy space with a sunny view into a courtyard below.

Danforth stood by the window looking out, while Anderson handed Helen a package.

"A little welcome home gift from your friends here at the academy."

Anderson smiled widely, hovering by Helen's side as she unpacked it.

"Ahh, how lovely." One of the technicians said. "Bet they've missed her."

"You'd think they'd have brought some of her friends to greet her though, wouldn't you?" The other one was less convinced.

"Would've made for good television, that's for sure." The first technician exclaimed. "I mean, they must be dying to see her."

Noah rolled his eyes, certain that the last thing Danforth wanted was to show the state of the other girls at the academy. What a way to ruin the perfect picture they had just created. Moving to refill another sanitiser bottle on the wall just inside the entrance, he lowered his head as he passed the two technicians.

Noticing him, one of them stood up. "You almost done?"

"Yeah, we need to get back to work now." The other one stiffened, as though Noah might report them for slacking on the job.

Inclining his head, Noah filled the bottle of sanitiser as quickly as he could, then returned to the desk to collect his equipment. Restacking them on the cleaning trolley quickly, he wheeled it out of the way, indicating to the pair of technicians that he was finished.

As they moved back behind the desk, the reporter began winding up. "A place of learning and luxury. I know I've enjoyed this peek into the hallowed halls of Danforth Academy. Next up, a little preview of the plans for the memorial ceremony, which takes place tomorrow in..."

Noah bent his head low and hurried away. The ceremony had been looming over him all week; fears about Flynn's execution never far from his mind. That it would take place the next day was more than he could bear. Heeding Diane's words that the Resistance was implementing a plan to save his father, he'd tried to be patient. But speaking to Ella had not put his mind at ease.

There seemed to be no clear plan in place and, if he was honest, he wasn't at all confident that Madeleine would put Flynn's wellbeing ahead of that of her own goals. Now that Helen was gone, there seemed little point in him remaining undercover at the hospital. The few attempts he'd made to get close to the Fertility Wards had been thwarted by the huge security presence now guarding that wing of the hospital. There was no way he could get inside to find evidence of Danforth's experiments at the moment. But he'd received no further instructions from the Resistance.

Sighing, he hurried back to the supply building. The task board was blank. Large numbers of patients had been discharged over the past few days, and the emergency had been declared over. It was time to return to normal duties. But it didn't feel normal to Noah any more.

Nothing felt normal.

CHAPTER SEVENTEEN: FAITH

Someone was shaking her. Groggily, Faith opened her eyes. She was lying on the sofa under the library window. A set of papers lay abandoned on her knee.

She focused on the figure looming over her. Slowly, Lily's face came into view. A pale, tear-stained face.

"Faith?" She frowned. "You with me?"

"What is it?"

"You need to come." Lily's eyes darkened. "She's asking for you."

Faith was already on her feet, the papers on her lap cascading to the floor. Leaping over them, she followed Lily back through the library and down the stairs, knowing where they were headed without having to ask.

At the door of Sophia's room, Lily gestured for Faith to enter.

The room was dark. The curtains were drawn, and there was a faint sour scent hanging in the air. She was vaguely aware of Lily closing the door behind her, but as she stepped inside her focus was only on one person.

Allowing her eyes to adjust, her eyes sought out the bed at the far end of the room. The figure in it lay still. Too still. Dread took hold of Faith as she made her way towards it.

Anna, Sophia's current guardian, sat on the opposite side of the bed. She pressed a cold cloth to Sophia's forehead. As Faith approached, she glanced up.

Faith met her gaze. "Lily said I should come. Is she-?"

Anna's face was drawn. "She's taken a turn for the worse over the last few hours, I'm afraid. We've adjusted her fluids and upped her painkillers," she moved the cloth away from Sophia's face, "but nothing seems to be making a difference."

Faith hung back, horrified by the medic's words.

"She's become pretty much unresponsive over the last hour," Anna continued. She beckoned to Faith. "But when she does speak, she asks for you."

Hesitantly, Faith perched on the chair at the other side of the bed. For the first time, she looked at Sophia. Her friend's eyes were closed, her skin glazed with a sheen of sweat. Her face was chalk-white, and the only part of her which was moving were her eyes. Behind the lids, they danced back and forth, betraying the presence of troubling dreams.

"We can't keep her temperature down." Anna removed the cloth from Sophia's face. "And she's very weak. I thought if you sat with her, she might..."

"Can she..." Faith forced herself to breathe. "Is she actually able to speak to me?"

Anna nodded. "Just about. The painkillers are making her groggy, and she's been drifting in and out of consciousness, but she does come to occasionally." Anna stood up, gesturing at the cloth. "Would you keep an eye on her while I go and refresh this?"

Faith nodded mutely.

"Try talking to her. She might well respond better to you than to anyone else. The rest of us are pretty much strangers to her. Don't underestimate the power of a familiar voice."

Faith felt a panic overwhelm her as Anna began walking towards the door. "Shouldn't I let her rest?" Anna's footsteps halted. "I mean... doesn't she need that to help her get better?"

Anna retraced her footsteps until she stood by Faith's side. Placing the cloth on the nightstand, she knelt down beside Faith and put an arm around her.

"I'm not sure it matters how much rest she gets." Anna tightened her grip on Faith's shoulder. "I haven't left her side for the past twenty-four hours, more or less. I've never seen a sickness like this. The vomiting has mostly stopped, but only because there is little in her system to come back up. Her symptoms are worsening, and nothing we give her seems to make a difference." The grip on her loosened, and Faith felt herself being turned to face Anna. "Do you understand what I'm trying to say?"

Faith stared at her. "But she's... I mean, she's not–"

"I'm not a qualified doctor," Anna said, "but I've seen a fair amount of sickness over the years. This is... I don't know, it's like something is draining the life out of her." She leaned forward, placing her hand on the swollen stomach. "I'm not sure if it's the pregnancy, or some delayed reaction to the drugs, but–"

"Surely the drugs are out of her system by now?" Faith tensed. "I mean, she's been here for almost a week. Shouldn't she have started to recover by now?"

"I keep hoping that she will, but so far, she just keeps getting worse." Anna shook her head. "Aborting the foetus might alleviate the strain on her system, much as I hate to admit it." Faith knew she was thinking of her own desperate flight from Bellator whilst pregnant with Noah, a male who would have been automatically aborted under Danforth's law. "But it would be too dangerous. We don't have a doctor qualified to perform the procedure." She squeezed Faith's hand. "I'm so sorry. I'll keep thinking, but I'm way out of my depth here." She held up the washcloth. "Are you okay if...?"

"Sure." But the second Anna left the room, Faith missed her comforting presence.

She turned back to Sophia. *Where had her friend gone?* The fiercely intelligent, warm-hearted, curious girl who'd been by her side since the age of ten when they'd both started at the academy. The brains behind their partnership. The voice of reason. The girl who had supported her wholeheartedly, yet wasn't afraid to tell Faith when she had gone too far.

The girl who lay in the bed was a stranger. Faith shuddered.

Leaning forward, she reached for Sophia's hand. It was cold and limp.

"Soph?" Faith moved closer. "Can you hear me?"

There was no reply. Closing her eyes, Faith allowed her head to rest forward on the bed.

"Please, Soph," she whispered into the covers. "You have to stay with me. You have to fight this."

The body on the bed stirred. Encouraged, Faith sat up. Perhaps her words were getting through. Her eyes centred on Sophia. A low moan escaped her.

"Soph?"

The hand in Faith's tensed, its grip tight. Sophia's lids remained closed, but the movement of the eyes behind them changed, becoming jerky and chaotic. She moaned again, louder now, her free hand also tightening on the sheet which covered her.

Faith glanced at the door, willing Anna to return.

"Sophia?" She tried to shake her friend's hand loose, but the death-grip remained. "It's Faith. Can you hear me?"

"No-no-no-no-no-no..." The moans morphed into words. "I can't... please don't..."

Alarmed, Faith leaned forward, stroking a hand down Sophia's cheek in an attempt to calm her. "Sssshh... it's alright... you're safe, you're..."

But Sophia didn't respond. She didn't even seem present in the same space as Faith. Physically, she was. But mentally,

Faith knew she was back in the ward in the hospital, surrounded by the machines and the medics who had put her through so much.

Relinquishing her hold on Faith, Sophia thrust her hand out in front of her, clawing at the empty air. An expression of terror froze her features in a twisted mask.

Faith stood up, moving closer in a desperate effort to rid her friend of her demons. "You're okay. I'm here. Come back to me. I promise I won't let anyone hurt–"

Sophia screamed. An anguished sound, which echoed off the walls of the room. Her other hand shot out, making sudden, painful contact with Faith's face. She recoiled, clutching at her cheek and biting back tears. For someone who was so weak, Sophia packed quite a punch. Clearly, her nightmares were lending her brute strength.

Blinking back tears, Faith came closer again, this time, grasping both of Sophia's hands in her own. Pinning her arms by her sides, she spoke as loudly and calmly as she could.

"Soph! You're okay, you're safe. I'm here, you're okay..." Faith repeated the mantra over and over. "I'm here, you're safe. Come back to me, please..."

Slowly, Sophia's demeanour changed. She stopped trying to lash out. Her moans subsided and the movement of her eyes behind the lids stilled. Eventually, she fell silent and her entire body went limp once again.

Faith wasn't sure which was worse. The wildly tortured soul of a moment ago, or the shell of her old friend who lay there unresponsive. Sagging back in her chair, she let the tears come. At first, there was only a trickle of saltwater on her cheeks. But soon, violent sobs racked her body, a torrent of tears which showed no sign of stopping. Covering her face with her hands, Faith slumped forwards on the bed, her face in her hands allowing her emotions to overwhelm her.

When she felt a hand on the back of her head, she presumed it was Anna returning. Hauling in a deep breath, she sat up and found herself looking right into Sophia's eyes. Open, for the first time since Faith had entered the room, and filled with a calm which had seemed impossible only moments ago.

"You're–" Faith scrubbed a hand across her face. "You're awake!"

"Anna said you'd come." Sophia smiled weakly. "I've been waiting."

"Of course, I've come." Faith sat up straighter. "Are you-?" She took in her friend's expression. "How do you feel?"

"Been better." Sophia's voice was hushed. "I can barely lift my head."

She demonstrated, her body tensing. She managed to raise her head a small amount, but the effort took it out of her. When she let it drop, she was panting.

"What's *wrong* with me, Faith?" Her forehead creased with concern. "I'm like a newborn... no strength at all."

Faith's eyes dropped to her friend's swelling stomach. The irony that the baby inside Sophia was the very thing which was draining her of her energy was not lost on her. But she wouldn't point that out. Chances were, Sophia was already aware of it.

Once again, Faith wished that Anna would appear in the doorway, saving her from having the conversation she felt ill-equipped to have. She sat forward, searching for words which might offer her friend some comfort. She came up empty. What could she say? Sophia was one of the cleverest people she knew. And she wouldn't appreciate it if Faith lied to her.

"I don't know." Faith cringed at her answer, but Sophia seemed to appreciate her honesty. "Anna says they've tried everything they can think of, but since they don't know what's causing your illness, they're at a bit of a loss."

She took hold of her friend's hand again. This time the returning squeeze was not so vice-like.

"Don't lose hope, though. They're still looking for other solutions, trying to work out what else they could do to–"

"They won't find anything." Sophia sighed. "It's not like anyone else has ever been through this before." Her voice quavered. "I'm an experiment. A test case. I'll bet even experienced doctors wouldn't know what to do with me. No one's ever seen..." she gestured to her stomach, "*this* before."

"There has to be *something*–"

"Why?" Sophia's voice grew shrill. "Why does there? Because it's not fair? Because you don't want me to die?" Faith recoiled at the unfamiliar bitterness in her friend's voice. "Life doesn't appear to *be* very fair."

Faith bowed her head. "I'm s-sorry, Soph."

"No. I'm sorry." All the fight had gone out of Sophia. Her eyes were filled with regret. "I shouldn't take it out on you. It's just–" She swallowed. "They tell me to eat. To build up my strength. And I've *tried*. But I just..." her shoulders slumped. "I just can't. And I'm just... so... tired."

She closed her eyes again, the animation of a moment ago gone. Faith squeezed her hand, noting that the returning squeeze was far weaker than it had been only moments ago.

"Rest, then." She stroked her friend's hand, not knowing what else to say. "Just sleep. That's got to do you good, right?"

Silence fell once more. Faith listened to the sound of Sophia's breathing, fighting tears. She had failed her friend. Just when she thought Sophia had fallen asleep, her eyes flickered open again.

"At least..." the voice was even fainter now. "At least I managed the recording." She eyed Faith. "Blake's edited it ready for the ceremony, right?"

Faith forced a smile. "I'm sure she's working on it right now."

"And you'll make sure..." Sophia grasped Faith's hand a little tighter, "it makes a difference? To save Flynn. To convince the citizens that Danforth... that she's..."

"I will." Faith bit down hard on her lower lip. "I promise."

Sophia relaxed against the pillows. "Alright. If it's too late for me...then at least I'll have made a difference... done something..." her voice trailed off, "something... some–"

"Something heroic." Faith finished for her. "Something brave and selfless. But don't–" she choked on the words, "don't talk like that. It's not too late for you. You've got to–"

She broke off as the door behind them opened. Anna hurried in, an apologetic look on her face.

"So sorry. Madeleine collared me." Her eyes went to Sophia. "You're awake! How are you feeling?"

She crossed to the bed, handing the cool cloth to Faith. When she pressed it to Sophia's forehead, her friend sighed with relief.

"Better?"

"A little." A shadow crossed Sophia's face.

"What is it?" Faith frowned.

"Those pains again?" Anna took hold of Sophia's wrist, her fingers feeling for the pulse.

"What pains?" Faith tried to stay calm.

Nodding, Sophia groaned and clutched at her stomach.

"She's been experiencing some severe cramping on and off." Anna leaned in, her mouth close to Faith's ear. "I thought, with the pregnancy progressing so rapidly, that she might actually be in labour."

"*What?*" Faith went cold. "She can't–"

"She isn't." Anna tensed. "I've seen enough pregnancies in Eremus to know, and..." Her worried glance returned to Sophia. "I've checked her over several times. It's definitely not labour." Anna leaned over the bed. "Sophia? Your pulse is a little fast. Try and stay calm. I know it's hard." She turned back to Faith. "She's stopped vomiting now, but it seems like her stomach is still experiencing severe issues."

Sophia groaned again. "I can't... can't..." she panted. "They're... w-worse than before." She curled up on the bed in a foetal position. "Feels like–"

"Sshhh." Anna ran a soothing hand over her back. "I'll get you something for the pain."

She moved to the dresser where there were several bottles of the orange pills. Shaking one out onto her hand, she hesitated.

"What is it?" Faith asked.

"She had one a couple of hours ago. I shouldn't really give her another. Too many could adversely affect her blood pressure, particularly if her body is under an immense amount of strain. If we're not careful, she could... But..." Anna gestured to Sophia. Her face was bathed in sweat and she was crying quietly. "*Look* at her. I might not have a choice."

"No-oo-oo-oo."

Her moans were guttural now. This was no mental torture, no nightmare. Whatever was ailing Sophia, it was agony. Faith shifted from the chair to the bed, seating herself as close to her friend as she dared.

"Shh," she soothed, imitating Anna. "Anna's getting you something for the pain. You'll feel better soon."

But her words fell on deaf ears. Sophia's groans grew in volume, her face creased in anguish. Suddenly, she gasped.

"Faith! Faith– Aahh!" Her eyes were wide and terrified. "It hurts so much, I can't..."

"Anna! You have to do something." Faith pleaded. "Give her something. She's in such pain."

The Eremus medic made a decision. Taking one of the orange pills, she dropped it into the bottom of a cup and used a spoon to crush it up. Adding a little water from the jug, she mixed it around. She moved towards the bed, nodding to Faith.

"Can you help her to sit?"

Faith slid an arm around her friend, noticing how painfully thin she was. Managing to support her into a sitting position, she looked at Anna for further instructions.

"Sophia." Anna's voice was commanding, loud. "I need you to drink this. Swallow it all. It should help with the pain."

Something about her tone got through to Sophia, and she managed to nod. Anna brought the cup to her lips, tipping it up slowly. When Sophia swallowed, they both heaved a sigh of relief.

"Won't she throw it back up?" Faith asked.

Anna tilted her head to one side. "I hope not."

"How quickly will it work?" Faith nodded at the cup.

Anna shrugged. "Shouldn't be long. And sometimes the cramps come in waves. We might find the pain subsides in a moment anyway."

She was wrong. Though Sophia had managed to still herself for long enough to swallow the liquid in the cup, the pains soon had her writhing on the bed again. Faith found she couldn't bear it, and began pacing up and down at the foot of the bed.

"Can't you-?" She gestured at Sophia. "Isn't there anything else you can do?"

Anna shook her head. "A higher dose of the pills will kill her."

As Sophia's cries grew louder and more pained, Faith resumed her pacing. Looking at the figure in the bed was too hard. But then Sophia called out for her.

"Faith?" Sophia's eyes were wild. "Faith!"

Faith moved to the bedside again. "I'm here."

"It hurts..." Sophia's voice was faint now. "It hurts so much."

Clutching her friend's hand to her chest, Faith leaned closer. "I know. I'm so sorry."

"I can't..." Sophia's voice was only a murmur now. "Don't let me... Stay with me."

"I'm right here. I won't leave. I'm not going anywhere."

Sophia's eyes zeroed in on Faith's. The pained look faded and she seemed calm. For a moment, Faith was glad, but then the hand in hers went slack.

"No!" Faith bent closer, willing her friend to hold on. "Sophia, no!"

But the eyes staring back at her were vacant.

Sophia was gone.

Chapter Eighteen: Noah

Please note, at eleven a.m. there will be a two-minute silence observed for those staff and patients not able to attend the Memorial Day service this morning. All staff are to cease duties to pay their respects.

As Noah loaded a washing machine in the laundry, he felt sick. Flynn was going to die today. And what was he doing? Washing the Bellator women's clothes.

He had barely slept the previous night.

He longed to escape the hospital, to leave the drudge-disguise behind and head out to save his father. But without a plan or backup, what could he, an Eremus male, do? Alone, he'd be more likely to get himself killed alongside Flynn. Still, he couldn't stand idly by and do nothing.

As another drudge began loading the machine beside his, Noah returned his attention to his task. Adding the soap, he switched it on, hoping the man next to him hadn't noticed his complete lack of focus. But as he turned to leave, he felt a hand on his arm.

"S'me." Liam's voice was low. "Keep working."

Noah collected another laundry bag and returned to the machines. "What's up?"

"Overheard something." Liam didn't look at him. "Might be of interest."

Another drudge appeared. Noah worked at looking busy, until the man had passed them by.

"Know Sanders?" Liam kept his voice low. "Doc in charge of your friend's case?" Noah nodded. "She was on the phone to someone in the alleyway behind the building. I was on the other side of the bins, so she couldn't see me."

Again, Liam paused while another drudge collected several empty laundry bags and moved away with them.

"Long story short, she was complaining about the girl being taken. Ruining her experiment. Said Danforth was going to scour the city looking for her, but Sanders told her not to."

"What?" Noah had to force himself not to face Liam. "*Why?*"

"Whatever drug they had her on, it had to be given consistently. Regular doses of the correct amount. If not..." A shiver ran through Noah as he paused. "If not, there'd be *severe* withdrawal symptoms for the patient."

Noah felt like he'd stopped breathing. "What do you mean, *severe?*"

"I mean irreversible." He felt Liam shake his head. "The rats in the previous tests, in cases where they were taken off the drug abruptly, they died. All of them."

Noah went cold. Sophia had been taken from the hospital six days ago. Without a constant dose of the metraxilone, she was in real danger. And Anderson was giving the same drug to numerous girls at the academy. The second anyone figured out they'd been replaced by placebos, they were in real trouble too.

He stilled. "I have to warn them."

Beside him, he felt Liam tense. "Thought you might say that."

"They'll be at the memorial service today."

"You need to be there. Try and speak to them." Liam went back to his task, switching on the machine before he spoke again. "Know the alleyway behind the drudge dorms?" He paused, waiting for Noah's answering nod. "There's a section at the end which twists to the right. It's fenced off, but it's easy to climb, and there's no camera once you round the bend."

"So I can get out–"

"Without being seen."

"But I–"

"I'll cover for you as long as I can. Give you a chance to get clear."

"You're sure?" Noah exhaled slowly. "Thank you."

"S'fine." He felt Liam shrug. "You're not coming back, are you?"

"Probably not. But look on the bright side…" Noah found himself attempting words of comfort. "In a couple of days, you'll have Rowan back."

There was a silence, then Liam leaned close enough to bump Noah's shoulder. It was the closest drudges came to physical contact, the equivalent of a hug.

"Go safely, then." Liam's voice was gruff. "And… keep up the good work."

Nudging Liam's shoulder in return, Noah hoped it conveyed his gratitude. "Do my best."

Liam was already moving away from him. After waiting a few moments, Noah followed, shuffling at the usual drudge pace towards the exit his friend had suggested. If he was careful, he could get out of the hospital without being spotted.

Now all he had to do was make it to the ceremony, speak to a Resistance member, and pass on the information about the metraxilone withdrawal. None of it would be easy. But with so many lives at risk, he had to try.

In the back of his mind, he was glad to have an excuse to be in the square when Flynn was brought to the stage. If the Resistance rescue didn't go to plan, perhaps he could do something. He had no idea what, but at least he'd be close enough to mount an attempt to save his father.

If nothing else, at least he'd get to see him one last time.

Chapter Nineteen: Faith

"Faith?"

Somewhere in the distance, her name was being called.

"*Faith!*"

It was Ella's voice. Her friend was no doubt wanting to check on her. But Faith didn't want to be checked on. To be asked if she was okay.

Sophia was dead.

She would never be okay.

Not waiting to be found, she opened the first door she came to. Blake's office. The techie had just headed off for lunch with Robyn. The room would be empty. And it wasn't a place Faith had spent much time recently. Ella wouldn't think to look there. Not to begin with, anyway.

The darkness of the room welcomed her. Collapsing into Blake's chair, she closed her eyes, letting the hum of the equipment drown out the world. It was comforting. At least nothing in here would shoot her pitying glances.

But when she opened her eyes, they came to rest on the familiar screen to her left. A screen which, for so long, had been her only means of contact with Sophia. It was turned off. They'd had no further use for it since Sophia had arrived at the library.

Faith remembered the joy she'd felt, less than a week ago, when she'd discovered the rescue had been a success. Sophia had been *here*, within her reach. Faith had helped to save her, and all her efforts to escape Eremus and return to the city had been worth it.

Her heart contracted painfully. Now Sophia was gone for good. There had been nothing anyone could do to save her life or that of the baby she'd been carrying. Faith leaned forward, tracing a finger through the dust on the screen. Tears gathered in her eyes. For once, she let them fall. Silently at first, then faster and faster, until a sob broke free from her body and echoed through the stuffy room.

Raw pain coursed through her as she flung her head into her hands on the desk, allowing the emotions to overwhelm her. One sob followed another, until they racked her entire body, making her chest ache. Faith welcomed the pain. Anything was better than the numbness which had enveloped her since the previous day.

She didn't even hear the door open. She was only vaguely aware of the hand on her back, patting awkwardly. She glanced up, expecting Ella or Diane. Instead, she found herself gazing into Blake's eyes.

Startled, Faith tried to jump to her feet, but Blake held her in place.

"Stay." She moved to the other side of the room, switching on a datadev. "I'll work around you."

Faith wiped her face with the sleeve of her sweatshirt. Strangely, she wasn't embarrassed. Blake continued as normal, moving around Faith as though she wasn't even there. Her actions somehow made Faith's tears seem normal, an acceptable reaction.

That she hadn't rushed to comfort Faith said a lot. Allowing her to cry it out, to recover from the bout of sobs without judgement, comment, or even observation, made it alright.

By the time she had pulled herself together enough to move, Blake had settled on a stool at the opposite side of the room. As Faith stood up, she turned.

"Feel any better?" She slid one of the headphones off her ear.

"Not really." Not wanting to dwell on her outburst, Faith stood up and walked across to the techie. "What are you doing?"

"Final edits of Sophia's spee–" Blake glanced down at the datadev in her hand. "Sorry. Probably not what you need to hear right now."

Sophia's words came back to Faith. *Tomorrow might be too late. I have to do something, while I still can.*

Taking a deep breath, she shook her head. "It's fine. She would want it to make a difference."

Blake nodded her approval. "Then I will make sure that the finished product is as powerful as I can."

"Thanks." Faith frowned. "It'll be ready in time for the ceremony?"

"I'll make sure of it." She glanced at Faith briefly, her eyes shadowed with doubt. "I only hope–"

Faith narrowed her eyes. "You only hope what?"

Blake sighed. "It's not the speech that's the problem. It's hacking into the feed for the ceremony. Madeleine's convinced the interruption will provide the perfect distraction so our operatives can get to Flynn. But..." The doubt in Blake's tone sent chills through Faith. "I'm not sure I... that is, Danforth's security experts have put far more challenging defences in place since the last time I did this, and..."

"You're not certain you'll be able to break through?" Faith surmised.

Blake shook her head. "And if I can't do it..."

"The distraction won't work." Faith's heart lurched. "Flynn will die."

Blake shook herself. "This is me we're talking about. Of course, I can do it." She hesitated. "I'd just feel *better*... knowing that there was a backup plan. That we had something else, something just as shocking, to distract Danforth at the right time."

Faith nodded. "You've done it before. I'm sure you can—"

"You're right." Blake slipped the headphone back over her ear. "Don't listen to me. It'll be fine. Don't worry," she met Faith's gaze steadily, "I'll do Sophia justice."

As she turned back to her datadev, her wristclip emitted a loud beep. Tutting, she glanced down at it. "Madeleine." She removed the headphones altogether and pushed herself to her feet. "Better go see what she wants." Moving to the door, she glanced back at Faith. "Stay as long as you like."

Grateful for the unusual show of understanding, Faith managed a weak smile. As the door closed, she felt a stab of guilt. She'd been so wrapped up in Sophia, she'd forgotten that Flynn's life was also hanging in the balance. Her eyes came to rest on the shape she had traced on the blank screen with her finger and her heart stopped.

It looked a little like a letter S.

She pressed the power button, hoping to distract herself. As the screen flickered to life, it showed one of the hospital's many hallways. A couple of medics walked past, deep in conversation, passing by a drudge who was moving in the opposite direction.

She reached forward, about to navigate to a different camera when something made her stop. She waited, hardly breathing, as the man came closer to the camera. Though his head was bowed low, something about his movement was familiar. And then she knew.

It was Noah.

Noah, who she wished more than anything she could be with right now. Noah, whose posture suggested a misery beyond that of an ordinary drudge. Noah, who right now must be terrified for the life of the man who had been there for him ever since his birth.

He passed beneath the camera and the hallway was empty once again. Faith's heart ached for him. She was so sick of watching the people she cared about suffer and being powerless to do anything about it. But what could she do? The entire Resistance was struggling with how to rescue Flynn. She was just one person. And a wanted person, at that. Someone who risked attracting a lot of attention if she was spotted in the city.

Blake's words came back to her. *"I'd just feel better knowing that there was a backup plan... something else... just as shocking, to distract Danforth at the right time."*

The seed of an idea started to form. Rooting through the mess of belongings on Blake's desk, she located a pen and notebook, hastily scribbled a note, and tucked it behind the charging unit which she knew Blake only used at the end of the day.

That done, she opened the door and peered out. At this time of day, most of the Resistance members would be in the hub having lunch. Hurrying into the empty hallway, she headed for the dorms, praying she wouldn't meet anyone. Once she had gathered a few choice belongings, she pulled on a dark hoodie and went back downstairs, backpack in hand.

One last stop before she left. Bracing herself, she slipped into Sophia's sickroom. Her friend's body was gone, but otherwise the room was untouched. Faith made her way to the empty bed. The nightstand was still filled with the detritus of the previous day. It took seconds to locate the items she wanted and slip them into her pocket.

Moments later, she was peering out into the empty hallway. Now came the tricky part. She couldn't get away with leaving through the tunnel. She'd have to cross the hub, and someone would question her. The side door was her only option, but there was always someone on duty there. Could she get past them without raising suspicion?

Leaving her backpack in the sickroom, she approached the little-used exit with caution. She pulled back the curtain which screened off the door, revealing a startled-looking Olivia on the other side.

"Faith! You made me jump." She narrowed her eyes. "Everything okay?

"It's Madeleine." Faith didn't have to fake her worried expression. "Something's happened. She needs you in her office. Now."

"She does?"

Olivia stiffened, and Faith wondered if she'd done something she didn't want Madeleine to find out. Playing on the woman's fear, Faith stepped closer.

"Yeah. Not sure what it was, but it sounded pretty urgent." She dropped her voice. "I wouldn't keep her waiting if I were you."

Olivia gestured to the door. "Would you...?"

As casually as she could manage, Faith nodded. "Of course. I can stay here 'til you get back."

"Thanks." Twisting her hands together, Olivia set off towards the hub.

Knowing she didn't have long, Faith darted back to the sickroom. Collecting her pack, she hurriedly donned a pair of sunglasses and pulled up her hood. Happy with her makeshift disguise, she retraced her steps to the exit. Sweeping the curtain out of the way, she slipped behind it and let herself into the street.

Outside, the square was busy. Too busy for anyone to notice a lone figure slipping out of the library's side entrance. When Faith reached the top of the steps without being stopped, she heaved a sigh of relief. She'd made it.

Lowering her head and hunching her shoulders, she slipped into the crowd.

Chapter Twenty: Noah

S o far, so good.

Noah had escaped the hospital with no issue, and with the streets so crowded for the memorial service, no one paid attention to a lowly drudge. The city's women were readying themselves for the ceremony, either hurrying home to watch the televised version or heading to the venue itself.

But as he got closer to the square, he ran into a problem. The streets around it were packed, and whilst Danforth's guards still appeared to be letting citizens in, every single woman who entered was stopped and had their bag searched.

Noah had no hope of getting inside without an accompanying citizen to vouch for him.

Instead, he slipped into an alleyway which ran along the rear of the square. The buildings here were mostly open to the public: restaurants, museums, a few offices, and a theatre. He peered at the doors leading out of the alley. Surely *one* of them would allow him access to the square?

One particular doorway had a noticeboard that was crammed with leaflets and flyers. It was suspiciously familiar. When Noah ducked into it to take a closer look, it hit him where he was. This was the alleyway he had hidden in with

Ella and Evelyn when he'd first entered the city. The door led into a restaurant of some sort. Probably one crammed with citizens hoping to catch a glimpse of the ceremony.

Taking a chance, he tried the door.

It clicked open, and he peered inside. The space beyond was empty. Praying that other drudges worked there, he tugged his mask higher and stepped through. At the end of the hallway was a busy kitchen, filled, just as he had hoped, with numerous drudges.

This was a place he could blend in.

Steam billowed from several ovens and there was the sound of pans bubbling on the hob. Multiple drudge feet hurried by, all moving with purpose. Standing still as he was, Noah did not fit in. At any moment, someone could ask what he was doing. And he wouldn't have a suitable response.

Bypassing the kitchen, he made his way further along the hall. What he needed to find was the main dining room. If he could make his way through it without attracting attention, he could find the front entrance and slip outside into the crowd. Then he'd be right where he wanted to be.

At the end of the hall, he found himself facing a pair of double doors. The hum of conversation coming from the other side made him hopeful. But when he pushed them open, he knew he'd made an error.

The dining room was filled with customers, as he'd expected. But, in stark contrast to the usual drab, grey uniform, the serving drudges were all dressed in a vibrant blue. The *second* Noah took a step into the room, gasps and whispers attacked him.

*"A **kitchen** drudge? "What's it doing in **here**?" "Place has really gone downhill."*

Following his instincts, he backed out of the room. He had to get out of here before someone questioned him and discovered he didn't belong. He headed for the exit, but before he could reach it a pair of drudges entered from the alley. Changing direction, he headed back towards the kitchen.

"Hey you!" The voice came from behind. "Stop!"

Cornered, Noah opened the one remaining door in the hallway. Finding himself at the foot of a set of stairs, he began to climb. On the floor above, there was what appeared to be the entrance to a second dining room. Not wanting to make the same mistake, Noah ignored the door and kept climbing.

At the top he reached a dead end. Praying that no one had followed him, he opened the two doors leading off the narrow hallway. Both led to storage rooms packed from floor to ceiling with boxes. Selecting the one which he knew would face the square, Noah made his way inside. Glancing down the empty hallway, he was grateful to see that no one had followed him as he closed the door behind him.

Navigating with caution, he made his way towards the only window. It was set into the gently sloping roof, but Noah hoped it might provide him with an exit. When he reached it, his heart pounding, he stood on tiptoes and peered out.

Beneath him, the square was packed. What seemed like thousands of women were still flooding in from both sides. The window gave him a side view of the stage, which was empty, yet set up with chairs, a podium with a microphone and, at the far end, a second platform whose purpose wasn't clear.

On the stage, a woman in a government uniform approached the microphone. Noah eased the window open as she began to speak.

"Good afternoon, citizens of Bellator. Welcome to our service of remembrance. Your chancellor will be onstage in a matter of minutes. Please be patient and find yourselves a space from which to watch the ceremony."

Noah shuddered at her words. Turning around, he snagged a box and pulled it towards him. Positioning it beneath the window, he planted his feet on top.

Please. He found himself praying. *Please let there be a way down.*

Hauling the window open all the way, he glanced at the building below. His heart sank. There was no fire escape. No handy rooftop which he could climb out onto. No awning below which might break his fall. Not even a drainpipe he could shimmy down to reach the ground.

Nothing but a sheer drop. He was trapped.

CHAPTER TWENTY-ONE: FAITH

Walking through the city was a surreal experience. After such a long time spent in the library, the fresh air and the freedom should have been invigorating. But Faith felt only a grim determination to get to the square and make sure Sophia's efforts had not been for nothing.

On her way, several of the posters declaring her a person of interest to the chancellor had taunted her. They were faded now, weathered by rain, but still there. A reminder of her precarious situation.

The first one she'd spotted had stopped her in her tracks. Her old academy photograph was front and centre. The girl staring back at her was a stranger now. A slight twist to the lips betrayed how she felt about having her picture taken. Remembering Sophia laughing at her discomfort, she fought to control her tears.

She kept her head low as she hurried through the streets. She couldn't risk being recognised. The posture was uncomfortable, and she understood for the first time the difficulty Noah had experienced adopting the drudge posture.

As she neared the square, Faith felt a trickle of sweat roll down her back. The streets were packed, and there were guards on duty at every entrance. Ducking into a doorway, she watched closely as every woman who passed through was searched. Her heart contracted painfully as she considered her options.

If she couldn't get in, her plan wouldn't work.

But a closer observation of the process revealed that the guards were doing little other than looking for weapons. There were so many women entering the area, they didn't have time to look closely at faces. And some guards were more thorough than others.

Hoping her disguise did enough to hide her identity, Faith approached with caution, choosing a youthful-looking guard who appeared to be quite distracted. Faith opened her bag ready for inspection and held her breath.

The guard gave her backpack a cursory search, keeping her eyes focused on the ever-growing crowd of women further down the street.

"Hope there's no trouble," she said to her partner as Faith had passed by. "I mean... I know Danforth wants a good crowd, but this seems a little–"

"Shut up and get on with it." The second guard had shot her a dark look. "We won't be popular if we can't check them all through before the ceremony starts."

Relieved, Faith had joined the growing crowd in the square, edging her way forward as more people arrived and the throng of people grew. The guards' concern was a good sign, she told herself, a sign that Danforth's protectors were wary of the Resistance. It gave her confidence as she picked her way towards the stage.

Faith spotted several members of Madeleine's army among the crowd: Robyn, Diane, Evelyn, and several others she recognised. The women were stationed at intervals around the square, blending in well with the other citizens but ready to move toward the stage when the signal was given.

How much of a difference could they make if their weapons had been taken from them, though?

Faith kept moving, dipping her head and changing direction every time she saw someone who might recognise her. Though she took care to avoid the Resistance operatives, she was comforted by their presence. She had to admit she hadn't been paying much attention to the final stages of the mission plan, but it seemed like the Resistance was throwing a lot of resources behind Flynn's rescue.

All around her, the crowd whispered. Bellator was more divided than ever. There were worries about further explosions, caused by the *villainous men* from the forest. Clamours for Flynn's execution, which Faith found hard to ignore. Intrigue created by rumours that Faith had created a second video. The last one gave her a small surge of pride.

Knowing that there *was* another video, one which would leave no doubt in their minds as to Danforth's true nature, kept her trembling legs moving. She would bear witness to Sophia's words along with the rest of Bellator. Make them count. Be there – *celebrate* – as the women finally saw Danforth for the monster she was.

Faith crept onwards, easing into the gaps between the women as the crowd shifted restlessly. Eventually, she emerged right at the front. The stage loomed ahead, the enormous screen at the back dominating the space. Shuffling across to one side, Faith positioned herself close to a set of steps leading up to the platform from which Danforth would speak.

Used for the annual Bellator Awards ceremony, the stage often had to be accessed from the crowd as members of the public were called forth to receive various honours. The steps would not be in use today, but the rope which discouraged the crowd from using them was flimsy and the entrance only had a single guard.

Sliding her hand into her pocket, Faith's fingers closed around her failsafe.

She was valuable to Danforth. The wanted posters proved that. Faith couldn't fight the chancellor with a traditional weapon. But she could damn well threaten to ruin her precious experiment. The handful of orange pills she had taken from Sophia's room were a last resort, but she had enough to terrify Danforth. To stop her in her tracks.

Especially if she took them all at once.

Glancing around, Faith decided her position was as good as it was going to get. Close enough to the stage, but far enough away for any of the Resistance to stop her from taking action. Pulling down her hood, she readied herself. If they recognised her now, it was too late to send her home.

Just when Faith was beginning to sway on her feet, Danforth appeared at the rear of the platform. She made her way forward, a suitably grief-stricken expression on her face. An immediate hush fell over the crowd as she gazed out at them expectantly. As the chancellor opened her mouth to greet them, a brief flash of light on the opposite side of the square caught Faith's eye.

It disappeared before she had the chance to react, but her eyes remained on the open window for several more minutes. It was a skylight in the roof of one of the restaurants which fringed the square. Someone was up on the top floor of the building, listening to Danforth's speech.

Perhaps it was one of the Resistance. It was a good viewpoint with little to no risk. She turned her attention to the stage as Danforth began.

"Six days ago," the chancellor's voice rang out across the square, "our beloved city suffered a *terrible* loss."

The crowd murmured in response. On the stage, Danforth bowed her head in reverence.

"We can never replace the citizens we lost. Our community still shudders with the impact of those *vicious* males, but we must not let fear of these men prevent us from moving forward. Today, we gather to remember the fallen, and also," she paused for dramatic effect, "to *punish* those responsible."

Faith shuddered at the chancellor's deceit. Glancing up at the screen, she glared at the magnified image of Danforth's face, twisted with false emotion. How could she try to comfort her people for a loss which she herself had created?

Faith clenched her fists as Danforth continued to mourn the city's devastating loss, beginning with a moment of silence. She then began reading a list of the fallen citizens' names.

There was no sign of Flynn so far, though the mention of punishment implied he would be brought out soon. But why he wasn't already on display, awaiting his fate with terror on his face? Surely that would provide maximum impact for the women in the crowd. It wasn't like Danforth to ignore an opportunity to crow about her victory.

But a glance at the crowd told her why. Danforth wasn't stupid. She had deliberately concealed Flynn's location since his arrest, knowing there would be those who wanted to liberate him. She was still keeping him hidden, knowing there would be resistors in the crowd. Every moment the Eremus man was on display was a risk. When the execution happened, it needed to be completed with swift and ruthless efficiency.

Until he appeared, the Resistance was powerless to act.

Faith thought of Blake. Back at headquarters she, too, would be waiting. Until Flynn was in sight, there was little point in her interrupting the proceedings with Sophia's video. The distraction might only have moments to take effect, and once the element of surprise was lost, it would be gone for good.

Faith braced herself. If the first distraction didn't work, she had to be ready.

Chapter Twenty-Two: Noah

On the stage, Danforth had finished reading the list of names. Nodding to someone out of sight offstage, she began to speak once again. Powerless, Noah clenched his fists. With no way to get down to the square, he was forced to witness Danforth's nauseating performance, unable to intervene.

It was torture.

"We are many different women," the chancellor began, "but I am certain we all agree on one thing. Whoever was responsible for the deaths of so many innocents should be made to suffer." Noah's heart twisted at her words. "These men behave like beasts. They *cannot* be permitted to take our sisters from us."

Beneath him, the crowd murmured in agreement. Noah bristled with fury. How easily swayed these women were! They'd forgotten Faith's words so quickly. Why couldn't they see that the woman who promised to protect them was the very woman responsible for so many of their deaths?

For what felt like the hundredth time, he glanced at the door to the store room, considering his options. While he hadn't been followed up the stairs, if he went back down to the restaurant, he risked attracting unwelcome attention again. The drudges working in the restaurant had specific duties, different from those he was accustomed to at the hospital. Without being sure of what those were, Noah knew he couldn't pull off the drudge act convincingly.

Even if he wasn't caught, there was no way for him to get through the restaurant and out into the square without one of the blue drudge uniforms. And a frantic search of the store room he was in had revealed it was used to store food and nothing more.

The window was his only access to the square. But there was still the issue of the thirty-foot drop.

All he could do now was watch. Wait. Bear witness to what was about to happen.

It was killing him.

As Danforth began to speak again, he turned back to the window, gritting his teeth.

"The citizens of Eremus must be *forced* to take responsibility for their actions." The chancellor turned to the back of the stage and gestured to someone who was out of sight. "I know you'll join me in hoping that our execution of this man today serves as a warning to them. To *anyone* who seeks to harm us."

With impeccable timing, as she finished speaking, Flynn was thrust onto the stage. Flanked by several well-armed guards, he was hauled towards a raised platform to Danforth's right. Noah clasped a hand over his mouth to keep himself from crying out at his father's appearance. Blindfolded and gagged, his hands bound behind him, he staggered rather than walked.

His skin was pale, and decorated with multiple colourful bruises. Clearly, those in charge of guarding him had been torturing him. A terrible thought struck Noah. Had Flynn kept quiet about Eremus? Or had he given away information which would jeopardise the cave community? Sagging against the window frame, Noah prayed his father had been able to stay strong.

As the guards pushed Flynn up onto the platform, he stumbled and almost fell. The women in the crowd jeered. They *wanted* him punished. Danforth had them convinced he was to blame for their loss, and they were hungry for his blood. Clenching his fists, Noah strained forward, praying the Resistance was ready.

Silence fell as Flynn was put into position. The guards stepped away, surrounding the platform in a semicircle, ensuring the crowd had a head-on view of his death.

"This man," Danforth turned towards her citizens, "is the mastermind behind the recent bombing."

Noah's eyes went to Flynn, his battered body stiffening at Danforth's words. He attempted to speak, his words muffled by the gag, which was so tight it threatened to choke him. One of the guards hit the back of his leg with a baton. Noah stifled a cry as Flynn crumpled. Regaining his balance though, he stood tall. He was determined to retain his dignity.

"This man," Danforth's eyes were glittering dangerously, "*deserves* death, for what he did. He–"

Tuning her out, Noah glanced at the crowd. Where was the Resistance? Surely, they had to act soon.

The square was full, but he focused on those closest to the stage. To even stand a chance of rescuing Flynn, the women would need to be close by. He ran his eyes over the faces of the citizens gathered around the steps to the left of the stage.

His heart stopped.

A familiar figure stood at the foot of the steps. She was wearing a hoodie and a pair of sunglasses, but he'd have known her anywhere. Her posture was tense and her eyes fixed on what was happening on the stage above.

Why was she here? Faith was a wanted woman, the first subject who had shown any promise in Danforth's experiments. And she wasn't a fighter. There was no way that Madeleine would risk her life. She was too valuable a pawn, too...

And then he knew.

Faith wasn't here with Madeleine's permission. And Faith wasn't intending to fight. Noah followed her gaze. She was paying Flynn no attention. Instead, her eyes were fixed on the screen at the back, waiting.

Waiting for another interruption. Another video, where she would give evidence of Danforth's crimes.

But anyone could see the increased security since the Liberation Day event. And Noah knew Faith. She was here because she was worried that Blake wouldn't be able to break through the additional security measures Danforth had in place. She was here to make certain that the women of the city heard her words.

And if the worst happened, if the video didn't work, she was prepared to deliver them in person.

Chapter Twenty-Three: Faith

T he screen at the rear of the stage flickered briefly. Hope surged through Faith as a puzzled ripple ran through the crowd.

This was it!

On the screen, Danforth's face dissolved, replaced with an image of a familiar sickbed. Faith's heart constricted as Sophia's face filled the screen. Her friend might not be here anymore, but she was about to get her wish. Today, the Bellator citizens would see just what their beloved chancellor was capable of. And Sophia would be the one to reveal the truth.

There was a loud buzz, followed by a crackling sound. On the podium, Danforth had abandoned her microphone and was shouting orders, her face creased with fury. An air of confusion hung over the crowd. Several Resistance members to Faith's left exchanged hopeful glances. As the achingly familiar voice rang out across the square, they began to creep forward.

"My name is Sophia. I am a student of the Danforth Academy... the Danforth Academy... the Danforth Academy..."

Faith's eyes flew back to the screen, where the image juddered horribly. Sophia's features lurched back and forth in a comical loop as the video stuttered, unable to play.

Please, Blake. Faith pressed her fingers into her sides to keep from screaming. *Work it out. You can do it.*

But Blake's concerns about repeating their earlier move successfully were being borne out right in front of them. Sophia's face flickered back and forth on the giant screen, the same words echoing over and over.

The women in the crowd stared upwards. But instead of a dawning horror at the atrocities Danforth had committed, they were simply bewildered.

Come on, Blake. Faith willed the techie to regain control. *Please.*

A long, metallic shriek echoed across the square. On the screen, Sophia's face froze.

And on the podium, Danforth hid a satisfied smile.

Turning to her people, she shook her head in mock-sadness. "My apologies. We seem to be having some... technical difficulties." She waved a hand dismissively. "But the ceremony must go on."

She turned her attention back to Flynn.

"I promised you *justice*," Danforth said. "I promised that those responsible for the recent atrocity would be punished. And today, you will see that I am a woman of my word. No longer, will these vicious beasts be allowed to hurt us. No longer, will they..."

Tuning Danforth out, Faith gazed up at her friend's face on the screen. Her eyes wide, Sophia was frozen in an earnest expression, her innocence and honesty shining from the screen. Faith swallowed hard. All the effort Sophia had put into the video, despite the pain it had caused her, so that the women of Bellator would know the truth.

She couldn't let it be for nothing.

She glanced at the guard on duty at the top of the steps. The woman was as distracted as everyone else, her gaze fixed on the chancellor. If Faith moved quickly, she wouldn't know what hit her. And once Faith made it to the stage, once Danforth recognised her, no one would dare attack.

Slipping off her sunglasses, she walked towards the stage, her hand closing around the pills in her right pocket.

At the bottom of the steps, she looked upwards once again. Danforth was shouting now, her face filled with fake fury, denouncing her *own* actions as those of the devil. The guard at the top was transfixed, her eyes fixed on the chancellor's performance. No one was paying Faith any attention.

She gazed at the screen one last time.

I won't let you down.

With a final promise to her friend, she launched herself onto the stage.

Chapter Twenty-Four: Noah

As Faith raced up the steps, he felt like his heart was going to explode. Straining forward, he saw her shove the guard at the top out of her way, sending the woman flying into the crowd.

What was she doing?

She appeared to be trying to save Flynn single-handed. Noah cursed under his breath. It was bad enough to have his *father* directly in the line of fire. Having Faith in danger too was more than he could handle. As she made a beeline for Danforth, he clutched the window frame, searching for some way to help her.

The skylight gave Noah a good view of the stage. If he'd had a weapon, he might have considered firing at those threatening Flynn and Faith, but he didn't. And, if he was honest, he wasn't that good a shot. Again, he considered making his way out through the restaurant, but discounted it. This was going to go down quickly. Even if he was prepared to risk getting caught, he would never make it to the stage in time.

He was stuck. Forced to witness the events, but helpless to change them.

He found himself thinking of his brother. Paulo could hit a moving target from several metres away, a skill which would have been very useful right now. But his brother was in Eremus. Possibly in grave danger, if Flynn's appearance was anything to go by.

And, he reminded himself, he didn't have a weapon.

Quashing his worries for the cave community, Noah forced himself to focus on the events happening below. When Faith had first reached the stage, shock and disbelief had immobilised Danforth. But a delighted smile spread over the chancellor's face as she recognised the young woman making her way to the podium. The first girl to show a promising response to her experiments was again within her grasp. A replacement for Sophia.

The chancellor gestured to the guards stationed on both sides of the stage, urging them forward. Noah watched Faith closely. Where he was expecting to see panic and fear, there was only an admirable calm. Moving closer to Danforth, Faith held out her right hand, uncurling the fingers slowly until the palm was flat.

Noah strained forward, unable to see what she was showing Danforth. He turned cold, though, when the chancellor backed away, stepping down from the podium with a fearful expression on her face. Whatever Faith held in her hand had terrified her.

As Faith stepped up to the microphone, Noah held his breath.

"My name is Faith H-Hanlon." A slight quiver in her voice betrayed her nerves. "I spoke to you once before," she gestured behind her, "from this very screen."

The crowd was silent, their eyes fixed on Faith. Danforth had moved to one side of the stage and was conversing intently with a small group of her guards. Keeping one eye on them, Noah tuned back into Faith's words.

"Last time, my words were discredited. But this time, I'm right here in front of you. And I *won't* be silenced." Shifting slightly, Faith glanced to her left, keeping her eyes on Danforth. "I'll have to talk fast, though."

She pointed at the screen again, her hand shaking.

"This is S-Sophia." Her voice shook, but she pressed on. "My best friend. She made this video—two days ago—in the hopes that it would help to persuade you that *everything* I told you before is true." Her face twisted in sorrow as she went on. "Yesterday, Sophia... d-died."

Noah clutched the window frame, his knuckles turning white.

"She d-*died*," Faith continued, holding a hand out to quell the horrified murmurs which ran through the crowd, "because of your chancellor's actions." Turning, she jabbed a finger at Danforth. "Sophia was given the experimental drugs I told you about. In *huge* doses."

She paused before continuing, shooting a sideways glance at Danforth, whose face was growing darker with every word.

"The drugs caused her to become pregnant." There was an audible gasp from the citizens. "Unbelievable, isn't it? A pregnancy without male seed." Faith leaned closer to the microphone, her voice bitter. "Danforth and her government considered Sophia to be a great success."

Noah closed his eyes. Sophia was dead. The metraxilone withdrawal had killed her, just as Liam had warned it might. She had paid the price for Danforth's experiment with her life. He opened his eyes, a hatred surging through him.

Danforth had paled at the mention of Sophia's death. Clearly, he wasn't the only one shocked by the news.

He turned his attention back to Faith, close enough to see the tears streaming down her cheeks as she continued to speak.

"Sophia's pregnancy was caused by the drugs." She was fighting to keep control, her voice hitching every now and again. "M-miraculous, perhaps. But the pregnancy did... did not progress in the normal way. Sophia's body c-couldn't cope with it. She got sick. And in the end, there was n-nothing we could do to save her."

Picturing Faith's gentle friend, Noah felt a weight of sadness settle over him. Sophia had never done anything to deserve the treatment she'd suffered. Danforth had used her. And, in rescuing her, the Resistance had unwittingly brought an end to her life.

His eyes fixed on Faith. She didn't even understand what it was that had *caused* her friend's death.

He vowed to get the information to her, whatever the cost.

Beneath the stage, the crowd had grown restless. Whispers ran through the group of Bellator citizens like a strong wind rippling through a field of corn. Despite his grief, Noah's chest swelled with pride. Faith's words were having a real impact. Many of the women were nodding and their feet had begun to shift restlessly as the tension grew.

But Danforth had recovered herself. She began moving towards Faith, flanked by guards on both sides. Her arms were outstretched, giving the impression that she meant no harm. Of course she wouldn't want her citizens thinking badly of her.

Noting the chancellor's approach, Faith's eyes widened. She spoke again, her words tumbling over one another.

"I *implore* you. Listen to me. I'm telling the truth. These experiments are *real*, and they're happening to large numbers of the girls at the Danforth Academy. We have to *stop* them." She turned to Danforth, her eyes wide. "We have to stop *her*."

As she turned back to the audience, Faith's eyes roamed the crowd wildly. He followed her gaze, knowing she was looking for the Resistance members, willing them to take action. He spotted Robyn, close to the front of the crowd on Flynn's side of the stage. Behind her were two other faces he vaguely recognised from the library.

They were all edging closer to the prisoner as the attention was focused on Faith and Danforth. Did they even have weapons? How were they planning on retrieving Flynn, or Faith, when they were surrounded by heavily-armed guards?

While he willed Faith to keep talking, he prayed she would be careful what she said. In her last speech, she had mentioned the Eremus people, shooting down another of the lies which Danforth fed her citizens. Today, that would be a bad idea. The moment Faith mentioned the men in the forest, people would turn towards Flynn.

And they didn't want anyone looking at Flynn right now.

Noah glanced at his father, still surrounded by an alarming number of guards. Flynn's body was tense, his head cocked at an angle. Listening. Noah had seen his father in the same pose many times, when they were hunting. For the second time in as many minutes, Noah wished he was back in the forest with his father and brother, stalking deer. His heart ached.

Silenced by the gag and blinded by the scarf which covered his eyes, Flynn was trusting his other senses. Relying on the skills he had honed throughout his life. When you worked in darkness, as the Eremus people were often forced to, it was essential to use your ears. Flynn wasn't stupid. He knew the interruption to the proceedings was a deliberate move on the part of the Resistance. He would be ready to act, when the time came.

Noah felt a tiny candle of hope light within him. But as he turned back to Faith, it was abruptly extinguished.

Danforth and her guards had reached the podium. Aware that time was running out, Faith turned. Unclasping her fingers again, she took something from her palm. Holding it up between her left finger and thumb, she raised it to her mouth.

Noah narrowed his eyes. The object was a vivid orange colour, shaped like a miniature orb. He glanced at her other hand, where she seemed to hold more of the mysterious items. They looked like sweets of some kind, or–

Noah's heart stopped. Faith was proffering a drug. And not, he was willing to bet, the kind which would cure sickness. For a horrible moment, he wondered if Faith was holding metraxilone. But she couldn't be. Danforth's reaction to the pills had been visceral. She'd been terrified that Faith would take them.

It didn't take much of a leap to figure out that the pills were a threat. If Faith swallowed them, Noah was willing to bet that they would have a devastating effect.

Faith knew how important she was to Danforth, *especially* now that Sophia was dead. The pregnancy experiment was close to success. The chancellor couldn't afford to lose the only other candidate who had shown promise.

When Faith had appeared on the stage, Danforth had been over the moon. To have her subject threaten to die, rather than return to the testing programme, was powerful. A bluff, Noah was certain. A distraction. But one, when delivered convincingly, that had sent terror into the leader's heart.

It was the reason Danforth hadn't had Faith hauled offstage in the first place. The move which had enabled Faith to speak to the crowd. But Danforth was changing her approach. Having witnessed the effect of Faith's words, the chancellor was determined to silence her.

Danforth was clinging to her reputation though. She couldn't be seen to treat Faith badly, not in public. She had to act with caution, or risk further damaging her reputation.

Noah's eye was attracted by a movement on Flynn's side of the stage. One of the women guarding him had moved away and was advancing on the podium from behind. Faith's focus was on Danforth. She had no idea there was a second threat. Noah's heart started pounding. Once the guard reached her, it would all be over. Without the pills, Faith was powerless.

His heart pounding, Noah racked his brain for a way to warn her. Below, the crowd was muttering, the noise growing in volume as they pressed forward, creeping ever closer to the stage. It would be useless to shout; there was no way Faith would hear him.

An idea struck him. He didn't have a weapon. But all he needed to do was attract Faith's attention. Make her aware of the threat.

Granted, his aim wasn't amazing, but if he could hit the stage with something, anything, it might give Faith a chance. And if she knew of the approaching guard, she might manage to regain control of the situation.

Glancing around, he looked for something he could throw.

Chapter Twenty-Five: Faith

Her hand was shaking and she willed herself to stay strong. Danforth was less than a metre away and, this time, she didn't look like she was going to stop.

Faith's hands were sweating. She could feel the pill slipping between her fingers. If she dropped it, she'd lose her advantage. There were more in her other hand, but she wasn't sure she could get them to her mouth in time.

Knowing that Robyn was close to the stage, she was hoping that her interruption gave the Resistance a chance to put their rescue into practice.

But now that her back was to Flynn, Faith had no idea what was going on behind her.

She was thrilled with the impact her words had had on the crowd. Even now, the square was filled with an angry muttering, and Faith had felt the women pressing forward. The movement had made Danforth nervous, too. It was the very reason the chancellor was currently advancing towards her.

Focus, she told herself. She moved the pill closer to her mouth, noticing that Danforth's eyes no longer flashed with panic. Fear prickled down her spine: something had changed.

A thwacking sound from behind startled her. Spinning around, Faith stared at the remains of an apple which had been thrown at the stage with some force. She glanced at the crowd. Was this the start of the Resistance rescue? Robyn was right at the front, but she seemed as bewildered as everyone else.

"What the–?"

And then she spotted the guard. Less than a pace away from her and advancing fast. Without thinking, Faith pushed the pill into her mouth and swallowed. But she had to do more. One pill wouldn't be enough.

A trickle of sweat made its way down her back. The remainder of the pills would make sure Danforth never used her again. But taking them...

Faith closed her eyes. Her breath came faster, panic threatening to overwhelm her. She didn't want to do this. But there was no other way.

Making up her mind, she raised her right hand to her mouth.

"Oh no, you don't." A firm hand closed around her wrist.

The voice was vaguely familiar. She searched her mind, trying to remember.

And then she knew. It was Danforth's right-hand woman. A vision of the woman taking charge of the attack on the Eremus citizens in the forest clearing came to her mind. Lieutenant Hammond, the lead guard who had masterminded the mission which had ended in Sophia's kidnapping. To her ending up back in Bellator, dosed with the drugs which had killed her.

A burning hatred surged through Faith.

"Let go." The grip on her wrist tightened, Faith cried out in pain. *"Now."*

Another hand grasped Faith's, prying open her fingers. Faith tried to resist, but Hammond was much stronger than her. Frightened her fingers would break, Faith relaxed her hand. The remaining pills tumbled to the ground. The guard who'd approached from behind smiled as she crushed them beneath her boot.

"That's right," she crowed. *"It's all over."*

Faith closed her eyes. She had nothing left to bargain with.

But it wasn't over. Faith glanced over the woman's shoulder. To tackle her, the woman had moved *away* from Flynn.

Which meant that, right now, he only had a single guard watching him.

It was the best chance they were likely to get.

As though she'd read Faith's mind, Robyn leapt onto the stage.

Faith's heart was pounding. If she could keep all eyes on her, prolong the distraction, cause as much trouble as possible, then maybe, just maybe, Robyn stood a chance.

For a moment, Faith relaxed, letting Hammond think she'd won. And then, as the lieutenant's hold relaxed, she fought. Kicking out at the guard in front, wrestling to free her hands, twisting her body around to scratch at Hammond's face, she made it as difficult as possible for the guards to keep hold of her.

She was vaguely aware of Robyn knocking the gun out of the hands of Flynn's only guard. Of Flynn, sensing the chaos, jumping down from the raised platform.

On the podium, Danforth was attempting to speak.

"Citizens of Bellator," she began, "please, remain calm. Let me reassure you–"

But the crowd was growing restless. There was the sound of stomping feet, a menacing rumble which grew in volume. Some brave citizens demanded answers from their leader, their voices strident and overlapping.

"Tell us the truth!" "Did this girl die?" "Let her speak."

Were the citizens actually rebelling?

Gratified by their support, Faith renewed her efforts, thrusting her limbs out in all directions. As she tried to scream, Hammond's hand clamped down over her mouth so tightly she could barely breathe. But she couldn't afford to stop. Not while Flynn was still a prisoner.

As Danforth screamed for reinforcements, a second apple hit the stage, smashing into pieces just to Faith's right. Had the crowd started to hurl things at their chancellor? She remembered the earlier missile and changed her mind. Whoever had thrown it seemed to have the same idea as Faith: distract the guards. Divert their attention.

This time, though, it didn't have much of an impact.

There were three guards holding Faith now, and she was tiring fast. As her struggle weakened, she caught sight of what was happening on the opposing side of the stage.

Robyn had succeeded in knocking out the first guard. Flynn had moved away from the platform and found his way to Robyn. The pair stood back-to-back, edging towards the side of the stage. But before they could get there, more guards appeared.

Faith glanced back at the crowd, her eyes searching for Robyn's backup. There was no way she could do this alone! But a wall of Danforth's reinforcements had surged forward, forming a barricade in front of the stage. Trapped, the other Resistance women were helpless to intervene.

The murmurs in the audience had gathered momentum, and now people were shouting.

"Rise up, citizens!" "Storm the stage!" "*Fight*!"

Faith was fairly certain the Resistance were the ones urging rebellion, but some citizens responded to the call. As more of Danforth's guard raced in from both sides of the square, the crowd pushed back against them. Faith could see fights breaking out, the noise of violence growing in volume.

Faith glanced back at the stage. Wasting no time, the new arrivals had sprung into action. One of the guards smashed the butt of her gun across Flynn's head, sending him reeling. The other guard leapt forward to tackle Robyn.

The Resistance fighter was ready, sending a kick directly at the guard's gun. Faith understood: having entered the square unarmed, Robyn's only chance of success was to disarm her opponent. As the weapon went flying, Robyn flung herself at the woman, pushing her to the ground. The pair grappled together on the floor, limbs flailing, evenly matched.

They rolled back and forth exchanging blows. Both women were bleeding, but Robyn appeared to be gaining the upper hand. Delivering a punch that sent the guard reeling, she began crawling towards the abandoned gun.

A few feet away, Flynn was being dragged back to the platform by the other guard. Blood was running down his face from a wound on his forehead. His blindfold had come loose in the struggle, and he swayed on his feet, blinking as he tried to orient himself. Spotting Robyn's predicament, he blanched. He made one final attempt to free himself, but was easily overcome.

Faith looked back at Robyn. If she could reach the gun, fire at the guards who surrounded them, the pair might stand a chance of getting off the stage. Robyn was bleeding from a nasty gash on her cheek, but her eyes blazed with determination. Inching forward, she took a moment to glance around her.

For a second, their eyes met. Faith expected to see fear in them, or anger. Instead, they were filled with sadness and a kind of acceptance. The situation was hopeless. Robyn could not win, no matter what she did.

With a bleak nod at Faith, she focused on the gun.

But before she could reach it, several of the guards on the ground leapt on to the stage, heading her off.

As Robyn's hands closed on the gun, they swarmed forward. Faith lost sight of the Resistance fighter as the guards surrounded her, outnumbering her. With every scrap of her remaining strength, Faith struggled against the hands which held her prisoner.

"No!" She bit down on the hand which covered her mouth. "Let me go! You can't–"

But she fell silent as a shot echoed out across the square.

CHAPTER TWENTY-SIX: NOAH

He recoiled from the window.

Things had quickly gotten out of control on the stage below. Initially, Noah had been encouraged by the crowd's reaction, but the number of guards who had stormed into the square out of nowhere made it difficult to see a way out for the three vulnerable people on the stage.

A shocked whisper ran through the crowd in the square. Creeping back to the window, he forced himself to look. To his relief, Faith hadn't moved. She stood in the centre of the stage, three guards pinning her arms to her sides. But the expression of horror on her face made him sick to his stomach.

Bracing himself, he scanned the stage. Flynn was now standing, well-guarded, on his original platform. But the guards who had been grappling with Robyn at the front were backing away. For a moment, Noah couldn't see the Resistance fighter.

And then the last guard moved and he understood the crowd's gasp. Robyn's body lay horribly still. She was twisted at an odd angle. The front of her shirt was stained with blood.

Her head faced the crowd and one arm was outstretched, as though she had been asking for help as she died.

Closing his eyes, Noah let despair consume him. There were too many guards in the square now, and not enough Resistance fighters to overcome them.

It was over.

When he turned back to the stage, Danforth had made her way to the podium again.

"I'm sorry you all had to witness that." The chancellor pulled herself up to her full height. "It appears that the Resistance situation is more serious than I thought." She gazed out at the crowd, her face taut with concern Noah knew was faked. "Let me tell you the *real* truth." She gestured at Faith, who had stopped struggling and was staring ahead blankly. "This young woman is extremely damaged. The Resistance has taken advantage of her vulnerability."

She glanced at Robyn's body.

"As I *keep* telling you, the rebels, both in Eremus and here in the city, are extremely dangerous. They prey on the weak. Faith here has been fed numerous falsehoods, facts which have been twisted to suit their dangerous aim: to turn you against me." Danforth paused, her face a picture of false shock. "If you begin to *believe* what they're telling you, they stand a good chance of gaining control. And after working for so long to shield you from the violent influence of males, I can't let that happen. I swore to protect you, and protect you I will. Whatever it takes."

She pulled the microphone from its stand and stepped down, moving towards the platform where the guards surrounded a defiant-looking Flynn.

"The males who planted the explosives which killed so many have obviously gained more influence over our own citizens than I had realised." She shook her head. "How they did this, I don't know. But I know their goal. It has always been the same: to regain control. They're attempting to do this by feeding you lies." She gestured to the lone figure on the platform. "Lies which will do nothing but destroy our unity, our togetherness, our strength."

Noah's entire body was shaking. The only thing keeping him upright was the grip he had on the windowsill. He kept his gaze fixed on Flynn as Danforth continued.

"Lies which will allow them to gain a stronghold over the women of this city. Force you back into the subservient role that women used to occupy." Danforth circled the platform, her eyes fixed on Flynn. "These people are *traitors*. We cannot allow them to threaten our community this way."

The crowd had begun to mutter again. As though she sensed she was losing them, Danforth hurried back to the podium to finish her speech.

"To demonstrate my devotion to your protection, this man, this... *traitor*, must serve as an example."

Time seemed to slow as Danforth stepped close to Hammond, whispering something in her ear. The lieutenant nodded in response. Assigning another guard to take her place beside Faith, she made her way across the stage to the platform. Waving a hand, she dismissed the other guards, who retreated to the rear of the stage without a word.

Hammond took up a position on one side of Flynn. Noah couldn't help but think she was making sure her audience had a good view of what was about to happen. Raising her gun, she aimed it at Flynn's head.

On the stage, Faith cried out, perhaps hoping for a last-minute reprieve. But Noah could see it was hopeless. A glance at the crowd demonstrated the guards' stronghold. Any attempt to break through their barricade would be suicide.

Holding his breath, Noah returned his gaze to his father, determined to witness his last moments. Flynn was looking at Faith, inclining his head slightly in a gesture of acceptance. Noah choked back tears. His father's last moments would be devoted to comforting another.

On the podium, Danforth gave a sharp nod. Hammond fired.

Noah clung to the windowsill, squeezing his eyes shut as the sound of the second gunshot ricocheted across the square and back.

When he opened his eyes, Noah had to fight the urge to scream. Flynn lay on his back to the side of the platform. His body had crumpled and seemed somehow smaller. The bandana which had fallen from his eyes was twisted around his chin, hiding the lower part of his face from view. But his open eyes stared up at the sky.

As the noise of the shot died away, everything happened at once.

There was a roar from the crowd, followed by ripples of movement which, from above, looked like waves. Fear and confusion reigned. Some people surged forward, threatening the guards at the front; others headed for the sides of the square, attempting to make a quick exit.

Danforth lifted her wristclip to her mouth, shouting commands. The guards who had been manning the entrances surged forward, their weapons raised. At the same time, those who had been protecting the stage began driving the crowd back. The ceremony was over, and the chancellor wanted the citizens to disband as soon as possible.

Forcing his eyes away from his father, Noah searched for Faith. Before the shots had been fired, she had been standing in the centre of the stage, flanked by two guards. Somehow, during the confusion, she had ended up on the ground. As she was lifted up by one of her captors, Noah feared she too had been shot.

She lay limply in the guard's arms. But as her captor carried her to the side of the stage, she shifted her head, resting it against the woman's chest. She was alive.

With a start, Noah remembered the small orange pill she had taken. It made sense that the drug was finally taking effect. But what would it do to her?

Unable to look anymore, Noah slumped down on the floor of the storage room. Beneath him, the restaurant was emptying out. Guards were calling for citizens to evacuate, to return home as quickly as possible. *Would they check whether the building was empty?*

His gaze fell on the box of apples. They were his only available weapon, and they hadn't been much use up to now. Picturing a guard storming in with a gun and being pelted by fruit, he fought the urge to laugh. Perhaps he was becoming hysterical.

He couldn't afford to lose control. Flynn and Robyn were dead. But Faith was still alive, and very much in danger.

Noah hauled himself to his feet. In the square below, the crowd was thinning, guards herding the women out of the square. A few citizens were struggling, arguing, but, on the whole, Danforth's army seemed to have the situation under control.

A glance at the stage revealed it to be almost empty. Both Faith and Danforth had disappeared, and there were only a few guards remaining. They were deep in discussion, motioning towards the bodies at the far side. Noah braced himself to follow their gaze.

When he did, he felt like someone had punched a hole in his chest.

Two of the guards stood over his father. Grabbing Flynn's legs and arms, they hoisted him up like a sack of grain.

A surge of rage threatened to overwhelm Noah. Once again, he stepped away from the window, unable to watch. Swallowing his fury, Noah strode to the store room door. Once he had adjusted his mask so it properly covered his face, he made sure that the stairwell was empty.

It was time to go.

Chapter Twenty-Seven: Faith

"Best get her out quick."

The voice came from far away. Faith was drifting, the earth below her shifting like it never had before. A pair of arms held her, but she didn't know who they belonged to.

"Could I...?" she tried. Could they even hear her? "I want to..."

"Hammond says there might still be Resistance in the crowds," the voice continued, as though she hadn't spoken. "This girl's important to Danforth. We have to keep her safe."

Faith forced her eyes open. The arms which surrounded her belonged to an older woman in a guard uniform. She was being carried.

"Where are you t–" she tried, but her voice didn't seem to be working. The woman didn't even glance down.

Faith's eyelids felt heavy, but she blinked, trying to focus. They were moving down a corridor, people hurrying past in both directions. Twisting her body, she tried to read a sign on the wall as they passed.

"Keep still." The guard tightened her hold. "If you keep wriggling like that, I'll drop you."

Faith sucked in a deep breath. Her chest hurt. As the guard strode onwards, she tried to resist. But her body would not obey.

"Better stay here until I confirm there's a vehicle waiting." A gruff voice commanded. "Don't want you to get her out on the streets with no waiting transport."

"I'll wait then." The woman hitched Faith up, as though she were getting heavy. "But don't be long. We've no idea what impact the drug she took will have. Let's get her to a medic as soon as possible."

Faith closed her eyes. She had to stay focused. Try...try to escape.

But the woman's arms were like a vice. And she was so very tired.

"What's happening with the other two?" The woman carrying her asked a passing guard.

"They're dead. Not a priority."

Faith's head swam. Flynn and Robyn were gone. All her efforts to save Noah's father had been for nothing. She hadn't even been able to share Sophia's dying message. And now she had fallen back into Danforth's clutches.

An overwhelming sense of helplessness took hold of Faith when the ambulance arrived. An ambulance meant she was headed to the hospital. Going to the hospital meant she'd be replacing Sophia in the fertility experiment.

As the woman carried her away, Faith stopped fighting.

CHAPTER TWENTY-EIGHT: NOAH

The pavement outside was crowded. Keeping his head down, Noah joined the throng of citizens moving away from the square. He was just deciding whether to return to the hospital or go back to the library, when an ambulance screeched past.

Instinctively, Noah made an about turn and followed in its wake. A few blocks past him, it stopped. Stepping back into the shadows of a doorway, Noah peered at the vehicle. For a few seconds, nothing happened. But then a door at the side of the street burst open. Noah spotted the same guard carrying a limp-looking Faith out into the street.

A medic jumped out of the ambulance and opened the rear door.

"Straight to Bellator General, okay?" Taking great care not to hurt her, the guard lifted Faith inside the vehicle. When she emerged, her expression was serious. "Danforth's orders."

Hammond appeared in the doorway. "There's another one coming, yes?" she demanded. "For the other two?"

"On its way." The medic raised an eyebrow. "Heard the others don't need such urgent attention."

"They don't need *any* kind of attention." Hammond waved a dismissive hand. "You'll be taking them straight to the morgue."

Noah closed his eyes and forced himself not to react. When he opened them again, Hammond was slamming the rear door of the ambulance.

"This one's particularly special to Chancellor Danforth." Hammond took a step towards the medic. "Make sure you take good care of her."

Nodding, the woman ducked around the lieutenant and climbed back into her vehicle. As the ambulance pulled away, its siren split the air again, hurrying people out of its path. Once the sound had faded, Noah emerged from the doorway. His entire body was shaking.

This one's special. That, he could agree with.

His thoughts turned to Sophia, then to Robyn and Flynn. Their blood was on Danforth's hands. *But there could be* no *more deaths*. The only way to save Faith from the same fate as her friend was to rescue her *before* the medics administered the metraxilone. There was no other option. He would return to the hospital.

He could only hope it was possible to sneak back in. That Liam would welcome him back. Be prepared to help him.

His mind made up, Noah marched off in the same direction as the ambulance.

Once he got away from the square, the streets were quiet. Most of the citizens had headed home, probably worried about further trouble. Unless Danforth had put a temporary curfew in place that had forced people indoors. It was a definite possibility.

Noah moved as quickly as he dared, concerned he would be stopped or questioned with so few people around. He stuck to the back routes, impressing himself with his knowledge of the city. Never had he been more grateful for Madeleine's insistence on stringent preparation for going undercover. The hours poring over maps had seemed tedious at the time, but now they were paying off.

When he reached the hospital, it was unusually quiet. Whilst the memorial ceremony had been disrupted, the minimal violence meant there would not be many casualties. Silently thanking Liam for the intel about the cameras, he located the exit he had used on the way out and managed to sneak back into the building undetected. Once inside, he made his way to the supply building and spent a few minutes stocking a trolley.

The ambulance would have arrived here much faster than him, so Faith was already in the building. Of that, Noah was certain. But he wasn't sure where they would take her. If they had decided she should go straight to the ward where they had kept Sophia, it would be almost impossible to get to her. But if she needed additional care *before* they placed her into the fertility ward, he might be able to get to her.

Wheeling the trolley through the hospital, his mind raced through possibilities. Faith would have been brought in via the Emergency Department. She might still be there.

He approached it with caution. Lowering his head, he pressed the buzzer on the door as though he was meant to be there. Hopefully, the drudge in charge of restocking the area had not completed his rounds yet. The technicians never looked very closely at the drudges assigned to their departments, so he stood a good chance of getting in. As long as he'd timed it right.

When the door swung open, the technician paused. "Didn't we already–?"

Her voice quietened, as though she were directing the question over her shoulder.

"What?" Another voice came from further down the ward.

"Did we need restocking?" She turned to face him. "I thought we'd…"

"Perhaps the higher-ups ordered more." The second voice again. "With the disruption at the ceremony and all."

"You mean they're expecting–?"

"More trouble?" The voice increased in volume, as though the second technician had moved closer. "Maybe."

The woman in the doorway seemed to accept the explanation. Stepping back from the door, she waved him inside.

"Don't be long." She pushed the door closed. "If we're expecting more patients, I'd like the ward clear."

Nodding, Noah moved past her into the main emergency area. He hadn't restocked this department before, but he knew what it would require. Multiple cabinets stood between the beds, each one needing to be ready for an emergency. All he had to do was move from one to another, taking a moment to peek behind the curtained-off bays as he did so. If Faith was here, he would find her.

The department was quiet, and the technicians were occupied with duties in their office. Noah attended to most of the cabinets without interruption, discovering the beds either side of them to be frustratingly empty. As he approached the final one, a rhythmic beeping came from behind the curtains.

Opening the cabinet door, he angled his body so his back was to the technicians' office. Holding his breath, he slid his finger around the edge of the curtain and eased it back.

His heart stopped. In the bed, hooked up to a machine which he knew monitored her blood pressure, was Faith.

Chapter Twenty-Nine: Faith

"*Noah?*"

Faith struggled into a sitting position. She had known that Noah was in the hospital, but she hadn't dared to hope that he would find her. Not so quickly, anyway.

But was it quickly? Since her arrival, she had been drifting in and out of consciousness. Who knew how long she had been in the Emergency Department?

Resting a finger on his lips, Noah stepped inside the curtain. "Hey."

"How are you here?" She leaned back on the pillows again. "And what time is it?"

"It's nine p.m.," he whispered, gesturing at the machine. "Are you okay?"

She nodded. "I must have passed out. At the memorial. Because of the..." She inhaled deeply. "When I left the library, I stole some very powerful painkillers."

"*That's* what you had on the stage?" He stepped closer, his face clouding over. "You took one, right? Are you–?"

"Wait." Faith blinked, trying to clear her head. "How do you–?"

"I was there."

"So you..." she swallowed hard. "Oh, *Noah*."

He dropped his head. "I knew about the execution. Thought maybe I could get to him. Do something." His shoulders sagged. "I was wrong."

"I'm so sorry." Faith struggled to find words. "It must have been... I mean, it was..."

"Awful." The reply was gruff. "Yes."

"I tried to... but I couldn't..." She reached out a hand. "There was nothing I–"

"Nothing anyone could have done." He took her hand in his. "But thanks. For trying, I mean. You and Robyn had more success than I did."

Faith bit her lip, trying to keep control.

"Robyn." Faith felt a physical ache inside her. "She was... she tried so–"

"I know." His voice faltered. "She was outnumbered. She didn't stand a chance."

"It was... terrible." Leaning forward, Faith thrust her free arm around his neck. "She gave her life for *nothing*."

"Not nothing." Returning her embrace, Noah put his lips close to her ear. "Means a lot that she tried so hard to save him."

They fell silent for a moment, drawing what strength they could from one another. When Noah pulled back, Faith resisted.

"Listen." He eased away, loosening her grip. "There's nothing we can do for them now. We have to focus on *you*." He stared at her, his gaze earnest. "Tell me more about those pills."

"I stole a bunch of them. To threaten Danforth. And it worked... for a while. But I only managed to take *one*. Not enough to..." Faith shifted position, remembering the moment she'd raised her hand to her lips. How certain she'd been. "And then Hammond–"

"Stopped y-you." Noah's voice broke. "I'm glad she did. Where did you get the pills?"

"Anna was giving them to Sophia."

"Ma?" He stiffened. "She's in the city?"

"Oh. Yes." Of course, he didn't know. "She came–"

"Because of Flynn."

"Yes."

He took a moment to digest the information, then nodded at her to continue.

"Anyway, the pills have a kind of... sedative effect. I guess that's why I passed out."

"How do you feel now?"

She closed her eyes, scanning her body. "Not as bad as I did. Just..." she tried to recall what Anna had said, "I guess even the low dose will affect me for a while longer. I don't feel faint anymore, but the medics seemed concerned about my blood pressure."

Noah's eyebrows leapt under his hair. "What's wrong with–"

She waved away his concern. "It's a little on the low side. Side effect of the meds, Anna said, when she gave them to Sophia." She nodded at the curtain. "From what I can tell, they just want to keep an eye on me, until I'm in better shape."

He shifted closer, brushing some hair away from her face. Laid a gentle hand on her forehead. Apparently satisfied that she was a normal temperature, he closed the gap between them again.

The sound of a door opening at the end of the ward made her stiffen. "Won't you be in trouble for..." she gestured at their closeness.

"The way I feel right now," he sighed, "I don't much care."

She pulled away from him. "Don't talk like that. I know... I know it's terrible, but you can't... *we* can't..." She frowned. "You'd be severely punished for this, wouldn't you?"

"If they caught me," he whispered. "But I'll make sure they don't."

For a moment, they both listened. There was a hum of distant conversation, followed by the slamming of a door. Then, silence again.

"See?" Noah pulled her close again. "All good."

Faith relaxed slightly, allowing herself to lean into him. Eventually, he pulled away.

"I should say... I don't want you to think I've forgotten..." He cursed softly. "I'm sorry about Sophia." He hesitated. "I know how much she meant to you. She... she didn't deserve to..."

Faith felt her eyes fill with tears. ""I was with her when... at the end. It was awful."

His eyes were on her, gentle, kind. But something was bothering him.

"What is it?"

"There's something I have to tell you."

A sense of dread settled over her. "Go on."

"I spoke to another drudge. Friend of Rowan's. He's been helping me. He heard something." When he reached for her hand, Faith got the sense he was trying to soften a blow. "The reason Sophia died... well, it's because she was taken *off* the metraxilone."

Faith stared at him. "What are you saying?"

"I'm saying that Sanders had done tests on animals before she started using metraxilone on human subjects. The rats who were taken off it... without warning, I mean... well, they all suffered withdrawal symptoms so severe that..." He couldn't look her in the eye.

"They died?" Faith inhaled sharply. "So when we took Sophia out of the hospital... when we thought we were *saving* her, we were actually... we were..."

"There's no way we could have known." Noah shook his head. "We had no access to the reports… to any documentation about the drug. It wasn't our fault."

"But it could have been prevented, if…"

"If she hadn't been subjected to the drug in the first place." He regarded her sternly. "Don't blame yourself." After a beat, he pushed on. "There are others to consider, though."

Faith's hand flew to her mouth. "The academy girls. Kemp was worried someone would start questioning why the metraxilone wasn't having an effect. If they figure out they're giving the girls placebos…" She shuddered. "I mean, there's a plan in place to rescue the girls, but if they don't do it soon—"

"They will."

"But you have to…" Faith curled her hand into a fist. "I'm no use to you now. Not stuck in here. You'll have to get the message through some other way." She sat bolt upright. "Go to headquarters. Tell them yourself."

"No way. If you think I'm leaving you here…" He held her gaze. "I'm sure Madeleine will send someone over here soon. Especially now *you're* here. I can speak to them then."

"No!" She grasped his hand as tightly as she could. "You have to go *now*. The sooner they know, the better."

"But—"

The door at the end of the ward banged open again. They both stiffened. This time, there was no mistaking the sound of approaching footsteps. Noah leaned close, his mouth moving against her ear. "I'll get a message to them somehow," he whispered. "And I'll get you out of here. I promise. I won't let them use you like they did Sophia."

"They'll *never* do that to me." She drew back from him. "I won't let them."

Outside, the footsteps were getting closer. Noah stepped away from the bed.

"I'll come for you." He mouthed the words. "Somehow."

A buzzing sound filled the air. The footsteps stopped.

"Could you get that, Carol?" the voice came from the other side of the ward.

Grateful for the interruption, Faith held out her hand, pulling Noah down until their lips met. Closing her eyes, she savoured the moment. Who knew when they'd be together again?

"I'll see you soon." He backed away. "I promise."

She managed a smile. "I'm going to hold you to that."

Chapter Thirty: Noah

Slipping out of the bay, Noah bent to attend to the cabinet again. As the technician approached, he stood up.

"You done yet?"

Nodding, Noah returned to his trolley. He wheeled it back past the empty beds, passing the other technician and exiting the ward without issue. Back in the hallway, he paused for a second to catch his breath.

He decided to return the trolley and complete some of his ordinary chores while he considered how he might get Faith out. He had to act quickly. Once she was on the fertility ward, he wouldn't be able to get near her.

More importantly, once Faith was in Sanders' clutches, she wouldn't waste any time. First, she'd administer femgazipane. And once that started to do its thing, metraxilone.

The drug which had caused Sophia's pregnancy. The drug which had led to her death.

He was heading for the supply building when he was joined by another drudge, who came out of a side corridor. Without looking at him, Noah knew something about his companion was wrong. For starters, he was far bulkier than the average drudge. The light was behind them, and the shadow the other man cast was far wider than Noah's.

The man's gait was different, too. Instead of the slow, steady steps of the drudge, the man appeared to hurry, taking large strides which made him stand out for all the wrong reasons. Puzzled, Noah chanced a brief sideways glance at the man.

His own step faltered as he tried to make sense of what he saw. The drudge wasn't a drudge at all, but a man. An Eremus man. And not one who had spent hours training, taking the time to properly learn how a drudge should act. One who had stolen an ill-fitting uniform, thrown it on, and entered the hospital with no preparation.

Harden.

Noah's mind whirled. His old enemy. A young man who had made his life miserable. Who had followed Jacob out of Eremus with his ma. And who was attempting, very badly, to disguise himself as a drudge. How he'd managed to get inside the hospital in the first place was beyond Noah.

His recent encounter with Sil came back to him. Her presence in the hospital had been odd. He remembered the store room he'd taken her to. Dammit, he'd even told her where the spare drudge uniforms were located. And now Harden was here. In the hospital. About to blow his cover.

Harden couldn't have been in the hospital for long. His disguise was so poor that he'd be caught within minutes.

Since the hallway was empty, Noah chanced some words.

"What are you *doing*?" he whispered, hoping the mask would hide his attempt at communication. "You look ridiculous."

He felt the man beside him flinch. Clearly, Harden had not identified the drudge he had been walking with. But his voice was familiar.

Harden turned his head. "Noah?"

"*Eyes forward!*" Noah hissed. "Someone will notice."

"You seem to manage the disguise well enough." Harden's tone was arrogant as ever. "I figured I could get away with it too."

"But you *won't*." Noah hissed. "You're too big. You're not even *acting* like a drudge."

There was a pause. "I'm not?"

"You're not." Beside Noah, Harden stiffened. "And you'll get caught. You'll get us *both* caught."

As they approached the end of the hallway, Harden hesitated.

"You don't even know where you're going, do you?" Noah felt him shrug. "This is madness. Let me get you out of here, safely."

"But Jacob–"

"Jacob nothing," Noah spat out. "Would he want you *dead*?"

Harden shook his head, all traces of arrogance gone.

"You'd better follow me then."

Abandoning the trolley, Noah changed direction, heading towards the camera-less exit he'd come through only an hour earlier.

"Why'd Jacob send you?" He couldn't resist asking.

"Sarah was in the square today. We know that Faith's here. He thought we might grab her... or find out more about her condition. I don't know." Harden sounded tired. "He wants to increase our hostage count."

"And he honestly believed you'd get away with snatching her from right under Danforth's nose?"

Harden didn't reply. As they reached the hallway leading to the exit, an alarm rang out. A shrill, repeating siren which blasted five times before a disembodied voice boomed through the hospital.

"Intruder alert. Hospital breach. All staff be aware."

As Noah picked up the pace, Harden hurried to keep up. "That me they're talking about?"

"'Fraid so."

Noah heaved a sigh of relief as they passed the last doorway in the hall and reached the exit which led to the outside. Noah yanked it open, thankful that the hospital hadn't yet locked the building down. Stepping through it, he turned back. Harden was hesitating on the threshold, his eyes wary.

"Get around that corner and there are no cameras. Climb over the fence and you'll be out of here." Noah jabbed a finger at the far end of the alleyway. "Either find a place to hide, or run like hell, until you get to safety. Got it?"

"How do I know you're not–"

Noah shook his head in disgust. "What would I have to gain? I'm putting myself at risk here too, or are you too dumb to see that?"

"I guess. Um..." Harden blinked, "thanks."

Noah shrugged. "Just get out of here."

He stepped back. As he opened the door wider for Harden to pass, a noise to Harden's right startled them both. Their eyes followed the sound. To Noah's horror, the office door next to Harden opened and a guard stepped out. Her eyes widened in surprise as she spotted the enormous drudge standing in front of her.

It took her no time at all to reach for the taser in her belt and hold it to Harden's chest. His body juddered violently with the charge. When she released him, he crumpled to the floor. Noah had frozen. But as the guard stepped away from Harden's lifeless body, her eyes turned to the open door.

She took a step forward, the taser stretched out in front of her. Slamming the door closed with as much force as he could muster, Noah knocked the woman down. Before she could recover, he turned around, checking the alleyway.

When he was certain it was empty, he ran.

CHAPTER THIRTY-ONE: FAITH

"Not sure we should administer any more sedatives."

"But Sanders recommended we..."

As the trolley moved along the hallway, Faith kept her eyes closed. She'd had a restless night in the Emergency Department. One of the technicians, a kindly woman named Carol, had hovered over her like she was dying. She wore a distinctive citrusy perfume, and as Faith had drifted in and out of consciousness, the intermittent scent of lemons had told her when the technician was nearby.

Every time she had attempted sleep, she'd been tortured by horrific images. Pictured Flynn's stoic face, waiting for the shot. Heard Robyn's scream of pain as the bullet tore through her body. The sense of helplessness had been overwhelming. She had done what she could to provide a distraction so the Resistance could mount a rescue.

But it had all come to nothing. Now, two more people were dead.

And the mention of Sanders told Faith she was being transported to the fertility ward. There was no denying it: she was about to replace Sophia as Sanders' guinea pig.

Faith still shuddered when she recalled the cold-eyed woman who had administered her first dose of femgazipane. Alone in her prison cell at the academy, she'd been terrified by the look on Sanders' face as she pushed the plunger on the syringe. The doctor was only interested in the success or failure of her drug concoctions. The potential damage it caused her subjects meant nothing to her.

The technicians in charge of moving Faith were worried. She had been given a pill *to help her sleep* the previous night, but it hadn't increased her blood pressure as they'd expected. What the technicians didn't know was that Faith hadn't taken it. She had kept the tiny pill under her tongue until the technicians had left. Spitting it out, she had hidden it in the hem of her hospital gown.

For now, at least, she was in control.

Faking sleep hadn't been difficult. She wasn't faking the low blood pressure though. And when she arrived in the fertility ward, there would be no resisting the sedatives.

"We shouldn't risk it." Carol sighed. "Not until her levels are more normal. She's been through so much."

"Were you in the square yesterday?"

Faith cracked her eyes open a little, squinting to make out the second technician's name badge. *Freya.* The woman had come on duty first thing this morning. Carol had been updating her on Faith's condition. She'd assumed the first technician's shift would finish soon after, but the woman hadn't shown any signs of leaving yet.

"I was sleeping." Carol shook her head. "Have to catch up when I've been on nights. You know how it is." She hesitated. "Was it as awful as it sounded on the news?"

"It really was. I've seen death before, in the hospital, I mean. I've never seen anyone executed like that though. Up close." Freya shuddered. "I mean... I *get* that men are a threat, but there was something about that guy. He looked so... resigned.

Like he *expected* that kind of treatment from the Bellator women."

"You mean, the way we expect brutality from them?" Carol glanced around as she spoke. Quickly, Faith closed her eyes again. "I've been thinking the same thing myself."

"It kind of made me feel..." Freya hesitated.

"Go on." Carol's voice was low and urgent. "Say it."

"...like we're no better than they are."

"Exactly." Faith felt Carol's hand on her arm, steadying her as the trolley rounded a corner. "I've been thinking this Resistance... maybe they have a point."

The women fell silent, and Faith heard voices, as though they were passing other staff. When there was quiet again, Carol continued.

"I mean... what about the woman?"

"You mean the one who tried to save him?"

"That's the one."

"I didn't know *what* to make of her." Faith could feel the woman leaning closer to Carol. "I mean, why would a Bellator citizen try to *save* a male?"

"Well, if I'm right and she was part of the Resistance..." Carol let the thought hang in the air for a moment as she stilled the trolley, "perhaps what they're telling us is true. And that woman was fighting to keep a good man... a good *person*... alive."

A familiar whirring sound startled Faith. They were waiting for the lift. She thought of Flynn. He *had* been a good person. One of the best people she'd ever known. As had Robyn. Picturing the Resistance leader's easy grin was painful. She hadn't deserved to die. Neither had Flynn.

But if her actions and his stoicism had caused these women to have doubts? If *these* women were asking questions, others would be too.

A shrill *ping*, followed by a swishing sound announced the lift's arrival. The trolley gave a jolt as it was loaded in.

"I can't believe that other girl's dead." Carol sighed as the doors slid closed. "Sophia, was that her name? I saw her being taken for a scan just last week." Scepticism filled the woman's tone. "She looked pretty sick, even then."

"You really think she died because of what they did to her?" Freya's voice hitched. "Here in the hospital, I mean?"

"Maybe." Carol had dropped her voice. "I think we've no idea what they're doing in those restricted access wards."

"Then..." The women's attention shifted to her, and Faith fought to keep her body relaxed. "You think this girl here... You think she's telling the truth?"

"You mean about the drug treatment?" Carol paused. "She might well be. I mean, why risk this kind of trouble without good reason?"

"Yeah." The other woman agreed. "Whatever's going on in those wards, they don't want us to know about it. I'll bet we don't even get through the doors today."

"For sure. Hey," Carol's voice took on a hushed tone, "did you see the news last night?"

Faith strained to decipher the women's words as they dropped their voices.

"I did. Can you *believe* it?"

"Heard the guards arrested more than forty women," Carol sounded impressed. "In *one* location."

"I know." Freya's voice was hushed. "Protests *against* Danforth? It's unthinkable."

For a moment, Faith's heart soared. Could her words have really had that kind of an impact? Uprisings were unheard of in Bellator. But if even a small percentage of the city's women were doubting the chancellor, it was a huge step forward.

If they were prepared to act, that was even better.

"After what I heard yesterday," Carol gave a disapproving sniff, "I was quite tempted to join them."

"Me too. There are rumours there'll be more protests today. All over the city." Freya lifted Faith's wrist, feeling for her pulse. "What happens if Danforth doesn't have enough guards to deal with them all?"

"That's what I've been wondering." Carol paused. "And if what this Faith girl said is true... if that Sophia girl died because of what Sanders did to her..."

"Pulse is still a little erratic." The technician replaced Faith's hand on the trolley. "I think you're right about the sedative."

"You'll back me, then? With Sanders, I mean." Carol's voice was filled with relief. "If we spin it that her body isn't reacting well to the sedative, and the other drugs may not work to the best effect, maybe she'll hold off."

"Yeah, best to make it about the success of the drug, not the patient." The technician's tone was sour. "We all know what matters most to Sanders."

"Yeah." Carol tutted. "Might buy the poor girl a couple of hours, at least. I really feel for her. I mean... if she is telling the truth, then–"

"You think sending her into those restricted wards is sentencing her to death."

Carol sighed deeply. "I do. But what can we do about it?"

Faith's heart sank as the lift doors slid open and she was wheeled out into a different hallway. Sanders was intent on pressing forward with the experiment, no matter what. A few hours did not allow her much time to escape, nor for the Resistance to rescue her. Could she risk asking the technicians for help?

Faith allowed her eyes to flutter open. "I..." she feigned sleepiness, "Where am I?"

"Bellator Hospital." Carol's kindly eyes gazed down at her. "We're just moving you out of the Emergency Department."

"How are you feeling?" Freya placed a hand on her arm.

Faith glanced between the two women. Their conversation had indicated a certain sympathy for her. An interest in the Resistance. Could she trust them?

"I'm tired," she began, aware of how quickly the trolley was speeding down the hallway. There wasn't much time. "Where are you taking me?"

The two women exchanged worried glances. Neither of them seemed to want to respond to her question.

"I'm in danger, right?" Faith stared at Carol. "You don't have to answer. But… if," she struggled up on to her elbows, "if you want to stop what happened to Sophia from happening again," the technician's eyes widened, "*please*, do something about it."

"What can we do?" As Carol leaned closer, the lemony scent grew more intense.

"Get a message to the Resistance," Faith racked her brains. She couldn't tell them to go to the library. "Find…" she ran through the people who would be easy to locate, deciding that Evelyn would be the simplest. "Find–"

"Morning!" Freya said loudly.

Carol's gaze jerked away from Faith's. A medic had just exited a door at the end of the hallway. As she made her way towards them, Faith settled back down again.

"Is that our new patient?" The medic stared down at her. "Faith Hanlon, right?"

"That's right." Freya said.

"She's a little on the pale side." The woman frowned. "I was hoping she'd have picked up overnight."

Faith disliked being spoken to as though she wasn't there. Narrowing her eyes, she glanced at the medic's badge. *Susie*. The medic was petite, and something about her was familiar. Then it hit her.

Susie was one of the medics who'd been in charge of Sophia. The woman who took blood from her every day. Who had controlled the doses of sedation she was being given. Faith went cold. There had been little doubt as to where the technicians were taking her, but the presence of this particular medic sealed her fate.

Susie walked with them to the end of the hallway. When they reached the ward door, she moved to take charge of the trolley. As predicted, she wasn't going to permit the technicians inside.

"Anything I need to know?" Pulling out a keycard which was attached to her belt on a kind of coiled spring, she tapped it against the keypad at the side of the door.

"Her notes are all there." Carol gestured to the file resting on the trolley. "But... you should know that her BP is still a little low." Concern filled her voice as she pushed on bravely. "I think she needs time to recover... before you begin any... treatment."

"Right." Susie nodded. "I'll pass it on to Doctor Sanders."

The medic began pushing the trolley into the ward. As her companions backed away, Faith could sense their reluctance. The doors swung closed behind her, and the last thing she saw was Carol's face. The technician looked anguished, as though she was abandoning a friend.

And then she was gone.

Chapter Thirty-Two: Noah

H e staggered out of the tunnel into the hub, blinking as his eyes adjusted to the light. Seconds later, a pair of arms closed around him. As he buried his head in his ma's neck, the scent of his childhood overwhelmed him.

"Shh." Her hand smoothed down his back. "Come sit down."

As she eased him onto one of the benches, Noah glanced around. It was good to hold his head up high. The hub was quiet. It was early, and most of the women were still in bed. His ma had always been an early riser, and he'd never been more grateful.

It had been a terrifying night. After fleeing the hospital, he'd been terrified he might not reach the library. Thanking his lucky stars it was already dark, he'd crept through the shadows of the city. With every step he took, he expected one of Danforth's guards to leap out and arrest him.

But it hadn't been as difficult as he'd anticipated. Some streets were deserted, with no evidence of citizens or guards. Other districts of the city had been very different. Ignoring the curfew, large numbers of women had taken to the streets, painting slogans on walls, chanting things, some openly argu-ing with Danforth's guards.

Noah had skirted the disturbances, grateful that they were keeping the guards occupied. By the time he'd reached the library entrance, though, he'd been on the verge of collapse.

Wiping the back of his sleeve across his face, he swallowed hard.

"M-a." He choked on the word, then tried again. "You know about... about Flynn?" Her eyes clouded over. "I tried to..."

"Wait. You were there?"

He gave a tight nod. "But I couldn't–"

His ma shook her head. "Of course not. Not when the whole of the Resistance couldn't..." She gripped his hands tightly. "You're just one boy... one *man*."

Appreciating the correction despite his grief, he returned the squeeze. "I'm so sorry."

"I know." An expression Noah had never seen flashed across her face. "He deserved better."

"Are you alright?" He leaned back, staring into her dark eyes. "Did you sleep?"

"Not really." She shrugged, her shoulders taut. "Danforth," her voice snapped on the word, "has a lot to answer for."

"His intentions were peaceful," Noah managed. "He didn't deserve–"

"Shh," his ma soothed. "I know. *We* know. Madeleine's as angry about this as I am. And though the memorial didn't go as planned, what Faith did, what she said..."

Noah closed his eyes at the name, dread taking hold of him again. When he opened them, his ma was watching him, her gaze steady now. Patient as ever, she waited for him to continue.

"Ma, Faith is..." He fought to keep the panic from his voice "They took her to the hospital. I was going to try and get her out but..."

"I'm so sorry." His ma squeezed his hand gently before pulling away. For the first time, she took in his dishevelled state. "Tell me what happened."

"They arrested her, after the memorial fell apart." His voice was steadier now. "I found her in the Emergency Department, but I think... I'm pretty sure they'll have taken her to the fertility wards by now."

"Why did you leave the hospital?"

"I had no choice." He shook his head. "Harden turned up. He was—"

"*Harden* was there?"

"Pretending to be a drudge. Like me." Noah sighed. "Only badly."

His ma rubbed a hand across her chin. "Jacob *must* be desperate. What did he want?"

"They heard Faith was there. Thought an extra hostage would help their cause." Noah ran a hand through his hair. "I tried to warn him... to get him out, but..."

His ma smiled bitterly. "Let me guess. He didn't listen?"

"He did, actually. I think he was scared. But..." Noah dropped his gaze, "by the time we got to the exit, it was too late."

His ma braced herself. "He's dead?"

"No. But... the guards caught him." The flash of terror which crossed his ma's face told Noah she was thinking of Flynn. "I had to run, or..."

"They would have got you too." His ma's eyes were wide.

"Yeah." Noah considered the potential evidence he'd left behind in the hospital. Papers that would link Danforth to the experiments. He closed his eyes. "I didn't even manage to—"

"How did you even make it back?" His ma shook her head. "The streets... they're—"

"I know. I saw." He paused, thinking back to the women on the streets. "It helped me, actually. Kept the guards busy. But Ma, people are—"

"They're *listening*. It's exactly what the Resistance has been working towards." She bit her lip. "Pity it came too late for Flynn and Robyn."

"And for Sophia."

They lapsed into silence. Noah leaned against his ma, laying his head on her shoulder. He was glad, at least, they were together in their grief.

"Ma," he bit his lip, "if Danforth has Faith, she's going to–"

His ma grimaced. "I know."

"And Helen, and the academy girls." He fought the rising panic. "Even *Harden*! It's not like we can talk Madeleine into helping *him*. I mean... she couldn't even rescue Flynn, and it's not like she'll be enthusiastic about helping someone who's on Jacob's side. Not now he's–"

He broke off, his hands curling into fists.

"Why do you care? About Harden, I mean?"

"I don't know." Noah shrugged. "I just... the lives of so many people are in Danforth's hands right now. I don't want there to be any more death."

"I'm afraid there may be a lot more death before this is finished." She reached for his hand again, as though she might soften her harsh words. She was shaking. "But at least you're not–"

A noise at the far end of the hub startled them. The door to Madeleine's office had opened. Blake was standing there.

"You're back." She eyed Noah. "Why?"

"Long story." He pushed himself to a standing position, his limbs aching. "I can't go back, though." He took a step towards her. "Blake, Danforth has–"

"Faith. We know. She left a note. After I found it, we tried to get to her before..." She shook her head, a heaviness weighing her down. "But we were too late. Are you up to coming to speak to us? We need to discuss our next moves."

Behind him, his ma tensed.

Turning, he laid a hand on her arm. "I'm fine. Come with me?"

Reluctantly, she nodded.

When they reached the office, Blake was pacing the room. Madeleine sat in the chair behind the desk. Noting that Evelyn had taken Robyn's usual seat, Noah dropped his gaze.

"Your cover's blown, then?" Madeleine began.

"It is." Noah didn't waste time apologising. "Do we have any new information about Faith?"

Madeleine gestured to Blake, who tapped on her datadev, bringing up a familiar image. "These are from earlier today."

"That's–"

"The room where they held Sophia." Blake cut him off. "Yes. They have Faith in there now. They haven't started her on the drugs yet, but we don't think it will be long."

"Then we have to get her out." Noah's voice notched up an octave.

"That's what we're here to discuss. If we–"

"You don't understand. The metraxilone…" Noah fought to keep his calm. "It's the reason Sophia died. A drudge friend of mine at the hospital overheard the medics discussing it. Once a patient starts receiving it, they can't just be taken off it. It leads to huge–"

"Withdrawal symptoms!" his ma exclaimed. "I should have known."

"So we *have* to rescue her as soon as possible." Noah stepped forward. "And the academy girls. Today, if–"

"Patience." Madeleine frowned. "There's more you don't know."

"Sit down." Evelyn gestured to an empty chair.

His ma guided him into it. Closing his eyes, he took a deep breath. When he opened them, Blake had navigated to a message thread.

"See this?" She jabbed a finger at the screen. "First contact we've had from Kemp in several days. She's obviously been unable to contact us. They may be watching her more closely than usual. This has been sent from a student address, but she's used a code which tells us it's her."

Noah leaned forward, trying to read the words on the screen.

"I'll sum it up for you." Blake interrupted. "Someone at the academy questioned the fact that the girls on the metraxilone weren't suffering any of the expected side effects. They sent a sample pill to the lab."

"The long and short of it is, they know the pills they've been distributing are placebos." Madeleine grimaced.

Noah's heart sank. "So they've started the girls on the real drug?"

"Not quite." Evelyn sat forward. "When Kemp and Arden took in the placebos, they dumped the entire supply of real metraxilone."

"So the school doesn't have any to give out right now?" Anna asked. "Do we know how long until they get a new supply?"

"Well as you can imagine they're eager to get the girls started on it." Blake tapped a finger on the desk. "Kemp thinks they've scheduled a large delivery for tomorrow."

"Do we know where it's coming from?" Noah asked. "Could we intercept it?"

"I'm afraid not." Madeleine huffed out a breath.

"So our only option," Anna wrinkled her lip, "is to get the girls out of there as soon as possible."

"It would seem so." Blake said. "But there are a lot of them."

"Plus Faith," Noah reminded them.

"And," Blake sighed, "we have very little time."

"You're right, it won't be easy." Madeleine shook her head. "But we have to act fast. If Noah's right, the moment a girl is given metraxilone, we have no idea how to help her."

Chapter Thirty-Three:
Faith

An hour later, Faith had resolved to do all she could to escape.

Susie had settled her into the tiny ward. After a short conversation with Sanders via her wristclip, she had left Faith without a sedative. Instead, she had made her eat a large bowl of porridge, loaded with honey. Leaving Faith with a large glass of water, Susie had told her to rest. The sustenance had rid her of the lightheadedness, but she was dreading the medic's return. The minute her blood pressure returned to normal, it was all over.

The ward was horribly familiar. Faith was even lying in the same bed that Sophia had been kept. The machines which administered the drugs had been pushed back, but were still there, waiting to be put to use.

Faith had been racking her brains for a way out. The ward was restricted and self-contained, with a bathroom and even a small kitchen unit. Faith knew without testing the theory that she was locked in. But she had to do *something*. Pushing herself up off the bed, she walked to the door and eased it open.

The lobby outside was empty. Slipping into it as quietly as possible, Faith made her way to the door labelled *Office*. Susie was staring at some figures on a screen, completely absorbed, Until Faith knocked.

"What are you–?" She jammed a finger on the datadev and the screen went blank. "Are you alright?"

Faith nodded, trying not to look too well-recovered. "I finished my water. Wondered if I could–"

Susie jumped to her feet. "You want some more?"

"I... could I maybe have a sweet tea?" Faith's eyes longed to roam the room around the medic, but she forced herself to wait, keeping them focused on Susie. "Might help my energy levels."

"Good idea." Susie hurried towards her. "Get back in bed. I'll make you one right away."

Pausing until the door into the tiny kitchen had swung closed, Faith moved back into the office. She tapped the button on the datadev, which lit up. Thanking her lucky stars it hadn't logged Susie out, Faith peered at the screen.

It was a report. Sanders' name was at the top, next to the title *Lead Doctor*. Below that, Susie Price, her current jailor, was listed as Sanders' assistant. With shaking fingers, Faith tabbed through the various pages, trying to take in the major details.

The first section appeared to detail the laboratory tasked with producing femgazipane and metraxilone. Huge amounts of them, by the looks of it. Faith shuddered as she recognised the name: BellaLab Corp. Memories of her disastrous mission with Evelyn came flooding back. Had the trucks leaving the premises that day been filled with the drugs?

Following her theory, Faith read on. Sure enough, beneath the BellaLab information, two warehouses were listed. Once the laboratory had created and packaged the drugs, this was where they would be stored until they were needed. Faith recited the warehouse locations in her head, trying to commit them to memory. If she could find a way to pass on this information, the Resistance would be far better armed to act.

On another tab, Sophia's name caught her eye. Clicking on her friend's report, Faith noted the dosages she had been given and scanned the notes the medics had made about the way her body had reacted. Words like *feverish*, *shivering*, *extreme temperature* occurred repeatedly. The results from Sophia's various scans were also detailed. Clearly, Sanders had kept a careful eye on her guinea pig.

Below all this was a section entitled *Next Steps*, which contained a table. The first column was simply a list of names. Faith recognised them with a start. They were all seniors from her class at the academy. Girls she knew well. The second column was titled *femgazipane* and the third *metraxilone*. An alarming number of girls were now being given both drugs.

At least Sanders believed they were. The placebos had been keeping the girls safe, so far.

When Faith reached the next column, her heart stopped. The header simply read *Academy Pendant*. Some students had a Y in that column. Others, an N. Clearly, someone had suggested that the necklace might be having an effect on the trial. Ever the scientist, Sanders was keen to test the theory.

Faith already knew what the results would be. Girls with the pendants would remain unresponsive to the femgazipane. Those without would respond well. And after her success with Sophia, Sanders would expect pregnancies. When they didn't occur, questions would be asked. After that, it wouldn't be long before the medics discovered the placebos.

Once the girls were started on the metraxilone for real, it would all be over. There would be lots of pregnancies. Danforth would deem the trial a success. But how many more girls would die?

Faith's eyes flicked to the door. In the kitchen, the kettle was boiling. Susie would not be gone for much longer.

Faith glanced around. Spotting a pile of papers in the corner, she hurried over and grabbed a few from the top. Scanning the desk, she prayed that someone in this office still used a pen. It was rare to find anyone writing physically these days, but there were still some people that preferred them.

Yanking open the top drawer of the desk, she rifled through it. When her hands closed around a long, slender object, her heart leapt.

Quickly, she slid the papers and pen into the waistband of her underwear. Reactivating rest mode on the datadev, she hurried out into the lobby. She had barely taken three steps when Susie reappeared, cup-in-hand.

She narrowed her eyes. "What are you doing?"

Faith gestured to a door on the left. "Needed the bathroom."

"Next time, wait til I can help you," she scolded. "You're still weak." Following Faith back to her bed, she placed the steaming cup of tea on the table. "Rest, now. You'll need your strength."

Settling back against the pillows, Faith closed her eyes. Feigning exhaustion was the best way to get rid of her shadow. But when the door to the ward closed behind Susie, Faith's fingers slid under her gown and closed around her contraband.

The risk had been worth it. Now, at least, she could warn them.

Chapter Thirty-Four: Noah

The conversation in the office was going around in circles. Far from making progress on a rescue plan, all the women seemed to be doing was arguing.

"We have to assume the information Liam gave Noah is correct." Evelyn was tense, her body coiled like a spring. "And get those girls out of the academy as soon as possible."

"But we haven't heard anything more from Kemp since that message." Blake argued. "How do we minimise loss of life if we don't have eyes on the inside? After Robyn, we can't risk–"

"We may have to."

Madeleine slapped a hand down on the desk. "Danforth's more desperate than ever to get a win. With all the unrest in the city, she has to make the fertility tests work... and appear to work *safely*. What we need is concrete evidence to corroborate Faith's words, to make sure that–"

"Does Danforth think the women of the city will just forget everything they've heard if she can make her experiment work? The miracle of birth without the need for a man." Blake spat out. "Like it will erase all the terrible things she's done?"

"She's an expert manipulator." Madeleine frowned. "If she can get the fertility trials to work, she'll find a way to spin it to her advantage. Proclaim her love for the women of the city. Emphasise how the experiment will allow her to create a safer environment for them all. Anything, to keep the women of the city onside."

"Or she'll lie through her teeth." Evelyn's voice was taut. "Make something up which will frighten most of the citizens into total submission."

"Madeleine's right. If we had proof that she was the one behind the bombing," Anna mused, "we could discredit her for good."

"Not before we get those girls out of harm's way," Evelyn insisted. "I've had operatives all over the city trying to find that kind of evidence for *days*. There's *nothing*. Danforth's too clever."

"No doubt she'll lay the blame at the feet of the terrifying males in the forest once again," Anna said bitterly.

"Those fears run deep." Madeleine's gaze was piercing. "You know that more than anyone."

"Sadly, I do." Anna shook her head. "Speaking of dangerous men, we shouldn't forget about Jacob. He's still somewhere close to the city."

Madeleine turned to face her. "You've heard from him?"

"No. But Noah saw Harden. In the hospital."

"It's why I had to run." Noah sighed. "He was captured by Danforth's guards, but–"

"The fact that he was in the hospital means Jacob's still planning something." Madeleine gritted her teeth. "If we knew where he was, maybe we could use him. Bring him back onside."

"He'll be even more desperate now that he's lost Harden." Anna shrugged. "He didn't have many supporters to start with. But he still has Avery. And he won't give up."

"Do you think Danforth *cares* about Avery? I mean, Jacob's holding her like she gives him power over the chancellor."

Blake's eyes flared. "But Danforth's never bothered with her before."

"Perhaps not," Madeleine mused. "But Jacob isn't thinking straight. He doesn't have all the information we do. All he knows is... Avery is Danforth's daughter. He assumes the girl means *something* to her."

"So, we need to remove the girls from the academy before Danforth can poison them all, rescue Faith, keep an eye out for Jacob..." Blake's tone dripped with sarcasm. "Anything else, while we're at it?"

There was a knock at the door. All eyes turned as it opened to reveal Diane, her face serious.

She didn't waste time on pleasantries. "I've been monitoring the cameras in Faith's room all morning." She was out of breath. Nodding at Blake, she pointed at her datadev. "Can you bring up the feed?"

Blake's fingers were already flying over the keys.

"She's still alive then?" Madeleine's even tone made Noah wince. "And they haven't sedated her?"

Diane shook her head. "She's still feigning weakness. When the medic was in there checking on her, she pretended she was sleeping. But when the woman left the room, she sat up and looked straight at the camera."

"Here we are."

Blake moved away from the datadev, revealing Faith. She was sitting up, as Diane had said, her head bent over her lap.

"What's she doing?" Madeleine squinted at the screen. "Is she... writing?"

"Looks like it to me." Diane gestured at the object in Faith's hand. "That's a pen... right?"

"She's writing a message. For *us*." Evelyn was nodding excitedly. "Think how many hours she spent staring at Sophia in that bed. She knows where the camera is. She knows we'll be watching."

"And if she's found out something useful..." Madeleine trailed off as Faith sat up again. "Wait... what now?"

With a brief glance at the door, Faith slid out of bed. Noah tried not to think about the risk Faith was taking. Beside him, his ma took his hand again, squeezing it gently.

Moving to the corner of the room where the camera was located, Faith grabbed a chair and pulled herself up onto it. When she was standing close enough, she held up the first piece of paper. Noah squinted, trying to understand the message.

"Is that a picture of a necklace?" Anna peered at the screen.

"She's trying to use code," Blake explained. "In case she's caught with the notes. It's sensible. Look – she's written DA. And something else..." Blake leaned closer, trying to decipher the next word. "Does that say... *knows?*"

"*Danforth Academy knows!*" Evelyn gasped. "They've worked it out."

"Worked what out?" Anna sat bolt upright. "What do they know?"

"Faith worked out the importance of the pendants the girls wear." Madeleine huffed out a breath. "There was always a risk that the medics at the academy would make the same connection."

"The pendants?" Noah sat up straighter. Faith's was still in his pocket. He carried it with him wherever he went. "They're important?"

"Turns out they're not simply given to the students as a symbol of their affinity to the academy. They're somehow infused with an intense hormone treatment. We think it's meant to enhance the girls' fertility." Madeleine's gaze was sharp. "But neither Sophia nor Faith were wearing them when they were given the femgazipane."

"So they *hindered* the drugs?" Anna narrowed her eyes. "Instead of working with them?"

"They did." Blake said. "It's why the femgazipane hasn't worked properly on any of the girls... until now."

"So once they've worked this out..." Anna let the thought dangle.

"There'll be a lot more unpredictable pregnancies." Madeleine shook her head. "And with no more placebos, there'll be no way to protect the girls from the drug's effects."

Noah felt sick. On the screen, Faith had replaced the first message with a second sheet of paper.

"What's this one about?" Blake stared at the screen. "Is that... a list?"

"Can't you zoom in?" Madeleine tutted.

As Blake adjusted the image, the Resistance leader leaned forward. "Looks like... another acronym at the top. Then maybe a set of locations?" She turned to Evelyn. "Do those mean anything to you?"

The older woman frowned. "Is that a letter B? And a C, maybe?"

"I think you're right." Blake continued to work on sharpening the images. "What's the middle letter?"

Noah leaned in. "It's an L." He was more adept at deciphering handwritten letters, since he was more familiar with them. It was one of the few advantages to the lack of technology that Eremus had. "B-L-C. Do those letters mean anything to anyone?"

"BellaLab Corp!" Evelyn slapped a hand on the desk. "Of course."

Noah recalled the name. Faith had told him about the laboratory, which was notorious for its links to Danforth. It was also the company Madeleine had been fired from for asking too many questions about their research. And Faith had been involved with a mission to investigate the company. It had culminated in a confrontation with security which had left Faith with several injuries.

"The labs must be linked to the experiments in some way," he mused.

But Evelyn was well ahead of him. "We've always had our suspicions about BellaLab, but we've never managed to get inside their headquarters." She glanced at Blake. "Those cloned keycards you were developing. Perhaps it's time to see if they work."

"What about these other locations, though?" Blake gestured to the remainder of Faith's message. "They must be important, or Faith wouldn't have included them." She squinted at the datadev. "Eliot Street. Acton Street. That's nowhere near the BLC headquarters."

"You're right." Evelyn frowned. "They're both in industrial districts on the outskirts of the city. I'm not sure–"

"Look! There's a syringe drawn next to both the addresses." Noah pointed to the image. "Maybe..."

A slow grin spread across Diane's face. "She's linking the drugs with the warehouses where they're *stored*. Perhaps in large numbers."

"That makes sense..." Blake's forehead was furrowed. "I've overheard Anderson talking about new drug deliveries at the academy several times." She punched the air. "Now we know where it's coming from!"

"If we can destroy her supply, we'll set the experiment back a *long* way." Madeleine clasped her hands together. "Long enough to–"

Suddenly, everyone was talking at once.

"Get the girls out, before..." "Rescue Faith." "Discredit Danforth for good."

After the cacophony of excitement died away, the silence was charged with electricity. For the first time since Noah had entered the office, he could sense real purpose. Hope. Determination.

He glanced at the monitor. Faith was still staring into the camera, her eyes hopeful. She was looking right at him. He held her gaze, trying to reassure her.

They could do this. Fight Danforth. Stop her terrible plan from moving forward.

"We have to act quickly." Madeleine's eyes gleamed. "Get the girls out. Destroy the warehouses. Then work on bringing Danforth down. For good."

Beside him, his ma leaned forward. "What can we do?"

But before Madeleine could continue, there was another knock at the door. "Come!"

Ella peered in. "Sorry to interrupt, but there's a woman at the side entrance. Says she has to speak to whoever's in charge."

Madeleine stiffened. "Who is it? Do I know her?"

Ella shrugged. "Says she's a technician from the hospital. Her name's Carol."

Chapter Thirty-Five: Faith

Faith's body ached with tension. After another restless night, she had been bracing herself for the worst to happen. At any moment, Susie could come in and hook her up to the machines which would flood her system with femgazipane. It was only a matter of time.

But the day had passed without the medic beginning the treatment.

She wasn't sure why Susie had delayed this long. Heeding Carol's warning about Faith's blood pressure, she had left Faith alone through the night, but this morning she had declared it to be normal. Still, she hadn't started Faith on the drug. It was almost as though she was waiting for something.

Faith had lain there all day, with the machines looming over her. She tried not to look at the horrible reminders of Sophia's fate.

It had taken her a while to work up the courage to send the message to the Resistance the previous day. She had been terrified that Susie would come in at any moment. But it had been all she could think of to do to help. Once she'd gotten back in bed, though, a sense of hopelessness had overwhelmed her.

Would Blake even see the notes? Was she still monitoring the cameras? Did anyone even know Faith was here?

Noah did. But the Resistance had not been in regular contact with him since he'd taken up his post at the hospital. She knew this, because she'd been longing for information about his wellbeing from the moment he'd left the library.

He'd refused to leave the hospital to get word to headquarters. And he'd promised to get her out. But what could he do? With the Resistance behind him, it would be difficult. But without their support? It was a death sentence.

There were hundreds of cameras spread throughout the building. She knew, from all the time she'd spent scrolling through them looking for Sophia. Surely, hospital security couldn't view them all at one time.

Still, it was a huge risk. If she was spotted, out of bed and signalling to someone via the camera, it would be disastrous. And not just for Faith. Questions would be asked about who she was trying to contact, and that put the Resistance at risk. Danforth would stop at nothing, now.

But if the message had been received, if the Resistance was acting on it, it was worth the risk.

The fertility ward had no windows, so Faith had no view of the outside world, but the skylight above her head told her night had fallen. Susie had brought her some dinner an hour ago. She had sat with Faith as she ate it, making sure she finished the entire meal. Before she'd left, she'd taken Faith's blood pressure, and declared it to be at an acceptable level, *at last*.

Knowing what this meant, Faith had been on edge ever since. But as yet, no one had come to insert the tube which would introduce the poison into her system.

She'd searched the room for a weapon. Anything which might allow her to fight, to attempt escape, to prevent them from overcoming her. But there was nothing other than the bed, the empty cabinet beside it, and the omnipresent machinery.

Perhaps there was time for one last act of rebellion. There had to be more classified information in the office where Susie had been working all day. If Faith could draw the medic out again, get inside, perhaps she would find more evidence. And if she could repeat her earlier trick, and Blake was her usual observant self...

Faith made up her mind. It might be too late for her, but, until they came to knock her out, she would do her best to fight on.

Sliding out of bed, she pulled the blanket around her shoulders. She shuffled towards the door and eased it open. The lobby was silent. The food trolley stood to one side, the remnants of Faith's meal still on the plate. Edging closer to the office, Faith readied her excuse.

But when she reached the door, it was empty.

Backing away, she glanced through the open door of the kitchen. There was no sign of Susie.

She walked to the door of the bathroom. Knocking loudly, she entered. Both stalls were empty, and there was no one standing at the sink.

Her heart racing, Faith returned to the lobby. Had they left her alone? She hurried to the exit, hardly daring to hope. But no matter how hard she hauled on the handle, the doors refused to open. She was locked in.

Abandoning caution, she hurried back to the office, beginning to rifle through the drawers. If there was a keycard, she was going to use it, before Susie returned.

But the search was fruitless. After several minutes of searching, Faith slumped back in the chair empty-handed.

"Dammit!"

She slammed a hand on the desk. The movement jerked the datadev to life, its screen still open at a document. Remembering her original plan, she leaned forward to read it.

The title at the top of the page read *Historical Fertility Data*. It appeared to be a record of Bellator's reproductive systems, going all the way back to the formation of the Women's Independence Party in 2085.

Faith scanned the information. Starting with Danforth's original plan to create a drug combination which might enable women to procreate without male seed, she worked backwards. There was a section about the existing reproductive system, which selected Bellator women to be impregnated with stored seed. Trailing a finger down the screen, Faith navigated back to the early days, to a time when the city had kept live male donors in captivity.

Clicking on a link titled *Male Subjects*, Faith was startled when a series of images appeared. Each picture showed a different man. Each one had an individual code underneath. Remembering the seed identification codes she had found in the *Genealogy* book, Faith's heart began to race.

These were the men who had been executed for rebelling. But before their deaths, Danforth had taken copious seed samples from each one and frozen them, creating Bellator's seed bank.

One of these men would be Faith's biological father.

Scanning the images, she searched for a visual clue. Would she know which man she was related to just by looking at him? But there was nothing familiar about any of them. They were just faces. Unfamiliar faces. Without facial expressions, personalities, or even names, the men she was scrolling past meant nothing to her.

Halfway down the page, Faith froze. There was one face she knew very well. One which set her very teeth on edge. The wide forehead, the set of his chin, the dark expression in his eyes. It was all so familiar. Her hands shaking, she scrolled down.

Don't let it be him. Please.

Back in the library, she had memorised as many of the codes in the record book as possible. Her own had been among the first she'd remembered, followed by those of the girls who had been in the caves with her. As the man's code came into view, she heaved a sigh of relief.

Jacob was not her father.

But his code was familiar. It matched one of the ones she had memorised.

Avery's.

The irony hit her. Jacob was on the run with a girl he knew was Danforth's daughter. A girl he was perhaps willing to kill, just to hurt Danforth. But what he didn't know was that his captive was also his own flesh and blood.

What would he do if he knew the truth? What would Avery do? In other circumstances, the discovery might have been amusing. The look on Avery's face when she realised she was related to the man she hated would be priceless.

But Faith didn't feel like laughing. Returning her attention to the screen, she continued to scan the other codes. How would she feel staring into the eyes of her own biological father?

A clicking sound from outside the office made her jump. Susie had returned. Leaping to her feet, Faith had not quite made it to the door when it was flung open.

But it wasn't Susie. And suddenly, Faith knew why Susie had delayed starting the treatment.

Standing in the doorway of the office, a satisfied smile on her face, was Danforth.

Chapter Thirty-Six: Noah

I t was late. As they approached their target, Noah marvelled that they hadn't run into trouble yet. Many of the streets were quiet: the curfew was still in place, and no one was supposed to be out in public after dark.

But not every Bellator citizen was following orders. The disturbances, which had begun in the hours following the memorial ceremony, had continued. Faith's words had struck a chord with the city's women. For the last two nights, disorder had broken out in various locations around Bellator.

The citizens wanted answers.

Initially, the chancellor had declined to add weight to *such vicious rumours* by responding to them. When pressed, she had reiterated her claim that Faith had been duped by the underground Resistance. As Blake had predicted, Danforth was quick to add that these *deluded* women were being manipulated by men.

Claiming that a number of *evil* males were always lurking on Bellator's outskirts waiting to attack, she had reassured them that they could depend upon the city guard for protection. For some of the city's women, the chancellor's words had been convincing.

Others continued to ask questions.

The disturbances had helped the Resistance to form a coherent plan. The mission was a complicated one, but if all went well, it meant they could tackle all their current issues. Rescue the academy students. Find concrete evidence of Danforth's deception and convey it to the citizens, ridding them of their doubt once and for all. And, after Carol's arrival the previous night, attempt to get Faith away from Danforth.

To begin with, Madeleine had issued a city-wide invitation. The Resistance had organised a protest march, beginning outside the ruins of Matriarch House. Citizens who attended would make their way through the streets of Bellator, finishing outside the gates of the academy at midnight. A candlelit vigil would be held, to let the girls inside know they had the support of the city's women.

The Resistance leader had been right. Danforth's guard forces had been depleted when Ruth had visited the city in disguise more than a month ago. Now, perhaps due to an increased lack of confidence in the chancellor, there were even fewer. Evelyn had been out and about listening to various conversations, and it seemed the show of force at the memorial ceremony had required most of Danforth's army.

Over the past few days, the guards had found the growing number of incidents in the city extremely difficult to deal with. The curfew had been a clever way of reducing the number of patrols needed at night, meaning there were more guards available for duty during daylight hours. But now the curfew was being ignored by so many, they were struggling.

Tonight, in addition to any disturbances, they would have the march to contend with. The Resistance was counting on it distracting the guards from the academy and keeping their attention firmly focused on the other side of the city. Evelyn was leading it. They'd received word from her an hour ago that more than two hundred women had arrived to show their support. There were rumours that many of them were calling for an election. A good portion of the Bellator citizens were doubting Danforth's claims.

The first part of the Resistance mission was going to plan.

Whilst Evelyn's march kept Danforth's forces busy, a smaller team would break into the academy and get the girls out of harm's way.

Back in his drudge costume and hoping it would help him blend in, Noah was part of that team. They were only two streets away from the academy. Beside him, Ella was shaking. Ever since Helen had returned to the academy, she'd been subdued. When Ella had learned of the new threat, she'd been distraught.

"I can't stand it!" She'd been pacing the hub the previous night, long after they'd been told to get some sleep. "Anything could be happening to her, and I'm not there to protect her."

She'd begged Madeleine to assign her to the rescue team. And though her combat experience was non-existent, she had proved herself during her time undercover. There were sufficient Resistance operatives with them who could fight. They also needed people who could keep the girls calm, reassure them they were being taken to safety. Ella was the perfect woman for the job. And it allowed her to help Helen in a time of need.

Noah wished he could be doing the same for Faith. Their mirrored situations meant both he and Ella were separated from the person they wanted to help the most. It was torture, knowing that Faith was stuck at the hospital under Danforth's control and being able to do nothing about it.

But Madeleine had refused to assign him to rescue Faith. She had other plans in that respect.

There were several missions in place, all running alongside one another. Missions they'd been pouring over for the past twenty-four hours. Missions whose objectives were intertwined, each depending on the success of the others to work.

First: the march. Draw the majority of Danforth's forces away from the academy.

Then, remove the Danforth Academy girls from harm. They couldn't possibly get all of them out, but Madeleine had instructed them to rescue the senior girls, those at most immediate risk from the testing, as soon as possible.

Next, make them disappear.

Anna had contacted Paulo, who had agreed that Eremus would shelter the girls, at least temporarily. Once Noah's team had retrieved them, they would be taken to the edge of the forest. There, they would be met by a team from Eremus. It was the second reason that Ella was perfect for this particular job. She would be the bridge between the academy students and their saviours. And, knowing that Helen would be with her, Ella was happy to return home.

Paulo and Ruth would meet them there, but they were coming *into* the city. Now that Faith had helped them identify where the drugs were being stored, Madeleine wanted them gone. Without the meds, Danforth's experiments couldn't continue.

After that, they would focus on cutting off the drug supply. Two teams would be heading for the warehouses tonight to get rid of the drugs for good. Olivia was heading up one team. The other would be led by Paulo.

Next to Jacob and Flynn, Paulo was the most experienced raider. He'd worked with explosives before. And he was desperate to be involved with the plot that brought Danforth down. He'd insisted that Ruth come with him. As a woman, she would pass under the Bellator guard radar more easily.

According to Noah's ma, Ruth had become Paulo's right-hand woman. In the absence of Jacob and Flynn, Anna and Paulo had kept things going. Organising the workforce, training the raiders, protecting and feeding the community, and keeping up morale. Ruth had been a huge help, and once

Anna had left, she'd become even more valuable to Noah's brother.

It was odd to think of the Eremus community continuing in his absence. What would it be like when he returned? Would it still feel like home, now that he'd experienced life in the city? It was an uncomfortable thought.

Pushing it to the back of his mind, he tried to stay positive. Tonight, he would see his best friend and his brother again. He didn't mind admitting that he'd missed them both. Knowing they'd be around over the next few hours was a huge comfort. As long as the first part of the mission was a success, he would be proud to accompany his brother on the next.

For now, he had to focus on the challenge ahead. The women of the city were already part-way to believing what Danforth had done to the girls in the academy. And Madeleine was determined to discredit the chancellor completely. Noah's role in the mission was to help Kemp with the piece de resistance: forcing Principal Anderson to publicly admit what she and Danforth had done.

The plan was brilliant: set up equipment to broadcast live from the academy. Hide a microphone on Professor Kemp, then send her in to confront the principal. Once the women of the city heard the words from Anderson herself, there could be no more doubt.

But there were so many things which could go wrong. The timing was extremely tight, for one. They weren't sure whether they could gain access to the academy's tech equipment, for another. In addition to keeping the microphone hidden, Kemp would have to goad Anderson into talking. As long as the principal was there, of course. There was no way they could guarantee Anderson's whereabouts at the time of the mission.

But they had to try. If they could pull it off, there wouldn't be a citizen in the city left supporting Danforth.

Noah knew it was vital to stay focused. But it was difficult to keep his mind on the mission when he was terrified for Faith.

She had not been in contact since she'd sent them the message about the pendants and the drug locations. Soon after they'd received it, the camera had gone dark. Repeated attempts to reestablish the link had been unsuccessful. Blake had come to the worrying conclusion that Faith had been spotted sending the messages. Rather than risk outsiders hacking into the camera, hospital security had blocked all access to the feed.

So they had no idea whether Sanders had started Faith on the drug regime.

Their only hope rested with Carol. As a medic at the hospital, she stood a better chance of getting near Faith than any outsider. Armed with a cloned keycard, Madeleine had sent her back to the hospital with the sole task of getting inside the fertility wards and doing what she could to help Faith.

The Resistance was stretched to a breaking point with the mission. They needed the support of ordinary citizens if they were to succeed. The fact that Carol had come to them in the first place suggested she wanted to offer her support. But Noah had his doubts. Would the technician be prepared to risk her life for a girl she barely knew? Would Madeleine, famous for her philosophy of the many mattering more than the few, make Faith a priority?

He shook himself. They had a job to do. Focusing on the mission was the best way to take his mind off Faith. There was no way he was getting back into the hospital now that his cover was blown. He had to trust that Carol would do what she could.

Ahead, Blake held up her hand. The group stopped as one. They were approaching the academy from the side, hoping to skirt the edges of the playing fields and access the building without attracting attention.

Anderson would be absent. Blake had overheard a conversation earlier which implied she was meeting with Danforth, to finalise plans for *Phase Three* of the testing. The very phrase sent a shudder through Noah. But with the principal out of the way, and minimal security due to the march, Madeleine was hoping that Blake's team would be able to get inside without any trouble.

Their task was to disable any guards, locate the senior girls, and get them out. After that, they would lead them through the city to the woods. By the time the march made its way to the school, the senior students would be long gone.

"It's almost time. Remember your roles." Blake commanded from the front. "And be sure to follow my instructions *at all times.*"

Noah took a deep breath and steeled himself. Time to focus. They had a job to do.

CHAPTER THIRTY-SEVEN: FAITH

Recoiling from the intimidating figure, Faith found herself at a loss for words.

"Well, well. Ms. Hanlon." The chancellor's voice dripped with sarcasm. "What an unexpected pleasure."

Faith bit back a reply. *Unexpected* was not the word. They were both well aware that Danforth was here to gloat. She had made them wait to begin the experiment so she could be here to witness it.

"Nothing to say? No clever response?" Danforth took a step towards her. "My, my! We are quiet tonight."

Faith dropped her gaze. Refusing to give Danforth the satisfaction, she concentrated on breathing in and out. But the chancellor was determined to provoke her.

"Thought you could get the better of me, did you?" The voice was oily, hatred hissing from her every pore. "Thought you'd outwit me, make me look a fool in front of my people?"

Still, Faith stayed quiet. Frustrated, Danforth took another step. She was only a pace away now, and coming closer.

"You won't get away with it. Not now that I have you here." The final step brought Danforth close enough that Faith could feel her breath on her cheek. "My original subject, back where she belongs."

Faith tensed as Danforth circled her.

"We know what we're doing now. How the drugs work. *Properly.*"

The plosive sound propelled a fleck of saliva out of Danforth's mouth. Faith fought the urge to move away as Danforth continued her rant.

"Dear little Sophia showed us how the drugs combined just to create the perfect storm. A pregnancy, borne of woman alone." Danforth moved away, entranced by her narrative. "A pity she was too weak to withstand the rigours of the pregnancy. But, no matter. She is gone, and now we have you."

Hatred seethed through Faith. She raised her eyes, meeting Danforth's gaze for the first time. The sardonic smile she received told her Danforth had won a point in their battle. She knew she had gotten to Faith, wounded her the way she wanted.

"With you it will be so much sweeter." Danforth returned to Faith's side, sizing her up. "You're a much stronger specimen." She took hold of Faith's arm, her fingers circling it. "I feel your pregnancy will progress much more successfully."

She squeezed the flesh so hard, Faith cried out. Danforth's grin told her all she needed to know: the chancellor wanted to hurt her. Faith was part of the machine which had put Danforth's plans in jeopardy, and for that she wanted Faith to pay.

Danforth's eyes glittered. There was something manic about her, something Faith hadn't witnessed before. A desperation to complete her mission, no matter the cost. As the chancellor leaned closer, Faith dropped her eyes, fighting the urge to recoil in disgust.

"Well, you're mine. Think Madeleine can help you now? The drudge she planted here? He's long gone." Danforth took hold of Faith's chin, forcing her to meet her gaze. "All the protest marches in the world won't make a difference when I hold the first baby born of woman alone. The Bellator women will worship me for what I've achieved." She leaned close, whispering the poisonous words in Faith's ear. "And you'll always know that you were the one who made my greatest triumph possible."

There was a sound at the door. Letting go of Faith, she took a step back.

"Chancellor." Sanders stood in the doorway. "I didn't know you'd arrived. I would have–" Her eyes narrowed as she spotted Faith. "What are you doing in here?"

"I..." Faith searched for an excuse, fear surging through her veins.

"Never mind." The doctor turned to Danforth. "Let's get you back into bed."

Danforth stepped back into the lobby. "High time we got started, I think."

Before Faith could react, Sanders had grasped hold of her arm. Faith struggled, but the doctor was stronger than she'd anticipated. And, as she was hauled out of the office, she saw Danforth was flanked by no fewer than three of her guards.

"It's really best if you just come quietly," Sanders muttered.

The situation was hopeless, but desperation lent her strength. Kicking out with her right foot, Faith managed to set Sanders off balance.

"You little–" the doctor cried out in pain.

Faith whirled around, her eyes searching the space for a way out. But Sanders was right. There wasn't one. Panting, she met Danforth's calculating gaze.

"Face it." The chancellor was enjoying Faith's struggle. "There's nowhere for you to go."

The guards leapt forward, grasping her arms. Within seconds, she had been lifted up and was being carried to the bed. Once in it, she found herself being pinned down while Sanders unlocked one of the drug cabinets. Faith gritted her teeth and squirmed, but the guards were too strong.

And then Sanders was looming over her, a syringe in hand.

"You'll just feel a tiny scratch." She smiled benignly. "And then, you won't feel much of anything. Not for a while, anyway."

Drumming her heels against the bed, Faith struggled to escape the vice-like grip of the guards.

Danforth stepped into view behind the doctor. For the first time since her entrance, her face was tense. "Keep her *still*!" she hissed. "We can't afford for anything to go wrong."

The guards tightened their hold. Faith gave up, wincing as Sanders pushed the needle into the delicate skin at the crook of her elbow. Her face devoid of emotion, she pressed down the plunger, emptying the syringe completely. Faith's gaze moved to Danforth, who was still peering over the doctor's shoulder. In contrast, her eyes gleamed with satisfaction.

Faith's eyes moved to the camera in the corner of the room. Surely, the Resistance would try to rescue her. They had to know what was happening to her by now.

Danforth's eyes followed. "Don't think your Resistance friends will come and get you." She leaned closer, her breath hot on Faith's cheek. "I've had that camera feed cut. Don't want anyone being able to interfere with our experiment this time."

As the sedative began to take hold, Faith could do nothing but stare up into Danforth's eyes.

"With any luck," the chancellor murmured, "when you wake up, you'll be pregnant." She turned to Sanders, who was pushing buttons on one of the dreaded machines. "You and I will go down in the herstory books for this."

The world around Faith began to fade. She fought to stay conscious, to keep her eyes focused on the ceiling above, the guards who'd imprisoned her, the triumphant expression on Danforth's face. But, in the end, the room began to spin and her eyes flickered closed.

Her last thoughts were of Noah.

Chapter Thirty-Eight: Noah

T he academy building was dark, Noah noted with relief. And this area of the city was silent, just as they had planned. He drew in a deep breath, attempting to calm his frayed nerves.

Blake was bending over the fuse box. A soft squeal of metal reverberated through the night as she levered it open. They all tensed, but when the silence continued, Blake eased the door of the cabinet fully open. Within seconds, she had disconnected the wires.

"Alarms are off," she whispered. "We shouldn't need to worry about them later."

When the Resistance had previously accessed the school, they had worked hard to get in and out without detection. Now they were intending to remove as many students from the school as possible, it would be impossible to hide the fact that they had been here. But it didn't matter. As long as they got the girls safely away, the alarms could wake the entire city. There would be no going back.

"I refuse to hide in the shadows any longer," Madeleine had declared. "Our actions tomorrow will change the face of Bellator *forever*. We may not win, but we will declare our intent to fight to the end."

With her words echoing in his head, Noah followed the group over the wall and across the lawns. It only took a couple of minutes to reach the side door of the academy. When they reached it, Blake knocked softly. It swung open. On the other side, a drudge stood in the shadows. Noah recognised him immediately.

"Arden," he whispered.

The Resistance spy had lowered his mask, revealing the whole of his face. He was grinning.

"Eight of the ten drudges here are with us." He jerked a hand behind him. "I've been working on them. The others won't help, but they won't give us away. The senior girls are being kept in the dining room. They've been there since there were too many of them to fit in the infirmary."

"At least they're all in one place." Blake nodded. "Where's Anderson?"

"She's not here." As Arden's grin disappeared, Noah's heart sank. "Professor Kemp thinks she's at some kind of meeting, but is due back soon. Kemp's going to coordinate the rescue for now, and…"

"…hope Anderson's back by the time we're ready to leave." Blake cast a glance at Noah. "You'd better stay with us for now, until Kemp gives you further instructions." Without waiting for him to nod, she turned back to Arden. "Where are the guards?"

"One at the front entrance, one at the door to the dining hall. Two more patrolling the building. We'll have to watch out for them. I'm pretty sure most of the professors are in bed already."

Blake jabbed a finger at Olivia. "Go to the front entrance and disable the guard. Then join us in the dining hall." She turned back to Arden. "You have someone to guide her?"

He nodded and beckoned to another drudge who stood beside him. Seconds later, the pair had disappeared around the side of the building.

"Where are we most vulnerable from the other guards? The ones on patrol."

"The dining room leads off a hallway from the main vestibule. If you post a couple of people on watch in that area, one at the foot of the stairs, the other at the mouth of the staff corridor, they should be able to warn us in time."

"Alright. Let's move."

With a swift nod, Blake set off. In a single file line, they made their way down the darkened hallway.

Noah gaped at the décor, trying not to get distracted. The walls were filled with enormous paintings, some of which stretched almost to the ceiling. The floor was made from highly-polished stone, and their footsteps echoed through the space, no matter how hard they tried to keep their footfalls soft. On either side of the hallway stood highly decorated pillars with abstract patterns swirling around them.

When they reached the end of the hallway, it opened into a circular space. The ceiling almost disappeared, soaring far above their heads. A magnificent chandelier hung in the centre, its crystals winking in the moonlight which poured in through the arched windows. The staircase which invited guests to ascend to the upper floors was wide and ornate.

An elbow in the ribs from Ella brought him back down to earth. At the edge of the space, Blake was muttering in the ears of two of the better Resistance fighters. Once she had stationed one at the foot of the stairs and the other on the opposite side, she beckoned for the rest to follow Arden again.

Darting down a hallway on the opposite side, he led them towards a door marked *Dining Room*.

Kemp was waiting for them. "Did Arden tell you about Anderson?"

Blake nodded. "Do you think–"

"Should be back within the next half hour." Kemp glanced at the hallway they had emerged from. "No trouble, so far?"

"None. Let's hope the evening continues that way." Blake turned her attention to the makeshift sick room. "What's the situation?"

"There are sixty seniors inside. I managed to switch the girls' evening sedation for the placebos Madeleine sent." Kemp's smile was tense. "They'll be sleeping, but not out cold."

"Good." Blake swept her gaze back down the hallway. "How many technicians are there?"

"Just one at night. And she isn't expecting any trouble." Kemp kept her voice low. "They do all their testing during the day. She's not a trained guard. She shouldn't be difficult to take down."

Blake moved towards the door, but Kemp put out a hand to stop her. "While most of them can walk, I'm afraid some of the girls are sicker than we anticipated. We might have to carry them." She shot a glance at the group. "I hope we can manage."

Noah thought back to the last time he had been involved in an attempt to take academy students out of the city. The kidnapping had been spur of the moment, and badly planned. The girls had been unconscious, so they'd *all* had to be carried. And they'd been heavy.

He found himself hoping there weren't many who needed that level of support tonight.

"I'll go in first. Take care of the technician." Blake was already easing the door open. "I'll signal when it's done."

Kemp nodded, and Blake disappeared. The group waited silently for their leader to return. Spotting Noah, Kemp nodded, clearly too tense to smile.

Beside him, Ella leaned close. "Pity we can't take the younger girls with us too."

"Would take too long, Madeleine said," Noah whispered back. "And as long as we destroy the drug supply, they shouldn't be in danger."

"Let's hope all goes to plan, then." Ella closed her mouth and stepped back as one of the other women glared at her.

The door opened a crack and Blake beckoned to them. "Let's get this done as fast as possible."

Noah followed the others. On the floor just inside the door lay a woman in the Bellator Hospital uniform. The technician. Her eyes were closed, as though she were sleeping, but her hands and feet were fastened together with twine. Madeleine had said the sedative would knock her out for several hours. Another obstacle eliminated.

The plan was simple. Wake the girls with minimum fuss. Have Kemp, who they trusted, explain the situation to them. Then, guide them out of the academy the way they had come, into the darkness of the city.

The plan would work. As long as none of them objected. Or panicked and raised the alarm.

Noah gazed around the room. It was packed with beds, ranged in rows along the entire length. In its current state, he couldn't imagine the room being used for eating. In every bed lay a young woman. Most of them were sleeping, but a few had begun to stir. Noah found himself glad that the femgazipane doses had been given to the girls via syringes so far. Unlike in Sophia's hospital room, there were no machines, no tubes for them to deal with.

He remembered how difficult it had been to disconnect Sophia's cannulas. The delay getting to the hospital meant that Robyn and Lily wouldn't have had time, so he'd had to do it. But Sophia had only been *one* patient. Here, there were large numbers.

Thoughts of Sophia and Robyn made him sad. Under other circumstances, Sophia might have helped with the mission planning, and Robyn would have been leading the charge into the academy. With a silent promise to live up to her example, he took another step into the room.

Blake materialised by his side. "You might as well keep watch for us for now, while you're waiting on Anderson. Stay by the door, though. The sight of a man might frighten some of them. Warn us if you hear anyone approaching."

As the others began to wake the girls, he found himself grateful that his own role was less physical. The room reeked of sickness. Even from his position near the door, Noah could see how pale and thin the girls were. *How could Danforth and Sanders think the drugs were having a positive effect?*

When all the girls were awake, Kemp stood in the centre of the room. Pointing a finger at her wristclip, which she had connected to the datadev, she accessed a series of messages she had created earlier. Each one appeared on the screens stationed around the room, meaning she didn't have to speak and possibly alert the guards in the building to their presence.

"We are here to rescue you," the first one said.

The girls gazed around at the strangers, a mixture of hope and distrust on their faces.

"What is being done to you is a criminal act."

A few of the girls nodded.

"Trust that we are taking you to a better place."

Kemp nodded encouragement, making eye contact with as many of the girls as possible. Noah could see that most of them accepted what she had said.

The last message gave specific instructions. "Please stand and prepare to follow us out of the academy. Stay quiet. Follow our lead, and you will be kept safe."

By the end of the sequence, many of the girls were already on their feet, gathering their belongings. Noah let out a breath. It was working.

He turned away, opening the door a crack so he could slip outside once again. Thankfully, the hallway was still deserted. He was about to go back inside when a shadowy figure followed him out. He squinted hard, recognising Ella.

Leaning close, he kept his voice low. "What is it?"

"Helen's not h-here." Her voice caught. "They must still have her with the juniors, because she's only just come back." She gripped his arm, fire burning in her eyes. "Noah, I can't just leave her here."

Noah glanced towards the vestibule, their exit.

"You want to look for her?" He didn't relish the thought. The academy was large, and neither of them were familiar with it. "I mean..."

They both jumped as the door behind them opened. Professor Kemp stuck her head out.

"Problem?"

Ella blanched. "Sorry... it's just that..."

"Helen's not here." Noah gestured back along the hallway. "Is she being kept somewhere else?"

Kemp took a few steps out into the hall, pulling the door closed behind her. "She's being kept near the staff offices. Anderson wanted to separate her from the rest." She glanced at her wristclip. "You've probably got time to go and fetch her before we're ready to leave."

"Is she..." Ella gestured back into the sick room she'd just left.

"She's fine." Kemp pointed over Noah's shoulder. "Go back to the main atrium – the one with the grand staircase. Take the hallway leading off it directly opposite this one. Follow it to the end. Got that?" She stared at them until they nodded. "You'll find a door on the left which has no name plate. That's where Helen is."

"*Thank* you!" Ella's face lit up. "We'll–"

Eager to return to the seniors, Kemp turned back to the dining room. "When you find her, ask her to take you to the control room. I'll meet you there."

"The control room?" Ella chewed her lip. "But–"

Kemp paused, her hand on the door. "Helen's not sick. And she'll be a useful asset when Anderson returns. I don't know why I didn't think of it earlier." The professor nodded, as though she had made a decision. "Blake will have to stay with the seniors, guide the team to the outskirts of the city. But we still have Anderson to deal with." She nodded at Noah. "Helen will know more about the tech stuff than you."

But Ella wasn't satisfied. "Sooo... we can get her out–"

"Once we've got what we want from our esteemed principal." Waving away any further protests, Kemp pushed open the door. "Keep an eye out for guards."

Without another word, the professor disappeared inside.

CHAPTER THIRTY-NINE: FAITH

Faint beeping sounds. The weight of a blanket as she lay on her back. The air, cold against her face.

She attempted to open her eyes. They felt heavy, sticky. There was a chemical scent in the air, like chlorine or bleach.

"M... I'm..." She tried to speak. "I'm..."

It was difficult to get the words out. Eventually, she gave up.

There was a new sound, hushed voices in the background. But she couldn't make out the words.

She slept.

Later, the squeak of a door being opened. A single set of footsteps.

She was lying on her side now, but couldn't remember moving.

As always, the beeping, punctuating the thud of the shoes on the tiled floor. Deadened, like the stranger wore running shoes.

A sense of heaviness. The inability to move.

Someone clearing their throat. A door closing.
Silence.

An alarm, its shrill tones cutting through her sleep.

A flurry of activity. Pillows being removed. Being rolled abruptly on to her back.

Someone lifting her arm, then a pinching sensation at the crook of her elbow.

Sudden peace as the alarm cut out.

She struggled to swallow. Someone leaned close.

Breath on her cheek. The scent of mint. A warm hand on her forehead.

Heaviness she couldn't shrug off.

The beeping sound resumed, penetrating the air around her.

A clicking sound. High heels, perhaps?

More voices, closer this time. Almost overhead.

"How's she doing?"

The voice, somehow familiar, sent shivers down Faith's spine.

"She's tolerating it. Sedation seems to be helping."

A rustling sound, like papers being shuffled.

"That's good." *Sanders*. The name was poison in Faith's head. "Let's roll her now."

Several pairs of hands took hold of her. Faith's body was rolled on its side. Pillows were adjusted to hold her in the new position.

The heaviness was ever-present, immobilising.

"Increase the dosage." A command.

"Are you sure she'll–"

"*Increase* the dosage."

"Of course."

The clicking sound again. *Definitely* high heels. The squeak of the door as *Sanders* exited.

A repetitive tapping for several seconds, followed by a whirring sound.

The same warm hand on her forehead. The minty scent close, once again.

"I hope you're ready for this, Faith Hanlon."

Retreating footsteps. The squeak of the door.

Silence.

Chapter Forty: Noah

As they crept along the hallway, his hands were shaking. Ella was a few steps ahead, following Kemp's directions as fast as she could. They passed numerous doors, one after another. Small rooms. Professor's offices, judging by the name plates on the doors. He hoped they were all in bed. He was suddenly grateful for the plush carpeting which deadened their footsteps.

They didn't have long. Kemp would want them in the control room by the time Anderson returned. She had to be due back soon, and they couldn't risk her going up to bed where the other professors were sleeping.

He said a silent prayer that Blake could get the girls out of the academy fast, and without Anderson's knowledge. They were heading back out of the side exit, to avoid attracting attention. But the sooner they got clear of the school grounds, the better.

When the marchers arrived, it would be far better that the girls were long gone. Then Anderson would be their sole focus.

At the end of the hall, Ella came to an abrupt stop. She gestured to a door on the left.

Noah glanced up at the door with no identifying signage. Had this been Faith's cell, originally? He shuddered as Ella turned the handle.

The door didn't budge.

"Dammit!" Noah could feel Ella starting to panic. "What now?"

Noah glanced around. A few steps further along the hallway was an alcove with a display cabinet. Thankful it didn't have a glass front covering it, he hurried over. The shelves were packed with trophies and awards of varying sizes and shapes. After weighing a substantial-looking statue in his hands, he made his way back to Ella.

"Stand back."

Ella moved out of the way. Taking a deep breath, Noah swung the statue at the door handle. A resounding crash echoed through the hall. Noah winced, but it had done the trick. The door had popped open, and its handle hung off at an obscure angle.

Ella seemed to have frozen. Grabbing hold of her arm, Noah pushed her inside.

Once the door was closed, he looked around. The room was small, and sparsely furnished. After the opulence of the rest of the school, it was surprising. A shaft of moonlight slanted through the window, outlining a figure sitting in the room's only bed.

"Hel-en?" Ella's voice cracked. "Is that you?"

The figure moved, swinging her legs around so she could stand up. She took a few faltering steps towards them.

"Ella?" She stopped. "What are you *doing* here?"

Ella closed the gap, and they flung their arms around each other. The pair held on to one another for several moments, their grip fierce and their breathing ragged. When their hold loosened, they moved back, staring at one another.

"You're okay?" Ella asked.

"I'm okay." Helen gulped in an audible breath. "A *lot* better for seeing you."

"Thank goodness." Leaning forward, Ella pressed her lips to Helen's. The touch was brief, but intense enough that Noah looked away.

"Sorry." Slipping out of Ella's hold, Helen turned to face him. "Hey, Noah."

Noah took a tentative step forward, remembering Helen's intense fear of men during her time in the tunnels. Thanks to the actions of Jacob and Paulo, she had been more skittish around males than any of the Danforth girls. Surprising him, she closed the gap between them and gave him a brief, but genuine, hug.

When she pulled away, her eyes were filled with tears. "I'm so glad you're here."

"How long have you been–?" Ella gestured to the bleak space.

"...their prisoner?" Helen's voice was brittle. "Since the day I arrived. It was clear Danforth didn't trust me not to run. They locked me up as soon as the cameras stopped rolling."

"That *witch*!" Ella hissed.

"They haven't drugged me. At least, not yet. I'm supposed to be their poster girl. That's what's kept me safe." Helen sighed. "It's horrible. The academy's so quiet. I've caught odd glimpses of the junior girls, but they seem..." she suppressed a shudder, "scared of their own shadows. And I'm so afraid for the other seniors. I haven't seen *any* of them. It's been," she glanced at Ella, "lonely."

"We're getting you out." Ella grasped her hand.

"But..." Helen faltered, gesturing to the rest of the building, "we can't leave the others."

"We won't be." Noah spoke quickly, anxious to get moving. "We're not alone. There are other Resistance members with us. They're getting the seniors out right now. But there's not much time. And we need your help with something before we go."

"My help?" Helen blinked. "But–"

"Kemp asked if you could take us to the control room." Noah gestured to the door. "You know where that is, right?"

"I do." Rallying quickly, Helen grabbed a sweater from the bottom of the bed. When she had pulled it on, she turned back to them. "Are we meeting the professor there?" She glanced at their empty wrists. "We won't get in without her."

Noah and Ella exchanged glances.

"She didn't tell you?" Helen paled. "We'll need her access code."

"She was... preoccupied with the seniors." Noah shrugged. "Let's hope she's got them all out already and is heading back here. Anderson's expected any minute."

Helen froze. "What's this got to do with Anderson?"

"It's part of the mission," Ella explained. "Kemp's going to get her to confess... say something damning about Danforth... so we can broadcast it."

"You mean..." Understanding dawned on Helen's face. "Proof of Danforth's crimes? So the women of the city will... will finally know?"

"Exactly." Noah took a step towards the door. "So shall we...?"

"Yes. It's not far. Just at the end of this hallway." Helen steeled herself. "Maybe she's there already."

Together, they crept towards the door. Easing it open, Noah peered outside. The hallway was silent and dark. Opening it wide, he gestured to Helen. She slipped out in front of him, a ghost in the shadowy hallway. Ella followed close behind. Easing the door closed, he set off after them.

But when they reached the control room, there was no sign of Kemp. Ella knocked softly on the door, but there was no response.

"What now?" she hissed. "I mean we can't just stay here. We'd be sitting ducks."

"I guess..." Noah glanced both ways down the hall. "Is there somewhere else we can hide until-?"

But before he could finish the sentence, they jumped at the sound of pounding footsteps. Noah tensed, but they had no time to react as a figure raced around the corner.

It was Kemp.

"There you are ," she hissed as she reached them. "Anderson's back."

"Where?" Helen's eyes were wide.

"Right behind me." Kemp shoved her pupil unceremoniously out of the way. "We need to get inside. *Now*."

She tapped her wristclip against the keypad. At the tiny clicking sound, she thrust the door open and hustled them inside.

For several seconds, they stood on the other side of the door, shaking. As Noah's eyes adjusted, he could see it was a tech-base of some sort. It was a lot like Blake's room back at headquarters. The large desk was filled with various pieces of technical equipment, and there were shelves either side stacked high with expensive-looking gadgets. There were numerous datadevs lying around, and cables snaking everywhere.

Kemp placed her ear to the door. After several seconds had passed, she let out a long, hard breath. "She's gone."

"Where to?" Ella enquired.

"Hopefully, her office." Kemp said. "Right where we want her."

Noah turned to face the professor. "Did Blake-?"

"Left a few minutes ago. Managed to take all the seniors with her." Kemp frowned.

"Does Anderson know they're gone?" Helen asked.

"Not yet." Kemp kept her voice low. "Once she does, she'll be straight on to Danforth. Our chance will be gone. We need to act fast."

"Better get started then." Noah ran his eyes over the equipment. "What do you need us to do?"

CHAPTER FORTY-ONE: FAITH

"Faith!" An urgent voice. "Faith! Can you hear me?"

Hands, shaking her. Not gently. A new presence, leaning close. The scent of lemons, fresh and sharp.

"Come *on*." The tone grew panicked. "Please!"

But she was paralysed. The weight on her was leaden, and refused to lift.

"*Please.*"

The woman's voice was vaguely familiar, but she couldn't place it. She was on her side again. She tried to stir her limbs, open her eyes, speak, but there was nothing.

Sighing, the figure moved away. Faith strained her ears, apparently the only part of her that was working. There was the familiar tapping sound. The same, odd whirring noise.

The woman was beside her again.

"I've reduced your sedation." The voice seemed to come from far away. "But it will take too long for it to wear off. There's no time to–"

She broke off, her breathing ragged.

"Do you *hear* me?" The woman shook her again. "They'll be back any minute. I can't stay much longer."

Placing a hand on her chest, the stranger bent her head closer. "Your heartrate's steady. You're breathing evenly." She sighed. "I don't think you're in immediate danger."

There was a pause. The sound of something being unzipped. A clinking, like metal instruments striking one another.

"I guess it's plan B, then."

Faith felt a pressure at the back of her neck. Something cold, being wiped over her skin.

"I'm sorry," the woman whispered, close to her ear.

There was a sharp pain as something sliced into her. A searing, burning sensation. And then, immediate relief as the instrument was withdrawn. A firm pressure as something soft and dry was pushed against the same spot and held there.

"All done."

The woman withdrew her hand. There was the sound of her packing away equipment. Rustling, the same odd clink of metal, the zipper being done up.

"It's the best I can do for you, for now."

A hand patted her arm. The lemon scent swirled around her again as the woman leaned close.

"Stay strong, Faith."

And then she was gone.

Silence.

For a long time, silence.

But somehow, the weight had eased. Faith was lying on her back again.

She forced her eyes open, recoiling at the light which pierced them. Clamping them shut again, she drew in a breath. This time, she opened them gradually, allowing them time to adjust.

The room spun around her. Sophia's room. Now hers.

As it came into focus, Faith assessed her situation.

Twin tubes snaked out of her arms, attached to the machines on either side. The incessant beeping sound seemed to grow louder as her focus sharpened. A tiny red light blinked in time with the noise, drawing her eyes to a screen filled with numbers that meant nothing to her.

There was the sound of voices. Heart racing, Faith closed her eyes again. The squeak of the door as someone entered. But were they friend or foe?

Whoever it was, there was more than one person. And the pair were mid-conversation.

"...over *three hundred*, I heard, by the time they reached the square." The voice was hushed.

"That many?"

"Incredible, isn't it?" *Medics*, Faith thought, as the women removed her pillows. "Marching through the city *in the middle of the night*."

"What's Danforth doing about it?"

Hands took hold of her again. Forcing her body to relax, she allowed the women to roll her on to her side. When they had replaced the pillows, they continued.

"Not sure." This voice was familiar. *Susie*, Faith remembered. "There are guards on patrol, of course, but..."

"You think it might get out of control?"

"They're headed for the academy, apparently, so it's not looking good. Sanders has instructions to move her to the Eliot Street location if things get any..." Susie stopped talking suddenly. Rapid footsteps crossed the room. "Wait a minute!"

"What?"

"Her sedation's been reduced." Susie's tone was sharp. "Did Sanders sanction that?"

"No." The second woman sounded nervous. "Maybe it was an accident."

"Are you kidding? We *all* know how important this girl is." The familiar tapping sound commenced. "Better hope the doc doesn't find out."

As the machines whirred into life, Faith's hands shook.

"Faith?" This was definitely Susie. "Can you hear me, Faith?"

Keeping her body as relaxed as possible, Faith feigned sleep. After a moment, the shaking stopped.

"She's still out. Guess the dosage wasn't low enough to make a difference."

"Thank goodness." The relief in the other medic's voice was palpable. "That could have been disastrous. If..."

The heaviness was already returning and Faith heard no more.

But her strange visitor had come with the intention of helping her. *Who was she?* And, more importantly, would she return?

As Faith gave in to the darkness, a flicker of hope sparked inside her.

Chapter Forty-Two: Noah

"I'll be doing the dangerous part." Professor Kemp moved to the desk. Opening a drawer, she started rummaging through it. "It's good that you're here, Helen. You're more familiar with the tech. Sit here, please."

"Okay." Helen's tone was shaky, but as she settled into the chair she raised her chin.

"Put these on." Kemp handed her a pair of headphones. "I'm going to head to Anderson's office. If I'm right..." she checked the time on her wristclip, "The marchers will be arriving any minute. It's perfect."

"Marchers?"

"Long story." Kemp continued to tap at the datadev, navigating through various screens. "Basically, the Resistance are leading a protest march through the–"

"The women are rebelling!" Ella butted in. "Questioning Danforth."

"They're headed towards the academy." Kemp unplugged a cable and replaced it with another. "Any minute."

"So if we can capture Anderson admitting what she and Danforth have done..." Helen's face lit up as she understood.

"It's genius!" She gestured to the equipment in front of her. "Just tell me what I need to do."

"Turn that other screen on."

Helen obeyed, the screen to her left lighting up. As Noah squinted at it, an office came into view. Anderson was sitting at the desk reading something on a datadev in front of her.

"Bingo!" Kemp crowed. "We can see her."

Spurred on by her success, the professor moved to a cupboard at the side of the room. She opened it and took something out. Pulling her shirt out of her trousers, she pressed a button on the top of the object and slipped it into her belt. "Help me with this, Ella?"

Ella hurried to assist her. Kemp fiddled with the cable attached to the object.

"You need to thread it up the back of my shirt. We have to keep it hidden."

Ella did as she was told, flushing at the close contact with the older woman.

"What do I do with this?" She gestured to a tiny black sphere at the end of the cable.

"The microphone?" Kemp pulled a jacket from the back of the chair Helen was sitting on. "Put it in my pocket. She'll see it, otherwise."

Taking a pair of scissors, Kemp cut a hole in the jacket lining before slipping it on. With Ella's help, she fed the cable into the pocket from the inside.

"That's as close as I can get it without her spotting it." She gestured to Helen. "Can you hear me?" Helen gave her a thumbs up. "Good."

Satisfied that the microphone was hidden, Kemp moved to a different datadev, turning it on and navigating through some options like lightning. She was searching the academy security cameras. When an image of the front gates appeared, she pointed at it.

"This is where the marchers should be arriving." She checked her wristclip. "Any minute now. I need to get to the office. Helen, you should be able to hear our conversation. Once I'm in, hit this button to start recording. Okay?"

Pale but resolute, Helen nodded.

Removing her wristclip, Kemp slid a small cable into the side of it and attached it to the datadev in front of Helen. She clicked a few buttons. "We'll store the recording on my clip. As soon we have what we need, remove it." She held Helen's gaze, her expression serious. "Whatever you do, keep it safe."

"Got it."

"Noah, lock the door after me." Kemp went to a cabinet at the far side of the room. Wrenching it open, she took out a gun and handed it to him. "If anyone tries to enter, you use this. Alright?"

Noah's hands were shaking as he took the weapon, but he managed to nod.

"Ella," Kemp turned back to the other girl, "when the marchers get here, flip this switch. Make sure that dial is turned up as high as it can go. Okay?"

As Ella moved into position, the professor glanced around the room, meeting their gazes one by one.

"If this works, we could change the minds of the Bellator citizens. *Forever.*" She walked towards the door. "If I don't come back," she opened the door, "take the recording and get out of here. By *any* means possible. Take it to Madeleine. She'll do the rest."

Before they could respond, she was gone.

The silence that filled the room once the door had closed behind her was a heavy one. They had expected to get out of the academy well before the marchers arrived. Now they were stuck here, with vital roles in a job which could make all the difference to the Resistance's success.

Or its failure.

After several seconds had passed, Noah walked to the door. Locking it behind the professor, he gestured at the gun. "I hate these things."

They lapsed into silence again. Helen's eyes were glued to the screen, Anderson hadn't moved. Noah felt a seething hatred for the woman. She was supposed to be an educator, concerned about the young women in her care. Instead, she had knowingly put innocent girls through torture in the name of science. *How could she live with herself?*

"She's in!"

He jumped at the sound of Helen's voice.

On the screen, Kemp had entered the office. She was standing in front of Anderson.

Noah stepped closer to the screen, praying that Kemp had a plan to get the information out of the principal. Checking the wristclip was properly connected to the datadev, Helen hit the record button. It was tricky to make out Anderson's facial expression, but her body had gone rigid at the unexpected interruption.

"Want to listen?" Helen disconnected the headphones and Kemp's voice filled the room.

"...speak with you?"

As Helen fumbled with the volume, Noah had to admire Kemp's calm.

"Not a good time, Charlotte." Anderson's voice was quieter than Kemp's. She sounded tetchy. "Can't it wait?"

"No," Kemp's voice took on a tone of certainty. "It can't."

Anderson sat up a little straighter. "Go on then."

"I came to give you my resignation."

"What is she–?" Helen exclaimed.

"Shh!" Ella waved a hand to quiet her. "Listen."

In the office, Kemp was still talking. "...here to tell you I'm a proud member of the Resistance, working here undercover. I want you to know that..."

"She's blowing her cover." Helen frowned. She was gripping the table so hard that her knuckles were white. "I guess that's part of her plan, to deliberately aggravate Anderson."

"That's a dangerous strategy," Noah muttered.

"...no longer be allowed to get away with your crimes against the girls in this academy." Kemp ploughed on. "What you have done to them is..."

"They're here." Ella jabbed a finger at the screen.

Where the space in front of the gates had previously been empty, now a large group of people was gathering.

"Go on then!" Helen gestured to the switch. "Flip it! Then turn up the volume."

Startled, Ella obeyed. An impressive number of marchers was amassing outside the gates. As Ella turned the dial Kemp had indicated, the marchers on the screen began to react. Looking upwards, they frowned, looks of confusion on their faces.

In the office, Kemp continued to goad the principal. "These girls deserve *better*. The citizens of this city deserve to know the truth."

"We did it!" Noah stepped closer, pointing at the screen. "They can actually hear her."

"Genius!" Ella's eyes were like saucers. "Now if she can just get Anderson to admit to the bombing..."

"...the crowd will hear it live," Helen finished off.

The plan was working. Better than they could have hoped. A recording of Anderson admitting to the crime would be a powerful tool. But a live broadcast of a confession to a group of women who were already asking questions would be priceless.

The marchers were silent and still now, listening intently to the private conversation in the office. Noah refocused his attention on the conversation, praying that Anderson would admit to Danforth's part in the bombing, without discovering the microphone in Kemp's pocket.

"You can no longer be allowed to get away with this, Principal Anderson," Kemp's voice had reached fever pitch, building to a climax. "It has to stop, or–"

"Or what? You *traitor*." In the office, Anderson was on her feet. "How, exactly, are you going to stop us? The women of this city *believe* in Chancellor Danforth."

"Oh, yes?" Kemp leaned forward, her face a snarl. "Maybe that was true, in the past. Right now though, her position doesn't seem so secure."

Anderson came out from behind the desk. "The chancellor has done *everything* for them. She's always had their best interests at heart."

"Really?" Kemp's tone was sarcastic. "I don't regard the experimentation at this school as being in the best interests of these vulnerable young women."

Anderson took a step towards Kemp. "Everything Danforth has done has been for the good of this city's women. The chancellor has been forced to make the most difficult of decisions, at times, but she has never run away from them."

"Difficult decisions?" Kemp cocked her head to one side. "What kind of decisions?"

"Decisions," Anderson went on, "which have meant the sacrifice of a few for the good of the whole."

"Sacrifice?" Sensing victory, Kemp pressed on. "These girls weren't given a choice. They were selected for Danforth's trial without any information about what would be done to them."

"When the fertility drugs work, it will all be worth it. The *entire city* will benefit." Anderson advanced towards Kemp, her voice menacing. "They will *thank* her. And they will see what she has done has *always* been for them."

At the gates of the academy, the women of the city listened. Their gazes aloft, they focused on the voice booming out of the speakers at the front entrance of the school. And Anderson had no idea. If Kemp could steer the conversation in the right direction...

"Danforth thinks it's okay to sacrifice these young, innocent girls for the good of the rest of the city?" Kemp's voice retained its mocking tone. "She's okay with them *dying* for us?"

"She is. Because she understands that the end justifies the means." Anderson was almost toe-to-toe with Kemp now. The volume of her voice increased as she neared the microphone in Kemp's pocket. "It's not the only time she's had to make a tough decision because she knows it will ensure the right outcome for the women of this city."

"Really?" Kemp sneered. "On what other occasion has she deemed it necessary for citizens to *die* so that the whole can benefit?"

Noah held his breath.

"The recent bombing, of course." Anderson spat out. "Another necessary evil. To ensure that the Bellator citizens understand the importance of Danforth's work."

A shockwave ran through the crowd.

"And as long as the chancellor has Eremus to blame for this kind of evil act, the women of the city will remain confident in her ability to protect them." Anderson finished, triumphantly. "Danforth will never give up. She knows what's best for them, even if they don't know it themselves."

Noah sat back in his chair, his heart pounding. At the front of the academy, the marchers stood, openmouthed.

"I think that just about did it." Ella was grinning.

"Look!" Helen pointed at the screen in front of her.

The crowd had come to life. Their faces seething with fury, the women of the city were converging on the gates.

As the crowd descended on the building, the trio in the tech room stared at one another. Clearly, Anderson's words had had the desired effect. But the angry mob outside put them in a very vulnerable position.

"What do we do?" Ella whispered.

Noah shrugged. "Get the recording. Then get out of here."

Helen saved the file and removed the wristclip. She slipped it into her pocket and turned back to the screen. Having abandoned the conversation with Anderson, Kemp was attempting to leave. As she did, Anderson lunged towards her in a desperate attack.

"Think she's worked out what's happening?" Noah asked.

Anderson threw a vicious punch which Kemp failed to avoid. Rallying, the professor launched herself at the door. Anderson was hot on her heels. The pair grappled with one another, falling to the ground out of sight of the camera.

For a moment, the sounds of their struggle continued. Then, without warning, the feed cut out.

"Should we try to help her?" Helen murmured. "Or wait for her?"

"Not if it risks us losing the recording," Ella replied.

"But–"

"Look at the impact it's having." Ella gestured to the camera which focused on the crowd. They had managed to haul the gates open now and were pushing towards the school's front entrance. "It's *huge*. The entire city has to see this."

"I guess." Helen glanced back at the office camera, where there was no sign of the two women. "But I don't like the idea of leaving her."

"None of us do." Ella sighed, taking Helen's hand. "But it's up to us now. We can't let her down."

The pair joined Noah at the door. As they peered out, their concern over the escalating disturbance grew. There were distant cries, and a loud crash, as though the citizens were trying to break through the gate.

But the hallway outside the teacher's entrance was empty. Creeping into it, they cast desperate glances towards Anderson's office.

"Can't we just–" Helen began, but then her face brightened.

Kemp had appeared further along the hallway. She was limping slightly, and bleeding from a cut on her face, but she was alive. Joining them, she wasted no time in guiding the group back to the central vestibule, where the racket from the mob was deafening.

"They'll be inside any minute," she muttered.

Picking up speed, she turned the corner, heading back to the Resistance's original entry point.

Arden was waiting at the door. He nodded at Kemp with relief. Without a word, he guided them outside and through the grounds, leading them to an exit at the rear. As they slipped into the alleyway, they turned back to look at the academy. All the lights were on and the noise from the invasion carried across the field to them.

Helen's face was pale. "Think the junior girls will be okay?"

Kemp slid an arm around her. "Evelyn's with the march, remember? She'll make sure they're not harmed. I suspect," she gestured to the hallway containing the offices and tech rooms, "they'll head straight for Anderson's office."

Noah shuddered. He wasn't a fan of the principal, but the baying mob descending on her office was unlikely to treat her kindly.

Turning to Arden, he extended a hand. "Thanks for waiting for us."

The drudge bowed his head. "It was my pleasure."

"Shall we get going, then?" Kemp was already walking.

Their hands clasped together, Ella and Helen followed her. Sucking in a deep breath, Noah nodded at Arden. Together, they brought up the rear of the group, heading for the outskirts of the city.

There was more work to do before the night was over.

Chapter Forty-Three: Faith

"Shouldn't she be awake by now?"

"*Patience*, Susie."

It was Sanders, again. Faith kept her eyes closed. It was instinct now, to protect herself. If they believed she was out cold, they discussed things more openly. She could assess her situation better, without alerting them to the fact that she was conscious.

Something was different, but she couldn't quite put her finger on what. There was a scent in the air that she didn't recognise, and the echo which had existed in the room had been deadened somehow.

Around her, the conversation continued.

"But we can't administer the metraxilone until she's awake." Susie's voice was aggravated. "That's what worked with the other one. It's key that we start her on it as soon as possible. Danforth wants us to—"

"She'll come around soon." Sanders' voice was firm now. "Give her a few more minutes, then I'm sure we'll be able to get started."

Faith's heart pounded. *The other one* was clearly a reference to Sophia. The casual reference to her friend as a nameless subject was horrific. The mention of metraxilone was worrying, too. Once the second drug had been given to Sophia, the pregnancy had followed. And once she was on the metraxilone, there had been no going back.

Faith remembered her mystery visitor, the whispered words of encouragement. She had to find a way to resist the experimental meds until the Resistance could mount a rescue.

The voices had retreated slightly, so Faith chanced a quick glance at the room. She froze. Whilst she was still surrounded by machines, and in a bed, she was no longer in the hospital. The space around her was totally unfamiliar.

How long had she been out?

Realising her change of location meant the Resistance would have no way of knowing where she was, Faith felt sick.

"You're awake!" It was too late to snap her eyes shut now, as a slender face loomed over her. Susie. "How are you feeling?"

The medic was joined by Sanders, her face emotionless. "*Now*, we can get started."

"What are you going to do to me?"

Faith knew what was about to happen. But there was no harm in keeping them talking as long as possible.

"I told you before." Sanders smiled. "You're going to be my big success."

"I don't want to be your..." Faith tried to struggle, but the sedation had yet to wear off completely, and her limbs felt heavy. "Don't want any part of this."

She glanced around the room, her heart racing.

Sanders laughed softly. "Don't think you're getting out of here. That was the whole point of moving you."

"Where am I?" Faith willed herself to get up, but only succeeded in shifting her limbs a couple of inches.

"Never you mind."

As Sanders moved away from Faith, she glanced at her surroundings. The room she was in was small, but it didn't look like a hospital. The metal joists on the ceiling were exposed and the space seemed more industrial than medical. More like a warehouse.

"Her vitals are good, considering." Sanders nodded at Susie, pressing a button on one of the machines.

"So you're happy to start her on the metraxilone now?" The medic seemed greatly relieved. "Shall I put another line in?"

Sanders squinted at the screen. "Yes. I think so. We might give it another half an hour, but it's best that she's ready."

Susie opened a drawer at the side of the bed. She brought out a section of thin tubing and a wicked-looking needle attached to a plastic vial of some kind. Faith recoiled as the woman grasped her arm.

"That sedation's really wearing off now." Susie commented. She tutted at Faith. "Hold still."

"No!" Now Faith had regained some control, she writhed this way and that, making it as difficult as possible for the woman to take her arm.

Suddenly, Sanders was at her side. "Give it up." Stronger than Susie, she held Faith's wrist with an iron grip, pinning Faith's shoulder to the bed with her other hand. "It'll be worse if you fight."

Susie moved closer, steadying Faith's arm at the elbow. As she brought the needle towards Faith's skin, it glinted in the light. Forcing her body to relax, Faith waited until she felt the tip of it pressing into her skin.

Sanders' grasp relaxed just a fraction. Tensing her entire frame, Faith let out the shrillest scream she could manage. Susie fumbled, and the needle fell from her grasp.

"Dammit!" she cursed.

Sanders rewarded Faith with a stinging slap across the face.

"Quiet!" she demanded. Turning to Susie, she gestured to the door. "Did you hear something?" The medic shook her head. "Go and check who's out there."

Susie obeyed. When she was gone, the doctor leaned closer. "Listen to me." Little flecks of her spit hit Faith's face as she spoke. "We will get that cannula into you if it's the last thing we do. You *will* be my first success."

There was a disturbance at the door. Sanders let go, and the two of them spun to face the newcomer.

Danforth stood in the doorway, her face twisted with fury. Beside her, Faith recognised Hammond. The lieutenant was armed to the teeth.

"Chancellor!" Sanders stumbled forward. "We weren't expecting you yet. I–"

"Change of plan." Danforth barked. Her glance ran over Faith's body. "She's still a viable option for the treatment, right?"

"Of course." Sanders inclined her head. "We were just about to–"

"We had to move quickly." Danforth sighed. "Things are... not going quite the way I'd planned." Her gaze fell on Faith again. "Let's..." she gestured to the door, "speak privately."

Nodding, Sanders followed her out without a word. When the door had closed behind them, Faith allowed herself a small sigh of relief. A temporary reprieve.

She had better make the most of it.

CHAPTER FORTY-FOUR: NOAH

B y the time they reached the forest, it was late.

Their journey through the city had been a real eye-opener. There were citizens out on the streets in many places, some wandering aimlessly, others moving with more purpose. Several of the women had been carrying weapons. The group had managed to avoid several protests, where guards were struggling to force citizens back inside their homes.

"Down with Danforth!" There were chants everywhere they went. *"Stop the experiments! Save the academy students!"*

One woman had been giving out handmade leaflets. *Citizens call for a new election*, they declared.

The fabric of the city was unravelling fast.

As they approached the forest, a slender figure burst from the trees, propelling herself towards him. "Noah!"

Ruth's embrace almost knocked him over. But when she released her hold, he missed its reassuring familiarity.

"He-hey." Ruth choked on the words, then recovered herself. "S'been a while."

"It has."

He looked properly at her face. One eye was badly swollen and several cuts marked her cheek.

"Jacob?" He gestured to her injuries.

"Yeah. I'm okay though." She pulled her hood higher. "Take more than that to keep me down."

Aware of another figure melting out of the trees, Noah turned. As Paulo came into view, a fresh pang of sorrow washed over him.

He stumbled forward. "I'm s-so sorry." He stepped in to hug his brother. "Flynn... I can't... I couldn't–"

"I know."

Paulo squeezed Noah so tightly he couldn't breathe for a moment. Noah felt his brother swallow hard. And then, abruptly, Paulo released him and stepped away. He turned to Kemp.

"I sent the rest of the group on ahead. Some of the girls were..." He cleared his throat. "I figured getting them somewhere they could rest was the biggest priority."

"Thank you." Kemp nodded gratefully. "We appreciate your support."

He shrugged. "We'll do our best for them. But if any of them need proper medical care, you know we're pretty limited."

"We managed to keep them off the metraxilone. That's the most dangerous drug, but none of them were given it. They should recover from the femgazipane, with time." Kemp shook her head. "I'm hoping they won't need to be with you very long. Things in the city are... well, let's just say they're changing."

"What's going on?" This was a new voice, and one which Noah struggled to place.

A third figure stepped out from behind the trees. With shock, Noah recognised Charlie, the guard he had threatened in the tunnel confrontation between Eremus and Danforth's patrol.

He turned to Paulo. "What's *she* doing here?"

"She's here to help." Paulo shot the Bellator guard a look Noah couldn't identify. "She knows the city well."

"But isn't she..." Noah frowned. "One of them?"

"Not anymore." Ruth stepped in. "She's on our side now."

Kemp raised an eyebrow. "You were a guard?"

Charlie nodded. "Yeah. Things change, though." She glanced at Paulo. "Let's just say I've learned a few things since I arrived in Eremus."

"That's an interesting way to put it." Kemp narrowed her eyes. "Some might say you've been their prisoner."

Charlie shrugged. "At first, perhaps."

Paulo took a step towards Charlie, almost protectively. "She's come here to do what she can to help turn the tide."

"Excellent." Kemp gave the ex-guard an approving look. "The women of the city seem to be coming around to our way of thinking, and many of the drudges, but the guards are mostly loyal to the chancellor. Would be good to have your support."

"I'll do what I can."

"Do you know where the warehouse is located?" Noah glanced at Charlie, hoping his brother was right to trust her. "I have a map, but you might be more familiar with that part of the city than me."

Charlie nodded. "Eliot Street, right? In the industrial district to the east."

"That's the one." Noah turned to Paulo. "Thanks for your support on this. We have to destroy both warehouses. As *soon* as possible."

"Whatever we can do to help bring that witch down." Paulo's voice was taut, carrying the weight of his uncle's death in every syllable.

Noah wondered if Olivia's team had reached the other warehouse yet. They had left the library at the same time as his group, but there had been no explosion so far. He hoped they hadn't run into any issues.

He turned to Ella and Helen. "Think you're alright to get back to Eremus from here?"

"Won't be a problem." Ella nodded. "I know the woods well."

"And I'm not sick," Helen added. "We'll be fine."

Kemp stepped forward, smiling. "Well done tonight. *All* of you. We did a good thing. It will make a huge difference to a lot of people." She held out her hand to Helen. "You have the wristclip with the recording?"

"Here." Helen fumbled in her pocket and handed it to her professor. "Where are you going now?"

"To the library, see where I can help." Kemp shrugged. "My cover at the academy is completely blown, so I can't go back there." She pocketed the wristclip. "Madeleine will want to hear this. To pass it on to the relevant people. Need to get it back to her as soon as possible."

"Sure you'll be alright?" Noah felt a wrench as the older woman turned to leave. She had risked so much this evening, in the name of the Resistance.

"I'll be fine." She gave a wry smile. "I've been surviving this city and its monsters a lot longer than you have." Stepping close to Helen, she took the young woman's hand. "I know how hard the last few days have been for you. After tonight, maybe things might just get a little easier."

Helen managed a watery smile. "I hope so."

Kemp squeezed her hand. "Take care now."

Stepping back, she nodded to the rest of the group. Then she turned and walked away, disappearing into the shadowy streets of the city.

Paulo turned to the rest of the group. "We'd better be making tracks."

Ruth stepped close to Ella, pulling her close. The sisters had been separated for a long time. And just as Ella was coming home, Ruth was heading for the city. It seemed a cruel thing.

Paulo nodded a goodbye to Ella and Helen, but shifted from foot to foot, clearly anxious to get going. Noah ignored Ruth's curious stare as he hugged Ella goodbye. He'd grown close to her during their time in the city. The dangerous situations they'd shared had forged a bond he'd never forget.

"Lead the way then." A ghost of a grin crossed Paulo's face. "These warehouses won't destroy themselves."

As Charlie led them into the city, Noah tried to be optimistic. Finally, they were going to put an end to Danforth's experiments.

But he couldn't shake the feeling that the explosives in their packs might do more harm than good.

CHAPTER FORTY-FIVE: FAITH

G lancing down at her body, Faith assessed her situation. The crook of her right elbow was bleeding slightly, where the needle had scratched the skin. It wasn't a bad injury though. She glanced at her left arm, where a tube was already feeding drugs into her system.

Slowly, she eased into a sitting position. Investigating the cannula with the fingers of her other hand, she could feel the needle piercing into the flesh. The tube snaked upwards to a clear plastic bag mounted on the front of one of the machines. The label on the bag read *femgazipane*.

First things first. Faith steeled herself. Taking hold of the plastic sleeve which held the needle in place, she pulled. It was an uncomfortable sensation, but the needle came free more easily than she had anticipated. She pressed her fingers against the site, but it didn't bleed much.

Swinging her legs around, she pulled herself to the edge of the bed. Her head was spinning and the effort the movement required made her nauseous. She spotted some water on the bedside table. Edging towards it, she grasped the glass and raised it to her lips. She took a sip. Cautiously, at first. Then, when the water settled in her stomach without making her sick, she drained it.

Once she felt a little more stable, she glanced down at herself. Clad in a hospital gown, she wasn't exactly dressed for running. But she didn't have much choice. Pushing herself to her feet, she stood still for a few moments, making sure her legs would hold her.

When she was pretty sure she was okay, she crept towards the door. On the other side, urgent voices muttered. But no matter how hard she strained, she couldn't make out what they were saying.

Turning the handle slowly, she eased the door open a crack. The voices grew in volume.

"...academy was overrun." Faith's heart leapt. Had the Resistance freed the other girls? "...couldn't get to Anderson."

"We don't know what's happened to the girls yet." Danforth was pacing. "Citizens have been flooding down there ever since that damn Thane woman started broadcasting. We just can't get near."

At the mention of Madeleine's journalist friend, Faith found herself smiling despite her situation. Stella Thane had been forced into hiding after printing the leaflets which had started all the trouble. Danforth's words confirmed that she was as determined as ever to broadcast the truth from her safehouse.

"...only just escaped the new government base before it was overrun," Danforth was saying.

"...forced to head here." This was Hammond again. "To regroup."

Faith pulled the door open a little wider. No one was looking her way. It didn't sound like things were going well for Danforth. If the Resistance mission was finally working, she had to get away. But she had to figure out where she was.

She glanced around. The place looked like a warehouse. Though the inner room Faith was being kept in was clean and fairly small, the outer area was much larger. The ceiling soared high above, and the space had floor-to-ceiling shelves packed with boxes. Faith recognised the green star logo of the Bellator hospital on the side of some of them and it made sense. *This* was one of the locations the drugs had been taken to after leaving BellaLab Corp.

Clearly, she was being kept in one of the warehouses listed on the document she had found in Sanders' office. She felt a tiny ray of hope. If the Resistance had received her message, they might already be on their way to rescue her.

But she couldn't count on that. Sanders had said the camera had been switched off. There were no guarantees the rebels knew where she was. Straining forward, she spotted an exit on the opposite wall of the warehouse. It wouldn't be easy to get to, with Danforth and her guards in the way.

If she managed to reach it, it might be locked. And there were no guarantees she would know where she was if she managed to escape.

Faith cast her mind back to the locations she had scribbled on the pieces of paper. Eliot Street. And Acton Street. Which one was she in? Where were they in relation to the library? When she'd conveyed the locations, Faith had relied on the Resistance working out where the warehouses were. She had never anticipated having to find her own way out of the un-familiar industrial district.

She tried to focus. Warehouses were probably located on the outskirts of the city. If she ran, would she be better off heading back to Eremus or returning to the city? It seemed ironic that she was considering Eremus as a potential sanctu-ary when it had once been a place she was imprisoned.

"What's your plan, Chancellor?" Hammond's voice brought Faith back to the here-and-now.

"We'll have to wait until the chaos in the city abates." Dan-forth paused. "I've dispatched every available guard to quell the riots. They're well-armed." Faith recoiled at the suggested threat. "They'll resolve things, eventually."

"And then what?"

"Then we'll spin this in our favour." Danforth didn't sound quite as cocksure as she usually did. "I'll blame the Resistance, of course. Find a way to prove it's them who are lying, not me."

"You think they'll believe the Resistance falsified the evidence?" Sanders asked.

What evidence was the doctor referring to?

"By the time I'm finished, they will," Danforth sneered. "I'll broadcast a speech. From here, if necessary. Denounce the Resistance, and Eremus, of course." She sniffed, disdainfully. "They'll swallow it."

"They always do," Hammond tossed the comment over her shoulder as she moved towards the door, "as long as you make the men sound terrifying enough."

"You're right." Danforth shot a grateful look at her lieutenant as she cracked open the exit door, keeping watch. "They might take a little more convincing this time, though." She started pacing. "I may have to reveal the extent of the damage to the seed stores."

There was an audible gasp from Sanders. "Won't that cause panic?"

"Perhaps. But if I can provide the *solution* to the issues caused by the seed deficiency, I'll be the hero again." Danforth gestured over her shoulder. "That's why it's even more vital than ever that we get the fertility experiment to work." She held out a hand to stop Sanders from interrupting. "With the academy overrun, Faith's potentially our only subject."

The doctor was already on her feet. "We'd better get back to it then."

Faith drew back from the door as Danforth raised an eyebrow. "You haven't started the procedure yet?"

"We were just about to." Horror took hold of Faith as Sanders continued. "You want us to go ahead then, despite the situation? It will be difficult to move her, once–"

"Definitely." Danforth's tone was cold. "The faster we get on with it, the faster we'll have a success story."

Her heart sinking, Faith began to ease the door closed. They would come for her in a matter of minutes. And she could do nothing about it. Outside, Danforth continued to press Sanders.

"How soon before–" She stopped abruptly. "What is it Hammond?"

Faith tensed at her tone. At the door, the lieutenant was staring at a message on her wristclip.

"Intruders spotted at the far end of Eliot Street." She reached for her gun. "They'll be here any minute."

Chapter Forty-Six: Noah

The night air was chilly. Once they had started walking, they'd kept up a good pace, eager to get the job done. Noah had been glad to let Charlie guide them towards the warehouse location, but had found that much of the city was familiar to him now. Steering them along the back routes, the ex-guard had managed to avoid most of the citizens who were out on the streets.

"Y'okay?" Ruth nudged him with her shoulder as they walked.

It was a familiar gesture. For a moment, it felt like they were heading for their den in the caves, escaping from Harden and his buddies. How long ago that seemed.

"Yeah." He forced a smile. "I'm okay."

It was wonderful to be reunited with his friend, but his head was still reeling from the events at the academy. It had been a stressful night and the fight was far from over. Getting rid of Danforth's drug supply was a vital part of the mission.

But now that the academy girls were out of danger, all he wanted to do was get Faith to safety.

Ahead of them, Charlie paused as they approached the end of an alleyway, checking that the road was clear.

Noah leaned closer to his friend. "How come Paulo trusts her now?"

Ruth cocked her head to one side as they waited for some citizens to pass by. "Not long after you left, Flynn and Paulo set about making some changes to the way the prisoners were treated. Allowed them more freedom, included them more. Actually *talked* to them."

She stopped speaking as they crossed the road. When they had reached the safety of the alley on the other side, she continued.

"Turns out Charlie wasn't the most devoted guard. In fact, she regretted her decision to join the training programme almost as soon as she signed up."

"That's pretty much what she told me." Noah hesitated. "And we're sure she's on the level?"

"Pretty sure." Shooting Noah a sideways glance, Ruth grinned. "Charlie's one of the good guys. *Really*. Once we told her the truth about Eremus, about Danforth's lies, she was happy to help us. She's been working shifts in the caves, making herself useful."

They paused to walk single file as the alleyway narrowed. At the far end was a six-foot fence, which Charlie was already climbing. "Not to mention the fact that she's besotted with your brother." Ruth chuckled at the shock on Noah's face. "Believe me, she won't do anything to hurt him."

As Paulo followed the ex-guard over the fence, Ruth's words sank in. Noah closed his gaping mouth. "She and Paulo are...?"

"Oh yes. The feeling is *decidedly* mutual." Ruth smirked at him. "How could you miss the way they gawk at each other all the time?"

Noah recalled the looks the pair had exchanged. "I guess so. It's just–"

"What?" She gave his arm a friendly slap. "You can't imagine your brother in love?"

Noah blushed. "Not really."

"Not even," Ruth hesitated, as though she were afraid to finish the sentence, "when you feel that way about someone yourself?" Noah froze, unsure of how to answer. Ruth saved him the trouble by motioning to the fence. "Give me a boost, would you?"

As Noah bent to make a cradle of his hands, he pushed away his discomfort. Now was not the time to get distracted. Waiting until Ruth had reached the top of the fence, he followed. On the other side, Charlie was poised and ready to move off again.

"Not far now." She motioned to the street ahead, where there were fewer offices and more industrial-looking buildings. "Should be there in a couple of minutes."

She set off at a brisk pace, Paulo falling into step beside her as if it were the most natural thing in the world. Noah had to admit they seemed very much in tune. As he trudged along behind them, he became aware of Ruth's questioning glance.

"How have things been here?" She sent Noah a sideways glance. "I mean... how have you found being in the city? Pretending to be a drudge?"

"Tough." He sighed. "Not that I figured it was going to be easy, but..."

They walked in silence for several minutes. Eventually, Ruth spoke again.

"I couldn't believe it when I heard about Flynn." Her voice was quiet, the words hesitant. He got the impression she'd been working up to saying it, searching for the right time. "I'm so sorry."

Noah clenched his hands into fists. "I saw it happen."

"You were *there?*" Ruth jerked around to face him. "I can't..."

"Yeah, well," he glanced away, ashamed of his tears. "He didn't deserve it."

"He didn't."

There was a brief silence. They continued to walk next to one another, their shared grief enveloping them. Eventually, Ruth inhaled deeply.

"How's Faith?"

The abrupt change of topic told Noah she was trying to distract them both. Keep them focused. But the new subject was no better. Noah swallowed hard, trying to find the words.

"She's..." He drew in a breath. "Danforth has her... in the hospital." He felt Ruth stiffen. "And I was *right there*... with her... trying to work out how to rescue her, but..." He hung his head, the weight of the guilt returning. "I blew my cover."

He kicked at a stone on the pavement in front of him. It spun away, clanging against a metal gate on the other side of the street. Regretting the move instantly, he mouthed an apology at Paulo. When his brother's attention returned to their mission, he continued.

"We did have someone on the inside. A technician from the hospital. Madeleine was trying to get her to help... to support with a rescue."

He thought of Carol, the concerned tech who had showed up at the library door. Was she, even now, attempting to use the cloned keycards to get inside the fertility wards? *Would she succeed?*

"I've no idea if she'll get in. Security in the hospital is so tight now." He shrugged. "When we left the library, Madeleine hadn't heard from her."

"I'm sorry," Ruth frowned. "That's awful."

"Yeah. I just hope that, whatever the p-plan..." he cursed himself as he stumbled over the words, "I hope it works."

There was another silence.

"You know you love her, right?" Ruth didn't look at him. "I mean... it's obvious. You can't keep your mind on what we're doing, because–"

"Maybe." Noah quashed his embarrassment. "I mean, it's hard to concentrate, knowing she's in danger. And ..."

Ruth glanced away, giving him a moment to regain control.

He took a deep breath. "She's brave, you know? She went out of her way to get information to the Resistance, despite being Danforth's prisoner. The warehouse we're heading for?" He gestured at the road ahead. "One of three locations she discovered were linked to Danforth's experiments when she was in the hospital. She risked her life to share them with us."

"That sounds like Faith."

"Right?" Noah had a lump in his throat. "Because of her, we can cut off Danforth's drug supply. Even though..." he dropped his gaze, fighting for control, "even though Faith's probably being dosed with them herself right now."

Ahead of them, the rest of their team had stopped. Paulo peered around the corner of the building, while Charlie gestured up at the sign on the wall: *Eliot Street.*

Noah forced himself to focus. Whatever happened now, he had to be ready for it. Everything they'd worked for came down to what happened in the next few hours. Live or die, he couldn't let it all be for nothing. People were counting on them.

"Ready?" He glanced at Ruth.

"As I'll ever be." Grinning, she waved a hand at the street ahead. "Lead the way."

CHAPTER FORTY-SEVEN: FAITH

It was difficult to know what was going on outside. After Hammond's warning, Faith had retreated into the relative safety of the inner room. She had been joined moments later by an agitated Dr. Sanders.

"Get down." The doctor had thrust Faith into the space behind the bed. "And stay down."

With little choice, Faith had done as she was asked. Sanders had armed herself with a gun from a drawer in the cabinet at the bedside. Then, she had joined Faith. Together, they had waited.

At first, there was only silence. Faith could hear the sound of Sanders' ragged breathing mingling with her own. The woman she was trapped with was frightened. And she did not have Faith's best interests at heart. There was a good chance the Resistance knew Faith was in the Eliot Street warehouse. If they were here to rescue her, she had to let them know her location. But she didn't want to get caught in the cross-fire. For now, staying with Sanders seemed sensible. The doctor would want to keep her alive for the purposes of the experiment, if nothing else.

Faith glanced around her prison. Another way out might allow her to slip away, remove herself from the danger zone. But the room had no windows. The only escape was through the door. And while the femgazipane wasn't having as dramatic an effect on her this time, Faith was still a little disorientated. Rubbing her hands across her face, she tried to focus.

A resounding crash echoed through the warehouse, startling them both. It was quickly followed by the sound of thundering footsteps.

Faith imagined Madeleine, Evelyn, Noah, or Diane bursting in to save her. There was no point in trying to run if the intruders were here to rescue her.

Making a decision, Sanders began to creep towards the door, Faith tensed. Combat did not come naturally to the doctor. She held her gun in front of her, but her hands were shaking.

There was no way Faith could rely on her for protection. But she had limited options for defending herself. On the cabinet beside the bed lay the abandoned syringe. It was still loaded with the metraxilone, its end wickedly sharp.

Checking that Sanders' focus was still on the exit, Faith crept forward. Snatching the syringe, she ducked back behind the safety of the bed. She wasn't well-armed, but the needle was better than nothing. She held it in her fist, ready to stab it into an attacker if necessary.

She turned her attention to Sanders who was reaching for the door handle. But before she could touch it, the door burst open, knocking the weapon out of her hand.

The doctor cried out in pain, cradling her fingers to her chest. The weapon skittered away across the floor, coming to rest in the far corner. Faith eyed it. Was it close enough for her to get to it before the intruder spotted her? She glanced back at the door, but could see no one. The attacker was keeping her distance. For now.

Rallying a little, Sanders made a desperate leap for the gun. Before she could reach it, two shots rang out, deafening in the small space.

Sanders' body jerked in midair. Pulsed twice, as both bullets hit their mark. As Faith retreated behind the bed again, it struck her what an excellent shot the stranger was. There was a sickening thump as Sanders' body hit the ground a few feet away. The doctor lay at an odd angle, not moving. A small trickle of blood leaked from a wound in her head.

"Enemy down." The voice was harsh, and eerily familiar. "A medic, by the looks of things. Checking the rest of the room."

As a pair of heavy boots tramped in, Faith realised who the voice belonged to.

Sarah Porter.

Which meant the people invading the warehouse were Jacob and his group. Not allies. Sliding the syringe into the pocket of her gown, Faith steeled herself to face the woman who had held her captive once before.

CHAPTER FORTY-EIGHT: NOAH

"**I**t's the middle of the night." Noah stared at the others. "It was supposed to be empty."

His entire team wore similar expressions. Shock, disbelief, uncertainty. They were here to destroy the warehouse. But there were people inside.

And the gunshots suggested they were not friendly.

The group had crept the final distance to their target as one. Assembling in a shadowy doorway across the street, they had readied themselves. But as Charlie and Paulo had begun to unpack the explosives, the shots had cut through the night.

"What do we do now?" Ruth whispered. "We can't blow the place up if it's occupied."

"No." Paulo was scowling. "We can't. But there aren't enough of us to surround the place and clear it."

"I'll slip around back, see what else I can learn." Charlie hurried off across the street without hesitation.

The remaining trio waited in tense silence for a few minutes. Noah's mind whirled through possibilities. During their planning, Madeleine and Blake had been working on the assumption that too much was happening in the city for Danforth to keep a guard presence at the warehouse. But her stock of drugs was valuable. Too valuable, apparently.

It made sense that the warehouse was being guarded.

But the gunshots had been hostile. They implied a second force, one which was attacking those who guarded the drugs. Someone who had a grievance with Danforth.

There were numerous citizens all over the city who were angry. But they were unlikely to know about the warehouse. Even if they *had* learned of its location and wanted to act, they would have arrived mob-handed.

There was no crowd outside the warehouse. No clamour of protest, the way there had been at the academy.

This was a smaller, more organised group. One with some useful intel, and a personal grudge against the chancellor.

Noah turned to his brother, "Do you think it's—"

"Jacob?" His brother nodded grimly. "Could be."

"We can't know for certain." Ruth glanced between Noah and Paulo. "Not until we see them."

"We know he has limited numbers, at least." Paulo remained tense. "Without Harden, there are even fewer of them."

"But we have no idea how many of Danforth's forces are inside," Ruth countered.

"Could be one." Noah fought the rising panic. "Could be twenty."

"There were only two shots." Paulo frowned. "Doesn't sound like a massacre."

"More likely a stand-off of some kind." Ruth strained her neck, as though she might see through the walls. "If they had achieved their goal, Jacob's group would be out and running by now."

"You're probably right." Paulo rubbed a hand over his chin. "Either way, I'm not sure we should risk going through with what we have planned. Not without more intel. Larger numbers. More weapons."

Noah gestured to his wristclip. "Not without consulting Madeleine."

"Wait til Charlie gets back." Paulo was shifting from one foot to the other, his eyes searching for his partner's return. "See if she's learned anything useful."

"What if it is Jacob and..." Ruth hesitated, "and Madeleine tells us to go ahead anyway? Blow the place, despite him being inside?" She chewed her lip. "I don't know how I'd feel about that. About..."

"Killing him?" Noah shuddered. "Me neither. I'd hope she wouldn't want us to do that. The Resistance is about *reducing* the loss of life. *Saving* people, not killing them. But we're so close to our goal now. With the city in such chaos, Jacob puts our plans at risk."

"She might feel it's a necessary sacrifice." Ruth held Noah's gaze, her eyes intense. "Destroying these warehouses is vital. We do this, we stop the experimentation. Cut Danforth off. Make sure that–"

"That she can't continue to experiment on people." Noah nodded. "I know. It has to be done. But I don't want to do it at the expense of Jacob's life."

They fell silent. Several more tense moments passed before they spotted a shadowy figure hurrying along the street. When Charlie reached them, she shook her head.

"It's impossible to see inside. Place has limited windows, all of them covered. That's the main door," she pointed, "on the front of the building. There's a back exit, but it's padlocked."

"Hear anything helpful?"

She shook her head. "Walls are too thick. No more gunfire, at least. Looks like..."

Noah was distracted as his wristclip vibrated. Gesturing to the others, he tapped at the unfamiliar button and read the message scrolling up the tiny screen.

"It's Madeleine." He shrugged off the others, who were crowding in behind him. "She wants us to stand down."

"You think she knows what's going on in there?" Ruth was gazing at the warehouse intently, as though she might develop x-ray vision at any moment.

"Maybe. Instructions are to return to headquarters as soon as possible."

"But why?" Paulo reached for the clip. "Can't we ask her?"

"She says it's imperative we get out of here as soon as possible." Noah pulled his wrist out of his brother's reach. "We'll receive more information when we get there."

Paulo frowned. "But I thought she wanted this place destroyed?"

"She does. There must be a very good reason to call us back." Noah shrugged. "We'd better get going."

Scowling, Paulo and Charlie rezipped their packs. The group was ready to go within seconds. As they left the warehouse behind, Noah knew there was unfinished business inside. But they couldn't disobey Madeleine's orders.

They hurried through the streets as fast as they dared, keeping to the shadows where possible. As they reached the centre, a roaring sound split the air.

They turned as one. On the opposite side of the city, a thousand sparks flew skywards.

"The other warehouse!" Ruth's eyes were wide.

"One down." Noah inhaled deeply. "One to go."

But time was ticking on. For the plan to work, they had to get rid of both. And, right now, they had no idea why their mission had been aborted.

CHAPTER FORTY-NINE: FAITH

I t didn't take Sarah long to find her. Stalking through the room, the rebel's face lit up when she came across Faith crouching behind the bed.

"You!" Recovering quickly, she called back over her shoulder. "There's a *real* surprise waiting for us in here."

There was nowhere to run. Faith stood up, raising her hands above her head.

"Move it." Grasping her by the elbow, Sarah shoved her towards the door.

Faith kept her steps small. Her head was far from clear, and until the effects of the femgazipane wore off, she needed to take it slow. But her captor's iron grip was punishing.

She had a horrible flashback to her last experience with Sarah. The woman didn't have a compassionate bone in her body. She was fiercely loyal to her leader. And her son. But her cruelty towards her adversaries was legendary. The grip she had on Faith's arm was so tight it hurt, and she showed no signs of easing up as she thrust her prisoner through the doorway.

As she emerged into the warehouse, Faith took her time looking around. There was no sign of Danforth, Susie, or

Hammond. Were they hiding? But she had no more time to wonder as Sarah urged her forward.

"Found ourselves another useful hostage." Her tone was triumphant. "And she only had one guard."

"Well, well." A horribly familiar figure stepped forward. "Danforth's other favourite. This *is* fortunate." As Jacob studied her, his tone changed. "Better be on our guard, though. Could be a trap. I can't believe they've left her here with a single medic for protection."

Jacob was still a formidable figure, but he looked exhausted. His eyes were hooded and his face paler than Faith remembered. But the multitude of weapons he had strapped to his person filled her with terror. Tired or not, Jacob was dangerous.

Tearing her eyes away from him, Faith forced herself to take stock of the other people in the room. There were only two others, standing in the centre of the space. One, clearly, a prisoner.

Avery.

The other, her jailor. The man who stood behind her had a hand clamped on Avery's upper arm. With a start, Faith recognised Karl. Remembering the moment Diane had knocked him out to enable their escape from the Eremus cottage, Faith winced. Like the others, he was heavily armed. His face twisted in recognition, his eyes piercing Faith's cruelly.

Avoiding his gaze, Faith looked back at Avery. The change in her old adversary was shocking. Gone was the shiny blonde hair, the manicured nails, the perfectly made-up face. And missing, too, was the permanent sneer. Avery's skin was grey, her eyes bloodshot, and her figure almost skeletal. Her hair had been hacked short. She gazed down at the ground, her shoulders hunched.

"Avery?" Faith called out.

The older girl raised her head. Her eyes registered Faith's presence. There was a flicker of recognition, but she didn't speak.

"Are you alright?" Faith tried again.

Avery opened her mouth to speak, but before she could say anything she doubled over. A hoarse cough echoed out across the warehouse, the high ceiling amplifying the sound.

Faith attempted to move towards her old enemy, but Sarah's hold on her tightened. She struggled, but found herself being jerked backwards.

Faith glared over her shoulder. "What have you *done* to her?"

"She hasn't been harmed." Jacob took a step towards Faith. "We've all had to go without over the past few weeks." He narrowed his eyes. "Since I was driven out of Eremus."

"That's not what happened and you know it." Faith felt her anger flare, despite the dangerous situation. "You gave them no choice, the way you were acting."

"What would you know?" Sarah hissed.

A stab of fury lanced across the ex-leader's face, but he quickly masked it.

"Let's just say it's been... tough on us all. We've struggled to find food, supplies, safe places to sleep. And this little princess," he jerked a thumb in Avery's direction, "doesn't like being without her luxuries."

Faith kept her gaze on Avery, who sagged against her captor now the cough had subsided. "And her hair? Was it necessary to cut it all off?"

Sarah laughed, the sound unpleasant. "It isn't like we've had the facilities to wash properly."

Jacob nodded. "Long hair was just not... practical."

"Not to mention the little vixen tried to escape." Sarah was practically snarling. "We had to find a way to punish her."

"Without her coming to any harm, *of course.*" Jacob added.

That made more sense to Faith. A sanction for disobedience. It struck her, not for the first time, how similar Jacob and Danforth's leadership styles were. And how vindictive.

"Never mind that." Jacob shook his head. "We now have *two* valuable hostages. Things might finally be coming together."

Faith ran through Jacob's group in her head. More than four people had fled Eremus with the ex-leader. Where was Harden? Sil? And there was another man whose name she couldn't remember, she was sure of it.

As the outer door of the warehouse opened, they all turned. A man Faith did not recognise slipped inside. Perhaps the man she'd been thinking of. Tall and dark haired, his expression was steely.

"Trouble, Denton?" Jacob tensed.

Denton. That was his name. Faith glanced around the warehouse again. Were Harden and Sil guarding other entrances?

"Maybe." The stranger kept his gun trained on the door. "Thought I heard voices. Saw some figures in the shadows. Might be nothing, but..."

"We're not taking any chances. Not when we're this close." Jacob gestured to Sarah. "Take them both in there. Keep them out of the way 'til we work out what's going on."

Grunting her agreement, Sarah manhandled Faith inside the smaller room again.

"*Don't* try anything." Sarah's voice was harsh, quashing Faith's optimism. "Or I'll make sure you regret it."

Faith tried not to look at Sanders' body as Sarah shoved her down on the bed and fastened her wrists together with twine. Pulling it taut, she seemed to take pleasure in Faith's wince of pain.

Seconds later, Karl brought Avery in. As he thrust her on to the bed next to Faith, she could see that the other girl's hands were already tightly bound. Noticing Sanders, Avery paled, but she clamped her lips shut, saying nothing. She was a different girl. The old Avery squealed at the slightest discomfort, yet here she was bearing the sight of a dead body without a sound.

Satisfied their captives weren't going anywhere, Sarah and Karl backed away, pulling the door closed behind them. Faith's heart sank as a key turned in the lock. Taking a deep breath, she tried to think things through. Much as she wanted to hope that the disturbance outside was the Resistance coming to rescue her, Danforth was a more likely candidate. The chancellor had been here only moments ago. The intruders had spooked her, but she would never abandon her only remaining trial subject so easily.

Danforth's disappearance had to be a ploy. Perhaps she was, even now, surrounding the building with guards. Preparing to storm in and execute Jacob's entire group. The thought didn't bring Faith any relief. With Jacob gone, she'd be right back in the chancellor's clutches.

At least the interruption had bought her a little time. She fingered the syringe in her pocket. Now was not the time to use it. But she felt comforted knowing it was there.

Becoming aware of her laboured breathing, Faith turned to face Avery. Her old adversary hadn't spoken since they'd entered the room.

"You okay, Avery?" There was no response. "Look at me!" Avery dragged her gaze upwards. "I'm so sorry you've had it so rough. But you can't lose hope."

A flicker of the old spirit lit Avery's eyes for a moment. But it died away as quickly as it had appeared.

"What's Jacob planning?" Faith angled her head towards the door. "What can we do?"

Avery stared at her. The skin on her lips was chapped and broken.

"We can't do *any*–" her voice cracked. She dragged in a wheezy breath. "Anything."

"There must be *something*–"

"There. Is. Nothing." Avery shuddered. "These people are... they're *so*..." She didn't appear able to string a complete sentence together. "Not just... the *men*." Her eyes were wild. "The woman is worse." She broke off, coughs racking her body again. Her eyes were watering by the time she regained control. "Once Harden left, Sarah–"

"Wait!" Faith grasped her arm. "Harden's gone?"

"You don't know?" as Avery raised an eyebrow, realising she had something over her old adversary. "He didn't come back from a mission. Couple days ago." She nodded at the sound of raised voices on the other side of the door. "His mother's livid about it. His friend Sil disappeared a couple of days later, too."

Aware they were running out of time, Faith tried to bring the focus back to their situation.

"We have to find out what they're planning. You haven't overheard anything?" Faith wanted to shake the older girl. "Caught sight of any documents?"

But Avery's gaze had wandered towards Sanders's body.

"Who's..." she paused, fighting to keep herself from coughing, "t-that?"

"A doctor. One of Danforth's best." Faith felt no sadness at the woman's passing. "She was about to–"

Avery averted her gaze. "Trust me, it's easier to just... let it happen." She drew in another shaky breath. "Otherwise, we'll end up like the doctor there."

"You can't give up." Faith nudged the other girl with her elbow. "You're their hostage, right? They're holding you because you're valuable. It's why they've kept you alive all this time." She leaned a little closer, dropping her voice to a whisper. "Danforth's here. Somewhere in this building. At least, she was, not long ago."

Avery's eyes widened. "Really?"

"I don't know where she is right now." Faith glanced at the door. "But I think it's safe to say she's coming back. And that there'll be trouble when she does. It would be great if we could get out of here *before* that happens."

"Get out of here?" Avery's face had brightened. "But if Danforth's coming, she'll *save* us."

"You really think so?" Faith wanted to slap some sense into her. "After all this time, you think she actually *cares* about us?"

"*Us*? No." Some of the old arrogance returned to Avery's face. "But *me*? Well, let's just say I'm a little..." she paused to cough, "*d-different* than the rest of you."

Faith's heart beat a little faster. Did Avery *know*?

"If you say so." She considered her next words carefully. "Look, Danforth has bigger things on her mind, right now. Jacob is just one of her problems. How can you think she'd waste time saving two random girls from–"

"Because I'm not a random girl. I'm special." Avery tossed her head, then grimaced at her lack of hair. "She and I have a..." she hesitated, as though she knew she was sharing a secret, "a bond, of sorts."

Both girls tensed at the sound of shouting on the other side of the door.

"You think because she's your biological mother she'll protect you?" Faith felt a stab of satisfaction as the other girl's eyes flew wide. "Yeah, I'm aware of your connection to her."

"Well, if you must know, *yes*. Why do you think I always got better treatment at the academy?" Now that she felt she had an ally on the way, Avery's sneer was back. "I was only there to report back to her. K-keep an eye on the rest of you."

Faith had suspected as much, but the confirmation was still shocking. "So you were a *spy*?" She couldn't keep the contempt from her voice.

"I was." Briefly, Avery looked shamefaced, but the expression was quickly quashed. "Danforth didn't trust the girls at the academy. Some of the staff, even. But she trusted me." Again, she paused, wheezing, but determined to finish her sentence. "She *needed* me t-there. And she n-needs me now."

"Does she?" Insecurity flashed across Avery's face. "You think she truly cares about you? Or that you're even still *useful* to her?" Faith could see the impact her words were having. "Did she go out searching for you when you were first kidnapped? No." She pressed on, hating the pain she was causing. But she had to make Avery see sense. "What makes you think this will be any different?"

Avery opened her mouth to reply, but before she could, the door flew open.

Chapter Fifty: Noah

As they approached the library, the streets felt electric. Noah let his gaze roam, revelling in the sense of freedom. Bellator seemed to have tipped on its axis in the past few hours. Things were changing.

The Bellator citizens were out in force, either marching towards the academy or the new government headquarters. Every woman they passed was demanding answers. And whilst some of them recoiled from Noah and Paulo, many of the women regarded them with curiosity.

It was progress. Noah wished he could celebrate.

None of the women were brave enough to attempt a conversation with a man yet. But as a female, Ruth had been able to speak to several of them in passing.

News of Danforth's involvement in the Bellator bombing had spread through the city like wildfire. And the women were furious. There were whispers that the academy was overrun with citizens, curious to see it for themselves. The remaining students would be safe from Danforth, Noah reassured himself, because there were so many members of the public present.

Once the drugs had been completely destroyed, Danforth would have nothing left to test on the girls anyway. He glanced to the west, where the smoke of the Acton Street Warehouse still billowed into the sky. The explosions were supposed to happen simultaneously. But until they could work out what was going on inside the Eliot Street location, it was still standing.

There was a distinct lack of guard presence on the street. News was, they had abandoned the academy as a lost cause, and most of them had been called to defend the temporary government headquarters. The number of women protesting, some armed with banners scrawled with hasty slogans, some with actual weapons, was rumoured to be unmanageable.

Order was unravelling in Bellator. The Resistance was gaining power by the minute.

But with Faith's fate hanging in the balance, there was no time to celebrate.

At the top of the library steps, Paulo hesitated. "You sure we're welcome here?"

"They might be a little... surprised. They don't usually use this entrance, but..."

Noah had considered entering the library through the tunnel but wasn't sure that he'd be allowed into the shop across the square without a female Resistance member. And, he figured, with the city in such chaos, a small group entering the library through the side door would go unnoticed. At least, he hoped they would. Noting his brother's apprehension, he pasted on a smile.

"The Resistance knows what you've done for them. And there might be more you can do, if you're willing." He stared at his brother. "Don't tell me you're actually nervous?"

"I'm not!" The response came too quickly. Paulo blushed. "It's just... I've never dealt with Bellator women en masse before. Only with Madeleine, and occasionally Evelyn. I just..."

Beside him, Charlie was smirking. "We're not aliens, you know."

"Shut up." He threw her a dark look. "Just ring the bell, would you?"

Noah did as he asked. Paulo and Charlie were an unlikely couple, but he'd begun to revise his original opinion of them. Charlie was a different woman than the one he had disarmed in the tunnel. No longer acting out of fear, not bound by the guard rules, she was relaxed and lighthearted. She even teased Paulo, something which he'd never known anyone to get away with.

Perhaps she was just what his brother needed. And who was he to judge a relationship between an Eremus man and a Bellator woman? It was hypocritical of him, when he wanted the same thing with Faith.

His heart quickened as he thought of her again, and he pressed the bell a second time. When the door finally opened, he was thankful to see Diane on the other side.

"Glad you made it back so fast. Lots to fill you in on." She gestured at the smoky sky. "At least one of them is gone." She stared at Paulo, who seemed to have frozen on the doorstep. "Come on in, then!"

He obeyed stiffly. "What's going on?"

Diane closed the door behind them. "Madeleine will explain."

Refusing to say any more, she led them through a deserted hub.

"Where is everyone?" Noah stared around at the usually-bustling room.

"Out on missions." Diane threw back over her shoulder. "Except me, Blake, and Rowan. And Madeleine, of course."

The leader was pacing the floor when they entered her office. She stopped at their arrival, her face tense.

"Thank goodness you're back! We thought we might be too late." She ran her gaze across the group. Her eyes settled on Charlie and she frowned. "Who is this?"

Noah stepped forward. "This is Charlie. She was the sole surviving guard from the tunnel attack on Eremus." As Madeleine's face darkened, he hastened to add. "She's on our side now."

"She came with you from Eremus?" This was directed at Paulo.

"She did. And she guided us to the warehouse we were *supposed* to be destroying for you." Paulo's tone was defensive. "But if she's not welcome..."

Madeleine shrugged. "I didn't say that. We have to be careful, is all." She sat down in her usual chair and turned to Charlie. "Would you mind waiting outside for now? No offence, but I'm not happy with you hearing the precise details of our mission before I trust you."

"No offence taken." Charlie shrugged. "Just know that I have guard experience. And I'm on your side. If there's anything I can do to help, let me know."

Madeleine waited until she had exited. "Let me bring you up to speed. Things were going very well until the recent setback. As you know, Blake's team managed to extract most of the senior girls from the academy. You finished the job by getting Helen out and securing Anderson's confession. I've just had word from Eremus that the group arrived safely. They're being settled into the caves as we speak." She turned to Noah. "Your ma went ahead of them. She assures me that most of them are adjusting well."

"They will be, if Anna's there," Paulo said.

Noah swallowed hard. The faith his brother had in his ma was humbling. With the loss of Flynn, he had worried his brother would retreat into himself. Instead, it seemed he was drawing strength from his other relationships. Hopefully, Noah would be among those who his brother turned to.

"In terms of Danforth," Madeleine continued, "the truth is well and truly out. Thanks to your assistance, Anderson's speech was aired live to every single woman on the march. *Anyone* who was outside the school tonight heard her admission about Danforth's guilt."

For the first time, Noah found himself thinking of Kemp. "The professor was heading here when she left us." His heart beat faster. "Isn't she back yet?"

"Don't worry." Diane caught the concern on his face. "She's been and gone."

Madeleine nodded. "We duplicated the recording immediately. Kemp took a copy to Stella Thane a while back." A fleeting grin crossed the Resistance leader's face. "The woman's been broadcasting it on every frequency possible for the last hour."

"I don't think there's a citizen in Bellator who hasn't heard the truth." Diane whistled. "And these women are *angry*."

"They really are. We met a few on our way back here," Ruth explained.

Madeleine gave a satisfied grin. "There's no *way* Danforth can come back from this."

"So what's going on inside the Eliot Street Warehouse?" Paulo closed his hand into a fist. "We heard shots."

Madeleine froze. "Shots, you say?"

Noah's heart contracted. "That's not why you asked us to step down?"

Ignoring his question, Madeleine turned to Diane. "You'd better go tell Blake. See if she's managed to hack into any of the nearby security cameras." As Diane hurried to obey, the leader turned to Paulo. "Describe what happened."

For once, Noah was happy to let his brother respond. "We heard two shots while we were standing across the street preparing to plant the explosives. We were about to contact you to ask what to do when you sent Noah that message." He stared at Madeleine. "What's going on?"

The Resistance leader turned to face Noah. "You remember I reassured you that there was a plan in place to help Faith?"

"Yes." He tried not to panic. "Didn't it work?"

"Not exactly, no." She frowned. "Carol, the technician who came to us?" He nodded. "She agreed to help with our plan to rescue Faith."

Noah had known this already. "Did something go wrong?"

"We provided Carol with a keycard to access the fertility wards." Madeleine held up a hand at Noah's questioning gaze. "As you know, Blake and I have been working on the tech for universal keycards to give us access to any of Danforth's private buildings. We weren't certain it would work until someone tried it. Anyway, she managed to get inside. But Faith was heavily sedated. There was no way Carol could have moved her alone."

"What did she do then?" Ruth had been standing close to the door but took several steps towards Madeleine's desk as she spoke. Her face was pale. "Is Faith okay?"

"Honestly," Madeleine looked down at her desk, "we're not sure. Carol reduced Faith's sedation levels, hoping she might regain consciousness, but it wasn't going to happen fast enough." Madeleine didn't sugarcoat it. "Not to the level where she would be able to walk."

A weight settled on Noah's shoulders. Faith was still stuck in the hospital.

"We did, however, have a Plan B which Carol managed to execute." Madeleine's expression brightened. "Before she left, Carol implanted a tracking chip in the back of Faith's neck." The Resistance leader held a hand out to prevent Noah from interrupting. "A backup option, so we could keep tabs on where she was."

Paulo lowered his frame into one of the chairs opposite Madeleine's desk. "What has this got to do with the warehouse?"

"Quite a lot, I'm afraid. Since Carol left the hospital, we've been tracking Faith's chip." As Madeleine continued, a sense of foreboding crept over Noah. "Earlier today, she was moved."

Noah's hand started to shake. "Where to?"

He was pretty sure he knew the answer.

"Well, that's the curious thing," Madeleine turned the datadev screen in front of her around. They could all see a map of the city. "According to her chip, she's currently located in the Eliot Street Warehouse."

The world around Noah went fuzzy. He shook his head, trying to clear it. "*What?*"

"This is her." Madeleine pointed to a red dot which blinked on and off intermittently. "See?"

"You mean...?" Noah felt sick.

"I mean," Madeleine's body tensed, "if you hadn't received our message in time, Faith would be–"

The Resistance leader didn't have to finish the sentence. As Noah fought to control his rising panic, all he could think about was how close they'd been to blowing up the very place that Faith was being held captive.

And, if they had ignored Madeleine's orders, how close they could have been to rescuing her.

Chapter Fifty-One: Faith

There was no hesitation as Sarah entered the room, closely followed by Karl. Together, they grappled the two girls into a standing position. Sarah took charge of Avery this time, and was no gentler with her than she had been with Faith. The two hostages were thrust towards the door. Sarah eased it open a crack, wedging her boot in the gap so they could hear what was going on outside.

"I knew you'd show up eventually." Jacob's voice carried easily. "When you realised that I'd taken charge of your precious cargo."

"*Precious cargo?*" It was Danforth, as chillingly calm, as ever. "What on earth can you mean?"

Faith's instincts had been dead on. Danforth had not gone far. And she had returned swiftly to deal with Jacob and his group. But how many guards did the chancellor have backing her up? Sensing Jacob was readying himself for the big reveal, Faith braced herself.

"Well, *Chancellor,*" Jacob's voice dripped with false politeness, "we happen to have a couple of hostages you might be interested in."

Faith's mind was racing. What did Jacob hope to achieve? With so few allies, what did he think Danforth would be willing to trade that could possibly strengthen his position?

"What makes you think I'd have any interest in bargaining with you?" Danforth shrugged off his threat. "Whatever advantage you *think* you have. Doesn't seem like you have a lot of support right now."

"What about you?" Jacob's tone dripped poison. "I see you don't have your usual army around you."

"I can *assure you*, this building is surrounded," Danforth sniffed. "You have no hope of success."

"Well let's see, shall we?" Jacob was gritting his teeth. "Perhaps when you know which of your citizens I'm holding prisoner, you'll change your mind. I don't *need* a massive force behind me for what I have in mind." He paused for a moment. When he spoke again, his voice was chilling. "Bring them out."

At Jacob's command, Faith and Avery were pushed out through the doorway. Faith stumbled as she crossed the threshold. Karl yanked her upright, sending a lance of pain through her shoulder. Once she had regained her footing, she attempted to assess the situation.

The chancellor stood on the other side of the warehouse, just inside the door. Her body was strategically positioned behind three guards. Hammond stood front and centre, still heavily armed. Her gun was pointing at Jacob and the man he'd called Denton. The ex-Eremus men stood their ground, centre-stage, their own guns pointing at the group by the door.

The other guards had their guns trained on Sarah and Karl as they brought the hostages into the room. At the rear of their group was Susie, the remaining medic. She appeared to be unarmed and was dwarfed by her protectors.

Danforth's iron control remained as her eyes met Faith's. This, she had expected. But when she glanced at Jacob's second captive, her eyes widened. Her enemy had managed to surprise her.

Another bout of coughing racked Avery's body, cutting through the tension. As she struggled to control herself, Jacob shot her a look of pure hatred. She had ruined the drama of his big reveal, allowing Danforth time to recover her composure. More than that, her cough told the chancellor at least one of the hostages was less-than-healthy, reducing Jacob's bargaining power.

"I believe," Jacob pushed on, despite the interruption. "That these two young women are of great importance to you."

"Perhaps." Danforth shrugged delicately. "But you can't think that I'll let you get away with such audacious behaviour. *No one* threatens me." She shook her head. "I'll never agree to your demands."

"What makes you think I *have* demands?" There was a hatred burning in his eyes.

Suddenly, Faith understood. Jacob knew he didn't have the backup to beat Danforth. He'd given up on that goal. Which only left...

"All I want," he went on, "is to see you suffer."

Faith's heart sank. If Jacob wanted to punish Danforth, the best way to do it would be to destroy the people she needed to succeed. He was mistaken about Avery, she was certain. Daughter or not, Danforth did not seem to care either way about the young woman. But all the chancellor's hopes of success with the fertility experiments rested with Faith. Her death would be a huge blow.

With a sideways glance to check that his backup still had a gun trained on Danforth's group, Jacob stalked towards Avery. Sarah relinquished her hold on Avery, aiming her own weapon at Hammond. Grasping her arm so hard that she winced, Jacob thrust his prisoner to her knees. It was a position he'd once had Faith in. That time, it had been an empty threat.

This time, Jacob was deadly serious.

Avery's eyes flew to her mother. She really was expecting Danforth to save her life. Faith had no such delusions. The woman might have brought Avery into the world, made her feel special in her role as infiltrator at the academy, but she had failed to protect her when it mattered.

Looking back, it all made sense. Avery's superiority complex, her disdain for the other girls at the academy, her entitled attitude. Faith had hated her for it, in the past. Now, she pitied her.

"This young woman," Jacob went on, his voice low and threatening, "is your own flesh and blood, I believe."

He raised his gun, resting it on Avery's temple. She whimpered, the wheeze even more pronounced by her terror.

"And?" Danforth shrugged. "You think we live like you do in Eremus? That we have the same bonds with our biological offspring? The girl has helped me in the past, it's true. And she is my... *daughter*. But that means very little in the scheme of things. Here in Bellator we're about the good of the *many*."

Avery's face fell as the truth hit home. She had been fooled into thinking she was special to the woman who ruled over Bellator. But in the end, she was little more than a cog in a wheel.

"Oh, Abigail." Jacob's knuckles were white and his face had drained of colour. Grasping hold of the remnants of Avery's hair, he pressed the gun hard against her skull. "I think you're bluffing."

"Am I?" Danforth remained calm, but her eyes flickered to Faith briefly. "I think not. I've always been fascinated by procreation. It's true, this girl is my offspring. But I only had her out of curiosity. Wanted to know what it was like to bear a child."

She took a step closer to Jacob, her eyes on her daughter. Hammond moved with her.

"I had a medic inseminate me with seed from the bank. Chosen at random, of course." Her eyes stayed with Avery, who was chalk-white. "I wanted the experiment to be devoid of any kind of engineering. I observed the changes that took place in my body during pregnancy. At the birth. Postnatally. It was an extremely useful part of my research." Now she looked at Jacob. "But after she was born, I checked the records."

Faith went cold. She knew what was coming. As Danforth continued, she braced herself for the fallout.

"When I found out who her seed donor was, well…" a haunting smile graced her face, "let's just say I was less-than-happy."

"Her *seed donor*?" Jacob frowned.

"It was you." Danforth paused for a moment, letting the dust from the bombshell settle. "I lost interest in her after that." She didn't look at Avery, even when the young woman gave a moan of misery. "Until later, when I figured out that she could be useful to me at the academy."

"What?" Jacob's eyes were wild. "But… I didn't–"

"Oh Jacob," Danforth swooped in for the killer blow, her tone silky-sweet. "She's not just *my* flesh and blood. She's yours. *Now* are you going to shoot her?"

Jacob's hold on the gun went slack. Confusion and fury warred on his face. "You're lying." He thrust the weapon into Avery's temple again. She was crying now. Silent tears coursing down her face. Every breath she took sounded painful. "Bluffing, to protect her. Well, let me show you how far that gets you."

He cocked the gun. The clicking sound echoed through the empty space.

"No!" The word was out of Faith's mouth before she could stop it. "She's telling the truth."

Every eye in the room swung to face her. Faith cringed.

"How would *you* know?" Jacob frowned.

Danforth regarded her with interest. Her eyes reminded Faith of a snake.

"I read about it. In the records at the hospital." She took a desperate breath. "She's your daughter too. You can't kill her."

A heavy silence filled the warehouse. Jacob's breathing was heavy and ragged as he fought to take in the new information. His seed had been used to create hundreds of Bellator children, but he'd never known them. The news that the damaged young woman who knelt in front of him was his daughter had floored him.

Eventually, he lowered the gun and took a step back. A wide smile spread across Danforth's face as she sensed the change in her enemy. Faith tensed, dreading the moment when the attention returned to her.

"Not willing to kill your own offspring, then?" Danforth was almost laughing at Jacob's struggle. "You never did have what it takes, did you? Not like me. I assure you, I'm willing to do whatever is necessary to protect my people."

Faith recoiled at the words. The woman was a monster. How could she believe, after everything, that she had the best interests of her citizens at heart?

She refocused on Jacob, hoping Avery's reprieve wasn't just a temporary one. He was frozen, his expression haunted, fixated on the young woman who knelt in front of him. Would he make the right decision? After all he'd done, sparing his daughter might be the first step on the road to redemption.

But the chancellor wasn't finished provoking him. "My actions may seem extreme, but I assure you, they get results. I mean..." she paused, enjoying his discomfort. "I'm sure you already know how easily I *disposed* of your comrade."

At the callous mention of Flynn, Faith clenched her fists. How could the woman be so cruel?

Beside Faith, Sarah had stiffened.

"*Disposed of?*" she ground out.

Her reaction struck Faith as odd. Perhaps Jacob's group had yet to hear of Flynn's death. But did they care that much about him, after he'd pretty much run them out of Eremus?

Danforth ploughed on, oblivious to the tension. "I wasn't going to show leniency to a man who'd invaded my territory that way."

Sarah stepped closer to Avery again. Her face was twisted with a fury Faith didn't understand.

"*You killed my son?*" she hissed, her voice low and menacing.

"Your son?" Danforth questioned. "I don't–"

As the penny dropped, Faith realised the misunderstanding. But it was too late.

Narrowing her eyes, Sarah redirected her gun at Avery. "Let's see how *you* like it."

"No!" A cry escaped from Faith as the shot rang out.

Avery's body jerked once, then collapsed forward.

Faith found herself stumbling forward, dizziness overwhelming her. As Karl's hold on her tightened, she was glad of the support. It stopped her from collapsing.

Jacob stepped forward, bending down next to Avery. Gently, he turned her body over. Blood was gushing from a single wound in her chest. Her eyes were filled with horror as she attempted to breathe. Her breathing had already been laboured. Now, the sound was guttural. Faith recalled distant biology lessons. The bullet had punctured Avery's lung. And the effort it took for her to inhale suggested the damage was severe.

She glanced around. All eyes were fixed on Jacob and Avery. Even Sarah appeared to be frozen in place. Jacob's reaction had shocked her. As Faith returned her gaze to the pair on the ground, Danforth leaned close to Hammond, whispering something.

Jacob had his hands pressed to the hole in the middle of Avery's chest. They were soaked with blood.

"You're alright." He choked out. "You'll be alright."

But Avery's breaths were becoming less and less frequent. Her eyes sought Jacob's, and she lifted a hand, grasping at the air. Taking it in his own, Jacob brought it to his chest and bowed his head.

"C-can't't," Avery stuttered. "I c-c-can't…"

"Shh," Jacob hushed her, his tone unusually gentle. "Rest now."

Avery's eyes began to flicker. The blood flow from the wound seemed to have slowed, and she hadn't taken a breath for what seemed like forever. Faith was desperate to look away, but found that she couldn't.

There was a silence which went on for what seemed like forever. Eventually, Jacob bent to press a finger to Avery's neck. His body sagged.

"Gone," he said, releasing his hold on Avery's hand. He closed her eyes. "She's gone."

A shockwave reverberated through the room. Faith trembled. Behind her Karl had relaxed his hold a little, but she didn't even consider running.

Sarah stepped forward and placed a hand on Jacob's shoulder. Jacob jerked away as though she were contagious.

"Get away from me." He stood up, gesturing at Avery's lifeless form. "How could you?"

Sarah's eyes were wide with shock. "I'm sorry. I didn't think…" She paused, seemingly at a loss. "She doesn't *mean* anything to you. You've been cursing her for *weeks*." Reholstering her gun, she stepped closer. "So why…"

Jacob shook his head. Grief was carved into the lines on his face. "A child. *My* child."

Sarah blanched at his expression. "I'm sorry. I–"

But she didn't get any further. As Jacob's hand went to his belt, Sarah's eyes filled with horror. He raised his arm, aiming a gun at her head.

"No! Please, no." She stammered. "You're not thinking straight. You can't–"

For the second time in as many minutes, a gunshot destroyed the quiet of the warehouse. Sarah took a direct hit to the chest. Falling forwards, she hit the ground and lay still.

Danforth started laughing. The sound was vaguely hysterical. "You're hardly a threat if you're going to start taking out your own people," she sneered at the ex-Eremus leader. "I always said you were a little on the stupid side. You just proved me right."

Jacob faced her, his face twisted in fury. "Don't you care at all?" He thrust a hand at Avery. "Your own *child*, and her death has no impact?"

Danforth shrugged.

With a desperate howl, Jacob raised his gun again. He charged forward, his face scarlet with fury. But once he was clear of Faith, he lost his advantage. Hammond now had a clear shot at a man who was threatening her chancellor. She took it, firing a single bullet.

It hit Jacob right between the eyes.

As his body collapsed, Karl let go of Faith. He raised his hands over his head. Denton followed suit.

Jacob's rebellion was finished. But Danforth was still a threat. As the chancellor's eyes zeroed in on Faith, she recoiled. Her own suffering was far from over.

CHAPTER FIFTY-TWO: NOAH

The dot on the screen continued to blink.

On. Off. On. Off.

Noah fought the urge to scream.

His team had been back at headquarters for more than an hour. The Resistance knew where Faith was. They knew she was in danger. Yet still, Madeleine was hesitating, debating the best course of action.

It was infuriating.

Noah's team had been offered refreshments. While the others had eagerly accepted the offer, Noah had insisted on remaining in the office, eager to know when they would set out to save Faith. After grabbing some coffee and a couple of energy bars, Ruth had joined him. But when Kemp had arrived back from the safehouse, filled with tales of the various riots raging in the city, Noah had lost hope of them ever taking action.

As the conversation swirled around him, he focused on breathing, keeping his eyes on the tiny red light. He'd fooled himself that as long as the light kept flashing, Faith would be alright. Like the blinking red dot represented her heartbeat, still going strong.

"Message from Olivia," Diane interrupted the conversation, gesturing to her wristclip. "Acton Street Warehouse was decimated by the blast. She's on her way to join Evelyn now."

"Evelyn's moved to the temporary government HQ," Madeleine explained to Ruth. "Keeping an eye on things."

"I've just come from there," Kemp said. "Situation's really getting out of hand. There are more than a thousand citizens outside the building, all demanding to see their chancellor."

Madeleine whistled under her breath. "The guards must be struggling to cope."

"They are. And there's no sign of Danforth." Kemp frowned. "But they're refusing to leave. The women were preparing to storm the place as I left. Actually," the professor cocked an eyebrow, "it's not just women. There are quite a few drudges there too."

"The tides really *are* turning." Madeleine turned to face Diane. "Get Rowan down there. See if he's able to speak to the drudges... gauge their mood."

"Sure." Diane stood up.

"And check on Blake while you're at it, would you? We haven't heard anyth–"

But before she could finish her sentence, the door burst open. Blake stood on the other side, her eyes wild.

"Managed to hack into a camera... on a side street close..." She was out of breath. "Close to the warehouse. Not the greatest view, but–"

"Is something happening?" Noah tore his eyes from the blinking dot. "Have you seen Faith?"

"Not Faith." Blake shook her head. "But several of Danforth's guards appeared out of nowhere. They've surrounded the building."

"Surrounded it?" Madeleine barked. "When?"

"Couple of minutes ago." Blake shrugged. "They all arrived at once, like they'd been... ordered there... for a specific reason. They look like they're protecting the building. Or the drugs. Waiting for–"

A pinging sound interrupted her. Diane raised her wristclip, scanning the incoming message.

"It's another update from Olivia." Her eyes widened as she scanned the message on her wristclip. "She and Evelyn are *inside* government headquarters." She turned to face them. "Danforth's not there."

"I wonder if..." Madeleine turned to Blake. "You said these guards arrived together... like they'd been summoned." She swung to face the others. "What if they're not there to protect the *drugs*, but to–"

"...protect *Danforth*." Noah forced himself to breathe. "If she's not at headquarters, it would make sense that she's there... with Faith..."

"She's protecting her only remaining asset," Blake agreed.

"What's the point?" Ruth asked. "Does she really think she can change the minds of the citizens after everything they've learned tonight?"

"I think she's desperate." Madeleine shrugged. "And desperate people do desperate things. Think about it. She believes the only thing that can bring her people back to her is the success of her experiment. She'll do *anything* to defend it."

"But if Jacob's inside the warehouse," Ruth chewed on her lip, "things won't be quite so simple. She'll *need* the extra guards to–"

"We have to get down there." Noah sat forward in his chair. "Right away."

"We do." Madeleine waved him away. "But we'll have to be careful. It's a volatile situation. We'll need a large enough force to deal with the guards, and, potentially, Jacob too."

As Madeleine and Blake bent their heads together, discussing potential operatives for the mission, Noah heaved a sigh of relief. Finally, they were taking some action.

He turned back to the blinking red dot.

We're coming for you. He willed her to hear him. *Hang on.*

The dot kept blinking.

Chapter Fifty-Three: Faith

She was exhausted. The effects of the femgazipane had mostly worn off, but the night's events had taken their toll.

Once the remaining members of Jacob's gang had surrendered, Danforth had called in additional guards from outside. Jacob was no longer an issue, but it seemed she had bigger problems. One of the reinforcements had whispered something in Danforth's ear as she entered.

The chancellor's face had paled. "*All* of it?"

"The entire warehouse." The guard had hesitated. "There's nothing salvageable."

Struggling to recover her composure, Danforth had gestured to the prisoners. "Get them out of here. Put them in a holding cell, for now. And tell the tech team at HQ to suspend the comms network for the time being. Let's make things difficult for the rebels." As the guard obeyed, Danforth had turned to Hammond. "Keep an eye on *her*." She had nodded at Faith, then beckoned Susie across. They had begun speaking in low, hushed tones.

Standing amongst the bodies of Avery, Sarah, and Jacob, nausea overwhelmed Faith. Whilst none of them had been friends, their deaths had been so violent, so futile.

Jacob, finding a twisted connection with Avery. His abhorrence of Danforth was rooted in the way she had treated him. Using his seed over the years had forced him to father countless children with no control and no chance of ever knowing any of them. The idea must have haunted him every day since he had fled from Bellator.

To find himself face-to-face with a young woman who was *actually* his daughter had shaken him to the core. A young woman he'd spent the last few weeks treating terribly as a result of his hatred for Danforth. Someone he'd been prepared to execute as revenge for the chancellor's treatment of him.

It had been a cruel blow.

And Sarah, killing Avery in vengeance for Danforth killing Harden. An eye for an eye. Faith wasn't even sure that Harden was dead. The fact that the chancellor had instructed her guards to arrest Karl and Denton implied she didn't always shoot first and ask questions later. If Harden was still alive, Sarah's act had been a pointless one.

Witnessing Avery's death at Sarah's hands, only seconds after discovering the truth, had pushed Jacob over the edge. Executing his loyal secondary had been extreme, but Faith could see why he'd done it.

His last desperate charge at Danforth had been nothing more than a suicide mission.

The bond between parent and child was a complex one, Faith reflected. She had witnessed Sarah criticise Harden, yell at him, order him to take actions she was certain he was uncomfortable with. Yet, when it came to it, she loved him enough to kill for him. Jacob had no bond with Avery, yet learning of their connection had impacted him profoundly.

The Bellator way did not allow children to develop a deep connection with either parent. Yet most of the citizens Faith knew had developed extremely close friendships. Substitutes for what was missing from their lives. Bellator had it all wrong. Perhaps some of the Eremus family units were dysfunctional. But they had a far better system than Danforth had created. Most of their issues were born out of the way the chancellor had forced them to live. In hiding, fearing for their lives.

She thought of Anna and Flynn, the way they had created a loving family unit, despite the lack of biological ties between Noah and Flynn, and Anna and Paulo. They were living proof that a family could be everything to each other, no matter what. Faith sighed, hating the fact that Danforth had broken the best family she'd ever known.

The guards handcuffed the remaining prisoners, conversing in hushed whispers over their heads. It was difficult to make out what they were saying. But from the snippets of conversation Faith caught, crowds were causing problems all over the city. There had been outbreaks of violence in several different locations, and Danforth's soldiers were concerned about how many guards were coming under attack.

Faith knew she should be ecstatic. The Bellator citizens were coming together, rising up against Danforth's oppression. The Resistance's efforts were finally paying off.

But she had never felt so alone.

The guards left, taking Karl and Denton with them. Danforth and Susie disappeared inside the room where Faith had been held captive. Seconds later, a howl of frustration echoed through the warehouse. For the first time in several minutes, Faith remembered Sanders.

Hammond raced to see what was wrong, dragging Faith with her. When they reached the doorway, Danforth was standing over Sanders' body.

"I thought maybe she was... hiding." Danforth's face was twisted with fury. "She knows how important she is to the project. But she's..."

For a moment, Faith wondered if the doctor had been a close friend of the chancellor's.

"Dammit! We'll be working *blind* without her notes." Danforth's next words rid Faith of the notion. Her only concern was her experiment. "What do we do now?"

"She doesn't document her research?" Hammond was frowning. "It can't be replicated?"

Danforth turned to Susie. "Sanders doesn't save her research on the central system, right?"

"N-no." The petite medic chewed her lip. "She was always afraid of it falling into the wrong hands."

"Do *you* have access to it?" Danforth demanded.

"She saves it on her private server, though I wouldn't have the access codes for that." The woman's voice was shaking. "B-but I'm pretty sure she has paper copies of all her notes locked in her office at the lab. She's... *was* kind of old-fashioned like that."

"We have to move." Danforth spun to face Hammond. "*Now*. If we've *any* hope of recovering that research."

"Is that really our most pressing issue?" Hammond glanced at the door. "What about the trouble in the city, and–"

"It's our most pressing issue." Danforth cut in, her voice rising an octave. "We *can't* lose the research."

Susie gestured to the warehouse around her. "What about the drugs?"

"I'll leave a couple of guards to protect them." Danforth shook her head. "But, honestly, it's useless if all the metraxilone is gone."

Faith connected the dots. This warehouse was filled with femgazipane. Which meant the Acton Street Warehouse had contained metraxilone, the drug which had caused Sophia's pregnancy. Destroying it had to be the work of the Resistance, using the information that Faith had provided.

Her momentary burst of pride was quickly replaced with horror.

She had given Madeleine two locations. Was the Resistance planning to blow up this warehouse next?

She didn't have to worry for long. Ordering Susie to pack up any vital equipment from the medical room, Danforth dispatched Hammond to collect a small sample of the femgazipane to take with them. As soon as the two women returned, the group headed out.

As they walked from the exit to the waiting comcar, Faith glanced around. Were there, even now, Resistance citizens creeping towards this warehouse ready to blow it sky high? And if so, was there any way she could attract their attention?

In the darkness, she could see nothing. She was pushed into the back seat of a comcar with darkened windows. A final glance backwards revealed the pair of guards who had been left to protect the building. Danforth's forces were definitely depleted.

As Hammond slammed the door of the comcar behind her, Faith's hand closed around the syringe in her pocket. Aside from making sure she was bundled into the escape vehicle, her captors had paid her little attention. They were too concerned with gathering supplies and equipment.

Things were definitely starting to fall apart. The Bellator citizens were rebelling. The Resistance had demolished one warehouse filled with vital drugs. And Faith was certain they planned to destroy the second.

She felt a small surge of pride. She had played a huge part in the changes taking place in the city. If she wasn't getting out of this alive, at least she knew she'd made a difference.

But she wasn't going down without a fight.

CHAPTER FIFTY-FOUR: NOAH

The team was on their way to tackle Danforth and rescue Faith. Noah knew he should be relieved, thankful, grateful.

But Madeleine had forbidden him from joining the mission. He was too involved, she had said, too close to Faith to be able to act rationally. It was too much of a risk.

So he was stuck in the library with nothing to do. Madeleine had dispatched Paulo to the Eliot Street Warehouse. Diverted Olivia from the government headquarters to meet him, along with her original team and several of Evelyn's. There were enough of them, Madeleine had reassured Noah, to deal with the threat.

She had also dispatched Kemp and Charlie to government headquarters to join Evelyn. Between them, they would attempt to quell the crowd, whose mood was turning more violent by the minute. The professor would speak to the Bellator citizens. Reassure them that, while the chancellor wasn't there, the Resistance knew where she was. That actions were in place to track her down and bring her to justice as the women of the city demanded.

Charlie had offered to speak to the remaining guards. She would attempt to persuade them that Danforth's cause was far from just, appealing to them to stand down. If the guards laid down their weapons, the uprising would end peacefully. A satisfactory resolution, with no unnecessary loss of life.

Back at the library, Diane and Blake were monitoring the camera on the Eliot Street Warehouse. Madeleine was in charge of other communications, her eyes flicking between datadev and wristclip, a walkie talkie on the desk beside her. Ruth was keeping herself busy making coffee and sandwiches. Everyone had a job to do, except Noah.

All he could do was sit and watch the blinking light.

Every muscle in his body ached with tension. He had even begun talking to Faith inside his head. Voicing the endless questions which tormented him.

What's going on? Who are you with? Are you in pain?

There was one question he didn't dare to ask. He was too afraid of the answer.

Raising the mug of coffee to his mouth, he took a long drag. It was hot, but the scalding pain was a welcome distraction.

Dammit, Faith! He replaced the mug on the table so abruptly that the coffee slopped over the rim. As he grabbed a tissue to mop up the mess, he ignored Madeleine's glare. When he was done, his eyes returned to the tracking chip once again.

Please be okay. He was begging now. *Fight back, hide, play dead. Do whatever you have to, but promise me you'll survive.*

The dot jumped in response. Noah rubbed his eyes. He was exhausted. It had been so long since he'd slept, he was starting to see things.

Leaning closer to the screen, he narrowed his eyes. The dot jumped again.

That time, he was certain.

The tiny red circle on the screen was moving.

"Madeleine!" He beckoned to the leader. "Look."

She was by his side in an instant. She leaned over his shoulder. "What is it?"

He pointed. There was a brief pause as Madeleine squinted at the screen. Noah continued to follow the dot, which was now making slow, but definite progress away from the warehouse location.

"She has to be alive, right?" Noah asked tentatively. "I mean, if she's being moved?"

The leader frowned. "I'd say so."

"Could Paulo have gotten there already?"

"No. They're not close enough." Madeleine's jaw was tight. "This is Danforth. Whatever happened at the warehouse is over. They're taking her somewhere else."

Noah sat up, rigid. "Can we divert Paulo? Olivia?"

"Not sure." Madeleine was already sitting back at her datadev. "I can try. Go grab the others though. Just in case."

Several minutes of calling both Paulo and Olivia's team resulted in nothing. When Noah returned with the others, the Resistance leader was drumming her fingers against the desk, her eyes blazing.

"Can't get hold of any of them."

"Comms must be down." Blake frowned. "I'm on it."

"Is that Danforth's doing?" Ruth asked, as Blake headed back to her office.

"Her tech team, maybe. It's a good strategy..." Madeleine cursed under her breath. "Prevent us from communicating. Gives her a better chance."

"So what do we do?" Noah glanced at the door. "We have to do *something*."

"Blake, you stay here and keep trying to resolve the communication issue." As the techie stood up to obey, Madeleine turned her attention to Noah. "You're about to get your wish." She grimaced. "The four of us will take a comcar. Track Faith's chip. Follow her."

"You're coming?" Diane raised an eyebrow.

Madeleine hadn't left headquarters since Eremus had set off an explosion at her old home to disguise their existence. Allowing the people of the city to believe she was dead, she had retreated to the library and taken a less forward-facing role in the Resistance. But she was formidable in combat, and having her with them would make their success far more likely.

"I don't have a choice." Madeleine was already unplugging cables and stuffing her datadev into a backpack. "Grab a couple of extra battery packs, would you? And a walkie talkie. We can keep trying to reach the others on the way."

"Will do." Diane moved to obey, opening a drawer in the desk.

"After tonight, with the way things are going, I have a feeling it won't really matter. Either I won't need to hide anymore, or..." Madeleine didn't finish the thought. "And I can hardly let three teenagers set off to rescue Faith alone."

"If we could work out where she was being taken," Ruth mused, "maybe we could get there first. Lie in wait for them."

Noah had been racking his brain for any potential location Danforth would consider safe. "I think *I* might know." The others spun to face him. "BellaLab Corp."

"The other location on Faith's list." Madeleine nodded. "You're probably right. Government headquarters is out. It has to be somewhere with excellent security."

"And," Diane added, her tone laden with doom, "somewhere with the facilities for her to continue her experiments."

Madeleine nodded. "Does that fit with the direction they're taking?"

Diane glanced at the tracking chip. "Yeah. They're heading in that direction. BellaLab Corp would make a lot of sense."

Madeleine zipped up her pack and swung it on. "Then let's beat them there."

Chapter Fifty-Five: Faith

The vehicle windows were darkened, and it was difficult to make anything out as they moved through the streets. Faith tried to estimate how long she'd been held in the warehouse but she was so tired that time no longer had any meaning.

When the comcar pulled up at a building, she braced herself. Wherever they were, it felt like a final destination. Despite the other guards Danforth had brought with them in a second comcar, the chancellor had very little support. The attempt to retrieve Sanders' research seemed like a desperate move.

Faith had a faint sense of satisfaction that the chancellor's luck had finally run out.

If only her own would change.

No one knew where she was. Now that the women of the city had seen Danforth for who she was, the Resistance would have a million demands on their time. With the support of the Bellator women, they could finally rise up; finally free the city from its oppressor. And while Madeleine would be looking for Danforth, what were the chances of her being found quickly enough to prevent Faith from being dosed with fatal levels of the metraxilone?

The door beside her burst open. Hammond grasped her arm and hauled her into the cool night air.

They were standing outside a large, modern-looking building. A sense of dread weighed on Faith as she recognised it. BellaLab Corp. The lab where Danforth's reign of terror had originated. Its windows were darkened, the street quiet. No riots here, no Bellator women marching. No one who could help her.

Danforth turned to Hammond as the four guards exited the second comcar. "We don't want any unexpected interruptions."

"Understood." Hammond turned to the guards. "Surround the building. Keep a close watch. Report anything suspicious to me immediately."

As one, they nodded. Two of them disappeared around the side of the building. The others stationed themselves on either side of the entrance, facing the street.

Satisfied, Danforth gestured to Susie, who headed for the building's main entrance. Hammond hurried Faith in the same direction. At the door, the medic fumbled in her pocket for something, eventually pulling out a keycard. When she held it to the keypad at the side of the automatic doors, they swished open with barely a sound.

Susie stood back to let Danforth enter. The medic's head was down, and she was visibly shaking. She had barely spoken a word since they had left the warehouse. She was no Sanders, of that Faith was certain. And she was definitely the weak link in Danforth's little group. Faith had tricked her once. Perhaps she could do it again.

But as Hammond pushed her inside, the automatic doors swished closed behind them. A complex locking-system clicked into place. Faith's heart sank. Getting out of here would not be easy.

The lobby which awaited them was sleek and high-tech. Not at all like the loading bay out back, which Faith remembered from her failed mission with Evelyn. Its high ceiling soared above their heads and large screens dominated the space. They were dark, but Faith could imagine them playing sophisticated adverts promoting the company's products during business hours.

Money was clearly no object for the company. The few pieces of furniture scattered around the lobby were arty and expensive. Large terracotta planters around the edges were filled with exotic-looking trees and ferns.

An empty reception desk took pride of place at the rear of the space. Sleek and sophisticated, its metal surface gleamed in the moonlight shining through the glass of the front windows. Enormous silver letters proclaiming *BellaLab Corp* were emblazoned on the wall above it.

Faith froze. For a moment, she thought she saw movement reflected in the shiny surface of the lettering.

"Welcome to BellaLab Corp." An automated voice boomed out of nowhere, making Faith jump. "The home of the future!"

"Move it!" Hammond snapped, tugging on her arm.

She picked up the pace, not wanting to aggravate her captors. When she glanced back at the reception desk, all was still.

It made sense that the chancellor had employed Sanders at her own company. Danforth's devastation at the lead doctor's death indicated that she had clearly been the lifeblood behind the fertility experiment. Without her, all the chancellor's hopes of reinventing the procreation process were shattered.

Unless Danforth could retrieve her research notes. As a hunted woman it was a desperate move, but one she was clearly bent on making.

They reached a bank of lifts on the back wall of the lobby. Danforth punched the button.

"Which floor?" she asked Susie. "Sanders moved offices recently, didn't she?"

"Y-yes." Susie managed. "She's still on ten though."

Hammond glanced back at the two guards at the front entrance. She leaned close to Danforth.

"Are we expecting...?"

Faith strained, but only caught the first few words of the sentence. Danforth shook her head.

"...together... the research..."

Both women were keeping their voices deliberately quiet.

Faith gave up trying to make out what they were saying. Instead, her thoughts turned to the syringe in her pocket. How could she use it best? She had no real idea what effect it would have. And she only had one. She had to save it until she was left alone with one other person. The problem was, Danforth seemed intent on keeping them all together.

Gloomily, she glanced back at the reception desk. From this angle, she could almost see behind it. As the women around her continued discussing their plan, a movement caught her eye. She frowned, leaning further to her right so she had a better view.

Her heart stopped. There was a *person*, or *persons*, hiding behind it. She was almost certain. And if they were hiding from Danforth, they were not on the chancellor's side. Which meant that they were probably on hers.

"What are you going to do when you find Sanders' notes?" She spoke as loudly as she dared. "You think you can do this without her? I mean, now that she's *dead*?" The other women spun to face her. Swallowing hard, she forced herself to continue, hoping her questions would help the interlopers. "I mean, do you even have the *facilities* here to hook me up to the drugs again?"

Danforth took the bait, shooting her a disdainful look. "We have *state-of-the-art* testing facilities here. Sanders has a private lab on the eighth floor. Tucked out of the way at the back of the building. It will suit our purpose *very* nicely. Don't worry," she turned back to the lifts, dismissing Faith, "Susie will soon have you on a steady stream of femgazipane again. And this time, we'll follow through with the second drug. There's still enough of it left for a single subject."

A shrill *ding* echoed through the lobby, making Faith jump. Danforth was first in the lift, a nervous-looking Susie shuffling in beside her. As Hammond frog-marched Faith through the doors, she hoped the conversation would prove useful to whoever was hiding in the lobby.

As the lift doors slid shut, Faith crossed her fingers.

CHAPTER FIFTY-SIX: NOAH

He'd been right about Danforth's destination. Despite their uncomfortable position behind the BellaLab reception desk, when the group had entered, Noah had been cautiously optimistic.

Once Faith spoke, hope surged through him. She was here. She was alive. She hadn't been dosed with metraxilone.

Now all they had to do was get her out. Comms were still down across the city and they hadn't had any success reaching the others. As they'd left the library, Blake had assured them she would keep working on the problem. Noah was confident that she would resolve it, given enough time.

But for now, they were on their own.

They had worried they might be outnumbered when two comcars had pulled up outside. But believing the building to be empty, Danforth had stationed the guards on the exterior of BellaLab Corp. It made sense to assume that any threat would come from the streets. But the chancellor hadn't banked on them working out her plans in advance, or Madeleine's prior knowledge of the building.

He had imagined they would need to break into the laboratory. Arriving at BellaLab Corp, he could see that wouldn't be possible. The enormous windows were made from mi-croglass, an innovative material which Diane had informed him was incredibly thin, and pretty much indestructible. In addition, the laboratory had an advanced alarm system adver-tised on the side which claimed it was more formidable than a fire-breathing dragon.

Undaunted, the Resistance leader had made her way around the side of the building. Taking a small tool kit from her jacket, she had opened a complex-looking fuse box and set to work. She had seemed invigorated by the challenge. Noah could only assume it was because she had been holed up in the library, inactive, for so long. He wished he felt as confident.

Within five minutes, she had disconnected the alarm from a side door and deactivated the locking system, allowing them to enter the building without breaking anything, and, more importantly, without detection.

Once inside, they had concealed themselves behind the large reception desk. The building was enormous. With no specific information about Danforth's plans, their only option was to lie in wait, and learn what they could about the chan-cellor's intentions before taking action.

They hadn't had to hide for long.

As the group moved into the lobby, Noah had frozen, pray-ing Danforth's group wouldn't approach their hiding place. The gun Madeleine had armed him with weighed heavy against his side. Unlike Ruth, who had armed herself to the teeth, every inch the fearsome Eremus raider, he still hadn't felt confident that he'd be able to use it. But when he'd spotted Faith being shoved around by Hammond, the surge of fury he'd felt had changed his mind.

Desperate to check that Faith was with Danforth's group, Noah had shifted his position as they had approached the lifts. Diane's face had darkened at his actions, but the risky move had paid off.

Faith knew they hadn't given up on her. It had given her hope. And the hope had made her brave. Getting Danforth to announce their destination and her plans had been both genius and dangerous. But as the lift ascended, they were a step closer to their goal.

"So Sanders is dead." Madeleine was nodding. "And Faith's right. Without her, Danforth will struggle. I'm certain she was central to the fertility plan."

"Those notes Faith mentioned," Ruth mused. "They're Danforth's only chance of saving the experiment?"

"Sounds like it."

"Then we have to stop her, right?" Diane started to stand, but Madeleine pulled her down.

"We do. But we have to be cautious." Madeleine peered around the desk. "Danforth's desperate. Which means she's dangerous."

"What's the plan then?" Noah asked. "Do we go straight to Sanders' office? Or head to this lab and wait?"

"The lab, I think." The Resistance leader turned back to the group. "As long as we can find the right one, we can be one step ahead."

"Which way then?" Diane glanced at the lifts. "I assume we're taking the stairs."

Madeleine nodded. "Listen," she glanced at Noah, "we have two objectives now. First, we get Faith out safely." He was grateful this was her first priority. "But we also need to get Sanders' notes."

Noah froze. "*You* want her fertility experiment research?"

She caught his misunderstanding. "We have to destroy it." She shuddered. "Once this is over, I don't want *anyone* trying to recreate those drugs."

"What about Danforth?" Diane was frowning. "How do we deal with her?"

"We take her to the government headquarters to answer for her actions. Alright?" They all nodded. "Let's go."

Madeleine glanced back at the two guards. When she was certain they were facing the street, she darted across the lobby. For an older woman, she was certainly spry. Noah and the others followed. When they reached a door on the back wall, Madeleine led them through it.

They found themselves standing in a darkened stairwell. Diane and Madeleine activated the flashlights on their wrist-clips and they began to climb. Silence swirled around them, interrupted only by the sounds of their footsteps and their laboured breathing. Noah felt the tension grow as they neared the eighth floor.

How long would it take Danforth to find the research notes? What if she couldn't? Might Madeleine's group be hiding in a lab, waiting for a group who would never arrive?

Fighting to keep his breathing even, he glanced up at the signage on the stairwell as he turned another corner. Sixth Floor. Two more to go.

Perhaps Danforth had located the notes immediately. In the lift, it would have taken them no time at all to reach their destination. If they lost the element of surprise, how would they save Faith?

Ruth dropped back to walk beside him.

"Okay?" She raised her eyebrows, sensing his panic.

"Not really."

"We're almost there." She nudged him with her shoulder, a familiar gesture. They trudged upwards in silence for a minute. When she spoke again, her tone was low and urgent. "What are you planning to do when this is all over?"

He stared at her. "What do you mean?"

"If everything goes to plan, we Eremus folks won't be pariahs anymore." Her smile did not reach her eyes. "City life seems to suit you. I just wondered..." Again, she hesitated. "Are you planning on staying here? With Faith, I mean?"

Noah kept moving, trying to formulate a response. "I don't know. Maybe?" He imagined walking the streets of Bellator without fear, Faith by his side. "I guess I'd like that."

He felt her tense beside him. Glancing over, he nudged her right back. "I think there's a part of me that will always want to be in Eremus, though. You won't get rid of me that easily."

"I hope not." Ahead of them, the group had stopped beneath a sign which read Eighth Floor. "Here we are."

Noah narrowed his eyes and glanced at his friend. "Were you distracting me? So I didn't panic?"

"Worked, didn't it?" She grinned, this time for real.

Shaking his head, Noah returned the smile. "Actually, it did."

"I know you too well, Noah Madden."

But the smile faded. There had been more to her questions than a simple distraction tactic.

He held her gaze. "How have I managed without you all this time?"

Her eyes brightened at his compliment. "I've really no ide–"

"Shh!" Diane glared at them.

They fell silent, exchanging quiet smiles as Madeleine eased the door open. She peered through.

"All clear. Let's go." She beckoned to them before disappearing into the empty hallway beyond.

The floor was made up of numerous labs, but each one was clearly labelled. There was a faint hum of machinery coming from somewhere, and Noah shuddered at the experiments which might be taking place on the other side of each door.

At the end of the hallway, Madeleine stopped at a door which was much like the others, aside from the sign which read *Innovative Research Department: No Unauthorised Admittance*. Madeleine nodded to Diane. "The moment of truth."

Diane was already rifling through her pack. She brought out a keycard much like the one Noah remembered from the hospital. Hesitating for a second, she raised her eyes to the ceiling, as though praying for a miracle.

"Here we go."

She held the card up to the lock. For a moment, there was nothing. But then, a tiny light flashed green and there was a hopeful clicking sound. Pumping a fist in the air, she pushed the door open.

The space beyond was large and filled with an array of complex-looking medical equipment. As they walked inside, Noah didn't even know where to look.

He turned to Madeleine. "What now?"

"We hide." She closed the door behind them and reactivated the lock. "And we wait."

CHAPTER FIFTY-SEVEN: FAITH

They had been there less than half an hour when they found it.

When they had entered the office, Hammond had pressed Faith into a chair, whilst Susie and Danforth had turned the office upside down. With no regard for Sanders' property, the two women had ripped open cupboards, rifled through drawers and tipped out the contents of several filing cabinets.

When they hadn't immediately found what they wanted, Danforth had morphed into a feral animal. A terrified Susie had become ever more inventive, running her hands underneath the desk, knocking on walls, and even pulling up the carpet to find Sanders' hiding place. Eventually, she had started pulling pictures off the walls.

The great Chancellor Danforth had been hunkered on the office floor, skimming document after document. Desperation leaked from her every pore as she hunted for references to the fertility trials.

Had her own situation not been so grave, Faith would have laughed.

But when Susie let out a cry of triumph, she felt like crying. Behind an oversized painting of the BellaLab building that hung behind the desk, the medic had found a hidden alcove.

Danforth sprang to her feet. Crossing the room in seconds, she stretched her hand up to the empty space. Faith cringed as a smile of triumph came over her face.

"There's something here," she whispered, relief in every syllable.

When her hand emerged, it was clutching a large, leather-bound wallet.

"Bellator Fertility Trials, 2119," she read. "This has to be it!"

Flinging it open, she started reading the first page. But a moment later, the colour drained from her face. She beckoned Susie over.

"What is this?" She jabbed a finger at the text.

Susie had retreated to the opposite side of the room since the wallet's discovery. With trepidation, she crept forward.

"Let me see." She leaned over Danforth's shoulder. "Oh. It looks like it's written in some sort of... code."

"*Code?*" Danforth paled. "You can work out what it means, though. Right?"

Susie took the file with shaking fingers. "Let's see..." her forehead puckered as she pored over the symbols on the first page. "I think..." She turned to Danforth. "That is, I'm pretty sure I could figure it out... given a little time."

Danforth clenched her hands into fists. "We don't *have* time."

The room descended into silence. Moments went by. Eventually, Danforth inhaled noisily.

"Alright." She nodded, as though making a decision. "We'll take the folder with us." She walked towards the door. "Let's go and get started on Faith. As long as we have a successful subject, we can work on the methodology later."

The decision made, they set off for their final destination. Faith re-entered the lift, Hammond's ever-present hand on her shoulder. *Had she imagined the presence in the lobby? What if her exhausted, desperate imagination had conjured the movement up as a source of comfort?*

The eighth floor housed many different labs, but Danforth and Susie marched past them all. Hammond and Faith followed the pair, who didn't stop until they reached a door at the very end of the hallway. Faith read the sign with growing dread: *Innovative Research Department: No Unauthorised Admittance.*

This was it.

Danforth had showed no signs of letting Faith out of her sight, and Faith hadn't dared to waste the contents of the syringe with three potential guardians around. But the situation was getting desperate. Once they were inside the lab, there would be no more chances to escape.

Faith glanced at her wardens. She was confident she could overpower Susie, and Danforth was distracted. Hammond was her greatest threat. The one she had to take out, if she had any hope of success. As Danforth held her wristclip up to the laboratory door pad, Faith slipped her free hand into the pocket of her gown. It closed around her makeshift weapon.

Waiting until Danforth and Susie had moved inside, Faith twisted her body sharply to the left. She had been compliant for so long that the move came as a surprise to Hammond. For a split second, the Lieutenant relaxed her hold.

Faith struck out. Bringing the syringe to the woman's neck, she pressed it into the flesh as hard as she could. Hammond cried out, her hands grasping at her neck.

"What did you *do?*" she hissed.

With her remaining strength, Faith pushed the plunger on the syringe all the way to the hilt. Not waiting to see what happened next, she abandoned her makeshift weapon and took off down the hallway.

She hadn't gotten far when she heard thundering feet behind her. A familiar hand closed on her shoulder. Faith strained forwards, desperate to keep moving, but Hammond's grip was vice-like. With a last burst of strength, Faith surged forward.

And then, suddenly, she was falling.

She hit the ground hard. Winded, it took her several moments to recover. When she did, she sat back on her knees and turned to look back at the guard.

"Did you think this would stop me?" Hammond held up the syringe. "Hardly." Letting it fall to the ground, she crushed it with her boot. "Let's get this over with then."

Hammond hauled Faith to her feet and half-dragged, half-carried her along the hallway. Faith let it happen. Her final desperate attempt at gaining freedom had failed.

They reached the lab. Why hadn't Danforth come looking for them? Eager to get the experiment started, the chancellor had expected Hammond and Faith to be right behind her.

A similar thought seemed to strike Hammond. Pushing Faith in front of her, she eased the door open with caution.

And then it was clear what had held Danforth up. She was seated on a chair in the centre of the laboratory. Madeleine stood behind her, a gun trained on her head.

Faith took in the rest of the room. Susie cowered in one corner. Beside her, armed to the teeth, stood Diane. And on the other side of the lab, stood two more familiar faces. Ruth.

And Noah.

Hammond reacted before anyone had a chance to speak. Hauling Faith up against her, she reached for the gun in her belt. "I presume *this* is what you came here for?"

She jammed her gun against Faith's forehead so hard that she cried out. Noah took a step forward, his face a mask of horror.

"Don't come any closer." Hammond ground out. "Unless you want your little friend dead."

Noah stopped, his face pale. Holding up his hands in surrender, he backed away.

"Alright," Madeleine spoke for the first time since they had entered. "Seems we have ourselves a bit of a stand-off. How do you suggest we proceed?"

CHAPTER FIFTY-EIGHT: NOAH

H e had never been so afraid. And so angry.

They had prepared well. Waiting, armed, in strategic positions around the room. Madeleine and Diane either side of the door. He and Ruth in opposite corners, concealed behind a desk and a cupboard.

Their sneak attack had worked. Madeleine had forced Danforth into a chair at gunpoint while Diane had made short work of dealing with the medic. He and Ruth had moved forward to wait for Hammond and Faith.

But the pair had never entered.

They had heard a muffled whisper in the hallway, and the sound of running footsteps. Noah had wanted to investigate, but Madeleine had ordered him to wait. Hammond would not harm Faith, she had reasoned. Not when she was so important to Danforth.

But now Hammond had a gun to her head.

"How about a trade?" Madeleine's voice was calm, despite the tension. "You give us Faith. We give you one of our prisoners."

"A switch? I don't think so." Even with a gun to her head, Danforth was condescending. "Faith is of the *utmost* importance to me. I'm not going to give her up."

"I don't think you're in a position to argue," Madeleine said mildly. "Unless you want to lose your own life, that is?"

Danforth ignored her. "What do you plan on doing with me, if we surrender?"

"Take you to face your people, of course." For the first time, there was a hint of anger in Madeleine's tone. "I want you to answer to them. You know, the citizens you claim you've been looking out for all these years."

"You never understood the importance of protecting them against *themselves*, did you Madeleine?" Danforth twisted to face her old adversary. "Always wanting to give people second chances. Always so honest with everyone, no matter the cost."

"It's better than lying." A faint flush was rising in Madeleine's cheeks. "Abusing their trust."

"I don't call it an abuse of trust. Not when they didn't know what was good for them." Danforth sighed deeply. "Let's face it, Madeleine, you're weak. I mean," she glanced at Noah from under her eyelashes, "look at you, fighting alongside a *male*."

"Tell me," Madeleine snapped, "how uniting with a *like-minded person* to achieve my goal makes me weak."

"Asking a man to protect you?" Danforth jeered. "It's pathetic."

"It's not about asking for protection." Madeleine was fighting to keep her tone civil. "It's about us supporting each other. As *equals*."

"Equals!" Danforth snorted. "Do you *honestly* believe he's on your side? That he'd defend you, if the need arose?"

"Yes." Madeleine pressed the gun into Danforth's head, forcing her to look forward again. "I do."

"You're a fool." Danforth laughed softly. "In more ways than one."

Noah tensed. What did the chancellor mean? He and Faith exchanged nervous glances.

"What will it be then, *Abigail?* Do you surrender?" Madeleine gestured to Faith. "Are you prepared to let another innocent citizen die for you? Surely, you don't want to face your people with *more* blood on your hands?"

"Oh, but I won't have to." Danforth brought her wrist up slowly. "See this?" She indicated something on her clip. "That's an alarm. It notifies the guards I have waiting outside that I need help." Madeleine's face fell. "Oh, yes. I activated it when Hammond entered, so they're *well* on their way. Why do you think I kept you talking for so long?" She tapped a finger against the clip. "I'd say you have... ooh, about a minute before my reinforcements arrive."

There was a stunned silence. Noah felt his heart contract. Had they come this far to be cornered by the chancellor's remaining guards?

His eyes met Faith's. Her expression was resolute. Whatever happened, she was grateful they had tried to save her. That was what mattered. Behind Faith, Hammond gasped. Noah turned his attention to the lieutenant. She didn't seem her usual invincible self. Though the room wasn't warm, she was sweating profusely, beads of moisture were forming on her forehead. And the hand which held the gun was shaking.

"W-what–?" She pressed her free hand to her stomach. "I can't–"

But before she could finish the sentence, Faith shook herself free. Stepping away from Hammond, she placed a well-aimed kick at the hand holding the weapon. The gun tumbled to the ground.

Noah swooped forward. He picked up the weapon and put the safety on. By the time he was standing again, Ruth had lowered a sickly-looking Hammond to the floor. Noah heaved a sigh of relief. If Hammond wasn't capable of standing, she was no longer a threat.

"What did you *do* to her?" Danforth's eyes were blazing.

Faith took a step closer. "I gave her a taste of your *medicine* out there." She jerked her head at the door to the hallway. "Took a few minutes to kick in, but it seems to be doing the trick now." She stooped down to look at Hammond. "Doesn't look like her body is reacting well to it, mind you."

Before Danforth had a chance to respond, the shrill *ping* of the lift echoed from further down the hall.

"Lock the door!" Madeleine cried, as the sound of multiple footsteps thundered towards them.

Noah leapt forward, slamming the door closed and activating the lock. Seconds later, the guards tried the door.

"Chancellor?" They began hammering on the solid metal. "What's happening?"

"Well," Danforth had recovered herself now that help had arrived, "it seems I have more support than you bargained for."

"Be quiet." Madeleine removed Danforth's wrist clip. "They're on the other side of the door. You have no way to let them in. And now," she pocketed the device, "you have no way to contact them."

Danforth fell silent, glaring at the Resistance leader.

"What now?" Ruth muttered.

"Come here." Madeleine beckoned her across. When Ruth stood by her side, she jabbed a finger at Danforth. "Keep this one under control, would you?"

"With pleasure." Ruth levelled her gun at the chancellor's head.

"It's about time I called for some backup of our own." Madeleine stepped away, tapping commands into her wrist-clip.

Noah prayed that Blake had managed to sort out the comms. If she hadn't, there was no way to call for backup. And they could only bluff for so long.

He glanced down at Hammond. The lieutenant was still sweating profusely, and her eyes were closed. Bending down beside her, Noah searched for additional weapons, removing another gun from her belt and several concealed knives. When he was done, he backed away, training his gun on her just in case.

Now that Hammond was out of action, Faith had moved to a counter a few feet away. She leaned heavily against it, looking pale and exhausted.

Noah wanted to fold his arms around her. But the danger wasn't over.

At the door, the guards were still attempting to break in. Having exhausted their fists hammering on it, they were now attempting to smash the lock.

"I'll bet you're regretting all that hardcore tech right now," Diane taunted the chancellor. "If it wasn't for the unbreakable glass and your sophisticated locking system, those guards would be through that door already and we'd be dead."

As Danforth shot her a dark look, Noah hoped she wasn't tempting fate.

Suddenly, the ground beneath them shook. The hammering at the door stopped momentarily, and the occupants of the room stared around, startled, as a booming sound echoed through the city.

"I think," Madeleine's gaze bored into Danforth's, "that's the warehouse on Eliot Street going up in smoke." Danforth paled as Madeleine continued. "How do you think you're going to continue your little experiment now that you have no drugs left?"

A high-pitched beeping at her wrist made her glance down. Noah heaved in a breath. *Had Blake finally managed to fix the comms?*

"What is it?" Diane asked, her eyes flashing to the Resistance leader.

A broad smile spread across the leader's face. "Charlotte Kemp just finished speaking to the crowd at the government headquarters." She paused, her voice softer than Noah had ever known it to be. "As did... *Charlie.*"

"*And?*" Diane came a step closer.

"And," Madeleine managed, "a miracle happened." Sensing their confusion, she explained. "Looks like she managed to convince large numbers of guards to stand down."

"Stand down?" Ruth exclaimed, her gaze shifting to Madeleine. "You mean they're not a threat anymore?"

"Well, *some* of them are," Madeleine gestured to the door, where the women were still attempting to break through. "But Danforth's forces were already depleted, and if a good number of them have laid down their weapons, we may well have control of the city."

"That's amazing!" Diane was choked up. "It's... it's over, then?"

Madeleine glanced at her clip once again. "Evelyn's leading a group over here now. Paulo and Olivia are headed this way too. They should be here in... fifteen minutes?" She glanced at the door. "All we have to do is sit tight, and hope that door holds."

Chapter Fifty-Nine: Faith

Faith felt almost faint. Could Diane be right? Was it almost over?

Sanders was dead. The genius behind the fertility trials could experiment no more.

Whilst the noise at the door hadn't abated, the microglass was holding. The guards seemed no nearer to gaining entry than they had been five minutes ago.

Hammond was in no state to protect her chancellor. Noah had secured her hands behind her back, just to be sure. But despite the terrifying delay, the metraxilone had taken effect, totally incapacitating the lieutenant.

Susie hovered in the corner of the lab, her fingers fluttering nervously. She wasn't a threat, even though Diane was no longer standing over her.

Best of all, Danforth was powerless. Her drug supply was all-but gone. She had no victims left to experiment on. Madeleine had taken possession of the wallet filled with Sanders' research. And the chancellor was their *prisoner*. Tomorrow, she would be forced to face the wrath of her people.

Faith turned back to Madeleine. A sudden movement caught her eye.

"Look out!" she cried.

But it was too late. Taking advantage of their distraction, Danforth had shot to her feet. Grasping Ruth's hand, she twisted the gun towards Madeleine.

"No!" Faith screamed.

She launched herself at them, pushing the weapon away. For a moment, they were falling. She fought to keep her balance as a gunshot split the air.

As the three of them crashed to the floor, the weapon skittered out of Danforth's hand. Madeleine rushed forward.

"Oh no, you don't." She pushed the chancellor flat on her back and thrust her knee into the centre of her chest. "You're not going *anywhere.*"

Faith scrambled up, gasping for breath. Beside her, Ruth moaned.

Faith turned to her. Noah's best friend was clutching her side, where a wound was leaking blood.

"Ruth!" Faith pressed her hands against the wound. "How did you–?"

"My knife." Ruth gestured to a small blade on the ground beside her. "I f-fell on it."

As the blood continued to ooze between Faith's fingers, she searched for something to stem the flow. The hospital gown she wore was too flimsy.

"Faith!" Noah was already pulling off his sweatshirt. He tossed it to her, his face white. "Press hard. We have to stem the bleeding. 'Til we can get her some help."

Faith caught it with her free hand. Balling the garment up, she pushed it against the wound as hard as she could.

"You'll be okay," she murmured, her eyes glued to Ruth's pained face. "They'll be here soon. They'll sort you right out." She leaned closer. "It's a good thing you were here, really. The Bellator medical facilities are far superior to the Eremus ones."

Ruth managed a smile at the feeble joke. Squeezing her hand, Faith turned to scan the room again.

The guards at the door had stopped hammering. Faith found herself hoping that they'd given up. Hammond had passed out. Noah's worried gaze was fixed on Ruth. Madeleine had her gun trained on Danforth now. The two were locked in a staring match, their eyes filled with hatred.

"Excuse me?" Faith's eyes settled on Susie, whose face was paler than ever. "Your friend. Diane, is it?"

As a group, they turned. One by one, their faces drained of colour. A few feet away, Diane lay on the ground, her body ominously still. A pool of blood had formed underneath her, pouring from a wound in her chest.

"I think... the bullet..." Susie began. "It was over very quickly."

Sensing the others' grief, she fell silent.

Danforth was far less tactful. "Not quite my intended target," she drawled, "but at least my bullet found a home somewhere."

"Really?" Madeleine swung to face her. "She's barely twenty years old!"

Danforth rolled her eyes. "Does her age make a difference? When all's said and done, she was a trial subject." She spoke slowly and deliberately. "In the grand scheme of things, Madeleine, she doesn't really matter."

The Resistance leader's eyes flashed.

"Ignore her," Faith pleaded. "She's trying to bait you. Don't—"

But it was too late. As the second shot in as many minutes reverberated through the room, Faith recoiled, covering her face with her hands. When she forced herself to look up, Danforth was dead.

Madeleine sat back on her heels, her face white. "I'm sorry..." Her voice shook. "But I couldn't... I just couldn't..."

Faith had never seen the Resistance leader so emotional. But she understood why. Listening to Danforth's poison, with Diane's body not two feet away, had been too much.

They had wanted Danforth to face her people. To be tried by the women she had betrayed. But by taunting Madeleine, the chancellor had secured herself an easy exit. Denied them justice.

For a few seconds, the room was quiet. And then multiple footsteps pounded up the hallway towards them.

"Madeleine!" Someone was hammering on the door. "Madeleine, are you there?" A brief hesitation. "It's Evelyn. Can you let me in? We've neutralized the guard threat." Another pause. When Evelyn spoke again, her voice was filled with concern. "Madeleine? Unlock the door so we can come in and help."

The words were welcome. But as Noah stumbled towards the door, Faith felt no sense of triumph.

CHAPTER SIXTY: NOAH

The Resistance team entered, taking in the devastation on the other side of the door. For a moment, they were silent.

Then Evelyn took charge.

After that, everything was a blur. Ruth was prioritised, dispatched to the hospital on a stretcher immediately. Someone slapped a pair of handcuffs on Hammond, before sending her in the same direction. Danforth and Diane's bodies were covered with sheets while various medics and technicians came in to check on the rest of them.

Noah found himself being examined by Carol, the technician who had planted the tracker on Faith. She was very thorough, bending close to him, looking in his eyes, checking his pulse and blood pressure, running her hands over his body looking for wounds.

"I'm okay," he insisted.

Once she was satisfied he was only suffering from shock, she agreed to let him go.

"Rest," she advised, her eyes kind. "You've been through a lot."

He nodded, a sense of relief descending as she backed away. He looked around for Faith, but didn't see her anywhere. With a surge of panic, he pushed his way outside.

There were people everywhere. He was surprised to see some drudges among the rescue party. Rowan and Arden smiled at him as he passed, their masks absent.

Three of Danforth's guards were being cuffed and marched off down the hallway. One lay still on the ground. Noah averted his gaze. He had seen more than enough death for today.

He had begun moving towards the lift when a hand closed around his arm. Turning, he found himself face-to-face with Paulo.

"We came as fast as we could." His brother scanned him anxiously. "You alright?"

"I'm fine," he managed.

"You don't *look* fine." Paulo squinted at him. "Things go bad in there?"

"Yeah." Noah shrugged. "Danforth's dead though, so I guess, in the end..." he trailed off.

"Yeah." Paulo dropped his gaze. "Goal achieved. But not as peacefully as we'd have liked."

"What happened out here?" Noah frowned.

"Quite a lot." Paulo took a deep breath. "Let's see. The academy principal killed herself."

"*What?*"

Paulo grimaced. "She was trapped in her office at the school when the protesters invaded. Locked herself in." He sighed. "By the time they broke down the door, it was too late. She'd taken a whole stash of pills. Though it might have been a blessing. That crowd was pretty mad." He gave a low whistle. "I know what would have happened if they'd found her alive."

"I..." For a moment, Noah struggled to find words to make sense of it. "She..."

"Jacob's dead." Paulo did nothing to soften the words. "Sarah too. *And* Avery." He sighed. "The other Resistance team found them inside the second warehouse."

"Really?" Noah tried to take it in. "All of them?"

Paulo nodded. "Seems like they tried to ambush Danforth. It didn't go so well for them."

More death. Noah swallowed hard.

"Was that sound... Did it..." He tried again. "I mean, did your team destroy the warehouse? The drugs?"

"We did." Paulo lay a hand on Noah's arm. "Though not before we removed the bodies. Jacob and his crew will get a decent burial."

"Really?" Noah was impressed by his brother's respectful attitude. "That's one good thing. What a mess, though."

"It looks that way right now." Paulo leaned forward, his eyes earnest. "But we did it, brother."

Noah frowned. "Did what?"

"Ma and Ella and that Blake woman saved the academy girls. Kemp and Charlie calmed the riot. My team destroyed the rest of the drugs. Your group defeated Danforth." Paulo slung an arm around Noah's shoulder. "There's still a lot of work ahead, but we changed things today. Together."

"Guess you're right."

"Damn right I'm right." Paulo's tone was proud. "Eremus stands a fighting chance now."

Noah closed his eyes. When he opened them, Paulo was smiling. "Flynn would be proud."

Noah's breath hitched in his throat. "He would."

"Saw Ruth on her way out." Paulo changed the subject. "Medics said she's going to be okay."

Suddenly, Noah couldn't speak. With a sensitivity he rarely showed, Paulo stepped forward, closing his arms around his brother. For a moment, they stood together, quietly drawing on what was left of one another's strength.

Noah was the first to pull away. Around them, the hallway was emptying of people, but there was still no sign of the girl he was looking for.

"Did you see Faith anywhere?"

Paulo nodded. "She could barely stand, what with the drugs they gave her, and then the shock. They took her to the hospital right after Ruth. Charlie went with her."

"The *hospital*?" Noah swallowed hard. "But she... she can't..."

"She'll be fine." Paulo leaned close. "Listen, I know that place has bad memories for you both. But Danforth's people aren't in charge anymore." He pulled Noah into his side. "They'll look after her."

"Maybe," Noah turned to face his brother, "but I need to see her. I have to make sure she's okay."

Paulo jerked his head towards the lifts. "Then what are we waiting for?"

Chapter Sixty-One: Faith

The hub was crowded, and a sense of anticipation filled the room. Faith hung back, not wanting to taint the optimistic mood. On the screen at the front, a news report was playing. Stella Thane was presenting a special feature on the recent changes in Bellator. Danforth's downfall meant she could broadcast publicly, and the smile on her face was triumphant.

Side-by-side on armchairs opposite the *Bellator Blade* reporter sat Madeleine and Kemp.

"We know that things feel very unstable right now," the Resistance leader was saying, staring directly into the camera, "but as your temporary leaders, we want to reassure you. We are doing our very best to bring order to the city as quickly as possible. We want to work together with you all to rebuild a Bellator we can be proud of."

"In the short term," Kemp took over, "this means repairing the damage caused by the recent explosions, the protests on the streets, and the riot at the government buildings." She too stared earnestly into the camera. "In the long term, though, we hope to restore more than just bricks and mortar."

Beside her, Madeleine was nodding. "As you all know, Chancellor Danforth died a week ago in a violent stand-off at her company, BellaLab Corp. We have all come to understand what a terrible hold she had over the citizens of Bellator. How underhanded she was. How her claims to have the women of the city's best interests at heart were utterly false. Her passing allows us to restore faith and trust in the city." She paused, her tone changing. "Better than that, it gives us a chance to create something new. A society which respects the opinions of its people."

"A society," Kemp chimed in, "which seeks to reestablish relations with existing males and rebuild trust between the genders." She shifted in her chair. "Men are *not* our enemies, and, in time, we hope you will all come to accept this."

Faith silently applauded the sentiment. The actions of people in both communities had paved the way for relationships between them to develop and flourish. She searched the room for Noah, finding him seated next to Paulo on the other side of the room. Their eyes met for a second before she glanced back at the screen.

As Kemp seamlessly picked up Madeleine's cues, Faith marvelled at their partnership. They had volunteered to run the city until democratic elections could be held, but Faith had no doubt that they would be elected.

Things ran smoothly under their influence. The professor did an excellent job of balancing out Madeleine's impulsive nature, and she, in turn, spurred Kemp into action. In the week that they had been jointly in charge, they had already made huge strides towards restoring order in the city and confidence in its leaders.

The bodies of Jacob and Sarah had been returned to Eremus for burial. As a mark of respect, as well as attending the small ceremony they had held for Avery in the city, Madeleine herself had travelled with the group returning them. It sent a clear message about the relationship she wanted to build with the woodland community. Sanders' research notes had been destroyed. Following that, working parties had been sent to clear the rubble from the warehouses, ensuring that none of the drugs remained.

There would be no more fertility experiments. The sense of relief Faith felt at the news was overwhelming.

Every single one of the girls rescued from the academy had survived. They were now being housed in specialised withdrawal units in the Bellator Hospital. The long-term effects of the large doses of femgazipane remained to be seen, but Madeleine had pledged the government's continued support. The girls would be given every available course of treatment to minimise the damage done by the drug.

Thankful that none of them had been given metraxilone, Faith was hopeful that the girls would all be able to make a full recovery. Hammond was the only one to have received the second, more drastic drug, and she had never been given femgazipane. She, too, was in the hospital, but so far it looked like the drug would not have long-lasting effects when given in isolation. Once recovered, Madeleine and Kemp had promised to transfer her to a secure unit where she could await trial for her part in the atrocities committed by the ex-chancellor.

On the screen, Kemp paused as Stella introduced a news report from the previous day. The video feed showed the academy seniors being led back into the city by Anna. Supporting the girls were numerous Eremus citizens, both male and female. There had been some nerves amongst the Bellator women at the idea of the men openly walking the streets, but Kemp and Madeleine had managed the situation well.

The Bellator people had been informed of the event in advance, and given the chance to stay home if they felt uncomfortable. The route the group was taking through the streets had been well-publicised, as had the timing of the event. If the women wanted to avoid the proceedings, they could.

Despite this, hundreds of citizens had arrived to welcome the girls home. No incidents of violence had erupted on the streets, and there had been a nervous optimism in the air. Any citizens who objected to or feared males had simply stayed home. And the men accompanying the students had behaved respectfully, which had gone a long way towards restoring confidence.

"As you can see, the girls from the Danforth Academy were brought safely to the Bellator Hospital yesterday." Madeleine smiled into the camera. "We would like to extend a vote of thanks to the Eremus people, who concealed and cared for the students at a time when Chancellor Danforth had placed them in grave danger."

Faith was glad that the Eremus people were finally getting some good press. Having them shelter the seniors in the caves had been an excellent move. For once, they were being viewed as heroic in the eyes of the city. It had created a fragile bond between the two communities which Kemp and Madeleine were keen to build on.

Since delivering the girls to the hospital, most of the Eremus citizens had returned to their home in the forest, but Faith hoped it wouldn't be long before they were welcomed into the city again. Only by spending time with one another could they hope to move on from the years of fear and resentment.

A few notable members of the forest community had remained in the city. Ruth was still in hospital, though she was recovering well from her injury. Faith glanced across the room at Ella, whose eyes were shining with pride at the positive reference to her home.

The young woman had returned to Bellator with Helen the previous day. They had gone straight to the hospital to visit Ruth. When she had arrived back at the library later, Ella had hugged Faith tightly. She and Helen were so grateful they would have the chance to be together now that the barriers between the communities were breaking down.

Perhaps, Faith hoped, the same could be true for her and Noah.

To Ella's left, his face as dark as hers was bright, sat Harden Porter.

When the Resistance had gone inside the temporary government headquarters, they had come across Sarah's son locked in one of the cells, unharmed. He'd been brought back to the Resistance headquarters, but when he'd learned of his ma and Jacob's deaths, he hadn't known where to go. Like Hammond, both Karl and Denton were locked up in the city's jail, awaiting trial for their part in Jacob's plot.

Harden's only remaining friend was Sil. She had fled to Eremus soon after his capture, begging their forgiveness. The community had allowed her back, but Faith suspected it would take years for her to regain their trust, if she ever did.

Proud as ever, Harden had refused to do the same. But with no real home or friends in the city, he had found himself in a sort of no-man's land. For now, he had accepted Madeleine's offer of shelter at the library. But he was far from happy living among the women he'd spent years hating.

"...so it's with great pleasure," on the screen, Madeleine was gesturing to her left, "that I introduce a third member of our leadership team."

The camera panned across to the final member of the Eremus community who remained in the city: Anna. She smiled gracefully at the camera, but the telltale tapping of her finger against the arm of her chair gave away her nerves to those who knew her well.

"As a woman who has experienced life in both Bellator and Eremus, Anna provides the perfect connection between the two." Madeleine was beaming. "She offers us a fresh perspective on the situation, and has already made multiple suggestions about ways we can improve relations between our communities."

Behind the smile, Anna looked sad. Madeleine had been thrilled when Noah's ma had offered to stay in Bellator. She and Kemp were hoping Anna's influence would ease the transition between the old world and the new, bringing them to a point where males were treated as equals, and might even serve on the Bellator government. Madeleine had praised Anna for her selflessness several times.

Faith knew there was more to it than that. Anna wanted to be a part of the new world as much as Faith and Noah. But moving to the city was also her way of dealing with her grief. Memories of Flynn were everywhere in the caves, and being there right now was painful. Working to bridge the chasm between the two communities was Anna's way of honouring his memory. If they made a success of it, he would not have died in vain.

Faith suspected Anna would spend the rest of her life making sure of it.

For now, Madeleine and Kemp were keeping the public leadership team female. Until the Bellator citizens were used to having men around, it seemed the sensible way to go. Few would object to the three women, if they continued to restore peace in the city. And, when the time was right, they could bring some males on board.

Kemp and Madeleine were already working with men behind the scenes. Paulo had proved himself extremely helpful over the past week, bringing in a team each day to help clear the rubble from the devastated warehouses. Charlie was always by his side. The ex-guard had changed him, and Faith suspected she was the reason he wanted to make a good impression on the women of the city.

Another male who had been extremely active was Arden. More confident than the ordinary drudge due to his years as a Resistance spy, he had shown a natural aptitude for organisation. He had already set up a support system for Danforth's slaves, some of whom were struggling to adjust to a life of freedom. And he had big plans to unite the network of drudges across the city, allowing them to play a more equal, important role in the community.

Things were changing.

On the screen, the camera panned back to Kemp.

"In closing, we would like to say how grateful we all are for the support and assistance of so many. If we hadn't been united, we could never have come this far." As she paused to take a sip of water, Faith could see her bracing herself to go on. "But we cannot forget that some of those people are no longer with us." She bowed her head a little. "We would like to take a moment to remember them."

Strains of gentle music swelled in the background. An image of Serene, the first victim of Danforth's experiment, appeared on the screen, followed by her age and the dates of her birth and death.

As Sophia's name flashed up, Faith turned away.

She wasn't ready to see the faces of her friends yet. The deaths of Sophia, Flynn, Robyn and Diane.

Hoping she could escape without attracting attention, Faith stood up and crept towards the door.

Chapter Sixty-Two: Noah

As Faith slipped from the room, his heart ached. Since she had returned from her two-day stint at the Bellator Hospital, she had been a little distant. Shock, his ma told him, could take a while to get over. Grief, he knew, would stay with her far longer.

Noah had been trying to give her space. But her face, as she left, had been haunted.

He followed her, but when he reached the hallway, it was empty.

"Faith?" His voice echoed back to him. "Faith!"

He stopped for a moment. Where would she go? Would she even want his company?

At the end of the hallway, a door stood open, the stairs beyond leading upwards. And then he knew.

When he reached the library, a faint sunlight was shining in through the windows. He walked through the empty space, the shelves of books solid as ever, a fortress of words offering shelter and protection. Of course, she would come here.

He rounded the corner into the records section. The table where Faith had sat to write her speech was empty. There was no sign of a figure standing at the shelves, browsing the books.

"Looking for me?"

The familiar voice came from the sofa beneath the window. Following the sound, he found Faith curled up in a ball.

"You okay?" He stayed where he was, not wanting to crowd her.

Faith sighed. "I just needed to get away." She sat up abruptly, gesturing to the empty square below. "It's hard to believe that things out there are actually going to change."

Noah waited, sensing there was more.

"I mean," her voice hitched slightly, "It's obviously great that Danforth's gone. That we can begin to rebuild... create the kind of Bellator I've always wanted..." she trailed off. "I guess we won, in the end. But it feels too soon. With Sophia gone... Flynn and Robyn," she turned to him, "and now... Diane."

"I know." He shook his head. "It's hard."

She stood up and walked to the window, pressing her fingertips against the glass. "Some days I think it's *too* hard."

A silence fell between them, as it had so many times since Danforth's demise. Noah took a deep breath, willing himself to find the strength to give her space, if that was what she needed.

"I'm sorry. Do you..." he paused, his eyes never straying from her, "do you want me to leave you alone?"

For a moment she was still. But then, as he was bracing himself for rejection, she turned.

"Actually, no." She took a tentative step towards him. "Listening to what Madeleine was saying in there... seeing how happy Ella and Helen are... it made me think." She dropped her gaze for a second, took a breath, then lifted her eyes to meet his. "They're right. We've suffered so many losses, but we've also achieved so much."

He held his breath.

"We have every chance now. *Every* chance to be together." She shifted from one foot to the other, as though she were nervous. "So, no. I don't want to be left alone." She gave him a shy smile. "I'd like you to stay. Will you stay, Noah?"

No more hesitation. He closed the gap between them. *I'll stay forever*, he wanted to say.

It was too soon for that. But with Danforth's reign over, they *did* stand a chance. With time, who knew what they might become?

He pulled her close, circling her with his arms. As she returned the embrace, he buried his head in her hair.

"Of course, I'll stay," he whispered.

It was where he was meant to be.

Epilogue: Faith

F lipping the switch on her datadev, she massaged a knot in the back of her neck. A noise at the door made her look up.

"Didn't you leave yet?" Kemp raised an eyebrow.

"I'm going. I'm going." Faith stood up and began packing her bag. "I was just finishing these papers."

Moving to the shelves on the far side of the room, Kemp cast her eyes over the selection of books.

"It's *Saturday.*" She mock-scolded, over her shoulder. "And a little bird told me you had special plans this afternoon. Go!" Kemp turned, making a sweeping motion with her hand. "And I don't want to hear anything else from you until Monday."

"Alright!" Faith held up her hands. "Who do you think you are, the principal?"

"Don't you forget it." Kemp laughed. "Okay if I borrow this? I never get tired of it."

She held up a book and Faith smiled. The volume was one of a few rare original texts which pre-dated Danforth's rule of the city. Discovered in the caves after the chancellor's death, the books had been donated to the academy by the Eremus council. Their pre-Women's Independence Party view on society was fascinating. Kemp and Faith shared an obsession with the books, and had read them all several times.

"Help yourself."

"Thanks." Kemp's eyes gleamed. "That's my evening sorted."

"See you Monday, then." Faith followed her old professor to the door. "Make sure you go home soon as well."

"I will." But Kemp was already retracing her steps to her office. "I just have a meeting with Blake's team first."

Faith rolled her eyes. As proud Principal of the Serophia Academy, Kemp never stopped working. A decade had passed since they had rescued the senior girls from what had been Danforth's institution. Following the turbulent events, the school had been closed down while the temporary government re-established order in the city.

When elections had been held for permanent positions, Charlotte Kemp had stepped away from her government role. Returning to her first love, she had worked hard to reopen the academy as a Centre for Further Learning. Named after Serene and Sophia, the two victims of Danforth's horrific experiment, it was open to anyone showing academic promise and the total opposite of the establishment Anderson had run.

Taking in a range of students from all over the city, the school was revered once again. And for the right reasons, this time. The student body was mixed gender. So far, the bias was still towards the female, but as more and more baby boys were born, the numbers were beginning to even out.

Kemp was most proud of their technology programme, which she had set up in conjunction with Blake. In the wake of Danforth's death, the Resistance's tech genius had set up her own company. One of its main objectives was to investigate future technologies and ensure they were used for good.

Everything Blake did was totally transparent. Working closely with Madeleine's government, she followed rigorous guidelines. They ensured that any trials and experiments her company ran were fair and did not abuse the trust of the Bellator citizens. Blake had worked hard to find positive uses for her company's advancements. She had also forged close links with Kemp at the academy, making sure that both her skill and her philosophy were shared with any aspiring IT geniuses. Faith was still intimidated by the woman, but her attitude was one to be admired.

Faith had been a professor at the establishment for six years. Taking over Kemp's previous role, she taught in the old Herstory classroom, though the subject was now called Theirstory. She was well-liked as a professor and loved her job, almost too much.

There were times when she needed to leave it behind. And today was one of them.

She exited the building, waving to Benjamin on reception. She still found herself faintly shocked, on occasion, to see men working alongside the women of Bellator. Despite knowing first-hand that women could be just as vindictive as men, the old teachings were ingrained, and difficult to shake.

Faith was grateful that, in another decade, the children she taught would be free of that prejudice. One of the reasons she was so passionate about her job was that it allowed her to educate the adults of the future about the mistakes of the past. That way, she was doing her part to ensure the same mistakes were never made again.

True to her word, Madeleine's government had spent the last few years rebuilding Bellator society from the bottom up.

Drudges had been freed, and now worked alongside the women of the city as equals with paid positions. Faith had stayed in touch with Arden, who had taken a position in Madeleine's government advising her on the very specific situation of the drudges. Many of them lived in shared houses, and stayed close to one another, their bonds closer because of their common experience.

Some of them had struggled to adapt to having independence, but, on the whole, they enjoyed a far better quality of life. Because of their specialised genetic engineering, they were unable to reproduce. It was odd to think that once this generation died out, there would be no more drudges. But those still living would enjoy a much brighter life than their predecessors.

The people of Eremus had been given the option to come and live in the city or remain in the place of their birth. But the cave community no longer had to hide. Instead, they travelled in and out of Bellator without question. A number of major routes in and out of the forest had been cleared, providing more rapid movement between the two communities. Some of the Eremus folk had even started trading with businesses in the city.

It hadn't been an easy journey, but, slowly, relations between men and women had improved. For the first few years after Danforth's death, the birth rate had fallen steeply. With no seed to continue reproducing in the old way, the city had struggled. But, after completing her medical training and taking a job as a medic at Bellator Hospital, Anna had found a solution.

She had proposed a system where Eremus men could donate their seed to the city's hospitals for use in procreation. The suggestion had initially come up against resistance. Many people feared it was a backwards step and would lead to Danforth's seed banks being reinstated.

Anna had been horrified at the implication. As a result, she had stipulated that the seed could only be given voluntarily and anonymously. After that, the proposal had been quickly accepted. And, once women began to take advantage of the new system, the birth rate had begun to recover.

Eventually, barriers had broken down completely. Men from Eremus and women from Bellator began to form relationships and, slowly, but surely, babies had begun to be conceived naturally. Gender testing had been banned early on, so every birth had an element of surprise. Best of all, children of both sexes were accepted and treated equally.

Collecting her bike from the rack at the front, Faith pushed it out into the street. *Things were so much better.*

Kemp's words came back to her as she mounted the bike. *A little bird told me you had special plans for this afternoon.*

She smiled to herself as she set off for the forest.

An hour later she hopped off the bike, wheeling it the last few metres before propping it up against a tree. Ahead of her, Swallow Lake glimmered in the afternoon sun. She inhaled deeply, stopping to take in the view.

"About time you got here."

She spun around. A pair of boots descended from a tree to her right, followed by a pair of legs, clad in denim. There was a thud as the figure leapt, landing on the ground beside her.

"You can take the boy out of the forest, but you can't take the forest out of the boy," she teased.

Noah laughed. Stepping forward, he swept her into his arms, kissing her soundly. When they parted, her heart was pounding. He could still do that to her, even after ten years.

"Sorry I'm late, I was–"

"I know," taking her by the hand, he pulled her towards the water. "You were working." Putting a hand up to silence her second apology, he pulled her down on the bank of the lake and settled himself behind her. "It's okay."

She smiled at his acceptance. It hadn't always been this way. For months after the fall of Danforth, they had struggled to find a way to be together which made them both happy. Eventually though, they had come to a compromise.

Their home was on the outskirts of the city. It meant that Faith's journey to work was longer, but allowed Noah to visit Eremus regularly. Spending time in the forest was important to him. And because of this, it had become a special place for Faith.

She leaned back against him, revelling in how solid his body felt, how tightly his arms clasped her to him. "We made it to a decade, then?"

He squeezed her tighter. "Seems like we did. Happy anniversary."

"Ten years," she marvelled. "Bellator's come a long way in that time."

He pressed a kiss to the side of her head. "So have we."

She laughed. "Remember when we didn't even dare to dream we could be together?"

He chuckled, the bass sound reverberating though her body. "About that..."

She twisted her body to face him. "Yes?"

"Well," he leaned backwards, fumbling in his pocket, "I wanted to do something to celebrate. To mark the occasion."

"Oh yeah?" Her eyes went to his hands, curious. "What have you got there?"

He put them behind his back, then held them both out in front of him. "Pick one."

She rolled on to her knees, her breath catching in her throat. Even now, he could surprise her.

She took her time deliberating between the two. Eventually, when he let out a groan of frustration, she tapped his left hand.

"Good choice!" He opened his palm to reveal a small package, wrapped in tissue. "For you."

She took it between her thumb and finger, sensing it was something fragile, something special. Unwrapping it carefully, she discovered an ornate silver pendant in the shape of the letter F.

"To replace the one I stole from you." His voice was thick with emotion. "The one which kept you Danforth's prisoner, though you didn't know it." He blinked. "Do you like it?"

"It's beautiful."

Faith bent closer, inspecting it. Once she had worn a gold letter *D*. It had fed poison into her system, identified her as property of Danforth's regime. Now, she could wear a delicate silver letter *F* and be herself, knowing that Noah loved her.

"Thank you." She leaned forward and kissed him. When they finally pulled away, she smiled. "Put it on for me?"

She turned around, pulling her hair out of the way. Noah obliged, laying the pendant over her heart as he fastened the clasp. He bent down, placing a gentle kiss on her neck.

"I don't think we have long," he murmured. "They'll be here soon."

As if on cue, there was a sound of voices in the distance.

"Or now." Faith pressed her lips to his one last time. "I love you. I hope we're still this happy in another ten years."

"We'd better be," he mock-growled, pulling her to her feet.

They stood together, waiting for the others to arrive. First came Ella and Helen, hand in hand as always, joined by their daughter, Lydia. At nine years old, she was a fiercely intelligent member of the academy, and one of Faith's favourite students. She travelled to school every day from Eremus, where Ella and Helen had chosen to settle.

"Did someone say picnic?" Ella teased, holding up a basket.

Faith knew it would be packed to the brim with lovingly-prepared food. No one in Eremus went hungry anymore. Ella began to unpack it as Lydia pulled her shoes off and waded into the lake.

Not long afterwards, Anna arrived with Paulo. She was fresh from a shift at the hospital. Reaching them, she kissed Faith on the cheek. Eyeing the pendant, she winked at her son.

"She liked it, then?" Without waiting for a response, she patted him on the arm and moved away. "Ella, Helen!" She embraced them both. "It's been too long."

Paulo glanced around, his eyes scanning the area. He was co-chancellor now, and Madeleine's equal. He worked hard in the city, but his loyalty always lay with Eremus, and he acted as their champion in all government discussions.

"Hey," Faith smiled. "Tough morning?"

"Too right." He grimaced. "I thought Madeleine would never let me leave."

"Well, I'm glad she did." Faith gestured to the ground. "Take a seat. They'll be here soon."

Charlie and Paulo lived and worked in the city, but made sure their children spent as much time in Eremus as they could. With Paulo working today, Charlie had taken their children, eight-year-old Flynn, five-year-old Matthew, and four-year-old Katie to spend the morning in the caves with the other children.

As Paulo sat down, she marvelled at how different he was these days. Even with the weight of his leadership role, things were so much better now. Paulo was more relaxed, less ill-tempered, kinder. More like his uncle. He even got along pretty well with Noah most of the time.

A few minutes later, the final members of their group arrived from Eremus. Flynn and Matthew raced in first, giggling wildly as Charlie chased after them. Katie lagged behind, her little face pouting.

"Wait for me, Ma!" she cried. "Wait!"

Ruth wasn't far behind, the two-year-old Sophia riding on her shoulders.

"*There* she is!" Noah hurried to meet them, scooping their daughter into his arms. "I missed you, pumpkin. Where have you been all day? With Auntie Ruth?"

"Roo!" The toddler stumbled over the name, as she always did, giggling with delight as Noah tickled her. "And Dun-dun!"

Faith turned to see Harden hovering just outside the tree-line. He was hesitant as always. No matter how many times they reassured him he was welcome, he was never certain.

"Come join us!" Faith took a step towards him. "There's plenty to eat."

He didn't look sure, until Ruth turned. "He's been keeping Sophia amused *all* morning." She smiled at the toddler. "Hasn't he!"

"Yee-ah!" Sophia wriggled out of Noah's arms and ran to Harden. Tugging on his hand, she moved him closer to the group. "C'mon Dun-dun!"

"Come and eat," Noah said mildly, "or she'll never leave you alone."

A combination of the childish enthusiasm and Noah's invitation seemed to work. Accepting Ella's offer of a sandwich, Harden joined the group, taking a seat slightly away from the others.

No matter how many years passed, he was still awkward in their company. One day, Faith vowed as they settled down to enjoy the afternoon sun on the lake, he would recover from the trauma of the past.

They all would.

As evening drew near, the sounds of shouting emanated from the trees. Grateful that any disturbances in the forest these days were caused by children's games rather than bombs and guns, Faith went to investigate.

She peered through the leaves, where Katie was lying on the ground crying. Her brothers stood off to one side, looking guilty.

"What's going on here?" she called out, walking over to the group of children.

They had been playing together beautifully all afternoon, but they were tired now. Holding out a hand to Katie, she pulled her up.

"Matthew pushed me over!" Her bottom lip was wobbling.

"I didn't!" Her older brother was quick to defend himself. "We were playing chase and I didn't stop in time. I knocked into her and she fell."

"*Didn't!*" Katie lunged towards him. "Did it on purpose."

Flynn stepped forward. "It was an accident." He said, his voice serious. "Matty didn't mean it."

"He did!" Katie turned to Faith, her eyes wide. "He pushed me, 'cos he's bigger, and he knows I'll fall." She turned to her brother, sticking her tongue out. "I hate boys. They're mean and horrid and–"

Faith pulled her niece into her arms. "Don't say that."

Katie was trembling with indignation. "Why not? S'true."

"No, it's not." Faith looked into Katie's eyes, searching for a way to explain. "Boys aren't *all* mean. They might play rough, and tease you, and make you angry, sometimes, but they can also be kind and gentle and... fun. And girls can be both ways too."

"But–"

Faith drew back, raising an eyebrow at the little girl. "Can't you think of a single time when you were mean to Matthew?"

Flynn snorted. "You tripped him after dinner the other day."

Katie regarded her brothers solemnly. "Only because he pinched me."

"That was because you stole my ice cream!" Matthew was indignant.

"Oh." Katie's brow furrowed. "I did."

Faith stifled a smile. "There you are. We're all capable of being both nice and nasty." Faith smiled. "But when it comes down to it, these boys are your brothers, and they love you."

"Love!" Now it was Matthew's turn to stick his tongue out. "Yuk." He wandered closer, though. By the time he reached

Faith's side, he was chewing his lip. "Sorry, Auntie Faith. I didn't mean to hurt her."

She leaned forward, whispering in his ear. Eventually, he nodded.

"I'm sorry, Katie." He squinted his eyes at her. "Are you alright?" Sniffing loudly, Katie nodded. "Wanna play chase again?"

Katie considered the proposal seriously. Then, with a burst of speed, she jumped down from Faith's lap and tore off through the trees.

"Only if I'm not it!" she called back over her shoulder.

The others catapulted after her, leaving Faith alone.

One day soon, Sophia would be old enough to play among these trees with her friends. Faith hoped she would grow up knowing that *all* people had the capacity to love and be kind, but also to be cruel and selfish. It was the choice to be one or the other that made a person who they were. And the way they were brought up had everything to do with that.

As the shouts of the children's laughter echoed in the distance, Faith was glad that the forest was filled with such pleasant sounds. It had witnessed too much pain and violence.

All they had to do now was keep it this way.

A NOTE FROM CLARE

Thank you for reading Alliance! Reviews make a huge difference to authors and readers. If you enjoyed the book, please consider writing a short, honest review on Amazon. I cannot tell you how much I'd appreciate it! (While you're there, click on my author page and follow me for more information about upcoming releases!)

I love building relationships with my readers. If you enjoyed Alliance and would like to receive updates when I have a new book out, sign up for my readers' club:

https://clarelittlemore.com/newsletter/

You'll receive a regular newsletter with giveaways, book recommendations, special offers, the occasional free short story, and (of course) details of all my new releases. I promise there will be no spam. I hate spam.

OTHER BOOKS BY CLARE LITTLEMORE

The Flow Series
Binge-read the entire series now!
Flow
Break
Drift
Quell

A drowned planet. A terrible secret. A girl desperate for answers.

In a world where sea levels have risen to unimaginable levels, an isolated society exists. Life in The Beck is tough. Floodwaters constantly threaten existence, and rules must be followed to ensure the survival of the entire society.

Sixteen-year-old Quin knows the Governor is hiding something. When she receives a sudden promotion to the Patrol Sector, she hopes the extra freedom will help her expose his lies.

Life in Patrol is not what she expected, though. The new recruits train hard, and failure is not tolerated. When she attracts the attention of the handsome, mysterious Cam, he warns her that asking questions could get her killed.

But Quin can't resist. She digs deeper and discovers that there's more to Cam than meets the eye. With her heart and her life on the line, Quin has to decide how far she is willing to go to protect the people she loves.

If you love The Hunger Games, Divergent and The Giver, this gripping dystopian series by Clare Littlemore will keep you up all night.

ABOUT THE AUTHOR

Clare Littlemore is a young adult dystopian and sci-fi author who thrives on fictionally destroying the world with a cup of tea by her side. The tea will often be cold, because her characters have a way of grabbing hold of her and not letting go until the final page of their story is finished. They regularly have the same effect on her readers. Clare lives in the North West of England with her husband and two children.
Come and say hello!

https://www.facebook.com/clarelittlemoreauthor/

https://www.instagram.com/clarelittlemore/

https://www.facebook.com/groups/lastbookcafeoneart h

https://twitter.com/Clarelittlemore

Acknowledgements

A lliance is the culmination of two years' work, and I owe a debt of gratitude to several wonderful people on its release.

As usual, I need to say a huge thank you to my editor, Beth Dorward. Alliance started off as part of Defiance, an extremely lengthy story which ended up being split into two entirely separate books! The manuscript underwent massive changes during the editing process. Throughout this time, Beth was always patient, practical and thorough, steering me in the right direction and making sure that my madcap ideas made sense as they travelled from my brain to the page.

Another big thank you goes to my designer, Jessica Bell, who created a cover for a book which was never meant to exist! Somehow, she always manages to maintain the central themes of The Bellator Chronicles, whilst creating an eye-catching new cover. (I love the green tones of the final book, hinting at the unison of the forest-dwelling Eremus folk with the more urbanite Bellator citizens.)

I also need to mention the wonderful Lyn Blair for her unwavering support with so many aspects of this series. She has read the book in many forms, from its most raw, 180k-word manuscript, to the final version (of both books 3 and 4). Her advice is always welcome, and she has helped me work through numerous plot twists which would otherwise have given me sleepless nights. Last but not least, to my mum, who always reads my books prior to publishing, proofreading for any last-minute grammar errors. With Alliance, she did this many times with several versions. I am eternally grateful for her catching all those little things which passed me by.

After that, there are too many people to name. So to those of you who you listened while I tried to work through a complex subplot; beta-read an early edition of Alliance or bolstered me when I was concerned I'd never see the book published: thank you. To those of you who brought me endless cups of tea and snacks while I tapped away at the keyboard (you know who you are); commented on early ideas for cover designs, or helped me to edit my blurb: thank you. If you considered my suggestions for titles; spotted an errant proofreading error; or waited until I'd finished the chapter I was working on before I helped you study for a test: thank you. If you bought copies of the earlier books in The Bellator Chronicles and waited for this one without complaint: thank you.

Finally, to my readers. Thank you for your patience. I know this book has been a long time coming! I hope you stick with me for many more to come.